Welcome Redemption Reagan Sinclair, FBI

Book Five

by JS Ririe

Jan Hill Books

Welcome Redemption -Reagan Sinclair, FBI
Book 5
by JS Ririe
Publisher: Jan Hill Books
ISBN: 978-1-7333027-2-2
Copyright 2019 by Jan Hill Books
Cover Image by: Fotoluminate
Cover Design by William Gensburger

Praise for: Welcome Redemption
Reagan Sinclair, FBI - Book 5

"Reagan's story is an action adventure tying the pleasures of a warm, spiritual and loving family into the intrigue of today's challenges and issues happening throughout South America and Mexico as the drug business continues to flourish. It reflects life-changing decisions that must be made and the effect they have on surrounding family, friends and colleagues.

~Elaine S.

Dedication:

In a very uncertain and unprecedented time, as we come together as a nation and world to fight an invisible opponent like the Covid-19 virus, my thoughts and prayers are with everyone who is trying to do his or her part. I marvel at the bravery and selflessness of doctors, nurses, first responders, truck drivers, government officials, church leaders and people still working in stores, restaurants, pharmacies and industry so our lives can go on in what has been termed a new kind of normal. I look in awe at others who are finding creative ways to help and keep in contact with family, neighbors and friends, and I feel sorrow and concern for those who are unemployed or have lost loved ones. This book is dedicated to them.

~JS Ririe

Chapter 1

The remainder of the flight to Mexico City was uneventful. I tried to keep my swirling thoughts still, but it was useless since I was heading into another unknown where it would be almost impossible to tell friend from foe. Even the woman sleeping in the seat next to mine couldn't be entirely trusted. Too much of what she had said on the flight was suspect. And I was finding it was impossible to keep the fact that she had willing allowed two people to be killed from affecting how I viewed our recently-renewed friendship.

Lila may not have cared what happened to Walter, but what Robert had told Angel in that garden led me to believe that she was in the same boat as her husband when it came to being discarded. Why else would he have told her that all her worries would soon be over? Lila wasn't dumb, and it would have been nearly impossible to miss the implication behind his double-sided expression of concern. It was just another anomaly I needed to understand before we landed.

I ran my hand through my hair as my brow furrowed into another expression of frustration. I wanted a few moments of freedom from overthinking problems to consider my complex relationship with Agent Fielding. I would love to give him another chance, and not just because he was Charlie's father. My feelings for him were strong for many reasons, but I hadn't heard anything about him for over three months. Entertaining the possibility of seeing him again would only cloud my judgment and quite possibly cause me to miss something important that would keep more than just me alive.

Besides, I had given Trey my word that we would talk when I got back. He might not be able to make my heart race the way Agent Fielding had done, but he had been with me through some horrendous times of trial, sorrow and self-growth. He was even helping to deaden some of the pain I felt over losing Neil.

The two agents accompanying us didn't try to initiate a conversation during the entire flight. They rose to their feet when the airplane landed at a small airstrip somewhere inside Mexico City's limits and made sure we were transferred into the right hands, but they climbed back up the steps leading to the plane's cabin once we were seated in the back of an embassy limousine.

Lila reached for my hand as we drove away from the landing strip. It was only 52 degrees outside, but beads of sweat were forming on my forehead and in the small of my back as I noticed the other cars in our procession move into formation. This was not a trip I wanted to make, and being plunged back into a case I had hoped to leave behind caused me to reevaluate many things—especially the grave reality of Charlie growing up without either of his parents.

The sky was gray and not because it was going to rain. Air inversion, combined with the exhaust from millions of vehicles, took away much of the beauty of a city that was home to picturesque cathedrals and palaces, beautiful parks and high-rise structures built from steel, concrete and glass. Some of the streets were lined with swaying pine and oyamel trees, and a few protestors could be seen waving hand-painted signs in the air.

Regardless of which direction I looked, there was something interesting to see from shoe-shine boys and candy-and-gum sellers to street performers. I knew there were parts of the city known as "cludaes peridas" or lost cities where electricity was not even available and people made their living by combing through garbage and selling their souls to the highest bidder. Alberto Rio had ripped innocent girls from their homes and transported them across the border into a form of bondage from which few were able to escape. But there was no evidence of that on streets we were traveling in a city of over ten million inhabitants.

"I suppose it's way past time for changing my mind." Lila said as we continued our journey. "Coming back seemed like a great adventure until we got here, and now I really don't want to face that part of my past."

"Even if it brings the person responsible for Angel's death to justice?" I asked. "I can understand ambivalent feelings about what happened to Walter. He was a despicable man who got what he deserved, but Angel was your friend."

I was hoping she would reply with something I could use to calm my troubled mind. I wanted to believe that all ties with her past life had ended so I could trust her when it came to helping me now, but she merely turned her head and looked out the window.

"Angel knew what would happen when she confronted Walter. I'm not saying she wanted to die, but she was definitely looking for a way out of the life she was living."

I decided not to question her any further until we were settled. Despite being formally summoned, I had no idea what our reception might be after the number of times I had forced myself into Director Phillips' operations without an invitation. My proclivity to state my opinions and offer suggestions had been the cause of several chastisements since joining the bureau, but I was learning how to control my outbursts. This time, I would do what was asked, try to keep my thoughts to myself and spend whatever free time I had looking for more answers on my own. Neither Juan Seville nor Agent Ross had died at their own hands or from natural causes. That meant something important was being kept from me, and I had to discover what it was before I was eliminated too.

When the gates leading to the embassy grounds swung open, I watched Lila lean forward to get a better look. The pleasant lawns and gardens of the fall had been replaced with brown, dormant grass and flowerbeds that had been made ready for spring planting. But I knew the dreariness outside would be forgotten once we entered the home to dignitaries and the people who worked with them.

The doors of the limousine were held open for us and our suitcases removed from the trunk. I walked beside Lila as we followed one of our escorts up the front steps and waited for admittance to the marble entry with glass chandeliers and the most opulent furnishings I had ever seen. Lila crossed the threshold in front of me.

"I think I'm going to enjoy living like this for a few days," she whispered as we were escorted down a hallway and through several doors before being told to wait in a room with red velvet, high-backed chairs, large metal sculptures and a highly polished hardwood desk.

"Will Director Phillips be joining us soon?" I asked the armed agent who had brought us there.

"I'm not sure what his plans are, Agent Sinclair. No one has seen much of him the past few days, but I was told to make sure you were comfortably settled. Someone will be with you soon, and I'll see that your luggage is taken to your rooms."

Lila immediately sat down and crossed her legs, but I remained standing until a servant I did not recognize from before brought a tray filled with exotic drinks for us to enjoy. I made sure mine was non-alcoholic before taking a sip, and then tried not to pace as we waited another fifteen minutes before the door opened again.

"I'm sorry Director Phillips or Ambassador Alexander couldn't be here to greet you in person," a lovely woman in a white blouse and black silk pants said as she literally glided into the room with her light brown hair pulled away from her face and her makeup flawless. "This wretched trial has everyone at the embassy on edge with all the constant delays and changes, but we are grateful you were willing to come. We know it is a sacrifice after all you have been through, but we promise to expedite your stay and make it as pleasant as possible. I am Genevieve Alexander, the ambassador's wife. If there is anything you need, please do not hesitate to ask. Dinner will be served at eight. Someone with the information you desire should be free to talk to you by then."

She was certainly polished when it came to diplomacy—hedging questions before they could even be asked—but I wasn't enamored by her finesse. I hadn't traveled thousands of miles to be kept waiting by anyone. The situation I had been pulled into needed to be explained before I said something I knew I would regret.

"Are you sure no one will be available to discuss why we're actually here before then," I asked. "I don't mean to be impatient or disrespectful, but wasting an entire afternoon is something I'm not prepared to do."

Her instant smile showed perfectly aligned teeth. "I understand your need to remain busy, Agent Sinclair, but there is really nothing I can do. Director Phillips will be busy with other matters until evening. I am simply here to greet you and make sure your stay is as pleasant as possible. Perhaps you could use the time you have been given to rest and unpack? I will have a light luncheon sent to your rooms. The rest of the household has already eaten."

"That would be wonderful," Lila interjected, giving me an exasperated look. "We don't want to put anyone out, but I am famished."

"Nothing is an imposition when it comes to our guests," Genevieve Alexander replied. "Feel free to enjoy your drinks before someone arrives to take you upstairs. I would stay to get better acquainted but have a pressing afternoon engagement. We will talk more this evening."

My drink was tangy and pleasant. I sipped it while we waited for our escort. Despite my rather brusque behavior, I quite enjoyed the surroundings. They were colorful, festive and in harmony with the city and country they represented. The paintings were replications of matadors fighting ferocious-looking bulls with rings in their noses and fire in their eyes; beautiful, young women with swirling skirts and dazzling smiles; and Aztec ruins and landscapes that symbolized a rich history of a proud people who respected their past.

It was all part of a carefully executed illusion that was meant to impress important people from around the world, but I did not fall into that category. I was here against my will, and all the memories associated with my last visit were staring to come back from the lavish dinners and ball to the terrors at the hospital. And it was impossible not to recall how hard it had been to get someone with authority to listen to my suggestions and give me clearance to act. I didn't expect preferential treatment now, but I needed to be doing something more than waiting around for the next shoe to fall.

"What's wrong? You're trembling like a leaf," Lila whispered, taking my arm as the woman who had served our drinks came back to escort us up the marble staircase to the rooms that had been prepared for our use. "You can't possibly be cold."

"I'm not," I replied, still trying to process the fact that I was here to testify, not help with a case. "I suddenly feel like a black cat has walked over my grave."

"That's ridiculous," she scoffed as the heels on her shoes made a highly-audible, clicking sound on the hard flooring. "Your life is much too grounded in reality to be influenced by superstition."

"Not anymore! I don't like all these reminders of a past that can't be changed."

"At least you know why you're here," she countered. "My interactions with Eloise were minimal, and she made no secret of the fact that she despised me almost as much as she did Angel."

"Was she was aware of your past relationship?" I asked as another thought seemed to intrude into my consciousness. If Eloise even suspected that Angel and Lila had a history she would use everything within her power to found out just what they had shared and how it might impact both present and future operations. And If Robert Evans was aware of the time they had spent together . . . Well, the havoc that could unleash with the formation of a new cartel was endless.

"Are you suggesting that someone believes I might know where the ledger Angel referred to was located? That's ludicrous because I didn't. I thought she was just spouting off to get our attention and sympathy when she mentioned having it. I really thought it was all in her head until I got to Washington D.C. and talked to you and Agent DeHoyes."

"I know you were trying to be careful, but are you sure no mention was made of your time together as teenagers? There were listening devices placed in every room in the house and likely near the pool. I found half a dozen in the bedroom Agent Fielding and I were using, and even the most innocent remark could have been passed on. When I saw Eloise and Juan arguing in the hall before the ball, I figured something had gone wrong with one of the shipments, but it could have been anything."

She reached for the railing as if her knees had suddenly become weak. "I didn't even think about that. Angel and I talked about Big Horace Green and a number of people who were part of a life we had left behind, but we never did it when other people were around. Even when we were out by the pool, I don't remember saying anything that could be used against us."

"I didn't mean to upset you, Lila, but there is a reason you are here," I said as we reached the top of the staircase. "Did you know Tristan Archibald?"

"You mean Archie? He was just a kid, but he would run errands for both of us and keep an eye on some of the men we were sent to entertain. Is he mixed up in this?"

I weighed what I should say carefully. Lila would know if I was hedging or telling a lie and clam up. "He's the one who told Neva to leave town. Someone within a very small circle told him about Angel's death because it's never appeared in any public record."

"Well, it wasn't me!" she exclaimed. "I've seen him a few times over the years, but once I left the projects, I didn't want to look back. Is he still okay?"

"As far as I know. Neva said he knew how to disappear."

"He was one of the most invisible people I've ever known, but if anyone associated with the Evans' family knew about him, disappearing might not be enough."

"Do you think Angel told Robert about him?"

"Maybe! She truly believed he would rescue her from the life she had created for herself. But I should have known he would never let her live once he had used her to get what he wanted. After all, he was his father's son, and the only woman he ever really cared about was his mother."

"Did you ever meet her?" I asked.

"Heavens no," she responded, giving me an annoyed look. "Guadalupe Evans was part of the echelons of society I never attained. Angel told me she was a formidable, egotistical and domineering woman who didn't like to be crossed. She was also very vocal with both stipulations and threats when Walter and Angel first got together. But once she knew her husband was serious about getting a divorce and marrying one of his escorts, she made her demands and left America behind. I guess got what she needed."

We had stopped in front of facing doors, and the maid indicated which room each of us should take, but leaving Lila when my mind seemed to be on fire again was hard. The amount of information she appeared to possess without conscience knowledge was astounding. She had basically given me confirmation that Lupe Evans and her son were close enough to plot revenge, and she had left her marriage with the resources she needed to start over again.

"Will you be alright for a few hours?" I asked.

"What you just said doesn't change the reason I agreed to come. I want to find out where Angel is buried and make arrangements for her body to be taken back to New York City."

"It's unlikely that will happen, even if we were allowed to leave the embassy alone."

"Why? I shouldn't be on anyone's radar, and Angel's body needs to be returned to her home. If anyone wanted to dispose of me, that could easily have been accomplished while I was still in the hospital. A pillow over the face like they tried to do to Sam, or something in my IV, would be silent and quick. No one would even know I had been murdered before my assailant disappeared."

Her reasoning filled me with horror, but the answer I had to offer would bring little comfort. Either she was being used by someone who still needed her alive, or she was more involved with the cartels than what she was willing to admit.

"Why don't we try to get some rest and talk later," I suggested, knowing I needed time alone to think.

"What about Angel's body? I won't leave it behind again."

"Let me check into it. I can't make any promises, but someone may be willing to help."

"I could take a run at the Ambassador's wife. She seems friendly enough."

"Let's not involve anyone else just yet. I want to figure out why we're really here first. I have a feeling we may be walking into a trap, and I want to be prepared."

"It wouldn't be the first one," she countered.

"Maybe not, but I would feel a lot better if Assistant Director Bridges had been able to come. I still can't believe Agent Ross is dead."

"After what he did to Charlie and you, I think he got off easy, but I know that's not what you're talking about. Still, I have to believe your boss would never have sent us here if he thought we would be in any real danger."

She kissed my cheek before vanishing into her designated room. The maid who had been accompanying us pushed open my door.

"Try not to be distressed, Agent Sinclair," she said in polished English. "I have worked here for many years and know you will be protected."

"And how would you know that?" I asked.

Her smile was not unkind. "My cousins both said you did not mince words. You probably know only one of them by name. She was at the hospital with you, Anna Garcia."

"Of course," I replied, pulling the small cross from underneath my shirt. "She gave me this. I don't often let others see it, but it helps me feel connected to her. She befriended me during a very difficult time."

"That cross meant a great deal to Anna. She got it as a child. I am glad you still wear it."

"Can you tell me where she is? I know she was being reassigned."

The woman standing next to me shook her head. "No one in the family has heard from her since she left, but we must never lose faith in the blessed Mother or her Son. We must believe that we will be reunited. It is the only way I can survive in such uncertain times. My name is Manuela. I know you do not feel as if you can trust anyone here, but I will not betray you."

"Thank you, Manuela," I said, touching her arm in a show of acceptance. "Your presence makes me feel less alone."

"Take some time to rest," she replied. "I will let you know what is going on."

I wasn't sure she was capable of doing that. Servants were aware of a great many things, but they weren't always allowed behind closed doors. Still, I was grateful she had taken the time to let me know I had an unexpected friend.

The room I had been given faced a courtyard that must be quite lovely during the warmer months when the shrubs and flowers were blooming, but I didn't do much more than glance out the window at white, iron furniture than had been covered with heavy plastic before starting to unpack. Like the rest of the embassy, my sleeping quarters were decorated in rich, dark colors and bold patterns. It was obvious that no expense had been spared when it came to the comfort of the occupants.

I had just put the last of my clothing into a dresser drawer when someone knocked on my door. When I pulled it open, Manuela glanced up at me with dark, apologetic eyes that reminded me so much of her cousin.

"Please excuse the interruption when you have just arrived, but one of the lawyers is asking to see you. There was no one else to deliver the message so I came myself."

"Don't apologize. That's why I'm here," I replied. I wanted my part of the trial over so I could return home, hopefully before my family found out I was gone. "Is Miss Rivers supposed to join us?"

"He did not say anything about her, but I am sure that was implied since you are both here for the same reason. I cannot wait until the Seville's evil reign has ended, then perhaps my cousin can come home for the wedding we have all been planning for her."

Her revelation was unexpected. While I had not known Anna well, upcoming nuptials were one of the first things girls chose to reveal.

"I had no idea she was getting married."

"Agent Lopez proposed right before she left and would have gone with her, but such a move would not be allowed."

"I met him when I was here before," I responded, recalling the young agent I had talked to several times while looking through some of the items that had been brought from the Rios ranch to the embassy. "Is he still here? I would like to extend my congratulations."

"He was transferred to the coast not long after Anna received her new assignment. We speak to him often, but I should not be talking about such thing with our guests. I do not want to be responsible for her being kept away indefinitely."

"Your secret is safe with me, Manuela. I will pray they can be reunited soon. Do you know where she was sent?"

"Colombia! That was all she could tell us. It is a big country with many bad people, but she told us not to worry."

"A not so simple request," I stated as my heart began to pound. Was she there to help Agent Fielding in his quest to find Alma Mendoza? That would only make sense if both Director's Phillips and Stevens believed that was where the reorganization of the new cartel was taking place. "Family is everything to me as well."

"You have a husband or lover?"

My head moved back and forth. "No, but I have a son who means everything to me."

The fact that I had made such an admission was alarming, but it also made me realize that I had accepted her offer of friendship.

"I have two sons of my own, strong and brave like their father. My one wish is for them to grow up in a world where they can play in the streets without fear of being abducted, recruited or killed. The cartels do not care about people. They only want to sell more drugs because it makes them even richer."

"That's exactly why I'm here. While it is impossible to eliminate the epidemic of drugs that is flooding both of our countries, I continue to hope that what each of us is doing will make a difference."

Once she told me where to meet the lawyer, I made my way across the hallway to knock on Lila's door. She had changed into a green, knit dress. I was still wearing the jeans I had traveled in.

"You look nice," I told her.

"I intend to take advantage of my time here. When I get back to my loft, I will be assuming the role of a non-traditional college student since, by God's grace, I have managed to pass the GED and will begin taking online classes. It's quite the foil for my checkered past, don't you think?"

"You have my congratulations for passing the exam, but why didn't you tell me sooner? We could have celebrated your accomplishment."

"It's not such a big deal. One of the girls in the twelve-step program was doing the same thing so we studied together. I got the letter in the mail yesterday, but you look like a woman who is not in the mood for frivolous conversation. Where are you going?"

"We've been summoned to the conference room to meet with a lawyer."

"I hope he's cute," she said, plumping her auburn curls as she stepped into the hallway. "Nothing is more dreary than spending the afternoon with some portly, old gentleman who smells of stale cigars."

"At least your sense of humor is still intact," I told her on as we made our way to the staircase. "I don't care what he looks like, or how he smells, as long as he's good at what he does."

"You're much too intense and predictable," she responded, glancing in my direction without smiling. "You didn't even change your clothes or freshen your makeup. Don't you know that he will work harder to help us out of this distasteful situation if we make ourselves as attractive and presentable as possible? First impressions do count."

"This isn't some popularity contest. People's lives are at stake."

"Then you need to be doing whatever is necessary to make every encounter productive. Carrying a gun and wearing a badge makes people uncomfortable, even if they haven't done anything wrong."

"And you're telling me this because of your vast experience in law enforcement."

"No, I'm speaking as a friend who learned her people skills on the street and working with men who were looking for someone to confide in. You need to lose the sour expression and lighten up. It does nothing to enhance your appearance, and it's a big turnoff to everyone."

"Wow," I said as we reached the main floor where a door to a large room stood open. "Why don't you tell me what you really think?"

"I'm not trying to be critical, but you're not the same girl I met in Mexico, and that concerns me."

"My life has taken a few rocky turns since then," I reminded her.

"You don't have to be pleasant all the time. That's impossible for most everyone, but you do need to be more approachable, especially now. The man in that room may have some of the answers you're looking for, but he's not going to divulge them if he thinks you're only here to criticize or make demands. And just in case you think I'm acting more like Angel than I should right now, I learned a great deal from her and will do whatever it takes to make sure I survive this little adventure. I have no intention of becoming the name of a deceased person in some confidential report, but I want the people who were responsible for Edward's death punished."

"Rios is already dead."

"You're deliberately missing my point, Reagan. It's not just the man who killed him, it's the society that makes such deaths commonplace and almost impossible to prosecute that I want to stop."

"That's not going to happen here. The best we can hope for is to keep Eloise in jail. I want you to stay as far removed from any legal proceedings as possible until we figure out why you're really here. There are too many temptations and unknowns, and you've come too far to let anything get in the way."

Her hand caught my arm. "I'm not going to mess with my recovery, but if I see an opportunity to make a difference I will take it. You're not the only one with a child. I may have walked away after my daughter's birth, but I've never quit loving her or wanting her to have the best life possible."

Her observations were so applicable they made me cringe. I had become obsessed with finding answers, and it had impacted every part of my life. Lila wanted me to understand what I might be up against if I didn't change some of my tactics.

"I'm sorry for acting more like a robot than a human being. That was never my intention. Like you, I just want to make the world a better place."

"Then let's do it together. I can butter him up with a few well-placed comments, and you can ask the difficult questions. I just want to see you happy again."

Without waiting for a reply, she walked into the room with the long, oval table and comfortable high-backed chairs, leaving me to wonder if I would ever really get to know my chameleon-like friend.

I can't say that I felt any better when I joined her. I had only expected to see one lawyer, but he was surrounded by several men in suits who looked ready to conduct business. This was a formal meeting, and it made me wishI had at least combed my hair. Lila found an open chair next to the most attractive man in the room, leaving me to sit only inches away from the door.

"We are glad you ladies could join us," the man standing at the head of the table with a huge stack of papers piled in front of him said. "I am Victor Vega from the law firm of Holston, Ramos and Vega. It is my job to prepare you for trial and keep you updated as we progress. For your own safety, you will not be allowed outside the embassy. The only exception will be to testify. I cannot express too strongly that what is discussed remains confidential. While we have taken every precaution, it is unrealistic to believe that everyone within these walls believes as we do that Eloise Seville should be punished for her crimes."

Lila looked over at me and rolled her eyes, but I knew that despite her bouts of bravado she was scared. No one was really safe until all of the Sevilles, and their connections, were permanently behind bars.

"Thank you for your consideration, Señor Vega, but there are a few questions we would like to ask before we begin," I replied.

He gave me a look of impatience that seemed to confirm the belief that our subpoenas were merely shams.

"I understand your eagerness to to know everything we do, Agent Sinclair, but I am afraid there is not that much to tell."

"Please do not insult my intelligence. We were informed before our flight that Juan Seville is dead. You cannot tell me that does not affect the trial."

"A short recess has been called while certain arrangements are being made, but we should be back on schedule in a day or two. Eloise does not want to postpone the inevitable. She seems quite eager to have her day in court."

"And why is that?" I asked. "Surely she has no reason to believe she will be a free woman any time soon."

"This will not be an easy win, Agent Sinclair. Although her older sons appear to have deserted her, Eloise has millions at her disposal and very competent legal representation working to secure her release. But we believe the truth will eventually prevail. People in this city are tired of being controlled by the cartels. They want their children to grow up in peace and safety. I do not like how pervasive some problems have become, but there are few residents of our entire country whose lives have not been adversity affected by the very thing we are trying to stop."

It was an empowering speech, but I wasn't sure just how strongly he believed what he purported. People might not like the cartels, but they kept money flowing into a desperate economy.

My next question was on an entirely different topic. "Are you aware of how Juan Seville died yet?"

"An autopsy is being performed, but it seems unlikely that he died of natural causes. My job is not to speculate on what may be going on inside the prison walls. My job is to prepare you for a trial that has already begun. Opening arguments have been made and several witnesses called. We have set the stage for your testimony, but you must be aware of what questions may be asked. The recording that was made when Eloise attacked you at the hospital will not be admitted as evidence, and your relationship with Agent Fielding is already being questioned. Eloise claims that she did not come to the hospital to stage an attack. She merely wanted to see if the child you claimed to be carrying had survived."

My eyes opened in disbelief. "You know that isn't true. She was there for revenge because her shipment had been seized and her youngest son incarcerated."

"Proving something is not easy when no one is willing to testify. Family members of some of the hospital employees have already gone missing, as have any records documenting your stay."

"Are you saying that the doctor who attended me is no longer there?"

"He seems to have relocated recently. We are dealing with people who have been circumventing the law for decades and have the connections and means to corrupt any legal proceedings."

"But why would Eloise voluntarily remain in custody if everything you said is true?"

"Perhaps something else is going on. I do not have the answers you are looking for, Agent Sinclair. I am merely a lawyer who has been engaged to prosecute a known philanthropist and revered member of her community—who also happens to be suspected of criminal activities."

This time, I was the one who rolled my eyes while looking in Lila's direction. I wasn't sure what to ask next since Victor Vega had failed to give me a reason to believe he was really a defender of the truth. In fact, he seemed to be nothing more than a figurehead who had even less knowledge about what was going on than I did. But Lila was ready to begin with her own kind of questioning, and it would be far less pointed than mine. She leaned forward in her chair while I leaned back in mine.

"I'm sure you are aware of my history, Señor Vega," she began, giving him one of her most beguiling smiles. He was an attractive man with sharp eyes, thick, black hair and no wedding ring. "I would never be considered an ideal witness, so I am having trouble deciding why I was even subpoenaed. I am in a recovery program and only want to stop others from going through what I have."

"I did not ask my superiors why certain witnesses were being called, Miss Rivers. Your name appeared on a list I received from the embassy."

"A list?" she asked, looking genuinely surprised. "I barely knew Eloise Seville."

"You stayed at the ranch owned by her brother for over a month where Eloise was a frequent visitor. You attended a concert, a night at an opera and the opening of an art gallery with her. You ate meals together, played croquet in the gardens during the day and games of chance in the library at night. You also rode into the countryside on horseback together several times and spent hours reclining beside the pool. It has even been brought to my attention that you helped arrange the initial meeting between Edward Peterson and Alberto

Rios and were aware of the activities he was engaged in as part of his initiation into the cartel. So please do not insult my intelligence by trying to make me believe that you have nothing to offer that might benefit the prosecution. We know our country has been targeted as the most cost-effective and efficient way of trafficking drugs and humans across the border into the United States. Sadly, we do not have the resources to stop what is happening on our own."

My eyes opened wide in surprise. Regardless of his deficits when it came to satisfying my curiosity or my demands, he knew how to stop Lila's advances. I didn't want her to learn everything Edward had done as part of his initiation from a stranger. She needed to believe that he had been faithful to her. Knowing that he had taken advantage of one of the young girls who had been sent across the border would destroy her last good memories of him.

"Señor Vega, could you tell us anything about the surprise Director Phillips was supposed to have waiting for us," I asked to redirect where his accusations may be heading. "We were led to believe it was some kind of secret weapon that could possibly keep Miss Rivers and me from testifying."

He gave me another intolerant look. "The strategies we employ cannot be shared, Agent Sinclair, nor can the identities of the other witnesses. I am sure you understand."

"What I understand is that you haven't told us anything," I responded, looking at the faces of the other men who sat around the table. Not one of them had made a comment or been introduced. They simply sat in their chairs with their fingers interlaced over yellow, legal pads of paper.

"Please talk to Director Phillips when he returns to the embassy," Victor Vega said as he rose to his feet and gathered a number of folders into his arms. "I came here today as a courtesy to give you a feel as to what might be expected when you arrive at the courthouse. I cannot tell you exactly when that might be, but I will return in the morning so we can begin preparations."

With squared shoulders and confident stride he lead the others from the room, leaving Lila and me sitting at the table feeling both annoyed and perplexed.

"Well, that was an interesting turn of events," she said as she dangled her foot in front of her chair. "I can't say that I enjoyed having my activities at the ranch broadcast. He made it sound like Eloise and I had become bosom buddies. We may have shared certain activities, but she only spoke to me when necessary. Nonetheless, he helped me remember something I had forgotten."

"Something useful, I hope."

"Not exactly. Rios wanted to make sure we had a good time, and business was never discussed in my presence. But I will say that Eloise seemed almost revered when we went into the city. People inclined their heads when she and Juan entered a building, and they were always given preferential seating. I read somewhere that they had given millions of dollars to the arts."

"You do know that you're supporting what Victor Vega said."

"It's rather hard to fault his logic when it comes to the place she held in polite society. Juan's death will garner the type of support she needs if her case goes to trial. No one will ever convict a woman who has as many friends as she does when her husband just died. That said, I'm more interested in the surprise you mentioned to Victor. Why didn't you tell me about it sooner? It would have given us something to talk about while we traveled. Do you have any idea what it might be?"

"I'm not sure there is one," I retorted. "It was probably some sadistic ruse intended to make our trip a little more palatable."

She dropped her foot unceremoniously to the floor. "Don't go all sinister on me now. I know Victor didn't make the best impression, but he might feel the need to be cautious. Still, it would be interesting to know what he's hiding. A secret weapon sounds Intriguing. Do you have any idea who or what it might be?"

I was in no mood for speculation. Too many thoughts about the deadly game we were playing were swirling around in my head. "All the people from our past are accounted for, unless you're still holding something back."

Her playfulness suddenly vanished. "I may have spent most of my life on the wrong side of the law, but I rode to the hospital with you, so Eloise wouldn't, when I believed you were losing a baby. I forgave you for the part you played in Edward's death. I even came to Washington D.C. to tell you what I had heard about Agent Fielding when I knew you could turn me over the the authorities. I think I've proven that I am trying to change, but you seem determined to believe the worst about me."

A wave of regret washed over me as I looked at a picture of the National Palace that hung on the wall. I was pushing too hard, and Lila would withdraw if I could't make her believe I was still on her side. That meant keeping my doubts to myself.

"I'm sorry. I know you didn't have to do any of those things. My nerves are on edge, just like you said, and I'm taking it out on you."

"Maybe, but you have to believe that not everyone is part of the enemy camp. Some of us keep secrets because it's how we survive. That doesn't mean we're intentionally trying to hide anything."

During what remained of the afternoon, I let Lila explore the embassy while I worked on the laptop I had been given trying to find something that would ease my mind and give me a better idea of what we might be facing during the next few days. It seemed unlikely that my two assignments with the DEA were related, except for the partner I had been working with. Agent Fielding was definitely a catalyst for change, but he had been missing for months, and no one seemed to hold out any great belief that he would be coming back. I needed someone with answers who was willing to talk to me, but everyone in a position to do so was unavailable.

Director Phillips did not return to the embassy that afternoon, and when I placed a call to Assistant Director Bridges, I was informed that he was in a closed-door meeting but would get back to me when he could. I understood his need to find out who was responsible for Agent Ross's death, but I was floundering in a bog of uncertainty with nothing to cling to. I even walked the halls hoping to see someone who remembered me and was willing to talk, but they were essentially deserted.

When it was time to eat our evening meal, I was more than ready to express my frustrations and concerns, but to my dismay, Genevieve Alexander was presiding at the head of the table.

"I am sorry we will be dining alone," she said as China plates, edged in a delicate strip of gold, were set in front of us. "Both my husband and Director Phillips have been detained. I was told to express their regrets."

"Will they be back later tonight?" I asked as as Lila gave me a warning look.

I knew she didn't want our hostess upset. They had shared a brief conversation in the conservatory before dressing for dinner where she had learned that both Genevieve and her husband had been born in Mexico City to influential families who still held numerous positions of authority in political circles. They loved their country but did not believe it was the best place to raise a family. That's why their two daughters, who were not yet teenagers, were attending school in Europe. They returned home for special occasions.

"Unfortunately, their exact plans cannot be determined, Agent Sinclair," Genevieve said, giving me a pleasant smile before taking a bite of her green, leafy salad. "Our country is in great distress, and there is much to be done."

"So there's nothing you can tell me?" I prodded.

"Please try to understand that while the problems you are facing seem quite new, they are merely issues we have been dealing with for decades. I wish there was more I could tell you, but I am not privy to most of what goes on within these walls. My responsibilities are seeing to our guest's comfort, chairing committees and hosting events that will help fund worthy causes. I leave the more weighty matters to my husband and the people who work with him."

While I knew that wasn't entirely true, bombarding her with more questions she was either unable or unwilling to answer would not be a productive use of my time. If I wanted to learn anything from her, I would have to take the approach Lila had.

The food was excellent, and the conversation covered a variety of topics like local tourist attractions, historical monuments and the history of the embassy. I offered what comments I could, but mostly, my mind remained focused on why we were really here and how I would get any answers when no one was available to talk to me.

We retired to a spacious library for after-dinner drinks. I asked for unadulterated fruit juice while Lila and Genevieve took large, crystal goblets filled with brandy. I watched them swirl the amber liquid between sips and wondered if my lack of sharing some of the niceties of life was really hampering the work I needed to do. People did seem to open up considerably after a few drinks, and it gave them something in common to share. But while they talked like old friends, I glanced around the room to see if anything had been left out in the open that might aid in my search for connections and bring a more speedy end to our time in Mexico.

I wanted to hold my son in my arms, express untold gratitude to every member of my family, and tell Trey that I was ready to give us a chance. He was a warm, caring and dependable man, and he could make my dream for having a real family come true. All I had to do was stop living in a world of fantasy that had no sure foundation.

After a brief discussion about fashion, to which I had little to add since shopping had never been one of my passions, Genevieve excused herself. She had correspondence to write, but we were free to enjoy the library for as long as we liked. I was ready to return to my room to see if Assistant Director Bridges had called, but Lila wanted another drink.

"Sit beside me for a few minutes and try to relax," she said, sitting down in an overstuffed chair in front of the fire that was merrily burning in the hearth. "I haven't been treated so royally since our visit to Rios ranch. That seems an eternity ago. Do you ever think about the way we met?"

"Quite often," I assured her.

"Me too. My first thought when I saw you on the arm of the man I believed to be Antonio Reese was that you looked like some innocent debutant who had become involved with a slightly older man and had no idea that he had gambled away your entire trust fund. I guess that's really why I volunteered to go to the hospital with you. I knew what it felt like to be used and what the realization of the awful truth could do. In my own rather jaded way, I wanted to help soften the blow. Edward often told me that he knew Tony wasn't the man he claimed to be."

"Really?" I asked, sitting down in the chair next to hers. "Did he give you any specifics?"

"Only that underneath that suave, confident persona he knew Tony had more experience than he did when it came to drug and human trafficking. He said he poor-pitied the woman who became involved with him because he would do more than just break her heart."

"I suppose you believed him."

"It was hard not to. Men who exude the kind of power and seductiveness he does are dangerous because they always know exactly what to do. That's why I know he isn't dead in some Colombian jungle. He's too smart to let anyone get the upper hand. Even Angel's blatant attempt at seduction didn't ruffle him. That had never happened to her before and may have been the catalyst in her deciding to pull the plug on Walter. If she couldn't control men with her body, what purpose did she have for going on?"

"That's a very sad assessment of her character."

"My intention is not to belittle the dead. Angel viewed her body as being her only real asset. If she couldn't use it as she had always done for both work and pleasure, what did she have left? If you really want to get inside the heads of criminals and bring them to justice, you have to learn what drives them to do unconscionable things. Mostly it's the desire for power, money and revenge, but sometimes people have simply been raised to view themselves as having no other alternatives. They follow the path of least resistance until it's too late to switch courses."

"Is that how you feel?" I asked.

"Sometimes, but I want to make it. That's why I'm willing to cut you some slack. I know you're not here to make friends and have fun. You're here to testify at a trial that has about as much a chance of being successful as me winning the lottery without purchasing tickets. That would make anyone tense, but what I want to know is just how concerned you really are about the opposing council using your relationship with Sam to destroy your credibility as a witness. I know Victor said we should both be prepared for anything, and you have more to lose than I do."

I let the air out of my lungs slowly. "Not many people feel kindly towards a federal agent who has disgraced his or her badge by crossing the most basic, moral line. All the defense has to do is plant a seed of reasonable doubt and nothing I say will count."

"But you didn't do anything wrong," she responded.

"We both know how convincing Eloise can be when she talks about family, loyalty and honor. A sympathetic jury—who was picked to rule in her favor anyway—will feel justified in rendering a verdict of innocent after she gets through telling them how I lied about carrying a child and was romantically involved with my partner. The recording, that has now been suppressed, would have backed up my story."

"That hardly seems fair after all the atrocities she's perpetuated."

"The premise that a person is innocent until proven guilty is the basis for any legal proceeding in a country founded on democratic principles."

"But the Seville cartel is the biggest one in the city."

"Unfortunately, she's not being tried as a member of the cartel."

"So what's the point of going through some bogus trial when there's no chance of winning? And why was a threat made against Charlie's life if Eloise is basically guaranteed an acquittal?"

"Some of my concerns precisely," I told her. "Nothing about us coming here makes sense, unless we're being used to further a different agenda. That's why I've been so pushy when it comes to talking to someone who can give us a few answers. Don't you think it's a little strange that the ambassador's wife is the only one who has given us a proper greeting?"

"I haven't wanted to look on this as anything more than a vacation because that would mean reliving everything that happened when we were here before."

"But that's exactly what the prosecution expects us to do before we walk into that courtroom. Victor Vega, or one of his associates, is going to ask questions that are meant to jar suppressed memories we aren't even aware of."

"I don't want anyone picking through my brain," she said, placing her empty glass on the nearest end table. "I loved Edward with all my heart, even if he wasn't perfect, and I will not allow his name to be dragged through the mud. Not wanting to relive most of my past is the reason I drink so much now. It helps deaden the pain that comes from losing everyone who had ever been important to me. I didn't have to worry about remorse, restitution and pain before I quite using, but I've been clean for nearly ninety days. If I relapse now, there won't be a next time for me. I'm not strong enough to go through withdrawals again."

"Then I believe we need to have a serious discussion about what these next few days will entail. The prosecution wants to win, and prepping for a trial can be stressful, intimidating and time-consuming."

"You sound like you've been there before."

"Only once, and it had nothing to do with my personal life. We already know Eloise's lawyers are going to blast my relationship with Agent Fielding, but we haven't talked about what methods they might use to to discredit you. Both sides will have done their homework regarding your time at the ranch and your relationship with Edward. While most of the questions are pre-determined, you can rest assured that anything in your past can be brought to light. Is there anything you haven't shared that can be used against you— any relationship, any act of conspiracy or any slip of the tongue? Your answers will be thoroughly rehearsed until you feel comfortable giving them, but you can't be prepared to defend something that isn't known."

Her frown let me know that she was thinking about more than just expensive liquor or invigorating conversation now. "Why do you keep pressuring me for things I don't know or remember? I've already told you everything I can."

"My intention is not to make your life unpleasant, but some lawyers are very good at forcing the person on the stand to incriminate themselves without even being aware of it until the cuffs are around their wrists. I don't want that happening to either of us."

"But you have nothing to hide now that everyone seems to know about both Charlie and Agent Fielding."

"I certainly hope that isn't true," I countered as the haughty and terrifying faces of both Carlos and Alma Mendoza's seemed to float before my eyes. "I haven't scratched the surface when it comes to enemies I've amassed that you know nothing about."

"I know more than you think I do. You believe Robert Evans and the Seville brothers have joined forces with Guadalupe because she went back to Colombia after the divorce. I also know that's where

Sam has been the past few months trying to infiltrate the cartel he once tried to bring down—the one whose existence brought Charlie into your life. I might pretend that I don't see or hear things because it's in my own best interest not to, but in truth, little escapes me."

"Please don't broadcast that fact," I told her.

"I won't. Unless convinced otherwise, my reason for being here is simply to help jurors understand that while you were playing your role at the ranch to perfection, you never crossed any lines with your partner. I can do that without lying because I've watched you wrestle with your feelings for Sam Fielding for months. If you had satisfied your longings, you wouldn't be in such a frazzled state now. You must be one of the last virgins—of legal age—on the planet."

"Hardly," I replied as my brow furrowed. "Lots of girls wear chastity rings, or do something else, as a reminder that they've made a commitment to save themselves for the man they marry. But it's late, and another heavy discussion is the last thing either of us needs. Why don't we call it a night and talk more in the morning? I've already said a number of things I regret."

"Oh, Reagan," she said, rising to her feet. "I'm such an awful friend. I get defensive about moral beliefs because I've lived most of my life without them. I want people to respect me the way they do you, but I'll never be the girl-next-door that every guy wants to protect. You can't deny that Sam was willing to risk everything to keep you safe, and there is no doubt in anyone's mind that you hold yourself to a higher standard than most people would even aspire to."

"Being different from the masses has its drawbacks, especially when it comes to being a federal agent, but I don't mind being considered odd. It's how I was raised."

"Do you think I'll be able to meet the rest of your family one day?" she asked as we made our way up the marble staircase in the mottled light coming from the enormous, crystal chandelier in the entry. "I know I might not fit in, but it would help me better understand the kind of life I've always wanted for my daughter. I just hope it's not too late to become part of what she already has. There's still so much from my past that could come back to haunt and hurt me."

I should have questioned her further, but it was late. And before I even decided to retire, I needed to place another call to the assistant director, report the day's activities and see what he had learned on his end.

"We'll make that happen when we get back, but some of them will seem even more old-fashioned than I do. I meant it when I said I came from a highly-committed Christian family. An exciting evening for us is sitting around the table playing board games and eating popcorn."

"No fancy drinks?" she asked.

"You won't even find a beer in the fridge. Alcoholism runs in our family, and we've all chosen to abstain."

Her laughter was instantaneous. "No wonder Sam finds you captivating. You're like this person from another planet."

"I'm perfectly human, Lila," I replied, reaching out to give her an impromptu hug as we approached the doors to both our rooms. "I know being my friend isn't easy."

"It's much easier than trying to maintain a relationship with Angel. She always promised the world but seldom delivered on anything. Still, I suppose that was part of her charm because she could make me believe an apple was purple, even when I could see with my own eyes that it was yellow, green or red. I was angry with her for such a long after she left me on the streets."

"How did that happen?" I asked.

"Angel was petite, blonde, beautiful and not afraid of anything. She knew how to get a man hooked on everything she had to offer, including illegal drugs. Big Horace Green recognized her value and after a few months working for him, he set her up in a lovely apartment away from the projects where her clients could easily find her. He gave her everything money could buy and even allowed Archie and me to live with her, as long as we vacated the premises when she had company. We didn't mind doing the work and running errands because we could sleep between clean sheets at night and eat more nourishing food. It was an unorthodox household since we were all minors, but it worked for nearly a year until Walter came along. He starting making demands because he wanted Angel for himself. Our benefactor became upset, and one morning when Archie and I came back after she had spent the night entertaining, we found that our keys no longer worked in the lock and our meager belongings had been left at the end of the hall. Walter had spirited Angel away and our employer had closed up shop in that part of the city."

"I thought you were working for Big Horace Green too?"

"I was, but my clientele was hardly in the same category as Angel's. I moved in with another girl who needed a roommate and never saw Archie again. I was surprised when you told me that Angel had found a job for him as a custodian in the building where she and Walter lived. She never reached out to me."

"Maybe she was afraid to."

"Not Angel! She was living her dream and didn't want anyone from her past messing it up. Archie was never a threat to anyone. He was just a boy who wanted to please a beautiful goddess with feet of clay. But the way things ended, I'm no longer sure which one of us got the better deal."

"I think you did. You're still alive, and you're still fighting. That's all any of us can do, and maybe tomorrow we'll learn something useful. I don't want to stay here any longer than necessary. Too much is going on back home."

"Do you think the FBI will ever figure out who killed Agent Ross? From what you've said, any number of people from the streets of Washington D.C. to the jungles of South America could have arranged the hit."

"We will get the people involved, and when do, I have a feeling that a very large stack of card houses is going to come tumbling down."

"On that less-than-cheerful note, I'm going into my room and order a bottle of Scotch. I figure the embassy owes me since we didn't get a welcome to the trial party."

"What about dinner? I doubt anyone here feels much like celebrating. The trial had barely begun."

Her look was one of resignation. "I prefer to celebrate every night for just having made it through another day without relapsing, but I won't get drunk."

"That would be much appreciated. There will be a lot of prepping to do tomorrow, and we need clear heads."

Chapter 2

Before washing my face, I placed another call to Assistant Director Bridges. A ringing sound pulsated in my ear until it went to voicemail. I sank down in the nearest chair and allowed my brow to crease. There was no need to leave a message. He would see my number and return my call, unless he didn't want to have his private number connected to an unsecured line.

He had warned me about using my cell when it was returned to me before the government plane left American soil. The GPS chip inside could easily be traced, but I needed to know what was going on back home. A lot could happen in eighteen hours, and the fact that I had yet to see Director Phillips was only adding to my belief that I should never have been forced to come.

I pulled the laptop from its case so I could start digging again, but it wasn't long before I realized that my lack of sleep was seriously hampering my cognitive abilities. I couldn't remember when I'd had a truly restful night. Worry over things I could not control had become my constant companion, and what was coming had the potential of testing my physical, spiritual, emotional and mental endurance to the limit. So instead of staring at a screen where images and letters kept moving, I changed into my pajama bottoms and t-shirt, slipped underneath the sheets and closed my eyes.

The stillness of the night was oppressive. The embassy was nestled in the heart of the city. The main building had been constructed of thick adobe bricks, and the distance between it and the outside walls acted as a barrier against any unwanted sound. From an outward appearance, it gave the impression of being impenetrable.

But the lack of armed federal agents made me me feel insecure. Either they were needed as part of some covert operation away from the embassy, or they were staying hidden intentionally. I rolled onto my side and glanced at the soft light that was visible around the edges of the door. There should be something I could do to get the information I needed so my stomach would quit churning and the pounding in my temples would cease. I hadn't come this far only to be left in the dark while someone else decided my future.

While I was contemplating my limited options, I heard a muffled noise in the hallway and saw a shadow pass beneath my door. I thought for a moment it might be Lila coming to talk, but when there was no knock or calling out my name, I grabbed my service revolver and tiptoed across the carpeted floor. I waited and listened. Sleep would be impossible until I knew if there was any reason for alarm. But when I pulled the door open, I saw Lila's face peering cautiously at me.

"What's going on?" she asked. "I was just enjoying some of the best Scotch I've had in ages when I thought I heard someone at my door."

"Go back inside while I check it out," I instructed, stepping into the hallway with my gun poised.

She gave me a frightened look. "I thought we would be safe here. That's one of the reasons I agreed to come."

"There's no reason to believe we aren't. Just lock your door and stay put. We'll talk when I get back."

I should have taken time to alleviate some of her fears, but only moments would elapse until whomever had been in the hallway disappeared. I hurried towards the marble staircase looking into each crevice as I passed it. My bare feet made no noise on the floor.

When I got to the top of the stairs, I looked down and saw a man in a heavy jacket hurrying towards the front door.

"FBI! Stop where you are and put your hands on your head," I shouted as I hurried down the cool surface as quickly as I could. When he didn't respond, I said it again. But he remained where he was, as if trying to decide what he intended to do.

I felt my heart lodge in my throat as I closed the distance between us. My gun was still leveled at the small of his back, but it wouldn't take much for him to overpower me. He was tall and powerfully built. The collar of his jacket was turned up, but I could see that his head was covered with a mass of dark hair.

"I'm not going to ask you again. Put your hands on your head and turn around slowly, or I will shoot."

The seconds seemed to last forever as we stood engaged in a battle of wills. My shouts had brought no one to help.

"I guess you have me at a disadvantage because it's not in my nature to shoot a woman," he suddenly said in a calm and disarming voice.

But instead of surrendering the way I had asked, he swung around with such energy that I stumbled backwards. With practiced precision, he pulled the gun from my hand as his eyes literally gleamed. My mouth opened, but it was impossible to speak when I realized who it was.

"I might have known my nocturnal visit would not go unnoticed. I wanted to talk to you but decided there wasn't time for some long confrontation."

DEA Agent Sam Fielding was standing in front of me and displaying that mocking smile that had been haunting both my waking and sleeping moments for months. I tried to take in his entire appearance at once. The dark circles beneath his eyes showed his lack of sleep, and his scruffy cheeks hadn't seen a razor for weeks, but otherwise he looked as healthy and strong as ever.

"It's you?" I managed to whisper as I struggled to remain standing upright.

"In the flesh, but I don't think it's wise for us to remain where we can be seen. Let's go into the library for a moment. I'm afraid that's all the time I can spare right now."

He guided me across the hall and through a doorway into the darkened room where after-dinner drinks had been served. But instead of turning on a light, he pulled me to one side where we would not be seen.

"I've missed you, Reagan," he said, taking my hands in his.

My relief at knowing he was still alive should have been enough to force civility, but I wasn't going to allow him to lull me into some sort of soothing trance.

"That's good to know, but I need you to tell me why you were skulking around in front of my door like some lowlife. Lila said you stopped in front of hers too."

"I don't suppose you would believe me if I said I was trying to decide which one of you would take my sudden emergence back into the land of living most calmly."

"Not for a minute," I responded.

"Well, it's true! But I came to the sudden realization that what you didn't know wasn't going to hurt you. I just got back to the city and needed to inform Director Phillips about what's going on. Although I am free to move about at will, my actions are carefully monitored."

I looked up at him with annoyance. "You're speaking in riddles. We all thought you were dead."

He laughed and then lifted my chin. Up close, he appeared to have aged considerably. Nonetheless, the playfulness that still danced in his eyes let me know that he had not changed inside. He was obviously enjoying our unexpected reunion.

"There's the little spitfire I've grown so fond of," he said as he took a step away so he could more easily see how much his presence was unnerving me. "Your often condescending, yet totally mesmerizing, face is what kept me going all these months in the jungle when every breath inhaled should have been my last. The thought of sparring with you again literally kept me alive."

I wanted to lash out at him with every ounce of strength I possessed. He had caused measureless amounts pain and anguish. "I hated you for leaving us the way you did."

He eyed me curiously. "It had to be that way. You're like a pit bull when you want something. I had already taken a huge leap of proverbial faith by coming to the States to set my affairs in order and couldn't risk anything more in case my entire mission went sideways. You already knew more than you should."

"I wasn't just anyone! I had been to hell and back with you on two assignments, and in case you've conveniently forgotten, we share a son. So please forgive me if I don't fall at your feet with relief."

"That is one thing I would never expect from you, Reagan. You're too levelheaded to let something trivial like emotional involvement cloud your practical judgment when it comes to a man. That's why I sent you a letter."

I leaned into the wall for support. I would not erupt into tears of frustration or sentimental release. He owed me an explanation as to why he had run back to his job leaving me alone with a baby and the command to look into Lupe Evans' life.

"Do you have any idea how worried I've been? And Charlie, I was terrified that he would never get to know his father."

"Charlie?" he asked, placing his hands on the wall—one on each side of my head so I would be unable to move—unless I managed to push him away. "I thought my son was named after me."

"It's a derivation of his middle name, and just one of the hundred things you've missed because you were too busy playing undercover games to be bothered with the child you helped to create."

I was being mean now, but it was better than falling apart. I didn't like being caught unaware, and the blood still pounding in my temples was making it hard to think. I had seen more desperation, fear, pain, loss and grief during the past six months than most people experienced in a lifetime.

"Did you know that he almost died?" I continued before my courage waned. His very presence seemed to envelope me in a deep and eroding fog. "I sat by his crib in the hospital for five days praying he would survive. I couldn't imagine how empty my life would be without him."

"But he's okay?"

"Only through the grace of that God you're not sure even exists," I responded as unwelcome tears filled my eyes. "You may believe that running back to Colombia to find Alma Mendoza was the best way to protect the innocent, but there is no one in this world more innocent, or more in need of protection and care, than your son. You don't give up the responsibilities that come with being a parent because it's inconvenient, even if you've just learned about it."

He was silent for the longest time. I could feel his hot breath beating down on my cheeks and wished I could move away, but his hands were still resting on the wall and my gun was dangling through his fingertips. When I allowed my eyes to glance down, I saw that he had a machine gun hidden underneath his coat. This wasn't a scheduled visit to the embassy. He was here to relay a message, and my appearance was keeping him from leaving.

Quite suddenly, I realized that all of my personal grievances and concerns about the past, present or future had to be set aside until whatever he was involved with had been resolved. He was an honorable and brave man any child would be proud to have in his life. I needed to stop thinking like a mother, or a woman whose feelings had been hurt, and resume acting like the agent whose door he had approached hoping he still had a friend he could rely on.

"I can't blame you for the way you feel about me," he finally said, standing upright and dropping his arms to his side. "I might not have handled things well, but I do love my son. It wasn't easy walking away from him, and the woman who had gotten underneath my skin. I've never had a reason to stay in one place before."

"But you should have trusted me more," I responded as a few tears slid from my eyes. "How do you think I felt when your lawyer had me sign papers leaving everything you had to your son? It was like verifying your death."

He returned my gun and then ran his hand through his shaggy hair. In a way, I liked it longer. It made him appear more vulnerable and approachable.

"Maybe I did take the easy way out by having Brad do all the explaining, but have you ever thought that I was afraid of confronting you personally because I knew exactly how you would react? In our line of work, goodbye usually means forever. It was easier to walk away and get on with what had to be done than confront feelings I'd never had before. I don't expect you to understand what drives my excessive behaviors, but I was at a place where turning back would have undone years of undercover work. That was unacceptable to everyone involved."

His honest admissions were chipping away at my anger. Every instinct told me to forgive before it really was too late. But if I told him how glad I was that he hadn't died, it might start something neither of us was prepared to finish.

"So what do you need me to do?" I asked before changing my mind.

"What I need you to do is go back to your room and pretend this encounter never took place, but since I know that directive will fall on deaf ears, I would suggest you talk to Director Phillips. He'll be in his office for the next few minutes and can fill you in on what I've told him, but I suggest you throw on a robe first. You have no idea how disconcerting your presence is when you're wearing the same nightwear you slept in when we were at the Rios ranch."

My arms instantly closed across my chest, despite the gun I now held in my hand. "What should I tell Lila. She knows someone was in the hall and is waiting for me."

"As little as possible. You were brought here for a very specific reason."

"One that has little to do with testifying at a trial," I interrupted.

"Your perception is spot-on as usual, but there isn't time to discuss strategies that may or may not see the desired result. You'll just have to trust me when I say that everything will become clear soon. Now, I really must be going. I've taken too much time as it is."

"Will I ever see you again?" I asked as he moved towards the door, leaving me in what felt like a deep and dreadful abyss from which their was little chance for escape.

"I hope so, Reagan. I would like to believe there is more to our story than this."

I watched from the shadows while he disappeared into the night. No alarm sounded and no person with a badge came to investigate. My first instinct was to run directly to Director Phillips' office, but the fact that Agent Fielding had climbed the staircase stopped me. He had not forgotten the people he had left behind, but he was committed to making sure that nothing distracted him from his mission. I needed to follow his example. That meant taking a deep breath, putting on something a little less revealing and speaking to Lila before barging in on a man who would not be happy to see me.

I hurried back up the stairs and rapped lightly on Lila's door while trying to decide just how much I should say. Lies had a way of multiplying and backfiring. Her soft footsteps from the other side let me know that she had not gone to sleep.

"You were gone for any awfully long time," she said, unlocking the door and then retracing her steps to the bed and pulling the comforter around her shoulders. "I was afraid you might never come back but had no idea whom I should call. This place seems more like a tomb than a residential office building where I imagined dozens of federal agents would be working."

I put my hand on her shoulder. A hysterical Lila might not be easily constrained, and what I had to say would be followed by questions I could not answer. "You did exactly the right thing by waiting and not sounding any alarms. Our phantom was a friend. Agent Fielding is alive."

She slumped backwards. "You're absolutely certain?"

"I talked to him personally. He was coming to speak to one of us but decided there wasn't time."

"So where has he been, and what has he been doing?" she asked. "Does he look as suave and debonaire as always?"

My lips curled into a weary smile. "You would never recognize him from a distance, but there wasn't time to discuss anything. Director Phillips is in his office. I want to get a run at him before he retires for the night."

"Not like that," she said, tossing a cream-colored, silk robe in my direction. "I want to know everything and won't go to sleep until you get back. Just tell me this crazy life will soon be back to normal now that Sam is back. I can hardly wait to see him. He's the only man, other than Edward, that I ever felt I could trust."

"What's normal?" I asked as a way of keeping the conversation from becoming too personal. "I shouldn't be gone long."

DEA Director Phillips was sitting at his desk when I impudently pushed open his door. There was no one around to announce my presence, and I was afraid he might not respond if I knocked. If he was surprised to see me standing there in a robe and bare feet, he never let on.

"I was wondering how long it would take for you to show up in my office," he said, dropping his pen on top of a stack of papers. "I had hoped word would not reach you until morning because I have important business to take care of before fielding any of your questions. Nonetheless, since you're already here you might as well sit down and make yourself comfortable. I'm sorry I wasn't available to greet you and Miss Rivers. I hope our staff had been treating you well."

"The stay has been pleasant enough, sir, but I need . . ."

"You've seen Agent Fielding," he interrupted as his eyes moved up and down my person. I was carrying my service revolver inside one of the robe's pockets, and the bulge was unmistakable. "I hope your little reunion didn't last too long. He slipped away from other responsibilities for the sole purpose of delivering an important message."

I looked over at him. Only the lamp on his desk illuminated a face that looked haggard and strained. Whatever they were involved with would not be easily explained.

"I saw him in the entry hall, sir, and told him to put his hands in the air. I thought he was an intruder."

His snort of laughter let me know just how concerned with other matters he really was. "I told Sam that having any contact with you prematurely wasn't a good idea. I was hoping he would take my advice and leave before anyone saw him. How did you even know he was here?"

"Both Lila and I heard footsteps in the hall. I decided to investigate since the number of agents in the building seems to have dwindled since I was last here."

"This building has never been left unprotected, Agent Sinclair. There are cameras everywhere and agents in the basement monitoring them every hour of every day. No movement, outside the confines of private quarters, goes unnoticed. However, you are right in assuming that most of our agents are involved with assignments elsewhere. There is no precedence for what we are dealing with, but we have tried to cover every   contingency possible. We want this situation resolved quickly and with as little bloodshed as possible."

"Agent Fielding alluded to that but told me to talk to you since he was pressed for time. I want to be included in the implementation of whatever plans are being made."

"Assistant Director Bridges told me you wouldn't accept testifying at a trial as a legitimate reason for being here once you'd had time to do a little sleuthing, but we needed Eloise to believed we were serious about pursuing a conviction. We want all ties the Seville cartel has to this city severed. That's been our goal for months, but we weren't sure that was even possible until Agent Fielding arrived tonight. He's key to everything we've been trying to do since Robert Evans and the Seville brothers made their big play for power."

"You do know that Agent Ross was assassinated last night while in federal custody. That doesn't speak well to any plans you may have been making."

"I'll admit that's something we didn't see coming, but past experience tells me that a hit like that didn't come from the people I've been trying to keep behind bars."

"Why not?" I asked as the muscles around my jaw tighten. "He was working directly with Agent Gibbons, and she's the one Eloise sent after me."

"I'm sorry that mission did not go as planned, Agent Sinclair, and my sincere condolences over losing your partner. But you have to understand that the dynamics of what we're dealing with keep changing. I hope the FBI can find the person who killed Agent Ross. We're all convinced he knew things that would aid in solving a number of ongoing cases on both sides of the border."

"But you really don't believe that's going to happen."

"It might, if the connections you've been postulating can be proven."

"You know about those?" I asked.

"You're not the only one who has been looking into Walter Evans' past as a way of discovering what his son is up to now. Guadalupe Evans has been a person of interest for decades, but she's a shrewd businessperson like her former husband. She knows when to attack and when to withdraw, and she uses other people to do the dirty work necessary for the kind of success she's achieved. The fact that one of the Seville brothers was seen entering Colombia gave Agent Fielding the impetus needed to pull off one of the biggest deep-cover operations this agency has ever seen."

"I'm afraid you're loosing me, sir. Whatever research I've done has been basically on my own. The assistant director doesn't even know everything I've found out because I haven't been able to reach him since I got here"

"He's been involved in investigations of his own but knows more than you think he does. Despite how we needed to make it appear, we have been working in tandem for the past few months. I want to thank you for stumbling onto Neva Jasper. That list Angel Evans managed to hide in such a brilliant way has been invaluable in locating some of the biggest players the DEA has ever been able to locate at one time."

"So arrests have been made."

"A few! Mostly, we're just waiting for the perfect moment to make our move."

"I don't understand, unless my belief that the Sevilles, the Evans and the Mendoza's are somehow working together is accurate."

"That is a correct assumption, although I doubt even you are aware of how intertwined the two cartels have become and why. I couldn't afford to have you poking around too much until everything was in place. I'm hoping you've kept most of your theorizing to yourself."

"Lila has been helping me make a few connections. She's been very free the past few days with information regarding her true relationship with Angel and what she overheard at the ranch. Angel got Walter to the pool so Robert could kill him. She also knew about the takeover."

"Our Miss Rivers seems to be a pool of useful information—when it suits her to be so. That's one of the reasons we didn't have her arrested the moment she showed up at FBI headquarters asking to speak you you. Despite how it appears, the DEA does not go lightly on people who escape our custody. But in her case, we felt she could do more good on the outside. That said, please do not be too liberal with any information you share. There are discrepancies in her story that need further investigation before I'm willing to trust her with any of our plans."

"I'll be careful," I told him.

He looked over the desk at me. "Sam told me your discretion could be assured."

"I would never leak information, unless told to do so, sir. I know from personal experience what happens when it gets into the wrong the hands."

"Once again, I am sorry you lost your partner, Agent Sinclair. I wish it could have been avoided, but we underestimated what Agent's Gibbons and Ross were willing to do. I wish he had answered a few questions before his demise, but I have been assured that no stone will be left unturned when it comes to solving his murder. Assistant Director Bridges has removed Agent Ross's wife and children from protective custody. They're not in any danger, but he needs her to believe she will become the next victim if she doesn't come clean. You see, Agent Sinclair, superiors are not above listening to their subordinates when they have something useful to say."

"I guess not," I replied. "I suppose that means you also know that my son's life was threatened if I came here to testify."

He cleared his throat before responding. "I have reason to believe that threat did not come from what's left of the old cartel either."

"Then where?" I asked, knowing that now was a time to listen and not ask unnecessary questions or state unwanted opinions. "It specifically mentioned Mexico."

"Perhaps it will make more sense if I explain what I can, but be advised that it can go no further. I'll preface my remarks by saying that I was surprised to learn of your involvement with Sam."

My resolve to remain silent while he talked was instantly overtaken by a need to defend my honor. "There was no personal complicity between us, other than the assignments we were given. We share a son who came into both of our lives quite unexpectedly. We just want to do what's right for him."

"I was not accusing you of anything, Agent Sinclair. Sam explained your relationship and how difficult it's been being away from a child he just learned was his, but it was imperative that personal involvements be clarified if this operation was going to work."

"Is that why Isabel and Luis Mendoza were taken captive by the DEA?"

"You don't mince words, do you, Agent Sinclair. Those children are in a safe environment where they are receiving the kind of attention they never got from family, but we needed the right kind of leverage. Director Stevens from our Colombian office found out that a plan was being made to get Alma out of prison and replace her with Carlos. It seemed like just another bid for attention until rumors started to circulate in the underground that the entire cartel framework throughout South and Central America was being restructured."

"That's ambitious," I interjected.

"It's what we've suspected all along but didn't have the information necessary to pursue anything until we learned that Mendoza and his people were going to be used to jumpstart the entire thing. Some of the key players needed to set things in motion were in prison, and Mendoza was the only one who could rally the needed forces."

"That doesn't explain why my son was used as bait."

"It might, if you'll just be patient for a few moments. We needed the right person on the inside. We had agents inserted into a number of them, but any change in routine would blow their covers, and we weren't entirely sure who was involved. Despite all outward appearances, Alma was devastated when the children under her care went missing. She considered Luis and Isabel the family she was never allowed to have because she'd spent her entire life grooming her younger brother to take over the family business—rather than seek out the life she really wanted."

"She didn't strike me as being a woman who had any maternal feelings."

"That's because you didn't know the woman we discovered she had once been. When she was young, she was betrothed to a man by the name of Alexandro Ramirez. He was an up-and-coming drug dealer in his own rights. Her father adored him and knew that a marriage would solidify a pact between cartels."

"So what happened to him?" I asked.

"As is the case with many young men who believe they are well-insulated against their enemies, he began to get greedy and got himself killed."

"That's a sad story, but I don't see how it advanced your cause."

"Did you happen to run across Guadalupe's maiden name during your research?"

"You know I didn't, or you wouldn't be asking."

"Well, it was Ramirez. They're not siblings, like you've found to be the case with some of the key people in both cases you've worked with the DEA, but they were cousins."

My head was starting to ache, but I knew what he was trying to tell me. A direct link had now been established between Robert Evans, the Seville brothers and Carlos and Alma Mendoza, but I still couldn't see why my son had to become involved.

"Sam let it be known that he had Mendoza's children and would return them if he was given a large enough cut in the proposed new business endeavor."

"Why would they believe that? He's always worked for the good guys."

"Let's just say that we made it look like he wasn't as squeaky-clean as everyone believed. Perception is everything in this game, and Sam is a master of deception and manipulation. I suppose that's a byproduct of what he's done quite successfully his entire career. We simply found the right person to help him pull off a rather ingenious rouse, and he took it from there."

"I'm afraid I still don't understand, sir."

"The specifics aren't important, but his story had to be believable enough that he wouldn't be executed on the spot when he found Alma and told her what he wanted to do. His proposal was simple. He would supply information about the DEA's plans in exchange for a modest percentage of the profits he managed to keep from being seized."

"So he basically became a spy for both sides."

"It's done all the time, Agent Sinclair, and he used his son's existence as source of collateral, if you will. Everyone knew he had no ties that would keep him from double-crossing anyone, but a family he cared about gave him the credibility necessary to have his proposal considered."

"But to barter with my son's life is unacceptable."

"The risk was substantial, but you have to understand that the wrong people already knew he had a son and who was taking care of him. Sam wanted to minimize his exposure to any more violence, and the best way of doing that was by putting himself in a situation where he might be able to stop another attack. It was a bold move, and one I wasn't entirely behind at first, but it has paid handsome dividends because we're getting information we need, and you and your son are still alive."

I shook my head in the darkness of room whose furnishings now seemed to be swaying. "That brings several questions to mind, Director Phillips, and none of them are pleasant."

"Fire away, Agent Sinclair. We're passed the point of my pulling rank on most things."

"Thank you, sir. First, I would like to know if Carlos Mendoza has made contact with the people he allowed himself to be incarcerated to find? That was a big sacrifice for someone who killed his wife, abandoned his children and left his former lover and unborn child to die just so he could stay one step ahead of the law."

"We're more than certain he has but, so far as we know from our contacts within the prison, no plans have been made to get anyone out. It's all about connections, money, power and making the right move at precisely the right time. Mendoza knows he's in no danger, and his militia will have him extracted the minute it is no longer necessary for him to be there. He's actually safer behind bars than on the outside while all the restructuring is taking place. His tendency to let others take the fall is well known in certain circles."

"But why get Alma out at all, unless he already knew what was being planned?"

He glanced away from me momentarily before resuming. "Carlos needed someone he could trust in control of his operation while he worked from inside the system. He might consider himself untouchable when it comes to almost everything, but he's no fool. He's in a pivotal position because he's already known as someone to be feared, and Alma is no stranger to the people who work for him. The Sevilles and Robert and Lupe Evans need both him and his connections to pull off this takeover, and he needed someone to protect his interests. An empire with a three-way head and combined resources would be a nearly impossible beast to stop."

"So how are you going to proceed?" I asked, realizing that while he might accept the role I was now playing, I still wasn't a member of his team.

"That's in the process of unfolding. Sam managed to convince Alma that he could get the Seville's out of prison without sounding any alarms. It seems that Lupe and Eloise had become quite close when their husbands were working together, and having her friend free was one of the conditions for the merger to take place. Lupe wasn't about to do it herself, and Alma needed to prove her loyalty."

"It seems rather bizarre that two powerful women would form such a lasting friendship."

"Apparently, both women spent their younger years raising families and sharing confidences. Another tidbit of information that you probably don't already know is that Walter and Lupe had a daughter. She was a few years older than Robert and used to accompany the rest of her family on business trips. She was killed in a drive-by shooting on her way to a club here in Mexico City when she was nineteen. Eloise helped Lupe during that difficult time and was even instrumental in making sure the man who pulled the trigger was punished."

"I'm assuming that means he was killed by one of the people the Seville's employed since they prefer taking the law into their own hands."

"The authorities were never able to determine if the attack was precipitated because she was in the car, but they were in gang territory and retribution is common for the cartels. If they can send a message, they're not above doing it in the most heinous way possible. But we're digressing, and there are certain things that must be done before morning. Suffice it to say that Walter was the brains behind the operation, and the Seville's supplied the product and the muscle. Sam came here tonight because he had information we needed, but his movements are being closely monitored. And some of the things he's been required to do will, of necessity, need to be covered up."

"Has Alma come with him?" I asked as another cold chill slid up and down my extremities.

"She's somewhere in the city, as are a great number of her people. Make no mistake that Sam is playing a very dangerous game, but he's one of the smartest agents I've ever had the privilege of working with, and his cover as a traitor is still intact. I'm not at liberty to divulge anything more than that."

My head felt like it had been caught in a vice, and my stomach was churning, but I couldn't just sit idly by while Agent Fielding was so deep undercover that any moment might be his last.

"I know I'm not an official member of your team, sir, but I would like to help."

"There's nothing any of us can do, except wait. Meet with Victor Vega and give him the cooperation he asks for, but do not tell him anything that we have discussed. I believe him to be loyal, but there are never any guarantees."

"I can do that," I replied.

"And one more thing," he said, looking at me with an intensity I had never experienced before. "If you're a praying woman, I would suggest sending a few extra invocations heavenward. Sam is up-to-date on what has been happening here simply because he has to maintain contact with us so his cover won't collapse, but that doesn't mean everything won't change by morning."

I left his office feeling more helpless than ever. I understood making sacrifices for the greater good, but Agent Fielding was gambling with more than just his life this time. If something went wrong, he would never see Charlie again, and I might not either.

But as my bare feet carried me over cool, marble floors, I realized that walking away wasn't an option for any of us because our lives had become intertwined—much like tiny flies caught in a large, sticky, inescapable spider's web. The amount of information the DEA had already secured was great, but they would not act on any of it until they could make a move that really counted.

My brow furrowed as I pondered my alternatives. I could continue hacking away in a mostly futile attempt to help, or I could do as I had been told and wait for an invitation to join an incredibly dangerous game as more than an observer. Neither option suited my personality or my training at Quantico, but without something more to go on, I was stuck in a place I didn't want to be.

The very walls of the embassy seemed to be closing in on me, but there was no place to go in the middle of night, so I returned to Lila's room hoping I would know what to say when I got there. She called out for me to come inside but didn't leave the warming confines of her bed. I sat down in one of the overstuffed chairs next to a barred window.

"You look like hell," she said, dispensing with any niceties. "What did our illustrious host have to say that made you more upset than you already were?"

"Director Phillips doesn't want to jeopardize whatever mission he's working on," I replied.

It was impossible not to think about my son's father who may already be back in Alma Mendoza's sinister lair. Despite wanting to live a different life, he was addicted to the excitement and danger of apprehending drug lords, and he was exceptional at doing it. No one in the DEA would ever encourage him to pursue a more conventional life.

"That's too bad," she said, giving me a look that was impossible to read in the dim light coming from her bedside lamp. "I was hoping he would go into all the juicy details since we know Sam Fielding is alive and could easily proclaim that fact to anyone who was willing to listen."

"Doing that would only jeopardize plans we know nothing about. The director wants us to sit tight, go over our testimony with Victor Vega, and be ready to walk into that courtroom whenever the call comes."

"I was hoping Sam's appearance would keep us from testifying. I don't want to see Eloise again. She always looked at me with contempt, but who is she to judge anyone? She helped create an empire that destroyed thousands of lives. I might not be able to offer anything that ensures she receives a lethal injection, but I certainly hope someone can. You could have knocked me over with a feather when you said Sam was here."

"Likewise," I responded.

I wanted to tell Lila everything because I believed her allegiance had changed, but too many questions remained unanswered. Once I was able to speak to Agent Fielding again, I would have a better idea of which direction to take when it came to her.

"There I go again," she said with a heavy sigh. "I seem to have a terminal case of foot-in-mouth disease, but you're like a little sister, and I don't want to see you get hurt. Sam Fielding could easily do that, especially where Charlie is concerned."

"You're right," I admitted, though I couldn't quite meet her eyes. "I've been so focused on whether he had been captured or killed that I've given little thought as to how my life would change if he made it back alive."

"But it's a good thing, isn't it?" she asked.

"It's what I've been praying for since he left, but I don't know what he's been through or what his plans for the future might be. I don't even know why he's here or how his presence will affect what happens to us."

"Life is never as simple as we wish it could be, but I think you owe it to yourself—and to Charlie—to sit down with him and clear the air."

"I plan to do that, if I ever see him again."

"But you're not sure that's going to happen."

"Seeing him tonight was a fluke. He came to our floor because he wanted to talk to one of us, but something changed his mind. I'm afraid we're no better off when it comes to knowing anything useful than we were a few hours ago."

"Now that's a crock!" she exclaimed. "You know that your son's father is still alive. The why and how are merely interesting questions that can be discussed later. What I've been wondering is how this will affect your relationship with Trey. I know you've had a few rocky moments recently, but I've seen the way he is with both you and Charlie. That's a man who wants to be part of something permanent."

"Trey isn't interested in pursuing a relationship where there isn't complete honesty and trust. I kept the identity of Charlie's biological father from him for over a month because I wasn't sure how I felt, or how he would react, and now he has a federal detail watching his every move. I'm not sure he'll even talk to me when I get back."

"He just needs time to decompress and think things through. He has to know that none of this is your fault. You were just trying to keep the people you care about safe, and Charlie's life had been threatened."

"That might have worked in my favor if he hadn't already been betrayed by his former wife. I can't offer him the kind of life he wants right now, and I get the strong feeling that he's tied of waiting around."

"I can understand exercising caution when it comes to matters of the heart, but betrayal isn't some inevitable disease. Sometimes it's necessary for survival."

"Tell me about it," I retorted as my thoughts returned to Agent Fielding and the fact that he was playing both sides against a middle where no parameters had been set. "My life was an open book before I became involved with the DEA."

"Welcome to the world of criminal activity and human depravity," she mocked. "I messed up the only thing of value my life ever produced by giving my daughter away. It was the best thing for her, but assuming that she'll ever understand and forgive might be asking a little too much."

"It all comes down to the same thing, doesn't it?" I responded. "No matter what comes our way through our own decisions, or the actions of others, having family and friends who are willing to stand by us is all that really matters."

"My family hasn't been part of my life since I was a child, and I can count the number of real friends I've ever had on one hand. I know your problems seem overwhelming, Reagan, but you have two men who would sacrifice most anything for you. All you have to do is decide which one of them you're going to give a fighting chance."

"It's not that simple, Lila."

"Opening your heart to love never is, but I would give all that I possess just to see Edward's face one more time. You've already had your prayer in that regard answered."

"We've talked about this before. Agent Fielding and I barely know each other, despite the roles we were forced to play."

"You know each other well enough. Nothing brings two people closer than a little life and death experience, along with some great chemistry, and you've had many such moments."

"Mexico was nothing like South America. I hated him because he was willing to let a woman and an innocent baby die, and he hated me because keeping us alive meant he couldn't finish his mission."

"How were you supposed to know what would happen when you went undercover for the DEA? You were a newbie agent who had never been part of an undercover operation before, but he certainly doesn't hate you now."

"Maybe he should! I didn't even tell him I was glad he was still alive. I just let my frustration and anger surface because seeing him again upset my fragile world."

"So you have to clarify a few things when you see him again. It's not the end of the world. I know you still hope things will work out with Trey because he's safe and predictable, but I'm here to tell you that he isn't the only man in the world worthy of your consideration. Sam Fielding is just about as good as they get."

"It sounds like you became much closer after I left the hospital."

"Let's just say that we had the opportunity to lay all our cards on the table, and we took it. He forgave my anger and blame because Edward died while trying to save his life, and he expressed profound gratitude that I had accompanied you to the hospital when he couldn't. He might be a complicated man, but I can assure you that he's worth fighting for. If he had any interest in me, I would certainly make every effort to see where it led."

I went back to my room shortly after that but didn't sleep well. There was too much to think about, and when the first rays of morning light hit my bedroom window, I took a long shower and dressed for the day. Despite many unanswered questions and concerns I couldn't address, staying cloistered in my room wasn't possible if I wanted to learn anything else.

Lila was waiting for me in the informal dining room when I went down the marble staircase to get some juice and a slice of toast. I wasn't sure my stomach would hold anything more.

"I'm surprised to see you up so early," I said as she filled a cup with hot, black coffee.

"My intention was to sleep until noon, but I'm glad I didn't. Did you know a big dinner party is being planned for this evening? I heard it from one of the servants a few minutes ago. It's caused quite a stir in the kitchen. Do you think it has anything to do with Sam being here?"

My surprise caused me to lean into the table for support. "I don't see how it could, but then anything is possible. Did you hear anything else?"

"Only that Victor will be in the conference room at nine, and one of us needs to see him. Do you care if I go first? I'm not much good at waiting, and I want to take a nap. I hope you brought more than what I've already seen you in to wear. Tonight is going to be special, and we need to dress up."

I almost told her there was no reason to believe we would be invited since our initial instructions were to remain in the background, but Director Phillips had mentioned that changes could be expected. This might be just another cog in a fast-rolling wheel that seemed to be gathering speed.

"I brought one of the evening gowns Agent Fielding furnished for me when we were at the Rios ranch. I haven't worn it yet."

"Then I hope he'll be here to see you in it," she replied. "It's my unwanted opinion that both of you have some serious explaining to do. Maybe you'll be able to convince him to come home with us."

"That would be nice, but I doubt he's in a position to even consider it."

She shook her auburn hair. "You can play the doomsday child if you want to, but I plan to enjoy myself for as long as possible. Now wish me luck with the suave Victor Vega. I wish you could be there to coach me, but I'm sure I'll do just fine."

I stopped by Director Phillips' office after leaving Lila in the conference room, but the door was locked, and there was no one around that could tell me where he had gone. I understood how busy he must be, but if he wasn't available to talk, I needed someone else who had clearance to hear what I needed to say. So I picked up a phone in his outer office and dialed Assistant Director Bridge's direct number. After several rings, it went to voice mail. I left a short message telling him I had information he needed to hear and could be reached at the embassy. I gave him Manuela's name and explained that she would know where to find me.

The bustle of activity associated with the upcoming dinner moved quickly from the kitchen to other areas of the ground floor. Since I needed a quiet place to strategize and think, I returned to my room and read through every note I had made and every printed piece of information I had brought with me to see what I had missed. If Agent Fielding and Alma Mendoza were in the city to spring Eloise and her youngest son from jail, I needed to figure out how and when it might happen and what that meant for my family and friends back home.

My anger over Charlie being used at bait to solidify a coalition between cartels had not lessened, although I now understood the reasoning behind it. Agent Fielding was using what he had at his disposal to make a calculated move, but I was tired of being manipulated without my consent. That meant discovering some leverage of my own. There was no doubt in my mind that I would it.

Chapter 3

The rest of my day was basically uneventful. I met with Victor Vega when Lila had finished. She seemed pleased with how their encounter had gone. I didn't ask for details because my own thoughts were still in disarray. Manuela had come to my room with a message from Assistant Director Bridges while I was rearranging names on a graph I had constructed on the laptop I was using. She told me I wasn't supposed to worry because everyone was safe, and he would get back with me when he could. It seemed like a slap in the face after everything I had been through, but there was nothing I could do except wait.

I was greeted with a handshake when I walked into the conference room shortly before noon. Victor Vega looked even more solemn and distant than he had the day before, but he had come alone. I couldn't help but wonder if he had received some disheartening news, but I didn't tell him that I had seen Agent Fielding or spoken to Director Phillips. That was something he needed to discover on his own.

His questions were specific, and I answered as honestly as I could. He already knew the defense's claims were bogus, but proving malicious intent would be difficult. Witnesses for the defense had come forth stating that my behavior at the ranch was suspicious, erratic and less than friendly, while Señora Seville had been affable and sympathetic to my concerns as a young bride who was going to have a child. I had rebuffed her kind overtures by siding with Angel Evans—a woman who had done nothing but flaunt her disregard for family values and fidelity—and lie about being pregnant. Lila's testimony as a character witness would not be enough to sway a jury into believing anything I said.

"You do understand that none of that is true," I said.

"Words can easily be manipulated, and Eloise Seville is already being a viewed with sympathy. She's an old woman, without a criminal record, who has been incarcerated for four months and whose older sons have abandoned her. When you add her husband's recent death and the fact that her youngest son is in prison on what she claims are trumped-up charges as well, it doesn't seem likely that the prosecution will be able to get anyone to rule in our favor."

"Then why not just call it quits and let the chips fall where they may?"

"That's not how the system works in Mexico. Eloise wants her case to be heard, but I am beginning to believe it is simply a ruse to keep the authorities busy while something else is being planned."

"Do you have any idea what that might be?" I asked, pulling my bottom lip into my mouth to stop any unwanted outbursts.

"My interactions with the DEA have been minimal. I am simply a court-appointed attorney who is trying to do my job. No one would voluntarily take on anyone associated with the Seville cartel. Although the old structure seems to have been dismantled, there are many sympathizers throughout this country whose livelihoods have been destroyed. They are not happy and will let their voices be heard."

I suddenly knew at least part of what was going on. It had to appear that the law was being upheld, but the Seville cartel still controlled much of the city and countryside. Eloise would get out of jail, and the DEA needed another plan ready before it happened.

No one approached me during the late afternoon hours, and I didn't seek anyone out. But I did see Manuela in the upstairs hallway where she was placing clean linens in a closet when I returned to my room.

"Are you ready for the festivities, Agent Sinclair?" she asked. "I have heard that entertainment will be provided by members of the Mexico City Symphony."

"I was not aware that I had been invited."

"There was no time for formal invitations, but a message has been left on your phone. Dinner will be served at eight with drinks in the library before and after. I have not been made aware of whom the other guests will be, but Madame Alexander is a great patron of the arts and her gatherings are not always scheduled in advance."

"So this isn't necessarily some random get-together."

"I cannot answer that, but I do not think you have anything to fear. The ambassador would not risk your safety. After all, you have only come to help us."

"Is there anything else you can tell me?" I asked.

She turned her back to the camera that hung suspended from the far corner of the hall. When she spoke again, it was in little more than a whisper.

"Please do not be alarmed, but I know an unexpected visitor came to your bedroom door last night. I also know that you chased him down the staircase and had a brief conversation with him in the library before he left the embassy. I will not ask who he was. His face was carefully shielded from the cameras, but please be careful. His unexpected arrival has given rise to speculation since none of the staff was advised of his coming."

"How do you know all of this?"

"My future brother-in-law is not the only close friend Anna made while working here, and some of the agents know who I am."

"Thank you Manuela," I said, knowing I should report what she had told me, but also knowing I wouldn't. She had come to me as a friend, and I had to respect that.

I watched her hurry down the hallway and turned to knock on Lila's door, but something stopped me. If Manuela knew Agent Fielding had been here during the night, other people on staff did too. One of them may even have reported what had gone on to Alma Mendoza. I should have left well enough alone, instead of chasing him down the staircase. My obsessive need to know what was going on may have inadvertently messed up whatever plans had already been made.

But I couldn't worry about what might happen next, or even who might be in attendance at the impromptu dinner. I could only remain vigilant, attentive and look the part I was expected to play. That's why I took extra care with my appearance—something not easily done with massive amounts of sleep deprivation and continual worry. The form-fitting evening gown I had to wear was exquisite, but pretending that recent events did not have me concerned would be nearly impossible.

It was hard enough knowing that Agent Ross had been executed in a cell while under federal protection, but seeing Agent Fielding again had awakened feelings I had been trying to disregard for months. I wanted to confront him about so many things, but he needed freedom from personal encumbrances until all of our enemies had been found, prosecuted and sentenced to places from which they would never be able to escape.

Lila went with me when we descended the staircase to the library shortly before seven. She looked well-rested and very elegant in a black gown that was cut conspicuously low in the front. Her hair was in a knot at the nap of her neck. It was evident that she was ready for more than just my company.

I was willing to be pleasant, and even try my hand at being charming, but every thought in my head disappeared when I saw Agent Fielding standing in front of the fireplace with a drink in his hand. He had showered and dressed for the evening but hadn't taken the time to shave. I wondered how he had explained eating dinner at the embassy to Alma. She wouldn't let him out of her sight, unless there was someone in-house to keep an eye on him.

"Well, if it isn't one of the most seductive men I've ever met," Lila said, hurrying across the room when she saw him. I followed numbly behind. "Reagan and I were talking about you last night."

"Were you now?" he questioned as she threw her arms around his neck.

I watched her freedom of movement with a certain amount of chagrin and alarm. We were not alone, and it was impossible to tell who might be friend or foe because the only person I recognized was

Genevieve Alexander. She looked ravishingly beautiful in a gown of red, and the tall man with silver streaks running through much of his hair must be the illustrious ambassador who had not even made an attempt to meet us. I tried to get a reading on the others in attendance, but it was hard to split my focus when I didn't want to miss what was being said right in front of me.

"It's good to see you too, Lila," Agent Fielding said, extricating himself from her embrace. His rather brusque movement made me wonder what he would have done if I had tried to embrace him the night before, instead of hold a gun to his back. "You look as if life has been treating you well."

"Lady Luck has been good to me the past few months, but I'm more interested in what you've been up to since we last met."

He glanced in my direction while she slid her hand through the crook of his arm. I was being left out of the conversation intentionally and couldn't help but wonder why.

"My life consists of little besides work, Lila, but when did you and Reagan become such good friends?" he asked as she reached for her own drink from off a silver tray that was being extended in her direction.

"It's been a few months. I decided a change was in order after that stint in the hospital, and she was the only person I knew who wasn't involved in what I was trying to leave behind."

"And how has that been working for you?"

"Amazingly well, until this very unpleasant summons came," she said, leaning towards him in much the same manner as Angel had done. "I'm going back to school."

"Now that is a change, but I've never doubted your commitment to anything."

She took a sip from her crystal glass while I stood watching their interaction. This was a side to Lila I had ever seen before. It made me wonder how much she had already had to drink.

"Change isn't easy, as you well know, Sam. I've actually met your son. He's absolutely delightful. I swear he'll be walking by the time we get home."

I felt my breath catch in my throat. Lila was treading on dangerous ground by talking so openly about Charlie, and Genevieve was moving in our direction.

"Nothing about that situation happened the way it should, but I won't make excuses for my behavior," he responded as I continued to listen. "I did what I felt was right. Of necessity, my work takes precedence over most everything, but that doesn't mean my son isn't important to me. My reasons for walking away may seem jaded, but I was only thinking about his future. Having me for a father doesn't give him much of a chance. I just wish a certain someone understood that better."

Lila shook her head as she glanced in my direction. "You're a smart man, and you've known many women in the Biblical sense. It shouldn't come as such a great surprise to know that most of us are ruled by emotions, especially when our hearts are involved."

I opening my mouth to object. Lila made it sound like I had spent the past few months pining away for him, and I had tried moving on with Trey. We might even be engaged if my secrets hadn't gotten in the way.

"There you are, Agent Sinclair," Genevieve said, effectively breaking my intense concentration on something that was really none of my business. "I've instructed Ava to bring you a fruit drink. Servants often have to be reminded of their duties when visitors have specific needs. But while we wait for her to correct that oversight, I would like you to meet my husband and a few of our other guests. He has just returned from a short business trip."

"Will Director Phillips be joining us as well?" I asked, falling into step beside her as she led me towards a group of people who were engaged in a discussion about a local artist. His most recent painting stood on a easel in the foyer.

"He should be here shortly. I am sorry we have not been able to spend more time with you, but our responsibilities are diverse. This dinner tonight is meant to move several pursuits in a more favorable direction."

Her comment made it sound like she was being open and hospitable, but in reality, she was trying to keep me from asking more questions. I had to give her credit for knowing how to be diplomatic, especially when she touched her husband's arm in a gesture that was meant to interrupt without appearing rude.

"Darling, I would like to introduce one of America's finest federal agents who has come to help us with this dreadful trial. She has been very anxious to meet you."

When our eyes met and his long and graceful fingers closed around mine, I knew why he had been placed in such a position of authority. There was something about him that commanded more than respect, and I felt completely insignificant in his presence.

"It is good to finally meet you, Agent Sinclair. My country thanks you for your willingness to lend assistance in such a disagreeable matter. Getting the drugs off the streets in our beautiful country is a never-ending battle, but with people like you willing to lend a hand, there is hope that we may one day be more in control like our neighbors to the north."

"I'm glad to be of service," I responded, not knowing what else to say.

More introductions were made, but as I glanced from face to face, I knew I would never be able to tell who was on our side. Most people were trying to live good lives and help where they could, but the forces of evil knew no boundaries.

Name cards had been put on the table indicating where each guest was to sit. Agent Fielding rose to his feet the moment I stepped into the dining room and pulled out the chair next to his. Lila was already seated across the table from him and the other chairs were filling up rapidly.

"I hope you're not disappointed in the seating arrangement," he said as his hand momentarily rested on my forearm.

"Not at all," I replied.

Lila just looked at me and smiled. Other than Genevieve, and three other women, we were the only females in what seemed to have grown into a rather large dinner party. That put me at a disadvantage, but Lila was back in her element since there were plenty of men to flirt with. Director Phillips soon joined us, but he was sitting next to our hostess while the ambassador sat at what I knew was the place of most prominence.

"Doesn't Reagan look lovely?" Lila asked Agent Fielding as I held my hands tightly together in my lap.

He had definitely slipped into a suitable role for the occasion, but I was having trouble deciding if I was supposed to act like a dinner guest, a federal agent or a woman with a lot on her mind. All I wanted to do was pull him aside and ask how his day had gone. His face was a mask that betrayed nothing. And when I looked down the table at Director Phillips, the shift of his eyebrow let me know that this was a social occasion—not a meeting where personal opinions or strategies could be discussed.

"I am so glad everyone could come on such short notice," Genevieve said as she brushed a lock of hair from her cheek with a bejeweled hand. "My plans are usually made in advance, but there are times when some of the nuances of polite society must be overlooked to accommodate last minute needs. Unfortunately, that meant our real guest of honor, Ernesto Velasquez, was not able to join us. I hope you have each taken a moment to view his latest painting. It will be displayed at the Gallery Grande in the morning. I have promised him that we will all bring our friends to enjoy it."

"I think it's perfectly lovely, as are our guest rooms," Lila said. "The entire staff has been more than gracious and helpful."

"Our wish is for you to have a pleasant stay," Genevieve said with a smile I didn't quite trust.

Women in her position made me nervous, and not because I had known many of them personally. While she might be exactly who she professed to be, instinct told me that she was the perfect person to leak information to the enemy. She oversaw most everything that happened at the embassy, and it seemed rather fortuitous that she had made time in her busy schedule to host a dinner on such short notice.

But instead of letting that thought ruin what appeared to be nothing more than a pleasant evening, I listened to what her other guests had to say. With the exception of Director Phillips, Agent Fielding, Lila and me, they were all patrons of the arts and sat on various boards throughout the city. The summer gala they were beginning to plan was expected to generate several million in support of theater productions, ballets, concerts and the ever-present, starving artist.

They talked about budgets, possible performers and other details that I found neither enlightening nor entertaining while we dined on squab that had been basted with a delicate sauce. Since I would not be around to enjoy any of the festivities, I allowed my mind to drift elsewhere.

Lila conversed knowledgeably since her time as an escort had provided the opportunity to attend many such events, but my remarks were brief and rather dull. While I enjoyed a good stage performance of any kind, what leisure time I had was usually spent with my family. I felt Agent Fielding grip my knee occasionally during the meal. It should have made me uncomfortable since strangers—any one of whom could be watching—surrounded us, but instead it brought a sort of comfort.

I wondered if Director Phillips purposely kept his wife and family away from the embassy. He never said anything about them, but from the picture on his desk I knew they existed. Perhaps they didn't even live in the country. That would be my choice considering what he did for a living, but it must be a very lonely life. I didn't want mine to become that way. He excused himself before dessert was served.

In all, it was a very uncomfortable meal that seemed to progress from course to course at a snail's pace. All I could think about, other than clearing the air with Agent Fielding, was holding my son in my arms and finding a way to make things right with my family and Trey.

On our way to the library for after dinner drinks and coffee, none of which I would consume, I put my hand on Agent Fielding's arm. "Do you have a few minutes so we could talk privately? I have a little apologizing to do. Director Phillips explained some of the obstacles you've encountered and what you hope to accomplish."

"You don't owe me any explanations, Reagan," he said, looking down at me while I watched Lila, and a rather short but affluent-looking man, stand in front of the small painting that had been brought to the embassy to be admired.

For the first time since meeting her, I caught a real glimpse into the life of a woman who had been painstakingly tutored into becoming a successful escort. She knew how to make men feel relaxed, appreciated and free to talk.

"Do you think she's going to be all right?" I asked as I noticed that he was watching her too.

"Lila is in her element, although I hope she doesn't return to her former life. The man she's with may seem harmless enough, but he's part of a cartel."

"How do you know that?"

"Because it's what I've done for a decade and a half, and they're easy to spot, if you know what you're looking for. The small tattoo between the thumb and index finger on his left hand communicates his loyalty to the old Seville cartel so he can be protected when altercations between rivals occur. No one has been able to determine which members have changed allegiance yet."

"Do you think Lila knows who he is?"

"It's hard to discern how much the charming Lila is aware of. She ran in some pretty tough circles. And while she claims to have told us all she knows, I'm sure she's holding a few things back. I hope you're being careful around her."

"She's been nothing but kind and supportive to both Charlie and me."

"I'm not saying she's out to hurt anyone, but the temptation to backslide might become too much now that she's been reminded of what she's given up."

"I don't believe that will happen. She has a daughter and wants to be ready to meet her with a clear conscience when the time comes."

"Unlikely parenthood seems to be all the rage these days," he retorted. "I know I should have considered the possibility that Charlie was my son. The timing was certainly germane, but I was so angry with Maria for becoming involved with Mendoza that I wanted to believe the worst about her."

"You can't blame yourself for her actions, and jealousy is a very human reaction."

"It wasn't jealousy! It was being the unemotional, hard-hearted, arrogant jerk whose tantrums you were forced to endure when we were in Colombia. Longterm commitment to anything unrelated to the mission was impossible. Maria and I both knew that. I suppose that may have been part of the reason she turned to Mendoza. She was all about family. You should have seen her with Isabel and Luis. If I hadn't known who she really was, I could easily have believed she was their natural mother."

I knew better than to ask anything more about the children I had been forced to leave behind. However, my own misguided and hasty choices had helped me better understand some of his. The work we did wasn't clearcut and sacrifices had to be made.

"Let me make our excuses to Ambassador and Genevieve Alexander," he said. "Then we can go to the solarium to talk. As much as I would like to believe no one is listening, that isn't the case, and what we have to discuss is too important to be overheard."

I leaned against the wall and watched long, purposeful strides take him into the library where I could hear happy chatter. He was a man of multitudinous contradictions, and while I wished I could believe that we might have a future together, nothing about us bespoke permanence. I did not doubt his feelings for Charlie, but being a father was a lifetime commitment, and he had already reiterated the fact that he wasn't into that.

Manuela passed by me carrying a large sliver tray piled high with fruit and small cakes as I stood waiting. She didn't slow her step to talk, and I didn't try to make eye contact. I knew she would come to me with anything she felt I needed to know.

"Are you ready to go," Agent Fielding asked as he put his hand underneath my elbow. "I think the ambassador suspects that we may have an interest in each other, although I'm not sure the director has included him in much of anything that is going on with the DEA. He's busy with his own affairs, and while they share the premises, it's mostly for convenience since much of what they do overlaps."

"I'm sure the ambassador appreciates the added protection of having armed agents walking the halls, regardless of the fact that his children live elsewhere most of the time. I couldn't do that. My son is too important to me."

"Don't you mean our son?" he questioned as he led me quickly down flagstone steps, across a small patio, and into a building constructed of glass and steel where we would not miss anyone's approach.

I shivered involuntarily as we moved between warm and cool temperatures. He was wearing a tuxedo, but my gown was strapless and made from light, billowy silk.

"It was a slip of the tongue," I said, breathing in deeply the scent of jasmine, rose and hibiscus. It was a clear night, and the stars were twinkling overhead, but this was not going to be a lover's tryst. It could easily be our last strategic planning meeting.

"This brings back fond memories," he said as we strolled among potted plants that were being kept alive through the use of space heaters and overhead misters. Our hands were close but not touching. It was safer that way. "I'll never forget how beautiful you looked the night of Ramon Rios' ball before all hell broke loose. You're a dammed fine agent, and equally as lovely now as you were back then."

"It seems like another lifetime. I doubt we're even the same people."

"Probably not. I just wish all the bad in your life wasn't directly linked to me."

"There's been some good too. I wouldn't have Charlie if you hadn't come back. You must think I've grown into a miserable, bitter person after my tirade last night."

"I've always appreciated your bluntness."

"Even I know there's a difference between being candid and being mean. I crossed the line, and I'm sorry I did."

"You never have to apologize to me, Reagan. I expected you to do things beyond your level of expertise and experience from the very beginning. Even the most seasoned agents are unable to control their feelings to the extent I do mine, but I don't want to be that haughty, sadistic man any longer."

I reached out my hand and touched his as the moon came out from behind a cloud. His fingers immediately closed over mine, and his core warmth seemed to envelope me, softening every angry thought I had ever entertained about him. We were connected for life through our son. But if I allowed honesty to override reason, we were connected as a man and woman too.

"You're a selfless, wonderful person, Sam Fielding, although you take too many chances with your life. Director Phillips explained part of the mission you've been on, but there's so much else I need to know."

"I was hoping you would never have to find out most of what I've been doing. I'm not proud of some of the choices I've been forced to make."

"He didn't share any secrets that wouldn't be covered in a written report. He just wanted me to know what all of us might be facing."

"And I wanted to contain as much of the anticipated fallout as possible. He told me about the note threatening Charlie's life. Do you know who slipped it under your door?"

I shook my head. "I thought it was someone connected to the Sevilles, but it could have been anyone. We seem to collect enemies like other people collect toys."

"That's certainly true, but we do what's required. Alma expects a complete report about tonight's activities before midnight."

"You're taking a mighty big risk with her. She isn't someone you can trust."

"Trust has nothing to do with it. We're using each other to get what we want. Contrary to what you might believe, I don't enjoy playing with people's lives, but my subterfuge has paid off. The authorities are going to discover when they do an autopsy on Juan Seville that he had stage four pancreatic cancer, along with certain drugs that were ingested to hasten his death. That's what the argument he and Eloise were having in the hall before the ball at the Rios' ranch was all about. They wanted to make sure all their bases were covered should one of them be captured or killed because they knew about the proposed takeover. Eloise was helping Lupe plan it."

"And Juan didn't take exception to that?"

"Our recently departed was in no condition to run his part of the operation, and Eloise wanted their investments protected. We're talking about narcissistic and psychopathic personalities, not run-of-mill criminals who only hope they won't get caught. These people believe they are above the law and that none of their rivals will ever be able to touch them now that they've joined forces."

"That seems a reasonable assumption."

"But they're not invincible, if the biggest weakness can be found."

"And you believe you can do that?"

"I think I may have discovered it already, but I'm not willing to stake my life or my career on it without proof. I believe family loyalty and true friendship, along with power and the ability to act without remorse, is at the center of running any successful cartel. But the people we're involved with have taken it a whole lot further. Lupe Evans wanted revenge because Walter used her connections and family fortune to built an empire, and then humiliated her by marrying a woman less than half his age who was a known junkie and hooker. Eloise wasn't fond of Walter because he flaunted his misdeeds and took all the glory while her family did all of the work. When Lupe asked for her support in a takeover that would benefit all of their children and get rid of someone who was making everyone look bad, she was glad to help out."

"And you believe a woman scorned can become the most formidable opponent of all."

"I'm not saying she planned everything, but someone had to get the ball rolling. Her relationship with Eloise was already set, and she knew she could secure the Mendoza cartel if she could get Alma on her side. But Alma was in prison, and she didn't trust Carlos."

"Director Phillips intimated that Carlos made the switch with his sister because he needed someone to protect his interests."

"I'm sure that was part of it, but Carlos liked the idea of becoming part of something bigger than what he had been able to create on his own. He was still running from the Colombian government, and a number of his key people had been caught while he was making his escape from the compound. From what I've been able to uncover, Lupe convinced him that she wouldn't play ball until he could guarantee delivery on all his proposals. That meant making a few personal contacts. I know it all sounds pretty farfetched, but I think what she really wanted was Alma in a position to get Eloise out of prison. Her original plan backfired when Eloise got herself incarcerated after attacking you."

"All of this is making my head swim," I reluctantly admitted.

"It's a complicated situation, and I could be wrong. But since we're here, and I'm still alive, I have to assume there is some credence to what I believe. She's using me to keep tabs on what the governing bodies are doing, and I'm hoping she'll let something worthwhile slip."

"And my being here helps you?"

"I needed her to believe I wasn't above using anyone from my past to further my own goals—even the woman who was raising my son."

"You do know it will be hard to forgive you for using Charlie as bait."

"I don't expect forgiveness, but I know how the criminal mind works. I had to give myself an area of supposed vulnerability, or I would never have made any headway with Alma. She hates you even more than she does me because you took something she believed belonged to her."

"She knows that isn't true now."

"Knowledge doesn't automatically erase hatred, and the idea of having you close enough to eliminate gave me a certain amount of credibility and leverage when trying to convince her that I no longer cared about anything except what money could buy. After all, why should I continue doing the dirty work without reaping any of the benefits? No one can save for a profitable future on a government salary."

"You make what we do sound as calculated as some of their actions."

"That was my intention, and my interaction with Agent's Gibbons and Ross helped. She couldn't be sure one of them hadn't recruited me. I'm still hoping we can get Eloise out of prison and under control before you have to enter that courtroom. There will be no way to protect you if that happens because I don't know who all the players are yet."

I felt myself go almost limp with anger and fear, but I would not give in to irrationality or tears.

"Using me makes a certain amount of demoniacal sense, but why involve Lila?"

"Because I know how the defense will try the case. They'll use our relationship to prove incompetency, lack of honor and a disregard for rules. Bringing Lila along served a dual purpose. Her testimony would only make it seem like they couldn't find anyone reliable as a character witness, and we would be able to keep an eye on her. We need to know if she'll make contact with someone from the wrong side while she's here."

"Has she done that?" I asked.

"Not to my knowledge, but her movements have not been highly monitored. Everything is up in the air right now, but in the few moments we have left, I want to know more about what happened with Charlie. The last time I saw you I found out I had a son, and this time I discover how close I came to losing him."

I touched the petals of a yellow-tipped, orange rose before replying. "From what the doctors have been able to determine, he picked up some latent parasite in the jungle that decided to start eating away at his lungs. They were able to identify the bug and treat the pneumonia, but there are no guarantees it won't happen again."

Without any warning, his arm slipped around my waist. I could feel his heart beating when he kissed the top of my head. "You should never have been forced to go through that alone. I'm sorry I was off playing hero as you so aptly call it."

"I had my family and some good friends, and while you may not believe there is a God, I can assure you that he is very real. There is no other explanation for Charlie's miraculous recovery."

"I'm glad you had that comfort. And who knows, maybe someday—when I can leave all this ugliness behind—I'll give religion another chance. But right now, I just want to savor this semi-peaceful moment."

"You know it won't last? That's why I need to know what I can do to help," I said, reluctant to leave the safety of his encircling arm and the warmth of his caressing breath. "You can't possibly do everything on your own."

"I already have a carefully-selected team in place, and I need to be with them when they return to Colombia. It's the only way I'll be able to find out if my theory is correct."

"So you're still going back, if you can."

"While Alma is capable of inflicting incredible forms of torture, she's the best chance we've got to stop this takeover."

"I can't begin to imagine what you've been through."

"We do whatever it takes to get a job done, but you haven't told me how things went in Maine. I only know that you weren't there for long."

I bit my bottom lip to keep from giving away the vast and powerful array of emotions I was feeling inside. He had gone through a great deal, but then so had I.

"Maine was beautiful, and Vestie Jennings was exactly as you described her—a woman with both passion and purpose who is very fond of you."

He picked a delicate orchid from off a vine and slipped it behind my ear. "Vestie went through a lot with her husband and son. I helped out where I could, but I'm more interested in why you chose to disregard my instructions to stay there until I made contact. I wasn't kidding when I said I would do whatever it took to keep my son safe."

"So would I, but situations change and adjustments have to be made. Working with you taught me that. I ran into Angel Evan's biological sister, Neva Jasper, at the town library."

"No kidding," he responded, giving me an almost stunned look. "I didn't know you'd continued with that search."

"You asked me to look into Walter's first wife if I got the chance. That's why I was at the library, but meeting Neva happened quite by chance."

"It must have made your head swim since I know you don't believe in coincidences. What was she doing in such an out-of-the-way town? Boothbay Harbor isn't exactly a tourist trap with abundant nightlife or the possibility of acquiring fortune or fame."

"She was there for the same reason I was, trying to escape killers who wanted something she didn't know she had."

"That illustrious book of names Angel hoped would save her life. Too bad her plan to destroy Walter and walk away a free woman didn't work. Her help would be invaluable in figuring out where Robert Evans and the Seville brothers have set up shop."

"So you still have no idea where they are."

"Not a clue! Lupe is living the highlife in Bogotá but keeps herself insulted from the outside world with armed guards watching her estate and traveling with her whenever she leaves. The people she employees have been with her for the past two decades, and we haven't been able to make any headway in getting one of them to turn. Nor have we been successful in getting anyone new into her household. She's a very suspicious woman. I've been pushing Alma for answers, but I'm not sure she knows anything more than her assigned part."

"Why not?" I asked. "She ran her own cartel for years."

"Because drug cartels and terrorist cells have a great deal in common when it comes to hierarchy and implementing plans. All factions work in tandem, but they don't communicate with each other. While one is assigned to obtain product, another supplies the weapons. Others lead raids, find backers and set up schedules for distribution. It's a complex system that works because one, highly-protected person calls the shots, and if a certain group is compromised there's little to fear because they really can't tell the authorities anything."

"And you still believe Lupe is in charge. I thought the objective of the takeover was get get someone new at the top?"

"Give them time. Robert will be the one in charge before long, but his mother wants to make sure his chance for success is optimal before stepping down. I'm sure ridding the world of her ex-husband has made the world a better place, but that wasn't her end game. She wants her legacy of power and wealth to outlive anyone in her family."

"Even her grandson?" I asked. "My understanding is that Robert's wife isn't exactly into that lifestyle."

"I'm afraid that poor woman will continue doing exactly as she is told, unless she wants to join her father-in-law in the ground. She was raised to be submissive, and her personality will not allow her to step out of line."

"It sounds like a miserable existence."

"Believe me, we've tried to get her on our side, but she's never in a position where we can even approach her. I know you think I exaggerate when I talk about what we're up against, but you've never tried to get inside such a close-knit circle. Trust is nonexistent, and one false move could mean the end for a lot of good people. Is there any chance you can reach out to Angel's sister again and find out what else she might know?"

"I've tried, but she's in protective custody, and no one will tell me where she is."

"Damned bureaucrats," he swore. "I know rules are in place for a reason, but they sure make it hard for those of us who are working outside the box of conformity."

"You seem to know what you're doing when it comes to playing both ends against the middle. I've witnessed your ability to dance with deceit and change course without missing a heartbeat more than once, but what you're doing right now is the stuff spy novels are built around. The energy and excitement is there until the last chapter, but the lead character usually ends up in a body bag or rotting away in some distant land. I don't know how you're able to keep all the lies straight."

His smile was less than encouraging, and I couldn't help but notice that his eyes were not on me. They were taking in all the colorful and exotic flowers that were used inside the embassy to brighten the surroundings and make guests feel welcome. A fresh bouquet had been put in my bedroom before my arrival.

"Practice makes perfect in just about everything, and Alma keeps me on a short leash. There is little room for error because I watch her as closely as she watches me. I just hope I see the bullet coming in time to step out of the way because, like you, I have a feeling this isn't going to end well."

"I wish I could run backup for you," I responded.

"While I would welcome the company, the best thing you can do is stay out of the way. People with kind hearts and strong family ties should never join government agencies like the CIA, FBI or DEA. First, they have trouble separating people from the actions they commit; and second, they put loved-ones in danger every time they accept a high-risk mission."

"Is that really how you feel about me?" I asked.

"I'm talking about anyone who takes an oath of allegiance to serve and protect. I've never questioned your loyalty, Reagan, but I know how much agony you go through wanting to believe the best about others and wishing your choices had not negatively affected your family. Believe it or not, I feel the same way and need to know that Charlie will remain safe until this nightmare is over."

"He's staying with an FBI agent who was hired to step in when situations like this arise."

"That doesn't mean he's safe. The cartels have people everywhere. They could be your neighbors, the clerk at the grocery story, even a fellow agent. We both learned that the hard way with Agent's Gibbons and Ross. I really didn't see that coming."

"If you're trying to scare me, even more than I already am, you're doing a good job of it," I said, looking up into his face.

His eyes suddenly seemed to bore into mine, and all traces of lightheartedness or subterfuge was gone.

"We should all be a little scared. These people leave no survivors, and there's no way of knowing what their next move will be. I want you on the first plane out of here. That way you can take care of your family and our son. Under the circumstances, you're the only one I trust to do that."

"What about the subpoena? I could end up in some Mexican jail."

"Since I'm the reason you're here, I'll see what can be done to get both you and Lila off the prosecution's list. I know you won't leave without her, and the only reason I needed you here was to convince Alma to bring me along."

"And you?" I asked.

Without any warning, the back of his hand brushed across my cheek causing spasms of sorrowful delight. "I chose my life years ago, and I did it with full knowledge that each mission could be my last. I've crossed too many people in the drug world to ever believe I can live a life of normalcy, but that doesn't stop me from wishing things could be different. Do you want to know what kept me going all these months while I was trying to convince Alma Mendoza that in was in her best interest to let me live?"

When I didn't give an immediate response, he tilted my face upwards until our eyes met again. I wanted to pull back, but for the first time since we'd me, I knew what our parting this time would mean. Alma Mendoza had no intention of allowing him to leave Mexico City alive.

"I kept thinking of all the times we almost got close enough to speak from the heart. I would give almost anything to go back."

"And do what?" I asked.

"Take the time to get to know each other; every nuance that makes us who we are. I want to fully understand why you won't drink cocktails, and why sleeping in the same bed—when we weren't going to do anything—bothered you so much. Perhaps if we understood each other better you would feel differently about me."

"My feelings for you have never been completely professional."

"I'm not taking about hating me because of my arrogance, or trusting me to keep you safe because it was part of my job. I'm talking about two people opening their hearts and not being afraid of what might happen if they do. I know you loved Neil, but you kept him at arm's length because something about true intimacy has you running scared."

"That's not fair," I responded, trying to fight back sudden tears. "Just because I won't sleep with a man doesn't mean I have intimacy issues. I just know what I both want and need."

"Even if you end up alone? I'm here to tell you that there has to be more to life than chasing bad guys all the time."

"That didn't seem to bother you until now."

"Maybe I've had time to reconsider a few things. What if we never see each other again? Can you really say that's all right with you?"

"Of course it isn't! I want you to survive so you can be part of Charlie's life, despite whatever complications it might bring."

His sigh was filled with frustration. "Are you really that obtuse, Reagan, or are you simply choosing to ignore what I'm trying to say? I'm talking about the chemistry between a man and a woman. I know something powerful is going on between us."

"I'm not sure our feelings are relevant right now."

"Why not? If I die, I want to know that my body will not be left to rot in some South American jungle. I want you to come looking for me, and I want you to put flowers on my grave and even shed a tear or two. If that's an about-face from the man I've always been, then I say it's about time I look beyond that macho attitude to the eventuality every man or woman on earth with have to face. Do you care enough to keep tabs on me? That's all I'm really trying to ask because I know it's neither the time nor the place to talk about a trying to build a personal relationship."

"You know I do," I responded as my lips began to tremble. "I want you to be part of our lives."

His fingers touched my cheek again. "Thank you for being willing to say at least that much. I know I'm not an easy person to be around. I'm demanding, self-centered and obsessed with my work. Those are not endearing qualities."

"Nobody's perfect."

"Maybe not, but I want to be perfect for you."

Suddenly, I felt the ice that had been put around my heart for protection crack. His eyes, that had always been filled with so much torment, seemed to dance in the light that came shining though the tall windows of the embassy. The scent of tropical flowers hung heavy in the air, and we were alone in setting that made me want to reach upwards until our lips were locked in a kiss that would melt our souls into one. Danger, expectancy and knowing that we might never see each other again was indeed playing cruel and enticing tricks with my head. All he had to do was throw his jacket on the ground, and I would know what it was like to be truly and completely loved by a man.

Just at the moment when his hands were caressing my bare shoulders, arms and neck, and I could feel the strength of his desire behind his touch, he pulled away.

"I would make you mine in every way right now, Reagan, but I know you'd regret such an impulsive act the moment it was over. I've never been an honorable man when it comes to women. One night stands are as good as it's ever been with me, and I enjoyed most of those encounters immensely. You deserve so much better."

"Maybe I've been wrong," I said, not wanting the moment to end. "I could never judge any of your actions too harshly because I've never walked in your shoes."

"Please don't give me credit where none is due. I've never cared about anyone, other than myself. Leaving Maria and you in that ramshackle hut was bad enough, but the most reprehensible thing I've ever done was belittling and turning my back on you. I should have helped you get Charlie out of the country."

"That wasn't your responsibility."

"But it should have been! I betrayed the people most in need of my help. If I had followed through with my original intention of going after Mendoza, I would have been responsible for my own son's death. How am I supposed to live with that?"

"The same way we all live with the awful things we've done. Maria couldn't travel any further with a bullet in her shoulder, and I had destroyed over four years of undercover work for you. Feeling angry is a very normal emotion."

"That's what I told myself all the way to the village."

"And yet you still came back."

"Not in time."

"Maria accomplished what she set out to do. Her son was born free."

"Thanks to you."

"Thanks to both of us. There's no way I could have delivered Charlie on my own or found my way out of that jungle. There were many times when I wanted to hate you, but how could I when you're the only reason I got to see my family again. What I did by accepting that first assignment was both reckless and foolish. I put more lives and livelihoods in danger than I dare count. Assistant Director Bridges is still putting out fires I'm responsible for starting, and Neil is dead because I allowed him to get too close."

"But I'm not Neil."

"And I'm not that starry-eyed agent you picked up at the airport in Bogotá. I grew up considerably before we made it back to civilization, but you were right about my incompetence. All the training in the world would not have prepared me for the outcomes of that experience. I still can't believe you wanted to work with me again."

"You were the most inexperienced, yet fearless, agent I had ever met. I guess I figured if you could handle my brutality in the Colombian jungle you could certainly play the part of my innocent, clueless wife. I'm not sorry I asked you to be my partner again, but I certainly wish . . . "

"There you are," Lila said, bouncing into the greenhouse with a look of triumph on her face. "I've been searching everywhere. That rather dismal party has completely broken up, and I'm not ready for bed yet. I do hope my sudden appearance isn't interrupting something important."

I pulled my hands away from Agent Fielding's as her stiletto heels crossed the small pebbles towards us. "Not at all. We were just talking about the past."

"Well, forget about that. I want to know what's going on now. Despite one nice dinner, home is looking pretty good to me right now."

"We're working on that," Agent Fielding told her. "The arms of justice move slowly at times."

"So we'll still have to testify?"

The look he gave me before turning to address her again let me know that most of what we had discussed could go no further.

"I'm not sure anyone knows what's going to happen with the trial right now. Juan's death put a crimp in some well thought-out plans."

"Well, of course it did," she retorted, seemingly unaware that he was trying to keep anything from her. "They were together for a lot of years."

He gave her a pleasant smile, but his fingers closed around my wrist for one last time. "Not to be ungallant when I'm in the presence of two beautiful women, but I need to speak to Director

Phillips before I leave. Don't forget what we talked about, Reagan. I really do have your best interest at heart."

"I bet you didn't even discuss business," Lila said as we watched him step through the glass door into the cold night air. "Did you tell him how you felt?"

"Not exactly. The timing wasn't right."

"Well, it might have been, if I hadn't interrupted. Did you find out anything useful? I'm not a great fan of secrets, and I would like to get back to my cat. One of the neighbors is checking on her, but she's going to be one angry feline when I return."

I linked her arm through mine as we lost sight of Agent Fielding amid the shadows. I was wearing his dinner jacket. He had slipped it over my shoulders when he noticed me shivering. Perhaps I would keep it as a reminder of the man I had allowed to get away. When I inhaled, I could smell his aftershave.

"The DEA doesn't operate like the FBI, Lila, and I'm not a member of their team. I haven't even been able to get the assistant director to return my calls. As for your cat, I'm sure all will be forgiven if you give her the right treats."

"That would be nice," she replied as we stepped inside. The embassy was eerily quiet, and our footsteps made a resounding clatter as they came in contact with the marble flooring in the main entry and up the stairs. "I thought I would enjoy living in luxury again, but there are too many restrictions, and I hate being told what to do."

I prepared for bed and then stood in front of the window with iron bars staring at the lights of a vast metropolitan city. Secrets, too numerous to count, were being successfully hidden from the only people who could stop the cartels. Once morning arrived, I would continue my search for connecting threads that might not even exist, but I couldn't do it now. I needed to commit to memory every detail of the evening—every thought, word, smell, touch and feeling—so I would never forget. My memories might be all Charlie ever knew about his father.

The mattress was firm and the sheets inviting, but even after I had slipped inside the soft whiteness, my mind refused to be silenced. I watched the hands on the bedside alarm clock move slowly around the top part of the dial and wondered what I may have missed that might help pull us out of the precarious predicament we were in. I didn't trust anyone connected to the cartels, and I was beginning to doubt some of the directives leaders gave. People on both sides of the law had agendas, and they were not afraid to sacrifice a few to save numberless others.

Just as I was about to allow myself the luxury of surrendering to tears of self-pity, there was a knock on my bedroom door.

"Wake up, Reagan," a voice loudly whispered. "We've got to talk."

Every nerve in my body seemed to ignite as I came close to stubbing my toe on the nightstand in my haste to open the door. Agent Fielding was standing in the hall, and the expression on his face let me know this wasn't a personal visit.

"What's wrong?" I asked as my eyes found his.

"Everything," he replied, running his hands through his hair as he motioned for me to step aside so he could enter the room. He was still dressed in what he had worn to dinner, but he wasn't the same man who had left me only hours before. "I've been a damned fool thinking I could pull this off when Carlos and Alma only made a switch so he could rally his incarcerated forces. The director got word while we were in the solarium talking that he's been sprung and plans to wreck havoc with every other drug cartel in Colombia."

"That's mighty ambitious. I thought you believed Lupe Evans was in charge," I responded, suddenly realizing that I as in my bed clothes again.

"I still do. She needs his army to squash any resistance. Robert would be useless in an attack since his skills, like his father's, lie in making the right connections for distribution. The Seville brothers can keep things moving when it comes to procurement, but they left their forces behind in Mexico. We don't have any details since it just happened. But Mendoza's men set off a bomb powerful enough to blow a hole in the outside prison wall and then went in with guns blazing. More than a few people were killed. It's all over the news and seems to indicate that the new and improved cartel is going to push its way to the top by any force necessary."

I sank down on the bed, my knees too weak to keep me upright. "Mendoza is an ambitious man, but he would never make a move like that on his own."

"No kidding! While he commands a respectable guerrilla force, this breakout took more planning and manpower than he's capable of directing on his own. Everyone finally agrees that we have three cartels working together now with Lupe Evans at the head, but bringing them down will be one of the biggest missions the DEA has ever supervised. The person with the most answers and experience working with the individuals involved needs to be in charge of the operation. Unfortunately, that's not the worst piece of information I came to deliver."

I looked over at him as he sat down beside me. "What could possibly be worse than being told you're going back to Colombia to take charge of everything."

"How about the fact that I let Alma get the upper hand by coming here tonight? She used my absence, and the information I gave her earlier today, to plan a little raid of her own. Eloise and her youngest son are in the wind as of twenty minutes ago. Everyone is searching for them."

"And you need to be among that group," I said, unable to grasp everything he had told me at one time.

"I'm in the best position to track them since I know where they've been and where many of their people are hiding."

"You're also the first one they will recognize as a true enemy. If you refuse to be reasonable, I'm getting my gun and going with you."

"That's now how this is going to work," he replied, grabbing my arm in a viselike grip as I tried to get to my feet. "The ambassador wants all civilians out of the building in case they decide to attack the embassy."

"I'm not a civilian!"

"In this case you are. You have no jurisdiction in Mexico without government permission."

"Then I'll get it! Where is Director Phillips now?"

"Too busy trying to keep the whole, damned ship from sinking to discuss anything with you. He's the one who told me to get you out of the building. Someone has been leaking information from inside these walls the past two days."

"Surely he doesn't suspect me!"

"He won't bring formal charges against anyone until he has proof, but you and Lila need to leave immediately. This is not open for discussion. Grab whatever cannot be left behind. I'll wait until you get a jacket and put something on your feet."

"What about Lila," I asked as he tossed a pair of sandals in my direction. I was busy putting the laptop and papers I had been going through earlier into a carrying-on bag I could slip over my shoulder. My clothing and personal items would be left behind.

"On her way to the helipad as we speak, I hope," he replied. "I wish we had more time. There's a great deal left I would like to say."

I felt horribly underdressed leaving the bedroom wearing only my pajamas and the suit jacket Agent Fielding had given me earlier in the evening, but he wasn't giving me another option. He hurried me down the hallway to a back staircase and then up several flights of stairs to a solid metal door that led onto the roof. It took his full weight to pull it open. From the other side, I could hear the pulsating clamor of blades revolving. But it was the gust of dry air hitting my lungs once we were outside that nearly stopped me from being able to breath without an oxygen mask.

Once I had blinked some of the dust from of my eyes, I saw that Lila was being helped into a black chopper with the embassy's logo painted on the outside. A pilot sat behind the controls, and the ambassador and his wife were already aboard.

"There's no room for me," I said, noticing that the passenger seats were already filled.

"They'll make room," he replied as two DEA agents with buds in their ears approached us.

"But it's not fair," I cried out loudly enough to be heard above the whipping wind. Throughout all the experiences we had shared— all the danger, the death, the fighting, the animosity, the deception, the horror of never knowing if the instant we were living in would be our last—I had never allowed my true feelings for him to surface because I knew he wasn't the right man for me.

"This isn't the time for hysterics, Reagan," he said, pushing me towards the helicopter. "I want you with our son, and I trust you to raise him to become a man I would be proud of."

"But he needs his father, and so do I."

"I know," he said, and I could hear the tenderness in his voice as his face came closer to mine. "You don't have to say anything more."

"But I do," I sobbed as unwanted tears rolled down my cheeks, only to be swept away by gusts of artificial wind. "I've never been entirely honest when it comes to my feelings for you."

"So, my fiery little agent loves me after all," he said, taking a moment to brush the hair away from my face so he could see it more clearly. "I was beginning to wonder if I was the only one who would ever admit what I was feeling inside."

"Never!" I said, standing on my tiptoes so our faces were nearly level. "I do love you, but it seemed so impossible."

"Not impossible, little one," he replied. "Don't you know that love conquers all?"

"But it hurts so bad."

"It hurts like hell, but it also gives me a reason to get out of this mess so I can come home to my family. Now, get on that helicopter before I decide I can't let you go."

"I want to stay and fight by your side."

"That's nice to hear, but you won't because you know our son needs at least one of his parents alive. Promise me that you'll let him know that I wasn't such a bad guy in the end. I plan on coming back, but fate may have other plans."

He leaned forward and kissed my trembling lips with such power and commitment that I knew he wasn't lying about anything now. He did love me. Maybe not the way he had loved women in his past with all the passion, danger and sneaking around, but with a love that could endure the test of time—if we were only given another chance.

"You are my life, Reagan, and my reason for going on," he whispered in my ear. "Don't ever forget that I loved you first and for always. You are my shining star. You make me want to be a better man."

He didn't give me a chance to respond. He just kissed my lips again and walked away. Neither of us looked back as we went in separate directions. I didn't know what he was feeling, but I had never felt such incredible pain. If an agent hadn't been offering support, I would never have made it to the helicopter and climbed aboard. He had to literally push me inside. By the time I glanced in the direction of the door leading into the embassy, Agent Fielding was gone.

Lila touched my hand and gave me a look of compassion and understanding as I moved behind her into the tail section where a stretcher had been strapped to the wall.

The deafening, relentless whirling of the blades above my head as we left the rooftop did nothing to stop the pounding of my heart. It only intensified the anesthetized feeling that seemed to flood my inner being as a cacophony of lights bounced and distorted below us. There was nothing tangible to keep me grounded. Not even Lila sitting just a few inches away.

Was it only moments ago that I stood on the helipad with Agent Fielding's lips pressed against mine, biding him a tearless goodbye, while people I didn't even know sat watching? To open my actions to the scrutiny of others was against my nature. But when faced with the probability of never seeing him again, I felt powerless as an unobstructed river running down a mountain.

From a purely professional point of view, I understood his need to stay behind in a city of strangers and go after the women who were now on the run from both the Mexican government and the DEA. He was the best man for the job, but he was also the agent with the biggest target on his back.

I clutched angrily at anything within reach as abrupt twists and turns made my stomach lurch and my body move across cold, uncomfortable metal. He should have allowed me to act as his backup. I wasn't afraid to walk into battle and had been trained for a life of danger just as he had, but I knew why he had insisted that I leave the embassy before our enemies arrived. Charlie did need one of his parents alive, but what if my walking away meant I would never know what it was like to make love to a man? I cared a great deal about Trey. In ways, I knew I loved him, but it was different from what I felt for Agent Sam Fielding. Trey made me feel safe, while the man I had just left behind made me feel alive.

If we were ever reunited, it would be through continued miracles I had no right to expect after the number I had already received. But in my humanness, I closed my eyes and prayed for more.

It was impossible to tell how long we were in the air after we left the confines of the city. My thoughts were centered on the American embassy and the people who might be fighting for their lives. It seemed incomprehensible that any sane person would storm a well-guarded structure after successfully accomplishing a bold jailbreak, but then I didn't fully understand the dynamics of ruthless revenge that had already cost Neil and so many others their lives. I just wanted to be with Agent Fielding, facing whatever came together.

We landed at a small airport that was miles away from where we started. The only thing I knew for certain was that we had not left Mexican soil. A mechanic in a worn, gray, one-piece uniform helped both Lila and me to the ground. The ambassador and his wife were already being escorted inside a corrugated metal structure that looked like it hadn't seen any recent repairs. For the first time since our strange nocturnal journey began, I felt a different kind of fear. What if the people with us were playing both sides of fence? We could be disposed of somewhere in the desert with some plausible explanation and our remains would never be found.

"Do you know what's going on?" Lila asked as we stood together on the hard-packed earth and the blades on the helicopter stopped revolving. Unlike me, she was still dressed in the gown she had worn to dinner. "I was relaxing in my room with a glass of the most expensive brandy I could find when one of the servants came running in and told me I had to leave. My Spanish is passable, but she was so distraught that I caught little of what she had to say. It was something about a breech and the inability to guarantee our safety any longer."

I shivered. The night seemed even darker and more nippy now that we were away from the city. "I was only told that Eloise had been sprung from jail and an attack on the embassy was suspected."

"But why?" she asked, pulling me towards the metal building. I could hear the sound of coyotes howling in the brush that wasn't far from where we were standing. "That place was locked up tighter than a drum, and why would they even bother with us if they already had what they wanted?"

"I wish I knew. Nothing makes sense to me right now, including the fact that Agent Fielding will chase Eloise and her accomplices to the ends of the earth if that's what it takes for them to be recaptured and punished. He wants Charlie safe for good."

"What about you? That kiss was far from platonic. Even Genevieve commented on how passionate and ill-advised it was under the circumstances."

I hung my head in remorse for a moment of weakness. "I didn't know it was going to happen."

"Hey, it was a long time coming, and it's not like you're breaking any rules. You don't even work for the same agency, but I am curious as to what went wrong when Sam appeared to be in control of whatever situation he was in."

I glanced over my shoulder before responding. The pilot had not left the helicopter, and Lila would know if I was lying. But I couldn't get Agent Fielding's words of warning out of my head. Someone, besides him, had been leaking information to the enemy, or Alma would not have made a such a bold move on her own.

"I really don't know any more than you do, Lila. Maybe the ambassador can enlighten us."

Her snort of doubt was far from ladylike. "It would be easier to get blood out of a turnip. For all his power and authority, Ricardo Alexander has the personality of a porcupine; always bristly and offish. He barely said two words to me, and I doubt it had anything to do with his wife being there. She was completely absorbed with her guests."

The overhead, florescent lights were almost blinding when we walked inside. The enclosure was nothing more than a large, drafty, metal shed with a five-foot partition separating the office area from where a single-engine airplane stood. I felt a sudden rush of nausea when I saw another mechanic making a pre-flight inspection. I didn't want to leave the ground in it after my experiences in the jungle but knew my desires would not be considered. I was a guest in Mexico, and Ambassador Alexander was in charge of building bridges between countries, not indulging witnesses that were being sent home because a legal proceeding had been unexpectedly interrupted.

He was talking on his cell phone, while his wife was sitting with her back erect on a worn, leather sofa. She was warming her hands with a cup of hot coffee and looked angry. Lila chose a chair across the room from her, but I remained standing near the door. I had a hundred questions to ask. The most pressing was why we had been spirited away in the middle of the night when we could have defended ourselves against an attack, even if most of the of the DEA agents were away from the embassy.

When the ambassador finished his conversation, he made a few comments to the man standing behind a cluttered desk and then turned to face the three women he had accompanied on the helicopter.

"I am sorry for the inconvenience. My wife is used to the uncertainty of my job, but I expect my guests to feel safe while they are in residence at the embassy."

"Can you tell us what happened?" I asked, trying to keep my tone light.

"Perhaps I should be the one asking what you know since you appear to be intimately involved with Agent Fielding," he replied, meeting my look with cold distain. "I was assured this would be an open and shut case once your testimony had been given. Now we have three fugitives on our hands, with no leads for apprehending them. I hope your Agent Fielding is capable of repairing some of the damage his ineptitude has caused."

"Please do not take your frustration out on Agent Sinclair," Genevieve Alexander told her husband, surprising me with her show of consideration after the methodical way she had conducted herself all evening. "Women do not always know what the men in their lives are doing, especially when it involves matters of national security. From what I have known of Agent Fielding, he would never allow anyone to stop him from completing an assignment, regardless of what personal feelings may exist. I am sure he is equally as upset as we are about this latest debacle."

The ambassador did not move to her side as I supposed he might to offer either comfort or support. He simply turned his eyes towards me. "I apologize for my outburst, Agent Sinclair, but I am not in the habit of being removed from my home without advance warning."

The numbness I had felt since getting on the helicopter was beginning to dissipate, and in its place was the raw awareness that came with indecision. Despite the fact that Agent Fielding had been caught unaware, and part of it was my fault, I needed to decide on a course of action that might prove beneficial before I was put on that that single- engine plane. To do that, I needed to gain the ambassador's trust.

"No apology is necessary, sir. You have a great deal on your mind, but I came here to help. Perhaps if we work together we can come up with something useful."

I watched as his jaw moved from side to side. No doubt he was assessing just how much he could relate without crossing lines that had been set in place to keep information secure. "Agent Fielding was taking a huge chance trusting Alma Mendoza. If he hadn't done that . . . "

"Understood, sir, but his actions were sanctioned by his superiors," I interjected before he could continue. Sam Fielding had risked his life countless times to make the world safer for others, and this time, he might be making the greatest sacrifice of all.

"Not all of them," he replied. "I have been dealing with the cartels for almost as many years as you have been alive. I know how they operate."

"I am not trying to undermine your expertise or your authority, sir, but I know how they work too. I also know Alma Mendoza and Eloise Seville on a personal level. They are vindictive, merciless and trust no one, unless it is advantageous to whatever monstrous plans they are hatching. That said, I believe you have bigger problems than worrying about what Agent Fielding will do to get the current situation under control. He believes there's a mole in your organization, and I agree."

He gave me a scathing look. "You honestly believe someone on my staff is leaking unsanctioned information."

"It happened before with Agent Gibbons. I know she didn't report directly to you, but there's a reason the escape was planned for tonight and why my former partner believes an attack at the embassy might occur."

"He could have instigated the entire thing for purposes of his own," the ambassador said. "It is as logical to believe that as to to say someone I trust is involved."

Lila put a restraining hand on my arm. "Don't argue with him, Reagan. He's just trying to get you to say something you might regret."

"You would do well to listen to your friend," the ambassador responded. "I have the power to ruin your career, or even have you incarcerated in one of our federal penitentiaries."

"Do you really think I care about my career, or my freedom, right now?" I challenged. "If someone in your organization is working for the cartels, don't you want to know who it is?"

His glare was icy cold, but before he said anything else, his wife was on her feet and closing the gap between them.

"Your job is not to fight this war against drugs and corruption personally. It is to bring people together so they can make the difficult decisions. Agent Sinclair is just overwrought because she has been forced to leave her lover behind."

I was good at deflecting, but Genevieve Alexander was a master, and I couldn't help but wonder what she was trying to hide. That fact that everyone lies had been drilled into my head at the academy, and on every case I had been assigned to work since.

"For your information," I said, not lowering my eyes from her face. "Agent Fielding is not my lover, nor has he ever been. We have a vested interest in the same people because we were partnered on two DEA missions, but then you already know that. I stayed at the embassy for a few days during the time Eloise was taken into custody, only you were too busy to make my acquaintance."

"I was just trying to help," she replied, suddenly gripping her husband's arm. "You do not think someone at our home is a spy, do you, my love? Everyone working for us was carefully selected."

"As much as I hate to admit it, Agent Sinclair has a point. Only a handful of people knew Alma Mendoza was coming to Mexico. You and I are among that select group, and what happened tonight was a well-organized and executed raid. When coupled with all the violence in Colombia earlier in the evening, it is obvious the cartels had help."

"You certainly do not think I had something to do with it?" she asked him with eyes open wide. "I have been far too busy with my philanthropic endeavors and planning our next trip to see the children at their boarding school in Switzerland."

"I know you would never become involved with something so reprehensible, but what I have not already told you is that a minor attack was made at the embassy after we left. No one was critically injured, but damage has been sustained to the building. Director Phillips believes it was a diversionary attempt to keep us occupied until the Sevilles were safety out of the city. A manhunt is underway, but with the number of sympathizers around to help, the probability is great that they will get away."

His cell phone rang, and he moved rapidly to the other side of the large, noisy enclosure. While he talked, Lila pulled me closer to the door and turned her back to the others.

"I don't mean to cast doubt where none should exist, but something about this doesn't sit right with me."

"It's a complicated situation, and we may never have the answers we're looking for."

"Even you?" she asked. "I know you're keeping something important from me, and that's okay. I don't have the right clearance, but I'm not stupid. Sam is a walking dead-man, and anyone associated with him will share the same fate if they're caught. That's the real reason behind our abrupt departure, isn't it? We weren't even allowed to pack what we brought."

The bile in my stomach rose to my throat, and I felt the room begin to spin. Telling Lila everything would be a huge relief, but that was unadvisable for many reasons. "I wish I could say something that would make you feel better, but you're right. Agent Fielding is the Seville cartel's biggest threat. He's spent the past fifteen years mingling with some of the most dangerous people on the planet, and he's only alive now because he's smart enough to know when to attack and when to withdraw. We should be grateful he wanted to make sure we were safe instead of questioning his loyalty or his methods of engagement."

"So no one is really interested in uncovering the identity of an informant right now."

"That issue will be dealt with eventually, but the presiding authorities are more interested in containing a potentially explosive situation. Eloise and Alma will not allow themselves to be caught without massive amounts of bloodshed."

"Who's Alma?" she asked.

My mistake was one even a rookie wouldn't make, but it was too late to make a retraction. "Carlos Mendoza's sister."

"Isn't that the man you thought was Charlie's biological father."

I glanced around the room to make sure no one was listening. "Yes, and she's even more ruthless than her brother. Agent Fielding believes more than just two cartels are involved in the takeover, but you can't say anything because he has no proof."

"My lips are sealed. Thanks for trusting me with at least that much. But if you're right, that means Sam is in even more trouble than I thought. What if someone tries to use Charlie to draw him out? Eloise already knows how to find both of you."

"So does Alma," I responded, fighting back unwanted tears. "Agent Fielding needed leverage to get close to her, and we were all he had."

"You mean he's been working with her the entire time?"

"Not all of it. Please don't ask me anything more. I've already told you more than I should. My first responsibility, before doing anything else for either the FBI or the DEA, is to get Charlie to a place where no one will ever be able to find him."

"You do know that's impossible."

"I still have to try."

"Then I'll go with you. We can use the money Edward left for me."

"I can't ask you to do that. Agent Fielding has made certain arrangements."

"None that aren't being closely monitored, I can assure you of that. Let me do this for you. I know Edward would approve."

Before I could think of a response to her kind and generous offer, the ambassador was motioning for all of us to join him. "No casualties have been confirmed on our side, and my orders are to get both of you back on American soil as quickly as possible. You will be leaving for the border once takeoff has been cleared."

"What about you?" I asked.

"That is none of your concern. However, in light of keeping public relations between our two countries friendly, I will tell you that my wife and I will be returning to Mexico City. There is much to be done to keep this from turning into another national tragedy."

"Does that mean there has been on word on the escapees?"

"All of the major ways out of the city are under surveillance, and you can rest assured that the Mexican government will not stop until they have been apprehended and brought to justice."

The sound of propellers breaking the silence of the night outside the metal building let me know that there wasn't much time until I would be back sky, and there was still much I needed to know.

"Will Agent Fielding be the one to go after them?" I asked, knowing I had already received confirmation of that fact.

"His Intel is critical in recapturing both women and shutting down the entire organization. He's needed on the front lines whether you like it or not."

"Well, I don't like it. There has to be a better way."

"I can assure you that everything possible will be done to keep him safe, but no guarantees will be made. You're young and emotionally involved, Agent Sinclair. I don't know the details of your relationship with Agent Fielding, but I do know a liability when I see one. Go home and get on with your life. Leave us to take care of the problems in our own countries. We are far better prepared to deal with them than you are."

He turned his back and walked away. I felt what was left of my fragile world shatter. I would not be included in anything now. My stubborn disregard for authority had seen to that.

Chapter 4

It was early evening by the time we reached FBI headquarters. As far as I knew, Ambassador Alexander and his wife had returned to Mexico City where they would deal with whatever fallout a botched DEA mission had brought. I had watched the television monitor in a larger airport where we had been taken in the small two-seater plane hoping for news from the embassy. But while video footage of the outside of the building was shown, not a great deal of information was made available to the public.

I understood the need to remain silent on a great many of the details since criminals who had been behind bars for months had escaped. It could easily lead to mass hysteria and groundless speculations as to who was at fault. A thorough investigation would be launched and someone would take the fall—most likely Agent Fielding since he was not an elected or appointed official. That hardly seemed fair, but it was how the bureaucracy worked. Those with the most power almost always came out on top.

Lila and I purchased matching sweats in a modest gray as we waited for our flight. We were both ready to wear something clean, even if it was less than attractive, and laughed as we twirled around in front of a full-length mirror in the woman's bathroom. It was reminiscent of my return flight from Colombia, but I was trying not to dwell on the past. My concern was for the present and future.

We tossed what we had been wearing into the trash, but I was unable to discard Agent Fielding's jacket. I would have it cleaned and hanging in a closet when he was ready to wear it again. Thinking about saving it for Charlie was much too hard.

While we were eating Chinese takeout from one of restaurants in the food court, I placed a call to Assistant Director Bridges. He apologized for not being able to send a company jet, but he had secured seats on a late afternoon flight and would have someone meet us when we arrived. He cautioned me to remain alert but didn't want to stay on the line. He would tell me what he could when we were standing face to face.

"This is not how things were supposed to play out when I agreed to let you testify," he said a few hours later when we were in his office. He motioned for us to sit in the two chairs that faced his desk.

Lila looked at me with concern, but there was nothing I could say to comfort her. We were at the mercy of government officials and any mercenaries who might come looking for us.

"Have you heard anything?" I asked, knowing I would have to defend my interactions with the ambassador, but I was tired of playing by everyone else's rules.

"I've been in contact with Director Phillips. He said the embassy sustained substantial damage from a bomb that was launched over the wall. It was similar to the ones used in Bogotá to get Carlos Mendoza out of prison. No one was killed, but a number of persons have been taken to the hospital in critical condition."

"I don't understand why they would do that, sir, since they already had Eloise and her son," I said as feelings of apprehension intensified. Manuela was still inside the embassy when we were taken to the helipad.

"The attack on the embassy appears to be a warning that they are now in control and any resistance will be met with violence and force. Were you able to uncover anything significant while you were there?"

I shook my head, unsure of how much I should say in front of Lila. "Likely nothing more than you've already been told. Director Phillips brought me up to speed on a few things, but mostly, there are more questions than answers. I wanted to stay and offer assistance."

"My directive was to have you out of there at the first sign of trouble, but I do understand your investment in this case. If you feel a need to work a few leads from this end, you and Agent Howard have clearance to do so for the next day or two, but I need you back on our cases after that. They just keep piling up."

"That's more than generous, sir. Have there been any new developments here?"

"Your family is fine. We've had agents keeping track of them. I think the threat you received was simply a strategy used to see if Agent Fielding would warn you about coming and expose himself in the process. His affiliation with two of the cartels involved seems to have been the catalyst in the events of the past twenty-four hours. I'm not entirely sure what he hoped to accomplish by going undercover again, but I suppose he had irrefutable reasons or his mission would not have been sanctioned by the DEA."

By sheer willpower, I kept my eyes from leaving his face. Most of Agent Fielding's actions had been validated after the fact, but no one needed to know that. "Can you tell me anything more, sir? Has Agent Ross' assassin been found?"

"We're still looking, but his wife has turned over account numbers in the Cayman and Cook Islands. She claims not to know where the money came from."

"Do you believe her?"

"She's already lost her husband and livelihood. We've even threatened to take her children away permanently if she doesn't give us what we need. It could be an act, but instinct tells me that she simply chose to look the other way."

"Is there anything I can do to help?"

"Maybe later. Right now, I have a team assembled in the conference room for debriefing and would like Miss Rivers to join us. When I think about the manpower and amount of coordinating effort it took to pull off two jailbreaks—in different countries—at basically the same time, it boggles my mind."

For the next four hours, men and women I didn't know fired questions at us. They wanted to know everything about the embassy, the people who worked there and who we had talked to during the hours we were waiting to testify. They seemed especially interested in Agent Fielding and why the FBI had not been informed about the role he had played in finding and working with Alma Mendoza. The entire ordeal left me wondering just how much communication went on between government factions, and if it was really safe to trust anyone besides my family, my boss and Agent Fielding.

"I can't endure another moment of this," Lila said as we left the building together at two in the morning. "I've made a decision. I'm getting out of this town as soon as my bags are packed. I thought it was tough being a junkie, but this crazy life you lead is far more dangerous than snorting coke. If you were smart, you would do the same thing."

I looked at her face in the lamplight of the darkened street. I had never seen such a determined set to her jaw, but it let me know that while she cared about Charlie and me, she wasn't ready to sacrifice her life for us.

"Where will you go?" I asked.

"I haven't decided, but we'll never know a minute's peace as long as members of any cartel know where to find us."

"What about school and your loft? You've worked so hard to make a new life."

"That new life isn't going to matter if I have to spend all my time looking over my shoulders. Honestly, Reagan, I think you're crazy if you decide to stay with the FBI. Assistant Director Bridges may think you have nothing to fear, but you and I know that isn't the case. A few hours ago, we believed Eloise Seville would spend the rest of her life behind bars. Now that she's free, there's no telling what awful things are being planned for the people who put them there. Sam should have come home with you."

"He did what he felt was right since he's the only one who knows where Alma's last base of operation was."

"What makes anyone believe she'll go back to that place? My bet is that they'll hunker down in some remote location where they can make plans that will rock the entire cartel world. They have to believe they're pretty much unstoppable now."

Her words sent a chill of foreboding down my spine. Working in their own countries, the Sevilles and the Mendoza's were entities to be feared but combined with Lupe Evans, they would be invincible.

"Where would you start if you wanted to destroy the competition?" I asked as several cars came down the street. It wasn't wise to be standing out in the open, but since it was late, I was going to crash at Lila's for a few hours instead of going back to my empty apartment. Two armed agents were only a few steps behind us. They would sweep the premises and remain in front of her door until morning.

"By taking out every known obstacle first," she said, increasing her pace. "I know that's not what you wanted to hear, but Sam should never have allowed his cover to be blown."

"And you think I'm responsible."

"Listen, honey! It's impossible to keep two magnetized objects apart, but the DEA's only real hope was having someone on the inside. Now that Sam's cover has been blown, they will close ranks. I wish I didn't believe there was another mole, but it's the only logical explanation."

"Did anyone at the embassy strike you as being capable of betraying his or her country?" I asked.

"No one seems entirely principled to me, but that's probably because my own life has been so duplicitous. Some people sell out for money and power, while others do it because they have no choice."

"I'm not trying to blame anyone," I replied as we rounded a corner and the trees along the sidewalk seemed to bend ominously towards us. "It's just that I'm afraid I'll never see Agent Fielding again."

She linked her arm through mine. "I understand your concern, but you have Charlie to think about. Thankfully, he's too young to know what's going on, but the people you're involved with don't forget, and they're vindictive as hell. That's why I suggested running while you still had the chance."

"It's not just Charlie," I said. "It's my entire family. I can't leave them vulnerable. Besides, where could we go that they wouldn't find us?"

"That's a fair question and one I can't answer, but what if the cartel decides to make a statement about their power on American soil? It would send a mighty strong message to the DEA, not to mention Agent Fielding, about just how impenetrable their organization has become. If they didn't know how he felt about you before, that kiss on the roof took all doubt away."

We walked the rest of the distance without saying anything more. Her words were running around in my head like freight trains waiting to collide. Had acting on my feelings inadvertently brought more danger into our lives? Agents were told not to become personally involved for a reason. It compromised missions and caused unnecessary mistakes to be made.

After the agents who had accompanied us made sure we were safe, Lila tossed a bottle of water from her nearly empty refrigerator in my direction. Since that fateful night when she had gone with me to the hospital her entire life had been overturned.

"Promise me that you won't leave without saying goodbye," I said. "You've become a very important part of my life, and Charlie adores you."

She took a sip before answering. "I would never go anywhere without letting you know. I just wish you would reconsider leaving. It isn't safe for any of us right now."

"Maybe not, but if I go, I will no longer have access to information that might be invaluable if a member of the newly-formed, mega-cartel chooses to make that bold statement you were talking about."

"Don't listen to me," she retorted. "I doubt they'll come looking for either of us any time soon. I'm just getting restless. It's not easy having my life under a magnifying glass when I know that people on both sides of the law are just waiting for me to slip up."

She made a bed on her sofa, but the rhythmic sound of breathing coming from the room above my head made it impossible for me to rest. My decisions had put everyone I loved in danger, but regardless of what might yet happen, I would never regret bringing Charlie home. Being separated from him was the most painful part of job.

I got up the moment the sun peaked its head over the horizon and folded the blankets I had been given to use. Lila had loaned me something to wear the evening before, so I showered quickly and ran a comb through my hair before pulling it into a knot at the nap of my neck. Then I pulled open the door and told the agents standing in the hallway that I could make it back to FBI headquarters without an escort. I stopped at the only bodega nearby—one that was open twenty-four hours a day—and purchased foundation and a tube of mascara. The dark circles beneath my eyes needed to be at least partially hidden.

Assistant Director Bridges had promised that he would tell Agent Cole of my return so I could see Charlie before my work day began. There were two cameras in the hallway just outside the door to the suite of rooms she used when there were children in her care. They gave an added sense of security, but after Agent's Ross' execution, I knew that nothing would stop mercenaries if the stakes were high enough.

I kept my face hidden until I had swiped my access card and stepped inside. She was holding Charlie's hands and guiding him across the floor. His squeals of delight tore at my heart. In no time at all, he would be walking, and I had missed most of the process.

"There you are, my little man," I called out to him.

At the sound of my voice, he gave me a broad smile that reminded me so much of his father. I closed the short distance between us and gathered him into my arms. "I can't believe how big you are."

"How did things go?" Amanda asked.

"Not good," I replied, grateful that I wasn't required to keep everything from her. "There were jailbreaks in two countries, and all of my enemies are now free to do as they please."

She shrugged her shoulders. "I hadn't heard. I was hoping everything would finally be settled so you and your family could start living somewhat normal existences again."

"My worries won't be going away any time soon," I said, kissing the top of Charlie's head. He was busy playing with the badge I had pinned to my belt. I had positioned him so the gun I carried would be out of his sight.

"Do you feel like talking about it? It won't go any further."

"Everything happened so fast I'm still trying to process."

"But you've been through debriefing? That was always the hardest part of any assignment for me. Too many people firing questions I wasn't sure I could answer."

"The process hasn't changed. We were at it until after two this morning. I'm afraid Agent Fielding is going to be blamed for everything."

"You saw him? The last time we talked you weren't sure he was even alive."

"He's been undercover with Alma Mendoza trying to prove that he'd switched sides."

"That's a dangerous game—double espionage."

"It's how he's lived most of his life, but she used the information he supplied to betray him. He's on her trail again, but I have a feeling it's not going to end well."

"You can't lose your faith now, Reagan. He's been in tougher situations."

"Maybe! I just wish he would leave the tracking to someone else and disappear."

"That's not who he is."

"Do you have any idea how many people want him dead?" I asked, knowing that hope was a necessity, but false hope was a liability that kept people from accepting the truth.

"I imagine the list would be quite lengthy. Have you decided what you're going to do? I know you won't feel safe until this whole mess is resolved."

"The idea of going into hiding has come up. I've done so many foolish things the past few months, but kissing Agent Fielding in front of witnesses, any of whom could be working for the cartels, has to be the most mindless of all."

"I'm not even going to ask how that happened," she responded. "You've been fighting your feelings for months, but if anyone wants to punish him, the best way to bring him out is to go after the people he loves."

Charlie had crawled off my lap to play with some of the toys that were scattered around the floor.

"So you don't think it's going to make much difference if I leave or stay?" I asked as he hit a xylophone with a plastic hammer.

"I can only speak from what I've observed over the years. I know keeping your family safe is a priority, but accepting the reality that comes with many of the choices we make is a must. You're in serious trouble, and it's going to take everyone who is willing to help to get you out of it. I've told the assistant director that I'm available to take care of Charlie for as long as needed. He said he didn't know what course of action would be pursued yet, but he appreciated my willingness to stay involved. Have you talked to your parents since you got back?"

"Not yet," I admitted. "I wasn't sure it was a good idea to use my cell phone."

"Then make the call from headquarters. I would suggest using the phone in my office, but I don't want anyone knowing where Charlie is. I'll be taking him back to my house the minute you leave."

The temptation to question her further about keeping Charlie safe was immense, but I knew every precaution was being taken. So I kissed my son goodbye and left him before the tears fell. I would make sure the footage showing my presence in the hallway was erased before it could fall into the wrong hands.

Assistant Director Bridges was in his office by the time I made my way through the bullpen and up the stairs.

"Good morning," I said after pushing his door open. "I hope I'm not interrupting."

He motioned for me to sit down. "I'm afraid there's been no further word from the DEA. Were you able to get any sleep?"

"No more than you, I'm sure."

"Hazard of the work I do," he replied. "Have you been to see Charlie?"

"Yes! Thank you for making sure he was safe while I was gone."

"I wish I could have done more. This entire situation with the DEA has become intolerable. It's left me questioning the advisability of allowing you to return to your apartment until we know what the new cartel's plans are. I will not have another agent's death on my hands."

"What would you suggest?" I asked. "Finding Lupe Evans is the only way we'll make any headway since it's common consensus now that she's leading the entire operation."

"And you don't think the DEA can do that? Their people are working tirelessly to stop the cartels."

"I'm not saying they aren't doing everything possible, sir, but their focus is on apprehending the people who got away. I know that emphasis will eventually lead them to the top, but I have a vested interest in how rapidly they can get there because it concerns the safety of my family. I still have forty-eight hours to investigate on my own, don't I?"

"It's more like forty-two now, but yes, you're cleared to use whatever resources we have. I would rather have you inside the building working on a computer than roaming the streets anyway. How would you feel about going to a safe house for a few days?"

My thoughts flew swiftly back to the farmhouse where Neil had lost his life. "I would rather take my chances in my own apartment, sir."

"Then I'll have a team assigned to your building. Don't try to take matters into your own hands, Agent Sinclair. The people you're up against have already shown what they're both willing and capable of doing, and we don't need more terrorists or assassins flocking to our city. But on a slightly different note, I understand that you and Ambassador Alexander had a few words. He can't press charges for insubordination, but he did suggest that you were too close to the situation to be objective."

"Maybe I am, but he wasn't exactly forthright with what he knew."

"You won't win brownie points, or get the answers you're looking for, by backing a superior into a wall. His responsibilities are somewhat different than ours."

"I understand his need for diplomacy, but he was purposely hiding things I had every right to know."

"You accused him of having a mole in his organization in front of his wife."

"That's because no one was addressing it."

"Do you have facts with which to prove your belief."

"Facts take time to collect, and I was whisked away from the embassy against my will in record-breaking time. Do you agree with him?"

"What I think has no bearing on what happened. Agent Fielding is your son's father. That gives you a personal interest in his welfare, but from what the ambassador said, the two of you appeared to be sharing a rather intimate relationship."

"You're referring to the kiss on the helipad."

He nodded and then folded his arms in front of him. "It's not exactly what I would expect from one of my people."

"I can't excuse my lapse in judgment, sir, except to say that he was going back to fight what might well be his last battle. I wanted him to know that he wasn't alone."

"For the record, I believe you've shown a great deal of restraint under some very difficult circumstances, but the ambassador has a point. Our actions must be above reproach when we're working in the field. Now, get to work. You don't have much time to put all the pieces together."

I reframed from asking that I be kept informed as new information was made available. My boss was more than understanding, but if charges were filed against me, proper channels would be followed to resolve them.

Agent Howard was the first one to greet me when I walked into the bullpen a few minutes later. "Am I ever glad to see you! When did you get back?"

"Last night," I replied.

"Well, don't hold anything back. I don't like it when I can't have my partner's back."

"I guess that means you haven't been listening to the news. There have been prison breaks in both Mexico and Colombia. Every member of the cartels I've been forced to interact with are now free to wreck havoc with the rest of humanity."

He took a sip of coffee before responding. "I don't like the sounds of that. Do the authorities have any leads?"

"Let's not talk here," I told him as I noticed a number of other agents watching us. I was trying to be more of a team player, but this case involved my personal life, and that wasn't open for discussion.

"The assistant director has given me permission to do additional research into the three families involved to see if anything useful can be found. He said you might be able to help."

"Then let's get to it. I heard about the bombing at the prison in Bogotá but had no idea it was connected to what you were doing in Mexico. You do know how to make enemies in all the wrong places, but I'll make damned sure they don't bother you or your son on American soil again."

We carried our laptops to a vacant conference room where I spread every piece of information I had gathered over the past few months out on the table so it could be easily accessed. Within minutes, Agent Howard was up to speed and ready to proceed on his own. While he tried to contact former associates who had spent time in Colombia, I began plugging names from each of the three families involved into genealogical research engines like Ancestry to see if anything popped up.

I already knew about Henrici Mendoza Montoya and Marianne Verde—infamous relatives of Carlos and Alma. And by noon, I had discovered that Lupe Costa Evans maternal grandfather was a man by the name of Tomas Rivera. Knowing birth years and the villages where ancestors had been born led me to other family members—all deceased. What we needed was a living relative, or even a former neighbor, who would be willing to talk.

Agent Howard sent the names, dates and places I uncovered to the only contact he had been able to find that was still in Colombia, but what he needed was up-to-date residential information if he was to be any help. So I scoured records of property transactions and holdings in and around Bogotá, and throughout the rest of the country, looking for recognizable names but found nothing useful. It appeared that more than a dozen families had basically disappeared. I even looked through Mexican marriage records for the Seville sons thinking that maiden names may have been used in acquiring land holdings, but each new lead came to a disheartening end.

I met with Assistant Director Bridges before leaving. He had made arrangements for me to stay in a nearby hotel for a few nights, with armed agents to lend support should the need arise. While I felt it was unnecessary, I agreed to his request, provided

Charlie could be with me. He said he had already taken care of that. Agent Cole would bring him to the hotel room and leave him with me until morning, but no one could see us together. He gave me a company credit card to use until the suitcase I had taken to Mexico made it back to the states.

When I asked why I couldn't just return to my apartment for what I needed, he gave me an unconvincing answer. He suggested I call my parents before leaving the office and tell them that the trial had been indefinitely postponed, but I was busy with another assignment and would not be able to contact them again for a few days. He also told me to replace my cell phone and get a new number. That's when I knew he was withholding something important.

I waited until Agent Howard had gone before making the call home. I hated lying to my parents, but over the past few months, I had become an expert at it. I told my mother what the assistant director had said and waited for her reply. She took it more calmly than anticipated, but then everyone in my family was giving me the space I claimed to need. She didn't mention anyone watching the house, so I knew the assigned agents were being careful. I hoped the ones watching Trey had done the same. I had a lot of explaining to do, but until clearance came, I had to play by the rules.

Two agents from another task force were waiting for me by the elevator when I was ready to leave the building. They would escort me to and from the hotel and take care of whatever needs I might have. I found it very disconcerting after being allowed the freedom to walk to and from Lila's loft but understood why Bridges was doing it. He had already lost two of his agents to the same cartel and didn't want to make it three.

I was taken to a suite at the Biltmore Hotel. While waiting for Charlie to arrive, I made a short list of the things I would need for the night. One of the agents went to the shops in the lobby to get them while the other one remained with me. I tried to be cordial, but smalltalk was impossible. I just wanted to hold my son and have time to think. So I went into the bedroom where a crib had been put and sat down on the edge of the bed. The entire situation had gotten completely out-of-hand, and I had to do something to stop it.

Amanda said very little when dropping Charlie off for the night. But from the look on her face, I knew she wasn't really on board with moving him back and forth. She had been able to keep him safe because no one knew where he was, but my insistence on spending more time with him could jeopardize that. I knew after our first few minutes together that I wouldn't ask for him to be brought to the hotel again. It was a purely selfish act.

After ordering room service for dinner, I fed and bathed Charlie and then played with him until his eyes became heavy. I watched him sleep for the longest time after that, all the while wondering how such a helpless, innocent and amazing child could be held accountable for the sins and actions of his parents. He deserved to have what I had promised Maria I would deliver.

With that thought in mind, I used the phone by the side of the bed to call Lila. I needed answers, and I was convinced that she knew more that could help me.

"Hey, you," she said. "I've been trying to reach you all day. Did you forget to turn your cell on?"

"Not exactly," I responded. "It's been brought to my attention that using it might not be wise. I plan on getting a new one tomorrow."

"Maybe I should too. I almost didn't answer your call. I take it you're not at home."

"The assistant director is being cautious. Don't you still have agents outside your door?"

"They've been there all day. That's why I thought you would be coming back to spend the night. Have you learned anything new?"

"Nothing about Mexico City," I said as I rested my back against the headboard where I could watch Charlie sleep. I hoped she wouldn't mention him because that would mean telling another lie.

"That's not what I expected to hear since Assistant Director Bridges gave you permission to look into things on your own. I've been racking my brain all day trying to piece together what we already know. As much as I hate to say this, the cartels aren't going to let Sam interfere again, and the government isn't going to stop him from trying. They need him to keep risking his life because there isn't anyone else capable of doing what he does. That leaves us to figure out something that might help him."

"I can't ask you to do that, Lila. It's basically out of our hands anyway since it's doubtful the DEA will ask for my input again. I seem to have become a thorn in their collective side."

"They should appreciate what you're doing."

"Perhaps, but most of them think I'm simply an interloper with a big mouth."

"So you speak your mind. That shouldn't matter if you're right."

My laugh was bitter. Her expressions of concern made it even more difficult to

believe she wasn't on the level, but my instincts would not keep people safe.

"I haven't been trained in their procedures, and I'm not an official member of their

team. That makes me a liability. I'll do what I can, but I want you to stay as far away from

this as possible."

"Have you talked to Trey?" she asked, abruptly changing the subject and leaving me to wonder why. "He's not going to be happy about that kiss on the helipad."

I had been trying to put that indiscretion out of my mind all day. The warmth, passion and feelings of hope and loss Agent Fielding's lips had brought as they pressed into mine had left me in a state of suspended animation. I wanted desperately to return to the refuge I felt in his arms, but that wasn't even a possibility now.

"Trey is the least of my worries," I replied. "He made it abundantly clear that he couldn't be with someone who keeps secrets, and my life is filled with them. But we really shouldn't be discussing any of this over the phone."

"I know," she said with a sigh of resignation. "The government is aware of everything we do. That means the cartels could be too."

"It's not as ominous as that. They only look if they have a reason to."

"We've certainly given them cause to do more than take a casual interest in our financial or driving records. Our lives have been irrevocably changed because of our involvement with the cartels, but that doesn't mean we have to continue being victims to their insanity. Have you given any more thought to leaving town until all of this blows over? I know Trey would go with you. He might not be as exciting as Sam, but he's handsome, considerate, kind and can give you what you say you need most because you share the same Christian beliefs."

I pulled my knees up to my chest. My life was a disaster, and anyone associated with me had already lost his or her sense of peace.

"Trey is a wonderful man. And maybe my feelings for him could grow into something lasting if I gave him a chance, but he wants a wife, a family and a chance for the perfect life. I can't offer him any of that."

"You were upfront with him about what you did for a living. He chose to become involved."

"And I chose to keep Charlie's paternity a secret from him. I'm not sure he'll ever forgive that, and I'm not sure it really matters any longer."

"So that kiss on the helipad really did mean something."

"It was a complication I wasn't expecting, but I'm not sure it really matters."

"Doesn't it?" she responded. "Sam knows what he has waiting for him, and he's going to do whatever is necessary to make it back. What you have to decide is if you really want to be with him. He's never going to offer a peaceful existence like Trey can, but I've seen the fire that exists between the two of you. Sometimes life offers us more than one compelling choice, and we have to make a difficult decision. I would never presume to tell you what to do, but I don't want you to wake up some day and realize that you've lost what mattered most when you didn't have to. Edward and I were not forced into meeting with Rios. We had everything we needed, but in searching for something more, we lost everything."

"I'm sorry he died, Lila."

"So am I, but somewhere during these past few months I've come to understand that I created my own destiny. We all do by the seemingly inconsequential decisions we make each day. Don't give up on what you really want just because it might be messy. The best things in life are the hardest to get."

Her perspective kept me awake most of the night. I didn't know what I really wanted. I had strong feelings for two men, and I wasn't ready to let either of them go until I made up my mind. That meant finding something that would allow Agent Fielding to come home so I could figure out if a future together was even possible. He was the most exciting, complex and dangerous man I had ever met, and he could easily destroy what remained of my life. Trey, on the other hand, was only looking for a commitment he could count on. He reminded me a great deal of Neil.

My allotted time looking for answers on my own came to an unsatisfactory conclusion much too rapidly. Through diligent effort, I could now prove that the four older Seville brothers and Robert Evans had arrived in Bogotá, Colombia within hours of the raid at the Rios ranch. Security cameras outside the terminal showed them being picked up at different locations. I used every technology available to determine the make, model and license plate numbers of the cars they were riding in, but the drivers knew what they were doing when it came to making identification possible. Once the vehicles were several blocks away they simply disappeared.

The authorities had known where Lupe Evans' villa was for years. They had people watching it continually, but unless there were secret tunnels leading to the outside world, no one unexpected came or went during the day or night. Persons of interest were brought into DEA headquarters and questioned on a regular basis, but no one had anything of relevance to share. That meant digging deeper into Lupe Evans' early life because she seemed intent on spending her remaining days away from the public eye.

Her family had massive land holdings in several parts of the country that included jungles, lowlands and oceanfront properties—all necessary for the successful cultivation, production and distribution of cocaine. The known estates of her ancestors, including that of Tomas Rivera, were thoroughly searched. But without strict building laws entire compounds could spring up almost instantaneously, and they were nearly impossible to find in regions of heavy vegetation.

I wanted desperately to go back to Colombia where I might be able to learn more. The Bogotá division of the DEA was doing what they could, but they were inundated with the aftermath of the bombing at the prison. Carlos Mendoza's escape had sparked a near rampage of protests, riots and looting. No one had heard from Agent Fielding since he left the embassy in pursuit of Alma and Eloise, and no one had come looking for me.

Believing I was in the clear after three nights spent in a hotel was easy, and it didn't take much to convince my boss that keeping such close tabs on both Lila and me was a waste of tax payers dollars. I had gotten a new cell phone and knew how to use my gun. But before authorizing my return to my own home, he insisted that an alarm system be installed. I had been contemplating doing that anyway. Charlie would stay in Amanda's care during the day.

Since our time for working a case unrelated to our department's responsibilities had elapsed, Agent Howard and I were assigned to an investigation involving jewelry store heists where over fifty million in loose and uncut diamonds had been stollen. The suspects had known ties to the Middle East, and three civilians had already lost their lives. I had never worked a terrorist case before but knew they could be every bit as ruthless as the cartels. In many ways, I was glad to be on active duty again. I had spent too much time looking for something I might never be able to find.

"Intel tells us that they'll attack in the Washington D.C. area next," Assistant Director Bridges said as we met with the rest of the team. "We suspect they'll show up at Hamilton Jewelers at the corner of fifth and Main some time today. A five million dollar shipment of loose diamonds is arriving before noon."

"Won't they suspect our involvement since it's so close to headquarters," Agent Hendricks, Neil's old partner asked. I had seen him in the bullpen occasionally, but he had never spoken directly to me. He still believed I was responsible for Neil's death.

"It will be too big a temptation to resist, and they have plenty of supporters willing to die for the cause. I need all hands on board for this one. I want this cell squashed before it has time to organize anything else."

Agent Howard and I were assigned to take the side alley where fire escape doors opened from several floors above the store's showroom. It was highly unlikely that anyone would come our way since it was such an indirect route out of the building, but no exit could be overlooked.

"I wish we were the ones going inside to browse," I said as we hurried to our post beside the dumpster where we would wait until we were needed or further orders were given.

Agent Howard adjusted his earpiece as he squatted down beside me. "I've been on the inside before. It may be more exciting than waiting to be bitten by some rodent looking for food, but I like going home to my kids at night. I figured you felt the same way so I didn't push for being closer to the action."

"You're right," I replied. "My first concern has to be for my son. I just hate waiting around."

"Most of us do, but this is a big part of what FBI work is all about. You just got off to a rather unusual start working undercover with the DEA. Are you sorry you're not affiliated with them permanently since their action seems to be nonstop?"

I looked down at the badge on my belt and the holster on my hip. Becoming an FBI agent was all I had ever wanted, but my perception of life was shifting. Instead of thinking I had plenty of time to accomplish every heart's desire, I knew my days were numbered. I needed to spend more time on the legacy I would leave behind. My relationship with my family was in shambles, my spirituality had eroded, and my son was in constant danger. Life couldn't get much bleaker than that.

"If it weren't for Charlie, I would say that becoming involved with the DEA was the worst thing that ever happened to me."

He touched my arm reassuringly. "It's always a temptation to compartmentalize so completely that we forget what's really important. I don't tell many people this, but I almost lost my family a few years ago. I was a go-getter who went after every dangerous mission available. I thrived on the unexpected and perilous and was gone from home for weeks at a time. The very nature of what we do isn't compatible with marriage and family, and my wife finally got sick of all the uncertainly. She said I was married to my job instead of her. It took a whole lot of readjustment and compromise to keep her from leaving, but I've never been sorry about letting someone else take the high-profile, glory jobs. There's still plenty for me to do, and most nights I'm home for dinner. A plaque on some wall for bravery in the line of duty isn't how I want my family remembering me."

"And you don't feel like something is missing?"

"I would be lying if I said I didn't enjoy an occasional rush, but the constant need for stimulation is gone. I've watched you the past few days. You have an incredible mind when it comes to putting seemingly unconnected pieces together. Most anyone can do legwork and shoot a gun, but not many people are blessed with a talent like yours. I'm surprised Bridges hasn't capitalized on it yet."

I thought back to my brief time in Agent Ross' position after he had been relieved of his duties. "I tried that once, but I hate being confined to an office all day."

"Maybe you'll change your mind. I would take a job like that in an instant if it was offered to me, but my brain isn't wired that way. I can see relationships when they're pointed out, but I sure as hell can't find them on my own."

I figured we would be squatting in the alley for hours, but apparently terrorists didn't like waiting around either. We heard the armored car carrying the diamonds arrive around ten. One of their people must have been waiting inside because the first shot was fired only seconds later. It was impossible to tell what was going on away from where we were, but our assignment was to stay put. That pause gave me a moment to think about the concept of dying for religious beliefs. I would certainly defend the right to worship as a Christian, but I would never murder and plunder to take something away from the innocent for a cause that only wanted to destroy.

It was by an act of grace alone that I looked up to see one of the heavy metal doors leading to the fire escape three floors above our heads open and a woman put her foot on the metal grate.

"Federal agents," I shouted up at her. "Put your hands in the air and come down without any rapid movements."

She stood where she was, as if trying to decide what to do. If she went back inside, we would lose her. I couldn't see her face, but her skin was olive-toned and she looked even younger than me. She had a small satchel slung over her shoulder and was nicely dressed in a business suit and sensible shoes.

By this time, Agent Howard had his gun pointed at her too. There was a five-foot drop to the ground at the bottom of the stairs. "No one needs to get hurt today," he said. "We just want to talk."

She reached behind her, but the door was locked from the inside. There was no place for her to go, and the gunfire from inside the building was growing louder. If this girl wasn't part of the heist, why didn't she just say so?

I took a tentative step towards the ladder at the bottom of the fire escape, but as I did so, her hand reached inside her pocket and she pulled out a gun. Agent Howard fired before I had time to open my mouth. She slumped down but not before taking two shots of her own. One hit the side of the dumpster, while the other one hit my partner.

Immediate thoughts of what had happened to Neil rushed through my brain, and I didn't hesitate in taking a shot of my own. Her body bounced down an entire flight before it stopped moving. Blood immediately began falling to the alley floor.

Additional FBI agents seemed to appear almost immediately. While two of them hurried towards the girl on the fire escape, I knelt down beside my partner. His face was drained of color, and he was clutching his arm. But he didn't appear to be critically wounded.

"Are you okay?" I asked.

He grunted his annoyance. "I should have anticipated that, but she looked too young to be involved."

"I'm not sure age matters," I said as I helped him to his feet.

"I suppose not. Terrorists recruit practically infants to work for them any more."

"Where are they?" the agent on the stairs above us demanded as he pulled the satchel from the girl's shoulder and opened it.

I felt my own knees start to give way since it was my bullet that had stopped the suspect from moving, but now wasn't the time to question my actions. Decoys were used for a reason.

"We need to search the floors above the shop," I shouted to anyone who would listen. "She may have stashed the diamonds or handed them off."

"You're not going anywhere," the agent standing next to me said before hurrying away. "You'll stay with your partner and the victim until the ambulance and coroner arrive."

"Do you think they'll find the diamonds?" I asked Agent Howard as I eased him down onto a filthy, frayed ottoman that had been left beside the dumpster.

"Hell if I know!" was his immediate response. "Since the gunfire seems to have ended, it means they've caught everyone who didn't get away. Damned good call about checking the upper floors. That girl didn't come out of that door for nothing."

"Still, I didn't mean to kill her."

"You can't think about it like that. She chose her life and knew how it would end. We gave her every opportunity to surrender. It was her choice to open fire."

The ambulance soon arrived, and I watched the young girl's body being zipped inside a black bag for transport. Agent Howard allowed one of the medics to look at his wound but refused to be coddled.

His angry mood didn't lift until the bullet had been removed, and he was waiting in his hospital room for his wife to arrive. He would be kept overnight to make sure no complications arose. His sacrifice of excitement to keep his family together caused me to reflect on where my own life would end up if I didn't start making a few changes. Charlie needed a mother who would be there to see him grow up, not one who kept bolting into danger.

When I got back to the bullpen everyone involved with the case was in high spirits.

"There's the woman of the hour," Agent Hendricks said as I approached my desk. "How's Agent Howard doing? I know this day couldn't have been easy for you."

I felt the tears come but didn't let them flow. It was enough that Neil's former partner had made a point of speaking to me. "He'll be out of the hospital tomorrow. His wife is with him now."

"At least he's still got one," an agent I couldn't name without looking at his badge said. "Some of the rest of us haven't been so lucky. This job is death on relationships, but we got the bad guys today, and the diamonds were recovered in an apartment on the third floor. I think it's time to celebrate."

I didn't care about details or celebrating right now. I just wanted to know if the shot I had fired had been responsible for a young girl's death. She may have been committed to faulty beliefs, but she had been willing to die for them. I could only ask myself if I was willing to live for mine.

"Are you coming with us to celebrate, Sinclair?" Agent Hendricks was asking when my thoughts returned to the present. "I know you don't drink, but this was your first big case with the team, and not everything they serve contains alcohol."

"I would rather get started on the paperwork, if it's okay with you," I said.

He took a step closer. "That can be done later. We've put in a hard day and need to relax."

He was challenging me after his brief comment of acceptance, but I shouldn't be judged as a team player simply by my willingness to spend time drinking with my colleagues at some local bar.

"Maybe another time," I said. "My son will be waiting or me."

I thought I saw just a hint of admiration as he turned and walked away. The men and women I worked with might never understand why I chose to live my life the way I did. I could only hope they would soon accept it.

Chapter 5

Agent Howard was released from the hospital the next day, but with an injured right shoulder he would be given desk duty until he was able to use his gun. That meant I was without an active-duty field partner again. It was the perfect time to talk to the assistant director about my plans for the future. I went to his office the morning after the jewelry store heist.

"You did a good job yesterday," he said as I approached his desk.

"Thank you, sir," I replied, as butterflies flitted through my stomach so rapidly I thought I might be ill. I had done nothing but ask for considerations during the past eight months, and I was still waiting to hear if there would be further repercussions from my time in Mexico City. Ambassador Alexander was taking the higher road now, but that could easily change. "It was a team effort."

"I'm not sure you understand the crucial part you played. The other floors might not have been searched in time if you hadn't given us a reason to do so. By the time our people got to the third floor, the last accomplice, who had the diamonds all along, was getting ready to hand them off to someone else."

"But who? The entire building was surrounded."

"No one pays attention to homeless people. There are far too many of them in the city. The final reports haven't come across my desk yet, but I have a feeling that's not why you're here."

"No, sir! I have legitimate concerns about my future as an agent. I'm not sure I have the heart for it any more."

He leaned back until his desk chair squeaked. "I thought we had tabled that discussion until this mess with the DEA was over? I think I've been more than understanding about your concerns."

"You have, sir, and I know this is where I need to be—for now anyway."

"Then what is it? You've proven your worth as a team player. Even Agent Hendricks' opinion of you is starting to change. And for what it's worth, I think you made the right decision last night. Not everyone celebrates the same way, and we need to stick by our beliefs. You've been through a lot the past few months, but your talents are undeniable."

"Thank you, sir. But how do I keep my personal feelings from interfering with the work I've committed to do? When Agent Howard was shot, I had flashbacks of what happened to Neil. I don't want to be a liability to anyone."

"Perhaps it's time for you to begin your sessions with Dr. Sylvester again. You need someone qualified who can help you make sense of a totally reprehensible situation. I think I may have been remiss in allowing that part of your healing to fall behind when your services were needed elsewhere."

"I would be more than willing to start therapy again, sir. I know outside circumstances aren't going to change any time soon, but shooting that girl yesterday and spending time in the hospital with Agent Howard let me know how fragile life is for all of us. We really are in this together, and every choice counts."

"That's a valuable lesson for every agent to learn. What we do is hard. We make split-second decisions that often have life-altering consequences, but you're not alone in how you feel. It might be a good idea to ask Dr. Sylvester about the support groups available for agents who have been through similar traumatic experiences. I'll set up an appointment, and we can go from there. How are things progressing at home now that you've been reunited with Charlie?"

"I love having him back in his own bed at night, but he's starting to get restless being transferred from one building to another without any connection to other people. Now that the weather is finally starting to change, I want him to feel less confined."

"Getting back to a normal routine is important. If there's any reason for concern, you'll be the first to know."

"Thank you, sir," I replied, rising to my feet. "And the new alarm system works like a charm. No one will get inside my apartment without being heard."

"That's excellent news. But before you leave, there's one more thing we need to discuss. Since Agent Howard will be out of commission for a few weeks, I want you to join him in-house in a more analytical capacity."

"Are we talking about doing Agent Ross' job again?"

"Not officially, but I could use the extra help. I'll have some files transferred to your desk within the hour. They're mostly cold cases that could use a fresh eye."

My heart was more heavy than usual when I left his office. We had been down this road before, but if the DEA needed my help again, or if someone new came looking for me, it would be advantageous if I could be easily found. And quite frankly, I didn't want another partner. Agent Howard and I were finally starting to understand each other.

That evening I took Charlie to the park across the street from my apartment building. It was a bold thing to do after all we'd both been through, but I couldn't keep running scared. He needed the normalcy I'd talked to my boss about. I was helping him across the grass when Trey called my name. The sudden loud noise made me jump.

"I didn't mean to startle you," he said, stopping beside us. "Charlie's getting so big."

"Yes, he is," I replied, not taking my eyes off my son as he teetered on his legs. I lowered him to the ground where he could run his chubby hands through the freshly mowed grass. He didn't have an aversion to it like so many small children did. "How are you doing?"

"Feeling like a fool for nursing a bruised ego instead of seeing how you were doing after our breakup. I'm not fond of rejection."

"I didn't reject you, Trey. You told me upfront what you were looking for, but instead of listening, I pulled you into my life that is still a mess."

"You don't have to explain anything, Reagan," he said, staring at some children who were playing on a maze of outdoor toys instead of looking at me. "I figured you were busy with work and other things. I wasn't going to come at all but didn't want to leave things the way they were."

"Am I that difficult to talk to?" I asked as I took a step forward. Charlie was crawling towards the group of children but had turned his head to make sure I was watching. "I never meant to hurt you."

"I know that," he said. "I over-reacted. It's not like you could stop what was happening. Under the circumstances, your job had to come first."

"It wasn't just my job."

He glanced quickly in my direction. "I suppose not. But regardless of how it happened, Agent Fielding and you share a son. That means he'll always be part of your life. Whether you make it more personal than that is up to both of you."

"That's true," I replied as I thought about the kiss we had shared on the helipad. I still didn't know what it meant, but I had been drawn into his life not so unlike Trey had been drawn into mine. Need was a powerful motivator, but it didn't always mean permanence.

"I want to give us another chance," he said as I tried to organize my thoughts. "I know it won't be easy because I have trust issues, but I'm willing to work on them."

"Why would you even want to do that after all I've put you through?" I asked, reaching out and pulling Charlie into my arms just as he reached the sand. I didn't want him to make it to the swings where he might get hurt. He was what mattered most.

"He's pretty good at moving around on his own," Trey said, running his hand over Charlie's head. "I've missed both of you so much."

I kissed my son's cheek as he struggled to break free. He wanted to explore his world without my assistance, but I wasn't ready to relinquish more control than I already had.

"Nothing in my life has changed, Trey," I said, spinning around so I could return to my apartment. Suddenly, I no longer felt safe out in the open where anyone could approach us. "We're still in danger, and that means anyone who has contact with us could be too."

He fell into step beside me. "I thought all of that had changed since the trial's been   indefinitely postponed? Your mom told me. We've kept in touch."

I knew then that I had to give him something more so he could make an informed choice that would be easier to live with. "Eloise Seville was sprung from prison by someone I became acquainted with while in Colombia. It's a complex story with twists and turns I'm still trying to figure out, but they're on the run with seemingly unlimited resources."

"Exactly what does that mean?" he asked.

"It means that the DEA is looking for them, but the possibility that they'll ever be found is minuscule. I seem to be in the clear at the moment, but the people I've upset are unpredictable and getting revenge is just part of what they do."

"But I want to be included in your life, whatever it is," he replied. "I'm not afraid of some drug lord with a vendetta."

"Well you should be, because I certainly am."

"Then let's go some place where we can't be found and start over. I've been miserable without the two of you the past few weeks."

I stopped walking and turned to look at him. His face told me his suggestion was sincere, but he was naïve if he thought my enemies would stop looking for retribution just because we moved to some remote place. Even Siberia might not be far enough.

"You're talking about going into hiding and never seeing our families again?"

"It wouldn't be forever—just until the authorities have whomever might want to come after you in custody."

"That's not how it works, Trey," I said with a shake of my head. "Once you commit to that lifestyle, there is no going back."

"I'm good with that," he replied as he caught hold of my arm.

"But I'm not! I refuse to spend the rest of my life looking over my shoulder and wondering if the next person I meet is a hit man or woman. The best option for me is to stay where I am and be prepared to fight back if necessary."

"That's insane, Reagan!"

"Maybe it is, but I have to think about what's best for Charlie. He deserves stability and family relationships. That's not going to happen if he's forced into hiding where he can never have any friends. Besides, he deserves to know his biological father."

"I thought that was a moot point because it's highly unlikely he'll ever be back."

"I can't predict the future, but he was very much alive until I left Mexico City a few nights ago."

Trey suddenly looked as if he had been sucker-punched and released my arm. "You left the country without telling anyone and saw him?"

"Everyone felt it would be best that way. He was in the middle of a mission that went sideways. I can't tell you anything more because it's a matter of National Security and ongoing operations, but he made me promise to protect Charlie, no matter what it took. I have to believe he'll make it back to his son."

"And back to you," Trey said with a heavy sigh. "I've always known that your relationship went deeper than what you were willing to admit. Is he the reason you don't want to start a new life with me?"

His direct question caught me off guard, and I hesitated longer than I should have before answering. "He has the right to be part of his son's life."

"Even if his presence means putting Charlie in more danger? I'm not stupid, Reagan. You wouldn't even be in this mess if you hadn't become involved with him."

"I accepted an assignment. I had no idea what it would lead to."

"You should have been able to guess," he said in an accusatory tone. "Even people who have no experience with the cartels understand how dangerous they are. Your Agent Fielding has devoted his life to taking them down and has amassed an incalculable number of enemies in the process. Charlie and you will be at the top of the list if anyone tries to get even with him. He should be doing everything possible to separate himself from you, and not keep drawing you back into the disarray he calls his life."

His clear assessment of the situation drove home the fact that I was deluding myself by thinking Agent Fielding could ever be part of our lives, even if he survived.

"If I hadn't gone, I wouldn't have Charlie."

"But you could have had other children with me!" he exclaimed, and I could almost see the desperation in his eyes. "I love Charlie and have no problem raising him as my own, but that doesn't change the fact that his very presence makes him the perfect target for some very bad people."

"He's just a baby, Trey," I said as tears slide from the corners of my eyes, and I pulled my son closer. "I wouldn't trade him for all the other children in the world. I know he was meant to be mine."

"I'm sure he was, but you can't miss what you've never known."

"Maybe not, but I accept full responsibility for whatever retribution my choices have unleashed. I'm not afraid to make a stand against evil people any longer. I've been doing it for months now, but I don't expect you, or anyone else, to understand. I have to remain visible so no one will go after the people I love to find out where I am."

"That's all very noble, but what about your right to feel safe and loved? That's the kind of life I want to provide for you."

I reached out and touched his cheek while Charlie squirmed in my arms. He would start fussing and want to be put down soon. "I love you for saying that, Trey, but this isn't your fight. I need to have this situation resolved before I even think about moving forward with anyone."

"Is that why you were so non-committal when we last spoke? I got the impression you weren't interested enough to fight for us. That's why coming here today was so hard. I know we can have a very happy life together, but it has to be what we both want."

When I looked at him, my eyes were swimming with tears. "I'm not in a position to indulge in personal wants right now. I know that's not what you want to hear, but did you even know that a detail was assigned to keep track of you while I was gone? It's standard procedure in cases like this. I haven't even told my parents I went to

Mexico City, and I need it to stay that way. My mother has become so traumatized over my life choices that she can barely function. I'm not willing to do that to anyone else. When I give my heart it will be completely and without reservations. That means this entire mess has to be resolved first."

We talked for a few minutes longer, and then Trey kissed my cheek. I felt a great letdown as I watched him walk away, but it wasn't enough to call him back. He had a few decisions of his own to make.

The next few days were a mixture of gloom and near despair. I talked to my parents on the phone again but made no mention of what was going on in my life—other than an overview of work and how Charlie was doing. They didn't ask about Mexico City or Trey. I could only hope that he respected me enough to keep what I had told him to himself. I hated what rules and self-preservation were forcing me to do, but I had to remain strongly independent when it came to the people I loved. Any misstep on my part could plunge them back into the unpredictable situation that was now the driving force behind my life.

With Agent Howard on desk duty, I accepted the assistant director's offer. Looking for something that might bring a cold case back to life wasn't anywhere near as stimulating as working in the field, and it was difficult maintaining focus. Whenever I had a free moment, or needed a mental break, I allowed myself to search for additional information about the cartels. If Bridge's knew what I was doing, he didn't mention it. I was giving everything I could my assignments, but dismissing what might be happening thousands of miles away was impossible

Much to my surprise, Trey called a few days after our meeting in the park to see how we were doing. He gave no indication of having come to any conclusions, but I knew he wouldn't wait forever. I vacillated between giving him the answer he wanted so I would have something to look forward to, and my need to see Agent Fielding again so we could talk about our ill-advised feelings.

Simple logic told me that I could be happy with Trey. He was an amazing man who was considerate of my feelings, took the time to listen and was always there when I needed him. His kiss was gentle and reassuring. I would want for nothing if we were together, except the expectancy and heart palpitations I felt when I even thought about Agent Fielding. He was the romantic warrior that went off to slay the dragon. Trey was the dependable blacksmith or innkeeper that remained behind.

Just as I was crawling into bed one night my cell phone rang. I hurried to answer it before Charlie woke up. He was going through another bout of teething.

"Hey, Reagan," Lila said. "I hope I'm not calling too late, but you told me to let you know when I came to a decision about leaving. Well, I've decided! An old friend has asked me to join him on a trip to Central and South America. He has business there, and I would love to see more of the world."

"You haven't mentioned an old friend before," I said, trying to keep my voice steady. She was the only real confidant I had.

"I had almost forgotten about him it's been such a long time since we last spoke, but I'm bored. Why not do something exciting and unexpected."

"What about your classes, your loft and your cat? You've invested so much time and energy creating the life you said you wanted."

She didn't sound like herself, and getting involved with another man until she had passed the first year anniversary in recovery could destroy all she had gained.

"I'm not leaving forever. It's just a few weeks, and I've already talked to my neighbor about taking my cat. Everything else will be fine until I return. I was hoping you would be happy for me."

If she wanted my blessing, she wasn't going to get it. Something about this sudden declaration of boredom didn't ring true. Every other time we had talked, she'd gone into considerable detail over how pleased she was with how her life was progressing.

"I am happy for you, but I'm scared too."

"Why?" she asked. "I know what I'm doing. This isn't some romantic tryst."

"Then why are you going?"

"My reasons aren't open for discussion. I need to get away, and this is a chance to do it. If you're worried about my recovery, it's wasted stress. I don't need a program to stay clean. I still want to meet my daughter, and I can't do that if I'm using."

"We all think were stronger than we actually are," I said, hoping she wouldn't take offense. Everyone who had ever fallen off the wagon had used that same kind of excuse. "Besides, you can't fault me for wanting you to stay. You're my best friend, and Charlie needs his Aunt Lila around."

"We'll still be friends, and you can kiss Charlie for me every day. I promise to keep you posted on all our adventures, but you're so busy you'll hardly know I'm gone."

"That's not true," I replied. "I know I've been preoccupied, but I still wish you'd reconsider. I don't have a good feeling about you going off with some random guy. Isn't there someone else you could go with instead?"

"You're my only girlfriend now that Angel is gone. I promise to be careful, but this is something I have to do. I can't explain why it's so important I take this step right now, but maybe in time you'll understand that I really have changed, and it's all because of you. True friendship is about giving with no thought of getting something in return. Don't deny me the chance to do something selfless. I've been focused on all the wrong things for much too long."

I wanted to believe her, but I knew she was keeping something important from me. "Then I suppose all I can do is wish you 'Bon voyage'. When are you leaving?"

"At the end of the week."

"That's only two days away."

"I know it's short notice, but I only decided today. Maybe we could meet for lunch or dinner before I leave. I'll call you with the details."

She hung up, and it wasn't until later that I realized she had done it on purpose.

Chapter 6

Lila had been gone for nearly three weeks before the next major event took place. Trey and I had been working on our relationship. He had taken me to dinner, and I had invited him over so he could spend time with Charlie. It was fun watching them together. My son's squeals of delight when Trey tossed him into the air warmed my heart, much like they had done when Neil was with us. This was the way family life should be—each member committed to the safety and happiness of the others. I looked forward to our time spent together but couldn't rid myself of the belief that if Agent Fielding came back everything we were trying to build would shatter.

Thoughts of him still consumed many of my waking and sleeping hours, but no word had reached us to where he was or if he was still alive. I was back in the same limbo where I had been before going to Mexico City. His promise on the helipad meant nothing if he didn't come back to fulfill it.

And how would Trey react when he came face-to-face with the man who had a legal claim on Charlie? He was the one who had spent time with him. He was also the one who had been at the hospital when he'd been so sick, and the one who was feeling more strongly each time we were together that he was Charlie's father in deed, if not in actual fact. And what was even more difficult to comprehend was the knowledge that I was beginning to believe as he did. Agent Fielding had been responsible for my son's birth, but Trey was the one who had been involved in his life.

What I thought I felt for my former partner was beginning to seem like a dream. We had spent little more than two weeks together and all of it had been under duress. Maybe Heavenly Father was giving me time to discover that my fairy tale ending would be different from what was found on the movie screen or in books. With all the anxiety and stress of my day job, it was nice to come home to the relative peace of a provincial family life when Trey was able to join us. Making it more permanent was becoming a consideration.

And then the tranquility I was beginning to accept as a possibility for my future ended. Assistant Director Bridges summoned me to his office.

"How well do you know Lila Rivers?" he asked, dispensing with any pleasantries.

"Well, enough," I replied. Lila had left without saying goodbye, and while she had sent a few very short texts, I had no idea where she was or who she was with. "Why do you ask?"

"It seems that she's been playing us and using you to gain information about the DEA."

"That's impossible!" I countered as a wave of disbelief swept over me. "Lila has been nothing but supportive since the night we met. She even went to Mexico City to testify."

"While I understand that this may be hard to hear, her name has come up in connection with a drug-related shooting in Presidio, Texas. It happened early this morning."

I stood rooted to the floor as my head began to spin. "Your source must be mistaken, sir. She's been traveling with a friend in South and Central America the past few weeks."

"I suppose you have proof as to where she is now?"

"No, sir, but she isn't capable of violence. She's a pacifist who is trying to get her life straightened out."

"I hope you're right," he responded, rising to his feet. "We have a video conference with the acting DEA director in Dallas. His predecessor was one of the men who was killed. We need you to be part of this because you've shared a friendly relationship with a person-of-interest recently. I would give you additional background on what is already known, but you need to hear this from the source."

I followed him numbly down the hall to a large room where a computer had been set up to stream the call and slipped into the nearest chair. The faces of the other agents in the room seemed to be swirling around so rapidly they were unrecognizable. What Bridges was suggesting was ludicrous. The woman I knew might be capable of deceit, but she wasn't a murderer. She had held my son in her arms and had a daughter she wanted to meet.

My mind was still in turmoil when the image of a man in a white shirt, sitting behind a cluttered desk, came into view on the large screen at the front of the room. Assistant Director Bridges was the first person to speak.

"Good morning, Interim Director Whitman," he said. "I have Agent Sinclair in the room with us. If you could fill her in on what happened this morning and why you suspect Lila Rivers is involved, then perhaps she can answer a few of your questions."

"Thank you for being willing to join us, Agent Sinclair," he said. "I apologize for pulling you away from the cases you're working, but we need your help. We lost DEA Director Barney Fairbanks and Agent Rico Gomez this morning in an attempt to stop a large quantity of cocaine from coming into the country. I don't have all of details, but surveillance footage of the incident has been sent to my office. One image is of a woman we believe was in Mexico City at the time Eloise Seville escaped from jail, but we need a positive identification before we proceed in tracking her down."

I gasped with horror as Lila's face appeared before me. She was dressed like mercenary and had an assault rifle in her hands.

"Do you recognize the woman?" Interim Director Whitman asked.

"It looks like Lila Rivers, sir," I replied in little more than a whisper. "But why would she be dressed like that and holding a gun? She told me she was going on a vacation."

"The details are still unclear. Do you recognize anyone else?"

I studied the few seconds of moving footage as closely as I could. Lila was standing in front of what appeared to be mechanic's garage.

There were piles of tires and wrecked cars everywhere. She didn't move and looked absolutely terrified. The two men with her looked like they were of Hispanic descent, but I was fairly certain I had never seen either of them before.

"I don't recognize anyone else, sir. But if that is Lila, it's obvious she isn't there by choice."

"We're not accusing her of anything just yet, but we still need to find her. This isn't an isolated incident. We've lost agents in Colombia, El Salvador and Mexico during the past two weeks, but this is the first time there's been an attack on American soil."

"Isn't Presidio a little off the beaten track for major drug trafficking?" I asked, trying to recall what little I knew about the area. "There can't be over a few thousand people in the entire area."

"Quite the opposite is true, Agent Sinclair. Small towns like Presidio are the perfect place for smuggling of every kind. Most of the residents are farmers with land that doesn't produce much. It's easy to sway both individuals and masses when they're hungry, and with the president cracking down on border crossings, the major cartels are branching out. They want us to know that what we do will never be enough to stop them."

"How did they get across? That town borders the Rio Grande River."

"They didn't come by water. They were in an ultra-light aircraft using all-terrain landing gear where they could take off and set down at will. I've heard of them being used in other parts of the world, but they're expensive to build and operate. We believe the cartels you have become involved with have completed their merge and this was their maiden voyage in letting the authorities know they're well on their way to becoming the largest crime syndicate in all of the Americas."

"But why use Lila to make a statement? She may be a former addict, but she's never had direct affiliation with the cartels."

"Maybe not, but her past isn't exactly pristine, and her former lover had some very dirty hands. We believe the airplanes are Robert Evan's contribution to the new enterprise. He's no longer the playboy who was only looking for a good time. He's getting ready to take his place at the top."

"Isn't he afraid of being caught?"

"The authorities have to find him first. And with the network of people he now has working for him, he'll remain as elusive as his mother. We believe he sent Lila as a way to get your attention."

"That's a mighty big assumption since I've never been directly involved."

"Your son's father has. Can you tell me when you last had personal contact with Miss Rivers?"

All the pieces seemed to be falling into a place of horror and regret that I didn't even want to sort out. "Almost three weeks ago. She called to tell me that she was going on a trip with an old friend."

"Do you know the name of that friend?"

"She wouldn't say."

"Our belief is that she's been with Robert Evans, at least until the last few days."

"Robert Evans," I echoed as my heart plummeted. "I'm not sure they've even met."

"Our Intel suggests otherwise, although we don't know why or how they made this latest connection. We only know that you're part of this puzzle, and we're going to need your help again to solve it."

I wanted to tell him exactly what I thought about the entire DEA and how they operated, but Assistant Director Bridges placed a restraining hand on my arm.

"What makes you think they've been together?" he asked. "Everything you have right now is purely circumstantial."

"We're still in the early stages of investigation, but they were seen entering the southern tip of Mexico together a few days ago. We need Agent Sinclair's help in finding Miss Rivers so she can be questioned. Right now, she's the only lead we have."

"I'll do it," I numbly replied. "When do you want me to come?"

"Immediately! I'll leave the details to Assistant Director Bridges. I want to thank you for your support before you arrive. It's not easy learning that someone you trusted may have betrayed her own country."

When the scene on the whiteboard disappeared, the assistant director made his way to the front of the room. I took that moment to glance around since I had not done so before. It was only then that I saw Agent Howard. He gave me a reassuring smile.

"Everyone here is part of a select team assembled to help Agent Sinclair from this end," our boss said. "We start by uncovering everything known about Lila Rivers. We need names, places and dates. Nothing is too insignificant when it comes to the people and activities she's been involved with in any part of her past. I've asked Agent Howard to report directly to me on anything that is found. He has the preliminary report, will fill in any blanks and make assignments. This situation will not resolve itself, people, so I expect you to give it everything you've got. I'll be back for an update once I have Agent Sinclair on a plane."

"Thank you for your continued support," I told him as we left the room. "I know this isn't your responsibility."

"We're family, and it's about time everyone in this division acted like it. I'll have a plane ready to take you to Austin within the hour. I don't know how long you'll be required to stay, but I would suggest that you try to contact Miss Rivers before you land. We need to figure out where she is but don't want to spook her before the DEA's plans are in place."

"You've met Lila, sir. Do you really think she's capable of doing what's being suggested?"

"Her past cannot be overlooked. If she was being used to get a message to you, it could be that Agent Fielding is getting too close, and his attempts need to be derailed."

"And getting me to Texas is part of that plan?"

"Like Interim Director Whitman said, the investigation has just begun, but I'll make sure Charlie is safe if I have to become his personal bodyguard."

"And the rest of my family?" I asked. "If what they're saying about Lila is true, we're right back where we started because she knows everything about them."

"We'll step up security and take them into protective custody if necessary. The key to their safety, and yours, lies in making Lila believe that you're here working as you've always been."

"I may be able to convince her that I haven't left the state, but she will know I'm aware of what happened in Texas."

"She doesn't know we have an image of her. That's your protection for now."

"I refuse to believe that she was a willing participant?"

"Desperate people are capable of just about anything. We might not know what her level of involvement is, but it's highly unlikely that she's merely a bystander. Maybe she slipped up, started using again and got in over her head before realizing what was happening. It wouldn't be the first time someone relapsed."

"Not Lila," I said, bitting down on my bottom lip to keep from rehashing what could not be proven. "She was fine when she left, except for being a little upset with me because I told her I thought it was a bad idea to go. If I could just get thirty minutes alone with her, I know I could get her to tell me everything."

"I hope you're able to do that, but for now, I need you to stick with the facts and try not to become emotionally involved. Lila is a shrewd woman and knows how to use the system. That may be one of the reasons she was pulled into this. She'll know something is wrong if your behavior toward her changes."

"It's already changed. She hasn't answered any of my calls, and her texts have been intermittent at best."

"That may be true, but you've got to try. If you don't, the DEA will do it for you. You're the only friend she's got right now—innocent or guilty."

While he arranged for my flight, I went to the locker room to get the backpack I kept ready in case an unexpected overnight assignment came up. I didn't want to go to Texas, and I certainly didn't want to leave Charlie alone again. But I couldn't change my mind now, so I stopped by Amanda's suite of rooms to see my son before returning to the conference room to wait for further orders.

"This is a surprise," she said, ushering me inside. "What brings you here in the middle of the day?"

"I came to tell my son goodbye. I'm being called away on another assignment with the DEA. This time, I'm going to Texas."

"I'm so sorry, Reagan. I don't know why they can't leave you alone. Charlie's taking a nap, but I'm sure he won't mind being awakened. Can you tell me what happened?"

"Another friend is in trouble and needs my help. That's all I really know, but I don't want to wake Charlie. He's been having enough trouble sleeping the past few nights. I just needed to see his face and tell him how much I love him."

"He knows how you feel, and I won't let him out of my sight while you're gone. Maybe his new teeth will have broken through by the time you get back."

"That would be nice," I replied, making my way to the crib where Charlie had a tight grip on the blanket that covered him. I touched his hand before bending over to kiss his forehead.

"It's going to be all right," Amanda said. "Assistant Director Bridges knows how to do his job, and I'm sure he'll have some news that might help before you get to Texas."

"He's the best boss anyone could ask for, but this is out of his hands."

She gave me a compassionate look. "You've certainly had your share of challenges the past few months, but I don't believe in fate. You have Charlie because it's what God intended. He'll make sure you're around to raise him."

"I hope so because my life just continues to spin out of control."

"You'll make it through this, and you'll come back a stronger woman."

I was about to reply when the outer door opened and Assistant Director Bridges walked in. He looked every bit as harried as I felt.

"I was waiting for you in the conference room but figured you needed to stop here," he said when we joined him. "How's Charlie?"

"Teething, but otherwise fine," I responded. "I thought I would have more time."

"That's one thing we do not have. I have an escort waiting to take you to the plane, and the DEA will have someone meet you when you land. I would suggest using what little time you have in the air to make a few plans. Agent Howard has a team on its way to Miss River's apartment, and we're already pulling more records. I'll let you know what is found, but I need you to promise me something in return."

"What's that?" I asked.

"If you feel something isn't going as it should, I want you to scream bloody murder, and then call me if no one listens. We can't always pick our assignments, but I will not have another agent's life jeopardized. Just do your job, and don't let anyone try to convince you that they have all the answers. They'll be making this mission up as they go."

"Thank you, sir," I replied. "Am I authorized to use my cell for anything more than official business?"

"I wouldn't advice it. If having Lila in plain sight was meant to deliver some message, you can be sure your movements will be watched. I'd refuse to let you go, but I fear that would only be postponing the inevitable."

I called Lila on my way to the plane. She didn't answer, but I left a message telling her I hoped she was having fun and asking if she had heard the news about the shooting deaths of the two DEA agents in Texas. It's what I would have said if I hadn't known about her possible involvement, but I wouldn't know until I heard back if my delivery was convincing. Compartmentalizing things associated with my job was coming more naturally now, but when family and friends were involved, it was an entirely different story.

Unshed tears tickled the end of my nose as I looked out the window at the blue sky and thought about the peace of mind and sense of security my work had caused me to lose. But instead of giving in to regrets or self-recrimination, I turned my attention to what I had been told before leaving D.C. If Robert Evans was in charge now, and if he wanted to send a message to the DEA, why would he do it through me? I was only indirectly involved with everything that was going on, except for my relationship with Charlie and Agent Fielding. What if the new cartel expected me to play ball with them and get the authorities to back off? I certainly had the most to lose, but they didn't know me at all if they thought I would give in to any demands without a fight.

An Agent Gomez met me at the airport in Austin. He was dressed in a dark suit and tie like ever other male agent I had ever met who was not involved in an undercover assignment. My attire was basically the same, minus the tie.

"Thank you for coming to get me," I told him as I settled into the passenger seat of the Black Suburban he was driving. I was surprised that he had come alone, but then if Robert Evans was using me to further some goal, he would make sure I stayed alive until he was through with me.

"My pleasure," he replied. "It was good of you to come on such short notice."

"Have we learned anything else about the shootings?" I asked.

"Nothing that I'm aware of. Interim Director Whitman has assembled a team, and we should know more when we get to our home office. Have you been to Austin before, Agent Sinclair?"

"No," I replied, thinking back to the night I brought Charlie into the country. "I've only been to Dallas, but I've heard it's a beautiful city."

"We're proud of it. I wish I could take you on a tour, but we'll be on our way to Presidio once briefings have ended."

Fortunately, it was a short drive to the agency. My supply of small talk was limited. I just wanted to see where things now stood so I would know how to proceed. I had no doubt that everyone involved was already aware of my friendship with Lila and my relationship with Agent Fielding. I would defend my way of thinking about both of them for as long as I could.

The red sandstone building that housed the DEA office was located on a relatively quiet side street. I was led to a conference room on the second floor where DEA Interim Director Whitman shook my hand.

"Thank you for coming, Agent Sinclair. Your help will be invaluable since you know one of our suspects personally."

I wanted to reiterate my belief that Lila couldn't possibly be involved, but I was beginning to learn how to pick my battles. Facts drove cases, and video footage from a surveillance camera proved that she had been at the scene. If she had done anything more than watch had yet to be determined.

"I'm glad to be of assistance, sir," I replied.

He made the necessary introductions and told me to sit down. "Just to get you caught up to speed, we've determined that the assault rifles used can be traced back to the Seville cartel. We don't know what they're calling themselves now that they've combined, but we feel this is just the beginning of the violence they're going to unleash."

The lines between my eyes deepened. Everyone in the room looked both distraught and angry, and I couldn't blame them for that. I had lost Neil to the cartels, and it was something I would never forget. "Was anyone else hurt in the attack?" I asked.

"Several of our agents are in the hospital. One is still in surgery, and two are in critical condition. The cartel—whatever they are called now—lost more than a dozen men. Most of them were itinerate day laborers who were here illegally. The ones who may have been able to tell us something either got away or are resting on slabs in the morgue. The plane touched down and was gone before we even arrived at the scene. We were able to secure most of the shipment but were unprepared for the number of people they had recruited on the ground. Lila Rivers is the only one we've been able to identify yet."

"I'll do what I can t help, sir," I said. "I've brought files of everything I know about both cartels, and the people who may be involved. I know this information was passed on to Director Phillips in Mexico City, but there may be something you haven't seen."

I pulled the manila folder from my backpack. It contained all the letters and pictures that had been confiscated from Angel's sister, Neva, along with the charts I had constructed and every piece of information I had uncovered on the Internet and from my partner's contact in Bogotá.

He looked at me with surprise. "Assistant Director Bridges said you'd been working a few angles of your own. I'm sorry we have to keep pulling you back into our affairs, but the truth is that you're the best shot we have right now. Lila Rivers is the only person we know of who has been brought in from the outside. We need to know why and how it happened."

"I'm sure you're aware that my involvement with this case goes far beyond my friendship with Lila," I replied. If members of the new cartel were already on American soil and were recruiting people whose identity could not be traced, it meant the people I loved were in greater danger than they had ever been.

"We have been apprised of your undercover assignments with our agency."

"Then you also know the Seville cartel was responsible for the death of my former partner and at least one documented threat against my son. The same thing applies to the Mendoza's. They will not let anything, or anyone, stand in their way. I want to see them stopped as much as you do."

"Not to make light of what you've already lost, or the current situation with your family's safety, but your passion and determination is what we're counting on. Once we get to Presidio, I want you to try to make contact with Lila again. But this time, I need you to tell her that you've been asked to help with the investigation."

"For what purpose?" I asked.

"Because it's been made clear to us, by a person who is unable to reveal his presence at the moment, that they already know you're here. Until we know otherwise, we have to assume her presence in Presidio was part of her initiation into the cartel. Play on her vulnerabilities. If she thinks you're still her friend, she might let something slip."

Agent Ramirez broke into the conversation. "You need to be aware that Robert Evans and Lila Rivers may have been working together since your time at the Rios ranch. We've pulled phone records that prove they've been in contact, but we don't know the nature of their conversations yet."

The implications surrounding his piece of information seemed to rock what was left of my fragile world. Angel would never have allowed Lila to move in on her man, and Lila had been totally committed to Edward. But if they had been working together for over half a year, her coming to Washington D.C. was no accident. She had been put in place to learn what she could, and the FBI had played right into her hands.

"You really think I can get her talk? She knows I didn't want her to go."

"If you can convince her that you know nothing about her involvement, we can use that to our advantage. Unfortunately, the cartel already has the upper hand. They'll be using whatever you give her to find out just how much we know and what our next move will be."

Interim Director Whitman took the lead again. "What we haven't told you is that a very convincing message was painted on one of the buildings next to the largest pile of bodies. They're taunting us because they believe they are invincible."

Before I could ask what it said, he put an image on the screen that hung from the wall in front of the room. The bone-chilling message read, "Death to all who stand in our way."

"You're sure it's from them?" I asked.

The interim director nodded his head. "The spray paint was still wet. They have the manpower to take down a small army. When you couple that with thousands of miles of unprotected border and only a handful of officers patrolling it, they can do almost anything they want."

"And you're counting on my friendship with Lila to tip the scales in our favor. If she's changed as much as you claim, I doubt she'll listen to me."

"We wouldn't do it if we felt we had any other choice, Agent Sinclair. They've already gotten one cocaine shipment across the border. It's only a matter of time until they do it again. We have to be ready before that happens."

My mind was swirling with both fear and dread, but I knew instinctively that Lila wouldn't hurt any member of my family. She would find a way to protect them, even if she had crossed over to the other side.

"Do you think Lila played a part in Eloise Seville's escape from custody?" I asked, hoping to bring my thoughts back into focus again.

Interim Director Whitman bit his bottom lip before responding. "Someone at the embassy was leaking tips to the cartels. We had several suspects in mind, but it was Agent Fielding who figured out who it really was."

The mere mention of his name made my heart race, but if I didn't want the true nature of our relationship broadcast to strangers, I needed to appear emotionally detached. "You've talked to him?"

"Not personally, but he's been instrumental in helping us get this far. That's why Miss Rivers was asked to accompany you to Mexico City. We knew she was involved in some capacity but had no proof. Having her there as a seeming witness for our side was the best way to give her the freedom she needed to hang herself, and she didn't disappoint us. The minute she arrived additional information made its way into the hands of the enemy."

"That's circumstantial evidence, not proof."

"You can take it any way you like, Agent Sinclair. I'm not here to argue. I'm here to uncover the truth."

"If you knew she was involved, why didn't you arrest her while you had the chance?"

"Nothing would be gained by having her in custody. We needed her to lead us to the people she worked for. I don't have all the answers, but you can ask Agent Fielding directly when we get to our destination. He's flying in from South America to lead this operation. Now, if there are no further questions, we'll be on our way."

I wasn't sure my knees would support me as I followed the men from the conference room, down the hallway and back into the warm, spring sun. I was told to throw my backpack into the rear seat of a Black Suburban and climb inside. Agent Gomez would be driving on our trip to the U.S./Mexican border, while Interim Director Whitman rode shotgun. Agent's Ramirez and Call would follow in a car of their own.

Keeping my mind from jumping to unrelated thoughts as city streets turned into open freeway was more than difficult. The hum of the tires on the asphalt, along with music softly playing on the radio, and my companion's lack of conversation gave me plenty of time to agonize and think. It angered me that no one had thought it necessary to keep me informed. Even if I wasn't a member of the DEA, my willingness to work with them was what had landed me in such an unenviable situation in the first place.

Knowing that Agent Fielding was still alive did little to lighten my spirits. It had been weeks since I'd left Mexico City. What kind of a man remained silent for that amount of time when he knew people were worried about him? He could no longer use being undercover as an excuse for not being involved in his son's life. He was avoiding us on purpose, and I had been a fool for believing the declarations he had made in moments of uncertainty and suspected loss.

I fretted over what I would say to Lila as the minutes ticked slowly onward. The day was stifling hot. I could see mirages of what looked like pools of crystal clear water on the highway in front of us when I rested my forehead against the car window. If Agent Fielding was right, then I was wrong in believing Lila that would not hurt anyone I loved. The possibilities of carnage that could unleash left me physically ill. I had always considered myself a good judge of character until now.

"We're heading straight to the field office," Agent Gomez said when we were a few miles away from our destination.

He had driven the entire way while Interim Director Whitman talked on his cell phone and glanced over the information I'd given him. He asked no questions, and while I caught fragments of his conversations, it wasn't enough to know if anything new had happened. I felt as if I was being stonewalled again, and it made me more angry than afraid.

We stopped in front of another adobe building, much smaller than the one in Austin, and Agent Gomez told me to get my bag. The suburban that had been following us pulled to the curb after we did.

I didn't want to get out of the car and face what lay ahead, but any delay on my part would only hinder the investigation. So I secured my backpack and hurried across the street as hot, dry air made rivulets of water form on the back of my neck and make their way down my spine. I could see nothing but sunlight and cacti in every direction from behind my dark glasses. The bleakness of my surroundings was almost suffocating. No wonder this location had been chosen. Not many people would live here voluntarily, and it was most certainly isolated.

The cold blast of air that hit my face when the outside door closed behind us made me involuntarily shiver. But I felt my knees almost give way when I heard Agent Fielding's deep, penetrating voice coming from somewhere down a hallway. There was no one in the outer office to greet us so I followed my companions until we came to a conference room where a number of people were already assembled. I hung back as I saw him standing in front of the group. He looked amazing for someone who had supposedly spent weeks tracking two illusive women.

His eyes briefly glanced over the men who were with me but, when they found mine, he stopped what he was saying. I could clearly see some of the color drain from beneath the tan on his face. Either he had not been informed of my arrival, or he was angry with me for leaving Charlie vulnerable after he'd made sure I got out of Mexico alive. He moved forward and shook hands with the interim director, but he merely touched my arm.

"I need to talk to you in private when we get the chance," he whispered.

I didn't respond. There were more crucial matters to discuss than our personal issues. If things went south, it wouldn't matter if we were on speaking terms anyway.

He resumed his place behind the podium. A white board and projector had been set up for the briefing. I chose a chair at the table next to an attractive female agent. We were the only women in the room.

"You must be the agent from the FBI," she said, scrutinizing my appearance. "Sam told me about you. I'm Agent Selena Diaz. He chose me to work this case with him because he knew I would do whatever was necessary to get the job done."

"Glad to meet you," I replied in less than a friendly tone. Why had Agent Fielding been talking about me, and why did Agent Diaz feel compelled to make it sound like she knew him in a very intimate way? If he had become involved with her that would certainly explain why he hadn't contacted me, but not checking on his son was unconscionable.

I tried not to think about her as Agent Fielding began speaking again. He explained that the entire area was being processed, but so far, nothing had been found that would tie any known cartels members to the attack. It was unclear just how much of the cocaine had left the site before the authorities arrived, but the amount seized would certainly be noticed.

"How did Lila get away when she was caught on surveillance footage just moments before the DEA arrived?" I asked. "From what

I've been told, a specifically designed, and very expensive, plane that was purportedly commissioned by Robert Evans to deliver cocaine was already gone. If she had joined forces with him, why would he leave her behind?"

He gave me an irritated look. "I'm sure you are aware that we believe she was there to send a special message to you about what they're willing to do to gain a firm foothold on American soil. How she managed to avoid us is still open to question, but with your help, we will find her and make sure she is punished for everything she's cost this agency."

"What Sam is trying to say is that the DEA wants the entire cartel destroyed, not just a single person who can be easily eliminated by either side," Agent Diaz interjected. "The message on the wall is very clear in its intent. This new cartel now has to means to do whatever they want, and they don't care how many hirelings die. There will always be more needy people to fill the gaps."

Her words were chilling in their accuracy, and they let me know that she and Agent Fielding had been equal partners on their joint mission. Whereas, I had only been picked for convenience and expediency when I had worked with him.

I didn't say anything more during the briefing. Agent Fielding knew my capabilities when it came to observation and making connections. He also knew that Lila and I were more than casual friends. After all, she had moved to Washington D.C. under the pretext of wanting to be around someone who could help her prepare to meet her daughter. The sad fact was that I had taken most everything she told me at face value. I hadn't even checked out her story to make sure she was really a mother.

My job, as it was explained to me during the next few minutes, was to keep reaching out to Lila so the call could be traced. I had serious doubts that anything I did would be successful. She was avoiding me for a reason. But even if she had defected to the other side, why had she done so through Robert Evans? He was the anomaly that didn't seem to fit, unless he had something on her that no one had discovered yet.

And then a sudden, terrifying thought entered my mind. Lila claimed not to know the identity of her daughter's father, but she had been a successful prostitute who didn't always know the name of her clients. What if, unbeknownst to her, Robert Evans had shared her bed? He was a womanizer who liked to party and wouldn't care about an illegitimate child when he already had a rightful heir, but the knowledge could certainly be used for leverage.

What if she recognized his face when she saw him with Angel, and that was the real reason she ran away from the garden. If he had gotten even a glimpse of her, he would automatically know how easily she could be compromised.

But I kept that thought to myself. I needed more to go on, and Agent Diaz seemed determined to keep me within reach. She was the one who took my cell phone so the necessary modifications could be made, and she was the one who sat beside me as we waited to see if Lila would return the call I had already made before I reached out again.

"I'm sure you have questions," she said as she tapped the ends of her fingernails on the surface of a long table in the conference room. "I'll answer what I can, but Sam likes to keep close tabs on who is privy to what. It's for everyone's safety. Still, it should be comforting to know that we'll have your back throughout the entire assignment."

It was hard to feel threatened when she appeared to be helping, but there was something about the clear, green eyes and the determined set of her mouth that told me more than words ever could. She wanted Agent Fielding, if she did not already have him, and I was a threat.

"Why don't you try again," Agent Ramirez said as he checked a connection on the machine that would be tracing the call.

I wasn't used to working under such restricted conditions, but the DEA was running this show, and any complaint on my part would be duly noted and reported. So I put the phone on speaker and tried to find that safe place by a mountain stream where my mind always went when it needed calming. The ringtones seemed to drone on forever, but to my surprise, Lila answered before the call went to voicemail. She sounded different, but maybe I was imaging it because I knew something she didn't.

"I should have waited for you to call back, but I couldn't," I began, hoping there was enough latent anxiety in my voice to be believable. "The DEA is hounding me again, and I don't know what to do."

"Slow down," she said. "You're not making any sense."

I paused briefly before replying, but I couldn't look up at the people who were hovering around me. They made me more nervous than Lila did. "Did you listen to the news this morning? Two DEA agents were killed in Texas, and I've been brought in to help."

"Why would they do that? You're not involved."

"Maybe they think I can be of assistance because I know both Alma and Eloise and have been one of their favorite targets. Leaving Charlie behind again was the hardest thing I've ever had to do. What if Bridges can't keep him safe this time? I wish you were here with me. I don't want to be alone."

The way I saw it, there was no need trying to play it safe. If Lila had turned, she already knew everything about me and would become suspicious if I acted evasive.

"I'm sorry you've become involved again, Reagan. But I don't know what I can do to help. My trip has taken me all over southern hemisphere, and I'm too far away to get back. We're heading to some remote island for a few days of snorkeling and fun. I have another call coming in, so I'll have to get back to you."

She was gone before I had time to say anything else.

"I tried to keep her on the line," I told my companions. "She's never hung up like that before."

Interim Director Whitman rubbed his hands briskly together as we waited for the signal that would tell us if our attempt had been successful. I didn't know where Agent Fielding had gone. He had simply left the room without acknowledging my presence again.

"I'm sorry!" the technician who had been monitoring the call finally said as he removed his headphones. "That signal was pinging off towers all over the world. The closest I got was some place in Central America. I should be able to determine the exact location when she calls back."

"It's crucial that you do just that," the interim director replied. "These people will not give up without one hell of a fight, and I don't intend to lose any more of our people."

His vehemence was understandable, but I wasn't one of his people. And I needed time alone to research and think. If my hunch about Lila's connection to Robert Evans was more than just a figment of an overactive imagination, she might have more to fear for than just her life.

"So, listen up the rest of you," he continued as my mind churned. "You're all on duty until we have the people involved behind bars. No one takes a day off, an extended lunch, or even a bathroom break without telling me first. Do I make myself clear?"

I couldn't help but wonder why Agent Fielding wasn't still taking charge since I had been lead to believe this was his operation. I hated his continual vanishing acts. But he was used to working alone, and other people were only a hindrance, unless he needed them.

While the other agents waited, the interim director made a list of assignments on the white board. I was glad my name didn't appear. Lila's abrupt ending to our conversation was something else I needed to ponder. She loved to talk more than anyone I knew. Either she was not alone in the room, someone had entered unexpectedly, or she was indeed answering an incoming call. I tried to recall every word she had said, and every intonation of her voice to determine if she thought I was trying to hide something.

But I hadn't been given the time to incriminate myself, and I had said nothing she didn't already know. Nonetheless, her comments—after saying nothing about where she had been or what she had been doing since leaving home—were puzzling. Traveling all over the southern hemisphere and getting ready to leave for some remote island for a few days of snorkeling and fun could be a lead she hoped I would run with. If it was, I needed more to go on. There were plenty of islands in, and around, Central America.

"Agent Sinclair," the interim director said, forcing me back to the reality of what was going on around me in time to see Agent Diaz exit the room. She was no doubt off to find Agent Fielding and see why she had been left behind. "I don't want you to get discouraged because this attempt at reaching out to Miss Rivers failed. We've just started."

"You don't know Lila the way I do. She was raised on the streets and spent most of her life as an escort. She knows when people have ulterior motives."

"That's the chance we take when we reach out to anyone this way. Agent Fielding seems to think you have a close enough relationship that she'll give you a chance, even if she doesn't quit believe you."

"Do you know where he's gone?" I asked.

He shifted his weight before answering, and I felt the temperature in the room rise. It was obvious he didn't like working with someone he didn't know. "He wanted to see the site for himself and check on the status of the autopsies. He's already familiar with the weapons both cartels use."

"How's that going to help if they're working together?"

"The cartel that takes top spot in the new organization will be calling the shots, and they'll want the more submissive faction to prove their loyalty."

His comment let me know that he knew less about what we were dealing with than I did. But my input would not be seriously considered, unless it was solicited. "What do you want me to do now?"

"Wait until Agent Diaz returns and then place another call."

"I don't mean to be disrespectful, sir, but that's not how the relationship Lila and I have formed works. We don't invade each other's privacy without being invited, and I never press for anything until she's ready. Any change in our routine will be noticed."

"Putting civilians in danger is the last thing I want to do, Agent Sinclair, but if she is involved with this, she didn't go into it blind."

I pushed my forehead into the palms of my hands. His attitude of superiority and denigration were unsettling, but he had every right to be upset. He had just lost his boss and at least one of his fellow agents. "Have you heard anything more about the agents who were taken to the hospital?"

His countenance softened. I had made the right call in changing the subject. "The ones who were not seriously injured have been interviewed. So far, no one remembers anything new."

"I'm sorry your boss was killed, sir. I can't imagine what would happen if something happened to mine."

"Director Fairbanks was the best man I've ever worked for. No one will be able to fill his shoes, but I will find out who pulled the trigger and see that person punished. I'm tired of the cartels trying to destroy so much of what Americans hold dear. That's why I'm allowing Agent Fielding to run this investigation, under my jurisdiction, of course. Other than you, he knows the people involved better than any of the rest of us."

"I'm not up-to-date on what's happening in South America, sir, but I do believe Lila is trying to help."

He snorted his right to disagree. "Even I don't believe she killed anyone, but her escape was built into the plan. That tells me she's more than a stooge."

"She may simply be a victim of circumstance," I replied. "I know I have a habit of speaking out of turn, sir, but many of my suppositions have proven correct."

"Your uncanny knack for upsetting your superiors was duly noted when I asked for your help. I'll try to forgive your lack of diplomacy, but I will not let you get in my way. This is a DEA case. You are here at our invitation. The minute your help is no longer needed, you will be on the first plane home. In the meantime, I'll instruct Agent Diaz to get you settled into a nearby motel when she returns. Until then, you can do whatever you feel is necessary."

"What if Lila calls after we've gone?"

"Agent Diaz knows how to run the tracer. We can set up an actual time for you to return the call if nothing happens in the next few hours, but until then, I need my agents looking for leads."

"Would it be possible to use use a computer until she returns? I have a few leads of my own I would like to pursue."

He gave his permission, and I was taken into an adjoining room where several work stations sat empty. A technician supplied the password and made sure I could log into the DEA's data bases before returning to his own assignment.

I spent the next few minutes scouring birth records in and around Washington D.C. Lila's supposed daughter was too young to have been born while she was still in New York City, and it was where she claimed to have seen her just a few months earlier. Without an exact date, or even a birth year, I knew my attempt might prove futile. But I had learned how to search records with nothing to go on. This time, at least I had a name.

Much to my surprise, I was soon looking at the birth certificate of Lila's baby girl who had been born in a small, rural hospital fifteen years earlier. No father's name was listed, but I had expected as much. My consolation came in knowing that not every part of my friend's life had been a lie. A few additional key strokes, and I was looking at her adoption record.

The next move was a little harder to make. I could either dismiss what might be an unfounded prompting, or let someone else know. I chose to contact Agent Howard. He had been looking into Lila's past all day, and his conclusion about her daughter's safety was basically the same as mine. Not because she could be related to Robert Evans —although he felt it was an interesting theory—but because she was a likely target for coercion or revenge. He had found her address in Lila's desk, along with a picture and a letter of correspondence that proved she had already made contact with the adoptive parents. He promised to place a call to the residence and take whatever measures might become necessary.

I leaned back in my chair and folded my arms tightly across my chest when our conversation ended. While I wanted to find the truth as to why Lila was on that video footage, I wanted to prove her innocence more. She had talked so often about the evils of drugs and how she wanted to stay clean and help others. So what possible reason would she have for becoming involved with any cartel again? It wasn't availability of drugs—should she decide to start using again. She could find them on street corners or at bars almost anywhere, and she claimed to be tired of living dangerously. I was missing something important, and I wouldn't stop looking until I found it.

By the time I returned to the room where everyone else was working, Selena Diaz was back. She looked like a thundercloud ready to explode. I should have been interested in her distress since it obviously concerned me, but that would mean inquiring as to just how intimate her relationship with Agent Sam Fielding really was.

I didn't want to believe him capable of the kind of deception it would take to be involved with someone else while claiming to have feelings for me. But if that was the case, she could have him. I was tired of worrying about him anyway and wishing he cared enough about his son to keep in touch. Trey was a much better man and could give me what I needed without having to change.

"I just spoke to Sam," she said, fixing me with a steady look that let me know she was ready for a confrontation. "He said the bullets removed from the victims may match the ones the Seville brothers were using in Mexico, but the angle they entered the bodies was the same kill shot he'd been taught while working for Carlos Mendoza. This was definitely a message to us about who's in charge and proves we're getting close to something big. He's on his way to the crime scene now."

"Did he say anything else?" Interim Director Whitman asked.

She seemed to puff up like a peacock. "Nothing pertinent to the case, except that he wants to speak to all the agents involved when he gets back. It's easy for things to be overlooked in the heat of a battle."

"My people work by the book, Agent Diaz, and it takes time to process a scene."

"Not to question how things are done here in the states, sir, but Sam and I have been in the trenches." she replied. "We know how these people operate away from civilization, and we know what to look for. That's the reason we were called. He'll keep us updated on everything he learns, but right now, he can't be hampered by procedures or rules that will delay his own investigation. The fact that everyone, who could be of any help in leading us to the heads of the organization, got away is a setback. But it also lets us know that this was just a trial run to see if we've got anything that can stop them."

"So this wasn't just about getting a shipment of cocaine across the border."

"Hardly, sir! This was about testing a new method of delivery, and it seems to have worked like a charm. They'll be coming across the border in full-force now, and there isn't anything we'll be able to do to stop them, unless we cut off the head of this dragon."

"I was told Agent Fielding would be overseeing the entire operation, not simply running one of his own. That's why he was brought here from South America," Interim Director Whitman told her.

"We came because we're the best qualified in bringing this new cartel down, but Agent Fielding has is own way of doing things. Just keep your people doing what they've been assigned. He'll let you know if he needs them to be doing anything else."

I usually liked people, but Selena Dias was fast becoming someone I wished would disappear. Her haughtiness in trying to take charge was making it nearly impossible for me to remain silent. I wanted to tell her that she wasn't the only one knew how Agent Fielding operated, but that wasn't the right move to make. Remaining detached was the only chance I had if I didn't want to get hurt.

"When can I call my family?" I asked, hoping to distract myself from the uncharitable thoughts I was having. "I want to know they're still okay."

Interim Director Whitman gave me an almost compassionate look. "Under the circumstances, I'm sure your boss is taking care of them. I need your line open for incoming calls the next twelve hours. If you haven't heard from Miss Rivers by morning, we'll revisit other options. Now, why don't you and Agent Diaz check out that motel. We can handle things here."

My quick glance around the room let me know that he wasn't getting off to a very good start with the agents now under his command, and Agent Diaz and my former partner were partially responsible. Dealing with the loss of a superior and another fellow agent was hard enough, but trying to step in and take control would test anyone's fortitude and ability to adapt.

Chapter 7

It was so hot outside that I took my jacket off the moment I stepped into the late afternoon sun. The street with its adobe and brick buildings was deserted. There was little but muted color anywhere. No grass, trees or brilliantly-tinted flowers like I was used to at home once the winter weather turned to spring. It made me wonder how humans could even exist in such a place where every living thing had to struggle for life, except perhaps scorpions, snakes and cactus.

But it did help me understand why so much of the border was unprotected. Most people couldn't survive in the heat and oppressive solitude for long. That made it the perfect place for cartels to move their product since animals, reptiles and water-deprived plants wouldn't put up much resistance.

"I hope you're ready to be roomies," Agent Diaz said as she slid her sunglasses onto the bridge of her nose and then unlocked the black suburban we would be using. "It wasn't my idea to share the same living space. But I'm the only female agent who knows what she's doing, and Sam told me to make sure you do your part when it comes to making contact with Lila Rivers. Friendship is no excuse for negligence or taking the law into your own hands. However, I am curious as to why you're so worried about your family. I'm sure the FBI is keeping tabs on them."

Her voice was cool and impersonal. It was her way of digging for information that would satisfy her curiosity about my personal feelings for Agent Fielding, but she had nothing to fear when it came to me. All I cared about was getting home to my son. He would be walking on his own soon, and I wanted to be with him when that happened.

"Your partner knows I'll follow through with any orders I'm given, even if I don't agree. As for my family, we're very close. Worry is just something I do. Don't you feel the same way about yours?"

"My family is the people I'm working with at any given moment, and I'll do anything necessary to make sure no one endangers what is trying to be accomplished."

The motel wasn't far from the field office, but that was to be expected since the town was small. As the tires rolled over hot pavement—and I felt the effects of the heat since it took a few minutes for the AC to begin working—my mind drifted to the residents of Presidio and other small towns just like it that were scattered along the border. They were raising families and attending church, and yet some of them had become involved with illegal trafficking in all its diabolical forms or the perpetrators would not have been able to make such a clean escape. How could they turn a blind eye to all that was going on around them if they really cared about their families? But finding sympathizers, who were not afraid to inform on their neighbors, would be nearly impossible.

I wished I was in a position to take a more active part in the investigation. I was trying to be a team player, but I still spoke what was on my mind, and my way of finding the truth was often frowned upon. Nonetheless, Agent Fielding understood how I operated and might welcome my help, even if he had moved on with someone else. But I would need to talk to him privately to find out, and I wasn't sure I could do that.

The neon sign outside the motel was broken, making the rundown building look even less habitable. It would not be a pleasant stay for many reasons, but I could sleep anywhere I had to for a couple of nights. I had done that already at Mendoza's compound, in cocaine processing huts, inside the monolithic structure in the jungle, at the safe house and even in Agent

Fielding's bed. But Agent Diaz needed to remain silent about her personal exploits because I didn't need any of my suspicions confirmed.

"This isn't exactly the Waldorf," Agent Diaz said while she was throwing her overnight bag, and the equipment that would be needed to trace a call, on the bed closest to the window. "You would think with all the drug money running through this town that they could afford to tear down some of these relics and build better places for people to stay."

"I've seen worse," I told her as I looked inside the bathroom with a small vanity and mirror. The fixtures were stained from a polished white ceramic to what looked more like mottled, tan marble. But the surfaces were smooth. That let me know that at least the room had been cleaned. It wasn't easy hanging my change of clothing and my jacket on the wooden hangers that had been left on a rod for guests to use, but it seemed safer that putting them in a drawer. I had already stepped on one peach-colored scorpion since my arrival. "I'm sorry you got stuck babysitting me."

She parted the drapes with one finger and looked out at the parking lot. The vast emptiness of the surrounding desert would make it easy to hear the sound of any approaching vehicle. Perhaps that was one reason this location had been chosen.

"It's all part of the job. Who's Charlie?"

Her question surprised me since I had made the assumption that she already knew everything about him. "He's my son."

"So, you're married," she stated as she turned to face me. "I didn't see a ring."

"That's because I'm single. Charlie's adopted."

"Why would you adopt a child? Doesn't the FBI keep you busy enough?"

"Charlie was a special gift."

"I'm not sure I want children. I guess I'm more career-oriented. That's always been satisfying enough."

I suspected there was more she had to say, but I didn't want to get into any conversation that might be misconstrued as bonding. If she and Agent Fielding were involved, as she so desperately wanted me to believe, he would have told her about Charlie.

"Families aren't for everyone," I replied.

"Maybe not, but I suppose I could be convinced to have at least one child if the relationship needed it to survive. Are you hungry?"

I hadn't eaten since morning, but the thought of food made me gag. "Not really. I just want Lila to call."

She closed the drapes and looked over at me before plugging in the machine that would trace the call.

"You really think she's innocent, even after seeing her at the place where the drugs were being made ready for transport? While I'll admit that she looked scared, it may have only been a reaction to holding a machine gun. They aren't easy to use, and she didn't look like anyone who had seen that kind of action before. That said, people don't change just because we want them to. Junkies and prostitutes always go back to using and hooking. Obsessive behaviors are part of their DNA."

It would be so easy to argue with her, but Lila could have given up the fight for freedom from drugs because it was too hard. However, that didn't explain hooking up with Robert Evans or the new cartel.

"I prefer to give her the benefit of the doubt until I've been able to appraise the situation for myself, Agent Dias."

Her smile was less than friendly. "I admire your depth of friendship, but I put all my cards with Sam. If he says she's guilty, then she is."

When I didn't respond, she pulled her cell phone from her pocket and began playing a game. I simply leaned back against the headboard on my own bed and let my brow furrow. I needed someone I trusted to talk to, but Neil was gone, and I had never felt that loss more deeply. He had always been there to listen—correcting when he thought I was in the wrong and giving support when no one else could. I wanted to cry out with the intensity of the pain that was consuming my soul again, but just as I was about to tell my companion that I needed some air, someone knocked on the door.

Our guns were poised by the time Agent Fielding announced his presence, and the change in her countenance was immediate. She was a woman in love, and everything about her exuded sensuality and intimacy. I swallowed back my anger at both of them for pulling me into their affair. Sam Fielding had the right to be with anyone he chose, but I had relived every encounter multiple times since our poignant goodbye on the roof. I had even come close to dismissing someone who had genuine feelings for me because I wanted to believe in what was nothing more than a fabrication of my disillusioned and trusting mind.

"I didn't know you'd be coming, Sam," she said, leaning seductively into the doorframe. "I could have shot you."

The way he smiled at her made the nausea rush to my throat. "I'm glad you didn't because we have work to do. But first, I need to talk to Agent Sinclair."

"I've done exactly what you asked," she replied, returning to her place on the bed but leaving plenty of room for him to sit down beside her.

He remained standing just inside the door. I could tell he was uncomfortable with the situation. Nonetheless, he was the one who had helped to create it.

"Alone," he said, without even glancing in my direction. "Why don't you grab something to eat? It might be a long night for all of us."

"I was planning on doing that later. Neither of us is hungry right now."

"Listen, Selena," he said. "I know you're my partner, but this is personal. Reagan and I have a few things we need to discuss in private."

She reluctantly rose to her feet. "I suppose I could get some coffee. Do you want some?"

He shook his head. "Take your time coming back. This might take a while."

All animation drained from her body at his less than comforting words, and I watched her walk out of the room with her shoulders slightly hunched. I almost felt sorry for her, but then realized that I was in much the same boat. We were both in love with a man who would never allow himself to be caught. Thank goodness I had not given in to my baser needs. My self-respect was still intact, even if my heart wasn't.

He waited until she was standing beside her car before closing the door and locking it. Then he turned his attention to me. I clenched my teeth, wanting to be cold and indifferent. This was not a conversation I wanted to have.

"I'm sorry for not contacting you, Reagan," he said as he ran his hands through his hair. It was an action I had once found endearing. "I kept meaning to, but we were away from civilization most of time. And when we had phone service, I couldn't think of anything to say. You have every right to hate me. All I do is disappoint both you and Charlie."

I made myself sit even more erect on the bed when he moved a few steps closer to me. It was a futile gesture, but I needed to feel as distant from him as possible. My cell phone with the cables attaching it to the recorder that would send an instant signal back to headquarters was lying on the maroon and green bed cover a few feet away. I wished I dared reach across that distance and throw it at him. It would certainly make me feel better, but I opted to draw my knees up to my chest and wrap my arms around them.

The position indicated an unwillingness to be open, but I had allowed him to state his case before and was always left feeling more confused and vulnerable. I needed to insulate myself so it would not happen again.

"There were times when I did hate you, but not for the reason you may think," I replied, daring myself to glance in his direction. "I can understand your becoming involved with someone else and not wanting to talk to me, but you have a son. Don't you ever think about him?"

"I think about our son everyday, just like I think about you. But I couldn't walk away from this case, and keeping our lives separate was the only way I could think of to protect you."

"Both cartels are aware that we share a son. If they wanted to come after us, nothing was stopping them. You put me in an impossible situation, and one that has only been complicated by forcing me to come here. From everything Agent Diaz has said, you share quite an intimate past, and I am nothing but a source of contention for both of you."

"Selena likes to make her opinions known. That's not so unlike someone else I used to work with."

"Please do not equate me with her. We're nothing alike."

"That's certainly true," he retorted. "She's willing to do whatever is required to get a job done, and she's not squeamish when it comes to making difficult decisions that may, or may not, involve certain archaic moral values."

"Just what are you saying?" I asked.

"I told you I wasn't working this case alone. I needed someone who was willing to play a certain part, and Selena was more than happy to oblige. We'd worked together before, and she knew how to follow orders."

"As opposed to me?"

"I can't see you playing my very passionate and highly affectionate girlfriend. Alma needed to believe I really had gone to the dark side for my plan to work, and that included divorcing myself in every way from both you and our son."

"But you used him as bait."

"That was a mistake. I was a killing machine who would never be hampered by emotional involvement, especially paternal feelings for a child I had once believed belonged to her brother. I needed a cover that couldn't be removed with another simple assassination. I spent a few days after I left you frequenting sleazy establishments in Colombia. I drank excessively, made a lot of wild statements and managed to convince a few key people in the underworld that I was tired of hanging around with the good guys. Selena was with me every step of the way. She'd had plenty of experience working undercover in Peru and was an instant hit with everyone because there was nothing she wasn't willing to try."

"And people actually believed you were into her."

"I know how to play a part and stay alive. Selena and I already knew how to have a good time, and I trusted her instincts. Once we made the right contacts, she went with me to meet Alma Mendoza."

"So she was with you when you came to Mexico City?"

It was a question I had to ask, but my heart certainly wasn't in it. He had been very apologetic and even remorseful about his relationship with Maria, but he didn't appear to be the least bit bothered by what he had done with Agent Diaz.

"Our cover meant we were together in every way—in and out of the bedroom. I couldn't exactly leave her behind. I'm not proud of some of my actions, but I am committed to getting a job done."

"I'm not sure Selena understands that. She thinks there's more than just work between you."

He looked down at the floor before addressing me again. "She went into this with her eyes wide open."

"But she knows you have a son."

"That was made clear when we entered our arrangement, but I've never said a word about you. I was trying to do what was right for the most people, and I will stand by that resolve until the day I die."

"You make it sound so clinical and easy, but that rationalization won't work on me," I replied, shaking my head. It was time to vent my anger and frustration before I lashed out at someone else. Despite his seeming bravery and selflessness, he needed to know that sometimes an individual was just as important as the masses, and his impulsive and careless actions hurt innocent people.

"If there's something you want to say, Reagan, now is the time. I might not be receptive later."

His cavalier attitude gave me the incentive necessary to continue. "Charlie isn't a baby any more, and he needs a father. You haven't been part of anything since the day you left us at the doctors in Colombia, hoping I would be smart enough to leave him there. If I had done that, you would never even know he was yours. But maybe it would have been better that way. At least you wouldn't have had to disrupt your life's work by concerning yourself with either of us. Leaving some money in a trust isn't being a parent. You deserted your own flesh and blood to go off and play hero again."

"Keep it coming," he said, motioning for me to finish what needed to be said. "I've been a terrible man and a horrible father. All I have ever cared about was my work until I met you. Do you have any idea how disconcerting it was to find out I had a heart that hadn't been completely corrupted? You turned my life upside down with all your compassion and high moral standards. You chose to take a baby out of a foreign country because of a promise made to his mother, but I wasn't given an option when it came to being a parent."

"You could have said you weren't interested when you found out and saved all of us a great deal of trouble. You have no idea how many sleepless nights I've been through not knowing if you were dead or alive."

"You would have been contacted if something had happened to me."

"Just like I was told that you were going to show up in Mexico City? You were like a ghost coming back to life when I went there to testify."

"I was a fool," he said, sitting down beside me. "I've always prided myself on being able to remain aloof. It's the only way I know of to survive. Emotions make people vulnerable. I couldn't risk that when there's so much at stake."

His physical closeness was making me forget how much I wanted to hate him for hurting me so deeply, but I had always known exactly the kind of man he was. He lived life on the edge, took what he needed and expected others to comply or get lost.

"Emotions make people human," I retorted. "I don't care what you do with your personal life, Agent Fielding. You can go straight to that place I don't even like to think about for all I care. But before you do, I need to know what happened at the embassy the night you forced me onto that helicopter. Along with the reason you think Lila is not longer trustworthy. I know you were harboring doubts about her loyalty, but I refuse to believe she's become a traitor without definitive proof. She's been nothing but a great friend to both Charlie and me, unlike some other people I could mention."

"You are still as forthright as ever," he said, getting to his feet and moving to the end of the bed.

"Like you, maybe I feel no need to change. I don't enjoy being condescending, condemning and unkind, but I won't apologize for my beliefs either. It's wrong to use other people and then cast them aside."

"If you really feel that way, then you need to quit your job and do something else because real agents do what ever it takes. I'm sure with your skills you wouldn't remain unemployed for long."

I felt the tears coming, but I wouldn't let them fall. My present tempestuous state had little to do with my employment. I was striking out because I was mad at myself for thinking I mattered to him. He used people and played games to get the information he needed to bring bad and powerful people down, but knowing he had a son should have sparked some desire to change.

When I didn't say anything, he moved across the room and sat down in one of the two chairs by the circular table near the window. "I know Lila has switched sides because I intercepted one of her calls to Robert Evans. I haven't yet discovered if she was working for him before Walter and Angel were killed, or if she was instrumental in anything that happened at the Rios ranch. But he needed help committing two murders and getting away before the authorities showed up. Lila may have only gone with you to the hospital as a way of keeping her part in what happened from being known. She and Edward were having trouble in their relationship. That's why he was sampling the merchandise."

"If that's true, why didn't you mention it before?"

"Things were happening too fast, and there wasn't time for one of our lengthy discussions about morality and the decline of civilizations. Edward didn't die immediately after he'd been shot. He whispered something when I knelt down to see if there was anything I could do to help."

"This just gets better and better," I replied.

"You can judge everything about the way I handle my life, Reagan, but it's not going to change any of the facts. What he said didn't make a whole lot of sense until recently."

"And just what was this revelation that helped him justify having sex with a young girl who was being sold into slavery?"

"He said Lila wasn't who she claimed to be, and I needed to watch my back because my wife was keeping secrets too."

"That's not exactly earth-shattering. Aren't you a firm believer that everyone lies?"

"Theoretically! But a dying man's last statement should never be entirely dismissed. I kept what I knew and suspected to myself until that call from the embassy was intercepted."

"But you knew about it when you spoke to me. I should have been informed. Lila was spending time with both Charlie and me."

"I weighed my options carefully. There was no reason to believe she would cause either of you any harm, unless she suspected you knew something. I couldn't risk having you slip up."

My chest was heaving with distain. "You really don't trust me, do you?"

"I trust you with the life of my son. Isn't that enough?"

I gave him another caustic glance. "What you're suggesting isn't plausible. Angel was into Robert, not Lila."

"You're making the assumption that every relationship is sexual," he said, giving me a look that showed just how far my attitude was pushing him away. "Sometimes bonds are formed for mutual needs that have nothing to do with pleasure or intimacy. When the two cartels merged, Robert became second in command to his mother, but he still needed help. Lila told him everything the two of you discussed the night you chased me down the stairs at the embassy. Something about that conversation tipped him off that I was playing both sides. That's why Eloise and her son were sprung without my knowledge and why an attack was made against the embassy. They wanted me to know that I had been made, and my actions were not going unpunished."

"If that's how things truly went down, why didn't you have Lila arrested instead of letting her go, and how did your partner get away? She didn't come to the party with you."

"First, we needed Lila to believe she was in the clear. From all the players we were aware of, she was the weakest link. As for Selena, she's a crafty little rogue who got wind of what was being planned and managed to get away while Alma and her people were busy elsewhere."

"But you've never suspected her of incompetence or betrayal."

"She was the one who told me what happened. Alma and Eloise had us chasing our tails over half of Central and South America for weeks. We know they're in Colombia, but with all jungles and uninhabitable areas it's been impossible to pinpoint their exact location. We've gotten a few decent leads, but they had always moved on before our forces were mobilized."

"I can see where Alma and Eloise would need to keep moving, but the Seville brothers have families. There has to be more permanent locations for their wives and children. Perhaps the leads you've been getting were simply meant to keep you away from the main compounds."

"That's why I figured you and I needed to talk privately. Despite the tongue-lashing I rightly deserved for my animalistic and less-than moral behavior, I know I can trust you to put aside our differences and give this case your undivided attention. We've been watching Lila since she left Mexico City, but you're the one who's had direct contact with her. Maybe something she said or did will give us a better idea of where she is and exactly what role she's playing—other than informant."

"Have you been tailing her personally?" I asked, not wanting to contemplate what he may have discovered if he had.

"I've spent most of my time in South America, but I did come back to the states once," he hesitatingly admitted. "I couldn't afford to be seen, but it was rather hard to miss the fact that you decided to move on with someone else, even after I told told you how I felt about us. Are you going to marry him? I saw you in the park. You looked like a real family."

"I don't know," I replied.

"But you've discussed it? How long have you been together?"

Everything fell into place in one gigantic realization that made me sick with remorse. Agent Fielding was going to contact me when he came to D.C., but he had seen me with Trey first. How cozy and contrived everything must have looked to him. While it didn't justify his physical relationship with Agent Diaz, it certainly made his attitude towards me more understandable.

"We met at Christmas but haven't exactly worked past the friendship stage. Why didn't you talk to me? You have no idea how hard it's been being alone all these months with a baby and no one to talk to. I've been so confused and miserable."

"You didn't look miserable, and what was I supposed to say besides congratulations on your new life? It was obvious he could offer you something I couldn't, and he's certainly been more of a father to Charlie than I have."

"You don't know what kind of father you would be if you had time to spend with him. Charlie loves people, and that includes Lila. Children are naturally intuitive. That's why I find what you're telling me so hard to believe."

"But it's still the truth, Reagan. She might not have pulled the trigger this morning, but she was definitely with the men who did. That's why we have to find her. I just wish it hadn't been necessary to involve you in any of this again. You deserve to happy with the man of your choosing, but I can't help wish it might have been me."

I rose to my feet and closed the short distance between us. Without even thinking, I placed my hand on his shoulder. His fingers immediately closed over mine.

"Nothing has been decided," I told him. "Don't you know that I wouldn't be dragging my feet if I felt it was the right thing for Charlie and me? Trey is a wonderful man, and he could give me everything I've ever wanted, except for one thing."

"What's that?" he asked.

"Filling the place in my heart that was always empty until I met you. I don't know if we even stand a chance because there's so much stacked against us, but I can't seem to let go of this fantasy that makes me put the rest of my life on hold."

He stood up and pulled me into his arms. "Do you have any idea how utterly irresistible you are right now and how much I want to kiss you? If things were different . . . "

I put my finger up to his lips. Agent Fielding was an enigma, a man who could make my heart beat wildly, but also a man who had brought me incredible pain.

"But they aren't, and we have no idea how any of this will end."

"You're right," he said, taking my hands and bringing them to his lips. "Still, you have to know that my feelings for you are genuine. I might not be able to give you the kind of life Trey can because I sense that it has more to do with moral convictions than anything else, but I would give you everything I possibly could."

"What about Agent Diaz? It's obvious that she's very much in love with you and believes you feel the same way about her. She thinks I'm a threat to her happiness."

"She's my partner. We've spent a great deal of time together—doing certain things I wish we hadn't to keep our cover intact—but I never gave her any reason to believe there was anything more to our relationship than that. You stole my heart the moment I first saw you holding Charlie and looking so Madonna-like, determined and scared. I kept putting you down because I knew you were the one woman who could break through the shell of indifference and contempt I had been hiding behind so I could do my job."

I was going to ask him if he was absolutely certain he hadn't given off any vibes she may have misinterpreted, but our time for being alone was over. Agent Diaz had returned and was knocking on the door.

"What's going on,"" she called out. "And why is the door locked?"

Agent Fielding gave me a frustrated look and kissed my hands again before unlocking it. "Security," he told her as she walked past him into the room.

I was glad the bed covers had barely been ruffled because her eyes seemed to take in everyone at once. I might not know or even like her, but I didn't want her thinking I would do anything inappropriate. My relationship with my former partner was still very much up in the air. She basically pushed me aside so a tote containing coffee cups could be placed on the table, along with a brown paper bag.

"I thought this might hold us until later," she said, handing one of the hot cups to Agent Fielding. "I didn't know what you liked in your coffee, Agent Sinclair, so there's sugar and milk in the sack along with some donuts. Sam and I take ours straight."

"Thank you for your consideration, Agent Diaz, but I don't drink coffee," I replied, forcing an unfelt smile. Despite our mutual dislike, I felt a certain amount of compassion because everyone deserved to feel loved.

"If I'd known, I could have gotten you some tea."

"Reagan doesn't drink tea or alcohol either," Agent Fielding said.

I watched as her eyebrows rose. It was an expression I had seen numerous times, but in a fallen world there were too many shades of gray. I could only remain strong if I didn't become careless or complacent about anything.

"That must be inconvenient, even for an FBI agent," she said, taking a sip of her own steaming liquid. "Sam and I would never survive what's required if we couldn't get real once in a while."

Her innuendos were becoming tiresome, but I understood why she was making them. "I'm not concerned about getting real. When I'm not at work, I'm spending time with my son."

"Having a child must be very restrictive. I'm sure Sam misses his, but he's pragmatic enough to know that family encumbrances only make agents vulnerable. That's why he chose a different tactic when going after Alma. I'm just glad I was available to go with him. He needed someone who can stand by his side in everything."

Little else was said, and Agent Fielding left before finishing his coffee. There was nothing more we could say to each other with a third party in the room anyway. Agent Diaz promised to let him know as soon as I heard from Lila and then followed him outside. I heard the door click so there was no way I could overhear what was being said.

Once the sky had turned from pinkish-blue hues to a deep, formidable blackness, Agent Diaz ordered pepperoni pizza. We ate it in our room. I had a soda while she drank three wine coolers. Apparently, she felt she was off duty, regardless of the fact that she had been ordered to stay with me. She received several calls, but I was unable to tell from her end of the conversation if they were professional or personal.

Not that it really mattered. I had enough to keep my mind occupied worrying about Lila. The woman I had known for over half a year was trying to get her life in order. If she was involved with Robert Evans, I needed her to return my call so I could hear her side of the story. It was the only way I would be able to clear her name.

When midnight arrived, I decided to turn off the bedside light and try to sleep. Agent Diaz had been lightly snoring for over an hour. It made me wonder how she could rest when there were so many unanswered questions. But she was used to working in the field—for months or even years at a time—without the comfort of knowing there were people around who could help if she got into trouble. Like Agent Fielding, she seemed to thrive on cutting things close, being on the run and never knowing what the next moment might bring. I could easily recall feeling like that as a teen who wanted to serve her country, but I was an adult now with a child to raise. My focus in life had changed, and so had I. All I wanted was to call home and make sure everyone I had left behind was still safe.

I tried to slow my breathing so sleep would come, but every time I felt like I might be drifting off something startled me into wakefulness again. I hated what my life had become. Deception and putting others in danger hung like an invisible net waiting to capture and punish. I didn't want to sacrifice my job. It's all I had ever wanted to do, but I couldn't have it both ways. My son needed a mother who came home every night and a chance to grow up in an environment where positive values could be instilled.

Something must be terribly wrong with my head if I thought I could juggle life to suit my own wants. As much as my heart yearned for the freedom to take a chance with Agent Fielding, it was impossible not to know that our relationship was doomed.

A car passed in front of the motel room window, bringing with it eerie shadows that made me long, even more, for Charlie and home. He was used to being with Amanda, but I liked to think he wanted to be with me more. When I envisioned his smiling face, chubby arms, and zest for discovering everything he could about life, I was reminded that no sacrifice was too great to be a good mother. Another job may be far less stimulating, but working for the FBI wasn't the only way to serve my fellowmen or my country. I could become involved with a humanitarian project, volunteer in a soup line, or man a hotline for battered women. There were plenty of ways to serve others the way Christ had done and leave of the intrigue and risks to people more suited to it than I was.

My cell phone rang as I completed another round of circular thinking that seldom got me anywhere. I grabbed it from off the nightstand where Agent Diaz had placed it before realizing that in so doing I had disconnected it from the tracing machine. I would be horribly reprimanded, and perhaps even lose my job, but it was too late to rectify my mistake. Agent Diaz was still soundly sleeping in the other bed. Perhaps the number of wine coolers she had consumed was responsible for that.

I jumped from my bed and raced into the bathroom when I saw Lila's name on the screen. I needed to have as honest a conversation with her as possible because she had some of the answers we so desperately needed.

"Did I wake you?" she asked once I had the door closed and was sitting on a towel on the edge of the tub. She sounded both tired and stressed, and not at all like the woman I had known in he past. "I wanted to call you back sooner but wasn't able to."

"That's okay," I replied as my heart continued to pound. I was knowingly violating everything I had committed to do, but the last thing I wanted was for Lila to hang up while adjustments were being made. "I was worried about you. Is everything okay?"

"Life's great, and I'm having a wonderful time," she replied. "We've just had a couple of long days traveling. Are you in Texas?"

"I am," I replied, trying to keep my voice steady. "They've put me up in this awful motel with stained bathroom fixtures and carpet that looks and smells like it's never been cleaned. You wouldn't believe the hideous colors. But I suppose the DEA is working on a budget, and I'm not exactly in a position to be asking for any favors."

"You poor thing," she said. "I know what a neat freak you are when it comes to your personal surroundings, but surely it won't be for long. You're as much a victim in all of this as Charlie's biological mother. I've been watching the news between flights and feel so sorry for the families of the victims. Have you been able to learn anything new?"

There it was! Either friendly curiosity or an attempt to get me to disclose classified information.

"I've only been here long enough to see pictures of the bodies and learn that most of the people involved made a clean getaway. What kind of monsters would kill without reason?"

Her pause was barely long enough for me to notice. "The DEA has no leads?"

"They know it was the work of the combined cartels. I'm assuming that's why I was summoned. The DEA doesn't exactly enjoy working with me. They would rather see me in a padded cell where I would be forced to keep my opinions to myself, but I do know both Eloise and Alma on a personal level. Did you know that a note was left on the side of a building saying this was just the beginning of their reign of terror? I don't know what they think anyone here can do to stop them. If they're using some specifically designed aircraft to take off and land, I would say they definitely have the upper hand."

I stopped talking so she would have time to process what I had said. I needed her to believe I had nothing to hide, but there was a fine line between drawing someone out and saying too much.

"I wish you didn't have to go through this alone. I feel like I'm deserting you at the worst possible time, but fate is often a very cruel mistress, and the past always comes back to haunt. I suppose nothing was found at the scene that could be used as a lead. You always told me that even the most evolved criminals make mistakes."

My whole soul was screaming out for me to tell her what I knew so she would be prepared, but that would be rightly construed as treason.

"Maybe something will turn up later, but right now, they seem to have covered their tracks exceptionally well. Would it be okay if we changed the subject for a few minutes? I'm having enough trouble sleeping and could use a lighthearted distraction. Perhaps you could tell me about some of the fun you've been having, and I can enjoy life a little vicariously through it."

"It's hard to think about personal enjoyment when other people are in so much pain," she responded. "Women should be home taking care of their families like you do with Charlie. He already has one parent missing. I wish you didn't have to be in Texas at. It isn't safe, especially if more attacks are planned."

The beating of my heart intensified. Was Lila warning me about what was coming? Two border crossings at the same location would not be anticipated. My next words must be chosen carefully.

"I'm sure you're right. For many reasons, this is the last place I want to be. Did I tell you that he's almost walking? I just want to stay home and be his mother."

"Then go home and marry Trey! Nothing would make me happier than knowing you were away from all this ugliness and enjoying the kind of life you've always wanted."

"I'm not sure the DEA would go for that? This wasn't a request. It was a direct order."

"They do have a tendency towards the dramatic, although it seems as if they do a lot bungling. Any news on Sam? I know you don't feel like you can go on with your life until things are settled with him."

Despite the retribution I would receive, I was grateful no one was listening to our conversation, especially Agent Diaz. It was far more revealing than I intended, but it was how Lila and I usually conversed.

"I haven't learned anything since we were whisked away from Mexico City, but then I didn't expect to. Ambassador Alexander made it quite clear that he was washing his hands of me."

"And yet the DEA had the audacity to ask for your help again. What gives them the right to keep disrupting your life when you've already told them everything you know? They need to back off or more innocent people are going to get hurt."

This time, there was no doubt that she was giving me a warning. We were skating on very thin ice for two women whose words and actions were most likely being monitored, but I needed her to reveal something specific that could be used in overthrowing the cartel. The trick would be doing it without disclosing classified information myself.

"They're just trying to do their job. Keeping drugs off the streets is in everyone's best interest. I don't want Charlie using them when he gets older."

"Nor do I," she said. "Addiction is horrible, but so is threatening people into doing things against their will. It shouldn't be that way."

Suddenly, I knew Lila was innocent, even if I couldn't prove it. She was telling me that she had been forced into working with the cartel, and I couldn't risk her safety by probing any deeper. A different approach was necessary if I wanted to learn anything more. "Where are you headed next, and when are you coming home? Charlie and I really miss you."

I heard her sharp intake of breath. "I don't know. We're supposed to visit some remote island off the coast of South America where there is nothing but sun, sand and some terrific nightlife at a fancy, but private, casino where the guest list is limited to a select few with the right credentials. I'm being told that it will be a chance for me to get a real feel for life away from modern civilization and meet some very interesting and influential people. But to tell you the truth, I'm ready to come home. I miss my loft, my cat and my classes at school. But mostly, I miss being on my own where I'm not at the mercy of anyone else's plans. How long will you be in Texas?"

"Only a day or two, I hope. The interim director wants to go over everything I can remember about both cartels. Maybe he thinks I've been hiding something."

"Have you?" she asked.

The directness of her question made me swallow back an onslaught of revulsion for the part I was playing in trying to find her. "I've told them everything I know, along with far too much of what I think. They don't want a repeat of what happened a few hours ago."

"No one can stop a dragon by simply cutting off one of its toes. This beast is too strong and powerful and is always looking for reinforcements from every walk of life. They're not going to stop until they've made a statement that no one can miss, and they don't care who gets hurt. I hope you know how much I love you and Charlie. You are my family. I would do anything necessary to keep you safe."

"Ditto," I replied.

"Listen, Reagan, while I would love to continue our conversation, the taxi is on its way to take us to the airport. I'll call in a few days to tell you about my adventures. This destination spot is supposed to be the perfect culmination to everything we've seen and done thus far."

"Wow!" I said, trying to come up with one last question or comment that would help me figure out where Robert Evans was taking her. "All I've seen recently are the streets of home and some funky-looking cactus and plain adobe buildings. I would love to travel to exotic places and spend time just having a little fun. It wouldn't matter how much time I had to spend on a plane."

"This leg of the trip won't require nearly as much time in the air as some of the other places we've gone. Just a hop, skip and a jump over the Equator, and I'll be basking in luxury of the most primitive nature. I wish you could join me, but I know you'll be busy looking for the people who managed to escape. There must have been quite a group of locals involved."

I had barely opened my mouth to reply when Lila abruptly cleared her throat.

"Your assistance in this matter will be greatly appreciated," I heard her say. "Losing a piece of jewelry is very distressing because it cannot be replaced."

The line went dead, and I felt my lips begin to tremble. If Lila had been alone while we were speaking, she certainly wasn't any longer. My mind was spinning as I rose to my feet, but before I had time to take a step towards the door, it flew open and a very angry Agent Selena Diaz turned on the light.

"What the hell do you think you're doing?" she shouted. "I just got a call from Interim Director Whitman. He said the tracking system had gone offline, and when I looked, your cell phone had been removed. If you think I'm going to let you jeopardize my career, you are sadly mistaken. We've been ordered to return to the field office immediately."

I took a moment to steady my nerves. My reply could mean the difference between freedom and spending the rest of my life in jail. I brushed past her into the bedroom knowing what I had to do, but hating the idea of using a fellow agent to cover my overt disregard for very explicit demands.

"I'm sorry if my actions have inconvenienced you, Agent Diaz, but what happened was an accident," I said as she stood in front of me with her eyes blazing and her hands on her hips. Her gun was just inches away, and I couldn't be sure she wouldn't draw it and force me to my knees.

"What you did was no accident. You were talking to Lila Rivers and didn't want your conversation overheard. You can kiss seeing that baby you claim to love so much goodbye because all I see in your future is a court marshal."

"If I end up in a cell, it won't be alone. I was drowsy when the phone rang and picked it up without thinking. That is a truth I will attest to in any court of law. The connection was lost, and I had to make a split-second decision. It might not have been the best one, but trying to reconnect it myself was impossible without detection, and you were sleeping so soundly it was impossible to wake you up. I don't know about the DEA, but the FBI has rules about drinking on the job. As I see it, we need to work together to resolve this, or I will be forced to tell both Agent Fielding and the interim director my side of a not-so-pretty story."

She gave me a look of complete hatred but didn't even try to make a rebuttal. "I will not be a party to blackmail, but I am curious as to what your proposal might be."

"I tell you what was said, and we get everyone to believe we were working together in trying to solve a very unfortunate accident."

"How will I know you're not lying to cover your tracks? I told Sam your loyalties were divided since Lila was a personal friend. What just happened only proves I was right."

"What happened proves nothing. We can stand here arguing semantics, but Lila was trying to tell me something, and I need a computer and a very detailed map to figure out what it was."

The trim of orange, green and gold chevron striping that hung close to the ceiling seemed to curl and slither like a snake as I pulled my change of clothing from a hanger and began to get dressed. Its fanciful movements seemed to remind me that heading down the wrong path often began innocently enough, but it didn't take long until one bad move grew into a noose that could both confine and destroy. I had been taking liberties for months, but I had stepped over the line this time.

I shifted my eyes so I could see Agent Diaz's profile as we drove the few miles towards the building where other agents were still working. Even in the semi-darkness of the car, I saw her lips twist into a sardonic smile. She would welcome the chance to ruin me for more than just work-related reasons, and I had made myself vulnerable to both ridicule and punishment. But I would do it again because Lila deserved freedom from her very evil captor.

When the tires on the suburban quit revolving, I mentally steeled myself for the first round of chastisement. Agent Fielding was standing on the sidewalk. His face was drawn, and I suddenly realized that I didn't much care what others thought about me, but I didn't want to lose his respect. He reached out and gripped my arm before I had time to put my foot on the first concrete step.

"Wait for us inside, Selena," he said as the muscles in his hand tightened. "There are a few things I need to say to Agent Sinclair before the official inquiry begins."

"Anything you need, Sam," she replied, giving him a smile that made my stomach knot.

I waited until she was out-of-sight before saying anything. "I know you have plenty of questions, but I never meant to cause any trouble."

"You never do, but I'm afraid I may not be able to help you this time," he said, releasing his hold on my arm and allowing me to walk the short distance to the bench that had been put along an outside wall. "What in the world possessed you to talk to Lila without waking Selena? She was there to make sure procedures were followed so there would be no chance of repercussions."

I opened my mouth to give an explanation, but his look of exasperation made me reconsider.

"You might as well know that phone records are being pulled, and while we might not get a transcription of what was said, we will know if you were trying to warn her. The people I work with believe you broke the connection on purpose, and I have no way of proving them wrong. What was so important you couldn't risk being overheard?"

I sat down on the bench in what could have been another romantic encounter. The not unpleasant odor of some plant hung heavy in the air, and being so far away from the city made every star in the heavens seem to shine twice as bright.

"I picked up the phone too forcefully by accident. You have to believe that. But when I saw that the call was from Lila, I knew I would never be able to speak freely in front of someone else. So I went into the bathroom and closed the door. Agent Diaz was sleeping so soundly she didn't even hear a phone ring until Interim Director Whitman called to ask what had happened."

"I don't give a damn about Selena, except as my partner who has willingly given everything she has to this cause. I've tried to keep you and Charlie safe, but your little escapade tonight may bring all of that to an end. I almost wish you had stayed home. I have enough worry and aggravation without having to put out another fire you've managed to start. If you had allowed Selena to do her job, she may have been able to guide the conversation so we had a few answers. Now, I'll be lucky to keep you from being thrown underneath the proverbial bus."

Any hope I may have had that he would be understanding was being rapidly shredded. "I did what I thought was best, and Lila gave me some information I believe can be used to figure out where she and Robert have gone. But I need time, and a computer, to work through it. All this unnecessary chatter is making me lose concentration, and I can't afford to forget anything that was said."

He leaned back his head and laughed, but it wasn't a pleasant sound. "No one likes to be around people who think they have all the answers. You should be listening and absorbing everything you can from people who actually know what they're doing. You've been working with the DEA for less time than anyone I know."

His accurate observation of my attitude made me cringe. Inside, I wasn't some know-it-all who thought she was better than everyone else, but I did have opinions and could see things that some of my colleagues missed.

"You accuse me of going off half-cocked most of the time, and you're right. I do act and speak without thinking, and I've made enemies on both sides of the law due to it. But I can't change the past. I can only move forward, making mistakes as I go."

"Then tell me what you know, and I'll see if it's enough to smooth a few ruffled feathers."

"Lila couldn't exactly tell me where she was, but she did give me some clues as to where they were going. I need time to put the pieces together, but she warned me several times that things are only going to get worse. This new cartel is out for money, glory and power. They're still recruiting members and are headed to some out-of-the way island. I think she may be involved as a way to protect Charlie."

"It always comes back to family with you, doesn't it," he said, slipping his arm around my shoulders. I wanted desperately to lean into the warmth and safety I knew could be found there, but our relationship wasn't back on solid ground yet. "I wish we had more to go on than your gut instincts, but I've never known them to be wrong. That said, you need to apologize and be convincing about it."

All of the agents I had met the previous day were in the conference room when we walked inside. Perhaps I should have acted more contrite because the icy stares I received could have cooled down an entire tub filled with warm sodas. While I was here as a courtesy to the DEA, I wasn't technically bound by any of their rules. My reckoning would come when I was forced to face Assistant Director Bridges.

The interim director broke off what I knew was a very revealing conversation with Agent Diaz when I approached.

"We'll continue this discussion later," he told her before turning his attention to me. "Right now, we all have great deal of work to do if we want to salvage any of this operation. With no thanks to you, Agent Sinclair, we've managed to trace the call back to a small resort town in southern Mexico. Our agents are on their way to the hotel, but it's doubtful they'll arrive in time. They're a hundred miles away, and the cartels have their own planes. It's going to take more than a miracle to find them."

"I'm sorry for not following protocol, sir, but Lila gave me some information that might prove useful. A great deal of our time together over the past few months has been spent talking about the ramifications of these particular cartels joining forces. While I accept that she's with Robert Evans, I do not believe it is voluntarily."

His eyes narrowed. "I'm here to see that justice is served, Agent Sinclair. Your friend, for whatever reasons, is working with some very bad people, and your diffidence in following procedures may well have cost us what little advantage we had."

He turned his back on me and walked away. I looked around at all the other agents and decided it was best to separate myself from them until I could sort out the supposed hints Lila had given me.

"Don't let anything Randall Whitman says get to you," Agent Fielding whispered in my ear as I headed towards a chair in a far corner of the room. "He's coming down hard because his boss was killed, and he's been given the task of finding out who is responsible."

"I understand how he feels. It wasn't that long ago that some of these very people killed Neil, and they've threatened my son's life more than once."

"He's my son, too, Reagan. I want to see these monsters behind bars, but causing discord in the ranks won't help. That's why I prefer working alone. I trust my own abilities and don't have to worry about someone else taking over and trying to steer me in another direction. In that way, I think we're very much alike. You can be obstinate and infuriatingly guileless, but your instincts are right on. I'm not saying that Lila is innocent, but I am willing to give you a chance to prove what you think you know."

"Then find me a quiet place to think. Lila said a lot of things I believe were in a code she hoped I would understand."

"You've got it," he responded, before allowing his hand to rest on my arm. The very weight of his fingers made me realize that he wasn't angry with me any longer, but when I looked away from him I saw Agent Diaz watching us. "Maybe someday we'll have time to sit down for a real conversation, but I have to finish this mission first. Drugs are coming into this country faster than ever, and Robert Evans seems to have no qualms about sending deadly messages. He's a dangerous man, and if Lila is with him, it means she's either in over her head, or she's been using you to get information the cartel needs. We're not going to know which it is until we find her."

He escorted me into a private office and left me alone. Had I dared, I would have exited the building and found a quiet place where I could speak my thoughts out loud. It was how I worked best, but he had already risk a great deal for me. It was my turn to do something of a more professional nature for him.

So I closed my eyes and allowed my mind to drift back to the conversation in the bathroom. I could hear the slow dripping of water from the shower head above the tub and see the pale green paint on the walls. I could even feel the hair on my arms stand erect as I heard the sound of Lila's voice. It took a few moments of intense concentration until I began to understand what she had been trying to tell me. Since she couldn't give me an exact location as to where they were going, she had given me clues that on the surface sounded like nothing more than idle chatter.

I pulled a notebook from my backpack and began listing everything I could remember. Assuming she wasn't working with the enemy to help set up some trap, she and Robert were heading to a remote island to meet associates he hoped would be amenable to backing him. That might be the lead we'd been looking for, was a huge lead, provided I could narrow down a viable location.

The coast of Colombia seemed reasonable since it was close to the equator and was the country where the Mendoza's and Lupe Evans ruled and the Sevilles had relocated. It seemed probable that they would go some place familiar where the locals could be trusted. That limited the possibilities since most islands had some form of law enforcement, but it also meant that Agent Fielding may have been there during the time he had worked for Carlos Mendoza.

A meeting of the size and scope I envisioned would be attended by some of the most merciless men and women in the underworld, and it would be held in a place that was easily accessible and free from interference. I pulled out my smart phone and soon discovered that there were a number of well-known islands such as the Isla de Providencia, Santa Cruz de Islote, Gogina, Malpelo and Isla de los Micos off the coast of Colombia. Each had gorgeous coastlines, crystal blue water for swimming and snorkeling, abundant animal, bird and sea life and plenty to do, but Lila had made a point of saying they would be out of cell phone service and only people with a certain kind of approval would be there.

I was too realistic to believe that we could take the whole cartel down in one sweep, but we might be able to take out some of its biggest players if we could get our people there in time. Lila had given no indication when the meeting would take place, but it had to be soon.

"Agent Sinclair," the voice of Interim Director Whitman broke into my musings. "I hope you've finished whatever Agent Fielding thought was necessary. He insists that you be part of whatever decision is made. I think it's absurd to allow an outsider to play an active part, but I am a reasonable man. I only hope our trust hasn't been misplaced."

I took a deep breath of hot, stale air and looked directly up at him. Despite my inexperience, I could bring something to the table. "I have a definite theory and an idea of where a very important meeting may be held within a day or two. It could even be as soon as the next few hours, but I need some help locating an island off the coast of Colombia. There's electricity but none of the creature comforts most people find necessary for a pleasant vacation."

He gave me a look that was less than tolerant and cleared his throat. "All the more reason protocol should have been followed. We don't need more riddles and speculations. We need answers."

I followed him back to the conference room where some very tired agents were waiting to hear what I had to say. This was going to be a tough crowd to convince that my beliefs were anything more than delusions because I wanted to believe my friend was innocent.

Agent Fielding gave me an encouraging nod. "Go ahead and tell us what you've been able to put together. We're all on the same side here."

Even a few weeks earlier, I would not have been able to stand in front of room filled with people, who obviously knew more about how cartels functioned than I did, and lay out a theory that had more holes in it than a block of Swiss cheese. But I no longer doubted myself as much as I had in the past, so I gave a synopsis on what I had come up with as quickly and succinctly as possible. While others in the room glanced around with looks of skepticism, Agent Fielding rose to his feet.

"I understand your misgivings, but we cannot underestimate the power of friendship. If what Agent Sinclair has laid out has even a particle of accuracy, we would be fools not to see where it leads. A new operation of the magnitude we're dealing with takes a lot of careful planning, and of necessity, will require support beyond what the cartels already involved can supply. They will want to capitalize on their strengths while spending the majority of their time in familiar territory where they are well-insulated from opposition. But if they are hosting an event to obtain additional funding, they will go somewhere neutral."

"You really believe that an undisclosed number of wannabe kingpins will go to some remote island just to get in on the ground floor of some new operation?" one of the agents asked.

I watched as Agent Fielding's eyebrow rose. "Unless it has already slipped your mind, I was Mendoza's right hand man for nearly four years, and I knew a great deal about his operation. The compound in the mountains of Colombia was his headquarters while I was with him, but he had other places all over the country. And his interests were not limited to drug trafficking. He was a connoisseur of fine wine, paintings, books and everything else of a cultural nature. It wouldn't surprise me if he owns several small islands. He used to take off for weeks at a time. When he came back, he was well-rested and always brought some treasure to add to one of his collections."

"I don't see how that helps us," the interim director said.

"Maybe it doesn't, but Agent Sinclair is offering a suggestion that needs to be taken seriously. We're not going to have any solid answers until we have someone in custody, but I believe the threat left of the wall was meant to keep us so focused on what might happen on U.S. soil that we overlooked the bigger picture. A meeting, like the one being suggested, would draw a lot of attention. And the organizers would need a diversion that kept the DEA occupied until it was over. I think it's worth checking out since it's the only lead we have right now."

The man I had been thinking about for months wasn't merely backing me up, he was adding to the believability of my theory, but we had to move quickly before Robert Evans realized what Lila had done.

"So what do you suggest we do?" Interim Director Whitman asked with the sweep of his hand. "If you know how to stop these people from killing more of our agents, I'm sure everyone in this room would be more than willing to help."

Agent Fielding cleared his throat before walking to the whiteboard in the front of the room. "First, we take a look at the region Agent Sinclair specified and figure out where this powwow is going to take place."

When a detailed map of the Colombian coast appeared, he took a dry erase marker and circled the location of the mountain compound and the old ancestral home I had seen a picture of in Mendoza's library. He went on to mark the Rios' ranch, the town Lila had called from, and several other places I had not known existed before.

Watching him work made me see just how valuable he would be in Washington D.C. training new recruits. His knowledge was tremendous, and he had the undercover experience needed to anticipate problems before they arose. If we survived this latest crisis, I would do everything in my power to persuade him to leave the fieldwork to others and take a job where he could get to know his son. Charlie and I could help him adjust.

"From my best recollections," he was saying when I forced my thoughts back to the dubious mission we were contemplating. "There are two places that meet the criteria Lila suggested as a meeting place for organized crime. The officials on those islands are paid handsomely to look the other way and offer protection to the cartels when necessary."

"How do you know that?" the interim director asked.

"Let's just say that I'm personally familiar with one them, and it meets all the criteria Miss Rivers alluded to. Mendoza sent me there to launder some of his money in a high stakes gaming casino where no one got inside the front door without a pass. The vegetation alone keeps the resort well-hidden, and no one would even know of its existence if he or she hadn't been personally invited to go there.

Everything on the island is run by generators, and the only way on and off is by boat."

"If it's that closely guarded, how do you expect to get there?"

"By accessing a beach on the far side of the island and heading inland after dark. It will mean making our way through some of the worst jungle I've ever encountered, but with the right people and equipment, it can be done."

"You're willing to risk your career, not to mention your life, when there's no definitive proof that a meeting is even being planned?"

Agent Fielding gave him an unforgettable look. "I would walk into the fires of hell if it meant putting these people behind bars. They deserve no leniency."

"Then we'll get our agents in that area mobilized and ready to move as soon as we have confirmation of any activity," the interim director said.

"That's not the way this is going to work," Agent Fielding replied. "I will not leave this in the hands of people I haven't worked with before. You can run things from here, but I will assemble my own team and lead the way through that maze."

"I'm with Sam on this, and I'm going with him," Agent Diaz stated as she rose to her feet and walked to the front of the room to stand beside him.

Her glance towards me was one of triumph. I wanted to be part of this takedown too but knew he would never agree.

Interim Director Whitman slapped his hand so hard on the surface of a table that most everyone in the room jumped. "I have my doubts about the advisability of going into this blind, but I admire your dedication and passion. I can have a chopper here to take both of you to the airport in a matter of minutes. Just make sure to keep me in the loop. We can use satellite images to coordinate our efforts."

"That would be much appreciated, but I have one request before leaving. I want Agent Sinclair to be part of this in an advisory capacity. I know you have doubts about the entire operation, but I've never known her impressions to be wrong."

His words left me speechless. After all I had done to complicate his life and his missions he still wanted me around to make sure nothing went wrong from our end.

"We'd be grateful for her help," the interim director said. "Who knows, Lila might get back to her again before you're even on the ground."

"A moment of your time before we leave," Agent Fielding said, taking my arm and disregarding Agent Diaz's look of disapproval.

I felt my heart literally skip a beat as he propelled me towards the vacant office I had been using before. Once we were inside, he leaned up against the door, put his hands on my shoulders and looked down at me.

"Please don't hate me too much for making another decision about your life without consulting you first, but if we can get these monsters behind bars for good a lot of innocent people are going to sleep better at night."

"I know I can't come with you. There's Charlie to consider."

"It's not just Charlie," he said. "I know we still have a lot to work through. But I'm not sure we can cheat fate again, and there is something else you need to know."

"You don't have to say anything more. I have your lawyer's number on speed dial. And regardless of what happens, I will keep Charlie safe, and he will know what a good man his father is."

"We've already discussed my tarnished character," he replied as he caressed my cheek. I forced myself not to shy away. "However, despite every reservation I have about being the kind of man who should even consider being part of a family, I want to come back to you and our son more than anything. But if that isn't in the cards, I want you to know that it's okay to go on with your life. I refuse to let either good or bad memories of me stand in your way."

"That isn't your call to make," I said, taking the hand that had been caressing my check and lifting it to my lips. "There will be plenty of time to talk about remaining issues when you get back."

"But in case I don't, I want you to marry this guy you've been dating—if you think he can make you happy. He's been more of a father to Charlie than I've ever been, and knowing me has already caused you to lose Neil."

The tears that formed in my eyes made it almost impossible to see his face. "Trey's a good man, but he hasn't asked me to marry him. I'm not sure what my answer would be if he did. All I can be concerned about right now is this mission. You have to promise me that you won't take any unnecessary chances, and that you'll protect Lila if you get the chance. No matter how this turns out, I'll never accept that she turned to the wrong side intentionally.

"I'll do everything I can to keep her safe, but someone is going to knock on this door, and there's something else I need to say before that happens."

I held my breath as he tipped my chin upwards until our eyes locked together. I had always known he was a passionate man, but the intensity of feelings I saw behind the carefully-guarded extremities made it impossible to do anything except get caught up in the fervor of the moment.

"You are the most beautiful woman I have ever met both inside and out. You have the capacity for warmth and tenderness that simply captivates me. Not an hour goes by when I don't think about the safety and peace I feel in your arms. You make me want to be a better man and believe in something greater than what I can see. I never thought I would say this to anyone, but I am totally and completely in love with you, Agent Reagan Sinclair. I hope you'll give me a chance to show you exactly what that means when I get home."

I opened my mouth as a sob escaped, but he put a restraining finger on my lips. "Please don't say anything. If I have to die, I want to do it remembering all the fantasies I've build in my own mind about us. I just needed you to know how I feel."

His declaration washed over me like a warm, comforting blanket until it reached every corner of my heart. I didn't want to care about him, but I could no longer deny how he made me feel either. Without conscious effort, I gripped his arm as he tried to move me out of the way so the door could be opened. I might be making the biggest mistake of my life, but it was by choice, and I would live with whatever consequences it brought.

"You're not going to walk away until I've had my say too," I protested. "You are a complicated man who has known far too many women and how to use that to his advantage, but I'm in love with you too. I didn't want to be, but underneath that often-irritating façade is a man with an incredibly understanding heart and the willingness to sacrifice everything he has for others. So you'd better come back to us, to me, because I want to show you that you have a family who doesn't want to live life without you any longer."

No further words were spoken. He simply encircled me in his arms and pressed his lips to mine. It was a kiss of both promise and desire that left me breathless for more.

"I will come back to you, my stubborn little agent," he said when it was over. "Just don't change your mind while I'm gone because what you just said will help me fight the battle of a lifetime."

"I'm not going to change my mind," I replied, wishing we could stay locked away in this room forever. My family might not agree with how I had chosen to live my life, but admitting that I loved Agent Sam Fielding would not come as complete surprise. I had always danced to my own tune and followed my own drummer.

"Tell Charlie I love him as much as I love his mother, only in a very different way. If there was time I would . . . " He put his hands on my cheeks again and kissed me very quickly. "I hope you know what you're getting yourself into. I'm not an easy man to love. That's why I've spent most of my life alone."

He was gone before I could respond. Perhaps it was better that way. What else could be said when we were facing the impossible whether he came home or not. The only comfort I could derive as the door closed behind him was that I had finally taken a chance with my heart.

Chapter 8

I'm not sure how any of us survived the next few hours. Interim Director Whitman was hesitant about leaving the scene where his boss and a fellow agent had lost their lives, but two of the agents who had accompanied us to Presidio volunteered to remain behind and make sure leads were followed and bodies processed so they could be returned to Austin where families were waiting for them. The equipment that was necessary for assisting Agent's Fielding and Diaz once they arrived in Colombia was in Dallas, and that's where we needed to be.

We packed up what few things we had brought and drove to the nearest airport where a plane was waiting. We didn't say much during the journey. What we were doing was more than a long shot, but we were without options, unless we wanted to wait for another call from Lila.

The miles in the air should have been at least somewhat reassuring since we now had a plan, but I didn't even have to close my eyes to see the triumphant look on Selena Diaz's face when I was told that I needed to stay behind. She would use any advantage to make sure the man we both loved couldn't get along without her.

The sky was overcast when we arrived in Dallas and considerably cooler than it had been in Presidio, but I barely noticed the change in scenery from dry countryside to thriving city. We were whisked away by car to DEA headquarters where a technical analyst and computer genius by the name of Agent Rosco Barnes was waiting with a live feed to the airplane Agent Fielding was traveling in. He was ready to give us an update on what he had learned during the hours since he'd left the states.

Satellite surveillance, complete with thermal imaging, was being made ready to pick up the action when they arrived on the small island where we hoped the meeting was going to take place. But even with all the support we could offer, I knew that he was the one taking all the risks. I believed in Lila's innocence and desire to change, but it wouldn't be the first time I had trusted someone when I shouldn't. I would never forgive myself if this mission turned out to be a trap.

The agents I would be working with seemed accepting of my presence, despite the fact that I was not an official member of their team. I had no idea how much they had been told, but I couldn't afford to act reticent now. Agent Fielding had asked for my help, and while I believed in technology and the expertise of the people I was working with, that didn't stop my continual prayers. Everyone involved could use a little divine intervention right now.

I was grateful not to be sitting in front of the computer where Agent Fielding could see me when his image was broadcast on the screen. Selena Diaz was leaning into him, their faces so near that I was sure their breath was intermingling. He looked tired beyond belief—while she looked radiantly alive. I wondered how many of the people watching the live feed thought they were a couple, in addition to being partners.

"How's it going in Dallas, Interim Director Whitman?" Agent Fielding asked as the lines in his forehead deepened.

"We just got here, but things will be ready on this end by the time you need them."

"That's good because my sources in Colombia are telling me that a number of private planes have arrived on the coast. There's no way of knowing their exact destination at present, but it seems to indicate that something is brewing."

"You'll have all the ground support the agency can supply, but I still have my doubts that we're going to capture anyone of real importance. Robert Evans will have plans in place for a speedy exit, and anyone else who shows up won't be able to tell us anything."

"At this point, I'll take what we can get," Agent Fielding responded. "The Evans, Sevilles and Mendozas need to know that their reign of terror is over. Any word on the aircraft they used to get into the states, or the people who were helping them?"

"We know several vehicles left the area after my men were shot, but surveillance equipment in that town is almost non-existent. The simple truth is that they knew we wouldn't be ready for them, and we weren't. We need someone on the inside who can give us a heads-up as to where they plan on striking next."

"That's why we have to follow through with this mission, even if it doesn't net the results we might be hoping for. My belief is that they plan on having more than one stealth airplane operating within the next few months. That takes a great deal of capital, but it can also pay huge dividends. Anyone who gets in on the ground floor could become more wealthy and powerful than ever imagined. This new conglomeration of drug lords could literally revolutionize drug trafficking for generations now that they've successfully gotten their people out of two federally-protected facilities."

"I hope for all our sakes that you're wrong, Sam, but I suppose we can't afford to minimize what they're capable of doing. I'll have my people start looking into every combination of known associates in our files to see if we can level the playing field."

"Make sure Agent Sinclair is involved. She's been working different angles of this case for months. And she believes—like I do —that Lupe Evans, Walter's first wife, has been highly instrumental in the kind of aggression we're seeing now. She'll stay out of the way, but she'll make sure her wants are known. If we get lucky enough, we may even capture her son."

"I suppose stranger things have happened," the interim director said. "That woman must be close to eighty by now."

"Age has nothing to do with it when a woman has sacrificed home, family and country to help the man she loves build a kingdom they were supposed to rule together," Agent Diaz interjected. "Guadalupe Evans desire for revenge only equals her drive for power that can never be taken away again. She has the patience, knowledge and connections to take whatever she wants, and from what I've seen, few people are exempt from the wrath she will release if they get in her way. What really surprises me is her seeming devotion to Eloise and Alma. Women like her usually aren't fond of other women."

I should have asked for an explanation. It was easy to understand how people could hate Walter Evans. He was a despicable, ruthless and cruel man. But I had a feeling her warning about a woman's commitment to keeping what she believed was rightfully hers had a more personal component. She wanted Agent Sam Fielding for herself. What she didn't know was that he had already declared his love for me.

It wasn't long until another call came into the the room where we were assembled—planning, praying and hoping that whatever assistance we might be able to offer would be enough. This time it was from the DEA field office closest to the airstrip on the coast where the plane Agent Fielding was on would land. Agent Auguste Parrella was in charge.

"I want to update you on the plans that are being made here since we'll be running this mission together," he said. "Sam and I have worked several operations together over the years and know who can be trusted. Due to the sensitive nature of this operation, and what we hope will be accomplished, no one outside these two offices will be included in our plans."

"Understood," the interim director said. "What can you tell us?"

"Sam and Selena are still pulling everything together. I'll know more of a specific nature when they arrive, but preliminary reports seem to confirm that Lila Rivers was right about a meeting being held on the island. Surveillance footage shows a woman leaving on a private yacht with the man known to us as Robert Evans, but we need a visual confirmation as to her identity."

I felt my heart settle in my throat when I saw Lila's face turn towards one of the cameras on the footage that had been pulled for us to see. The terror was gone from her eyes, and in its place was a look of total resignation. She knew what awaited her at the island. Her message on the phone had been her final goodbye to me.

"What else do you know about her?" I asked.

"Not much, Agent Sinclair," the man in a tan uniform, whose image was also on the screen, replied. "They arrived in town a few hours ago and had their luggage transferred immediately to the yacht. Their visit would not have been questioned if I hadn't received Sam's call. You have to understand what life is like around here. The locals rely on the cartels for everything. Their apathy towards much of what goes on comes mostly from fear, but they are well compensated for the help they offer."

"And the government can't intervene?"

"Our numbers are small. The best we can do is try to maintain order. The island they are going to was purchased by a very wealthy man as a retreat for members of any cartel who are willing to play by his rules. It is heavily guarded but is a popular gaming resort where massive amounts of drug money are laundered each month. We have tried to get our people on the inside many times, but their presence is always discovered, and they are executed in the most barbarous fashion."

Every hair on my arms now seemed to be standing erect. "So what is being planned has little chance of success."

"Sam knows what he is doing, and with your help, we will be able to keep track of where the bodies are. We will also try to maintain radio contact so he will know what we do, but signals are easily jammed."

"Can you be a little more specific, Agent Parrella?"

"Like I said earlier, Agent Sinclair, I will know more when Sam and Selena arrive. He has two other agents in mind to go to the island with them, but they have not arrived yet. A fishing boat will take them within a few miles of the island where they will drop anchor and wait. It is not safe to get any closer. They will swim the rest of the way, carrying whatever is needed with them. It will be a race against time, and there is much to fear in getting through the jungle without being killed or captured."

"Are you speaking about wild animals?" I asked, recalling my own time on the run through the mountainous jungles of central Colombia.

"Those will not be his biggest concern. It is more likely they will stumble across a land mine, quicksand or a trap set to capture anything that gets too close to the retreat."

"What can you tell us about that?"

"There is the main house where the owner resides, a hotel with approximately 50 rooms, a casino, and several buildings where workers live and guns and other supplies are stored. All our information comes from satellite images of the island. That is why we are relying on you to tell us what you see. Sam was very explicit in saying that no other office can know what we are doing, and we do not have any of the equipment we need for such an endeavor here. Without delays, they hope to breach the resort around midnight. The goal is not to go in with guns. It is simply to ascertain who is there and what plans are being made. While Robert Evans appears to be running this part of the operation, he's never had more than a parking ticket. Keeping him in custody when he is caught will not be easy."

"What about killing his father and Angel?" I asked as I watched Interim Director Whitman's eyes narrow.

Technically, he was the one in charge, but he was giving me enough rope to hang myself by doing what Agent Fielding had asked. And much to my surprise after all the warnings I had received about insubordination and keeping my opinions to myself, I was rising to the occasion. I would use everything I already knew and ask any question I felt was necessary to see my son's father return home. If I was fired for doing so, it would be a small price to pay for trying to save people's lives.

"No definitive proof has ever been found linking him to those deaths. This mission is to plant surveillance equipment and make a clean getaway. Teams will be organized to follow the major players once they leave the island, but there is little anyone can do while they are there."

"Nonetheless, your goal is to do so without any confrontations or violence," I said. "I understand that few people believe in Lila's innocence, but we wouldn't have come this far without her help."

"While I would like to feel as you do, Agent Sinclair, there is nothing to indicate that we are not walking into a trap. Miss Rivers may have been giving you clues to draw Sam to a place where he can be eliminated. She knows you work for different agencies, but she also knows how close you have become and how determined you are to stop the people who have threatened the life of your son. Sam told me about her past. If she has switched sides, she will use what she knows to make sure she does not become another casualty. You would do well not to place too much faith in her right now. If she makes no move against us, she will have nothing to fear."

I reached for the back of a chair as my knees began to give way and the screen went dark.

"I guess all we can do now is wait," Interim Director Whitman said. "I don't like running this part of the operation from so far away, but Agent Fielding was very specific in his demands. Satellite imaging will show us where everyone is, but without radio contact, we won't be able to help anyone on the ground. Is everything ready on our end, Agent Barnes?"

"Yes, sir," the young agent with the dark, inquisitive eyes said as he brought the satellite image to the screen. "Things will look different after dark, but this gives us the general layout of the island and how many people are already there."

The beach, the marina, the hotel, the outbuildings, and the swimming pool were clearly visible. Each person moving around in the sun or shade was shown as a blue or red figure, often outlined in yellow. That included the guards armed with machine guns and standing at intervals along the wall surrounding the entire compound. The chance of our people getting inside was minima. And finding a specific individual, like Lila or Robert Evans, would be impossible. I wanted to contact her again. We needed her exact location, but any attempt at communication would only increase her likelihood of getting caught.

"Can you get any closer?" the interim director asked.

"I can try, sir. What we really need is the ability to hack into the live feeds already established, but whomever is running them knows how to do his or her job. Transmissions are bouncing all over the place. If our people can penetrate the perimeter of the compound, we might be able to pick up their signal, but until then, we can only go with what we already have."

Since it was unclear how long we would have to wait until we were contacted again, I decided to keep digging into the lives of people we already knew were involved. All Intel gathered about Lupe, Carlos, Alma or even Eloise let me know that they would not make an appearance at the meeting. They were too well known, highly recognizable, and at the top of the DEA's most-wanted list. But the fact that Robert Evans could still move around unencumbered told me that I was missing something important.

He was an international playboy with known connections to several cartels, and yet he had never been brought in for questioning. In fact, he appeared to be nothing more than a minor player until the night he killed his own father. Was that simply a matter of family revenge or the event that catapulted him to the helm? I was still having trouble believing that the Sevilles or the Mendozas would become subservient to anyone. It was a conundrum I didn't have the skills or the information to solve, but Lila would be able to answer many of the questions I had if we could just get her out off the island alive.

Instead of going directly back to pile of papers I had gone through so many times in the past, I moved to a quiet corner of the large room where agents were feverishly working to make sure everything was in place when Agent Fielding confirmed that he was ready to make his move. I wasn't at all sure the mission would be successful, but I couldn't give in to doubt or uncertainty now. So I placed a call to Agent Howard to see if he had learned anything new about Lila that might help me convince the DEA that, despite how things looked right now, she was on our side.

His voice was filled with concern when he answered. "I'm glad you called, Reagan. Bridges has kept me appraised, as best he can, about what's going on in Texas, and it sounds as if you've run into a few snags. What can I do to help?"

"No words of advice or censure for getting in over my head again?" I asked.

"There's a lot I would like to say, but I know you're not the one calling the shots. I'm assuming you would like to know what I've uncovered about the illusive Lila. That woman has had quite an illustrious career when it comes to working with some of the people we've been trying to put away for years."

"Please tell me something I don't already know," I challenged. "Lila is on some island off the coast of Colombia with Robert Evans. We suspect a meeting to gather more financial backing is about to begin. Agent Fielding and his new partner are on their way to see what can be learned."

"So why aren't you on a plane headed for home?"

"Because Agent Fielding asked that I remain at DEA headquarters in Dallas until this mission is over. He wants me to be the one watching his back, so to speak. We'll monitor everything from the air, but it's doubtful we'll have radio contact. These people are smart. All audio and visual signals are being scrambled. The goal is to set up some sort of surveillance that will give us something we can use."

"That's not an assignment I would choose to be on, but I know you didn't call for my blessing," he replied. "We've been through everything in Lila's apartment, and I have to give her credit for being tidy and thorough. There wasn't a scrap of usable information anywhere, but it wasn't a complete bust. She had a key hidden underneath her mattress. It appears to belong to a safety deposit box, but there was nothing like that in her loft. You wouldn't happen to know what bank she uses? If she's trying to hide something, that's the only place we have left to look."

"I suppose I should have asked, but you can always pull her cell phone records. That's all most people use for transactions any more."

"Only because they don't know what we do. There isn't a system available that can't be hacked. I'll let you know as soon as I learn something more."

Our final communication with Agent Fielding was brief and came right before he stepped on the boat that would take him and his companions as close to the island as deemed safe. It was dusk. They would maintain radio contact as long as they could.

"Well, I hope they know what they're doing," Interim Director Whitman said when the line went dead. "From everything we've been able to learn about that island, they'll be lucky to make it to the interior alive."

"Please do not doubt his competence or his will to finish this assignment, sir," I said. "I've been with him in the jungle before, and he is fully aware of all the dangers they'll have to face."

"I meant no disrespect, Agent Sinclair, but I would feel a whole lot better if we had someone on the inside. I hate sending my people in blind."

Instead of replying, I looked around the room at the agents who were already gathering around the whiteboard where thermal images of everyone on the fishing boat had appeared. Spotting Agent Fielding in his wetsuit was easy, even from thousands of miles away. There was something about the way he moved that was unmistakeable. Each of the three agents with him was securing supplies in waterproof backpacks that would be carried while they swam to shore. As much as I wanted to be with them, I knew I would only be in the way. These people had been trained for missions far different than ones I would ever be sent on.

"Try not to worry," Agent Barnes said as he handed me an earbud so I would be able to hear what was going on once contact was made again. "While this isn't like dealing with something closer to home where we can pick up feeds from literally hundreds of different sources, maintaining visual contact won't be a problem."

"What's the point of being able to see where they're at if we can't alert them to potential danger?"

"Let's just take one step at a time, Agent Sinclair. I've been doing a little exploration of my own, and I believe there may be a way around some of the radio wave interference on the island—at least until our people are closer to the compound. I'm not saying what we're doing isn't without risks, but even in this office, Sam Fielding has become somewhat of a legend. He knows his way around more than just a jungle. He understands how the criminal mind works, and he's spent the past fifteen years infiltrating some of the most secure cartels in the world. He'll anticipate most everything, and we'll assist by letting him know everything we possibly can about what is going on inside the hotel and outbuildings."

"Thank you for not saying I have no right to be here."

"I remember my first year on the job. I went home most every night feeling like I had no right to be telling more experienced agents how to do their jobs. But the bottom line is that each person on a team has a crucial role to play. Agent Fielding wanted you here because he trusts your loyalty, outspokenness and ability to look outside the box. Now, let's get to work and see if we can't do something that will make sure all our people come out of this alive."

During the amount of time it took for the fishing boat to make it to the place where Agent Fielding and the others would jump into the ocean and swim towards the shore, Agent Barnes gave me a quick course about satellite surveillance and thermal imaging. We watched several yachts arrive at the dock and a number of persons disembark and head towards the hotel. Most of them were carrying weapons and had armed escorts.

By studying the topography of the island, we were able to identify landmarks and coordinates that would make the trek through the jungle less arduous and dangerous. And a closer look at the compound helped us locate the best point for getting inside. Once the fishing boat dropped anchor, I watched in silence as Agent Diaz put her arms around Agent Fielding's neck and kissed his lips before jumping into the water. The vessel would stay where it was until our people had returned. Nothing was said about what would happen if they couldn't return the way they had come.

By the time four bodies emerged on the shore, I was ready to come unglued. Interim director Whitman told them everything we had learned. There appeared to be about a hundred people inside the hotel and only four in the owner's house. It was impossible to pick out individuals, but at least one woman had been identified moving among the most recent arrivals in a way that led us to believe it was Lila. We suspected the meeting would be held in the smallest outbuilding since not everyone who had come to enjoy the amenities would have been invited to attend.

"Is there anything else you can add, Agent Sinclair," Charlie's father asked. I couldn't afford to think of him as being anything more than that until I knew he would be returning.

"Only that Lila expects us to show up. People here believe she is leading you into a trap. I can't tell you with certainty that she isn't, but my heart keeps insisting that she doesn't want to be part of any of this. I believe she is trying to protect someone—most likely her daughter. A father's name wasn't listed on the birth certificate, but . . ."

"Don't even say it, Reagan," he broke in. "I know how your mind works. I'll make sure Lila remains safe if I can, but you know how this game works by now. People are rarely who they claim to be, and we never know what's going to happen until it does. We'll try to place bugs inside the main house and in the office inside the hotel. Then we'll move on to the building you mentioned. I'm hoping you can give us more to go on by the time we reach the compound, but this signal isn't going to last."

I heard the line begin to crackle, and then his voice was gone.

"Hop to it, people," the interim director said. "I want to know if an insect hiccups by the time they make it to that compound."

My stomach was churning as I watched four bodies head into the jungle. Agent Fielding led the way, and I tried to stay focused as the movement of primary colors seem ed to contort and dance. Agent Barnes zoomed in as close as he could to the tree line, but they were soon lost to view.

"They should reach their destination in less than an hour. Let's use that time to see if we can learn exactly where this alleged meeting is going to be held. While I agree that the outbuilding would be a logical location, we have no proof. Get that for me as soon as you can."

While he walked to the other side of the room, I looked to Agent Barnes for help. I had not felt so lost and afraid since the day Neil was killed and Sam and I had faced our adversaries together. The mere thought of what I had lost made the tears surface, but the suddenly realization that I had called Charlie's father by his first name hit me with such force that I had to reach for the edge of the table to keep from collapsing. Maybe I was just taking my cue from everyone else, and maybe our declaration of love had been the turning point in our relationship. Either way, it didn't really matter. He was an integral part of my life and had been for a very long time.

"Over here," Agent Barnes was saying when I forced my thoughts back to the present. "I think we may be seeing exactly what the interim director needs."

There was indeed movement on the screen. Two men had left the hotel and were making their way across what appeared to be an expanse of grass towards the building we suspected would be the location of the meeting. A few minutes later, two others followed.

"What about Lila?" I asked. "Do you think she will be left behind?"

"Not if she's involved," Interim Director Whitman said. "And even if she isn't, Robert Evans will never let her out of his sight if she's being used as bate to get something he wants. I would suggest you give her another call, but I don't want to tip our hand."

"She already knows we're not far behind. My clues were as easy to read as hers."

But just as I finished speaking, I saw the front door leading into the hotel open and five people emerge. Two of them were in front of the others and walking very close together. I saw a glimmer of metal resting against the back of the smaller one's neck. It only took a moment to recognize who the person being escorted to a very unsatisfactory end was.

"There's your proof, Interim Director Whitman," I nearly shouted. "I can't be sure who the man is, but that's Lila being held at gunpoint. If that doesn't prove her innocence, I don't know what does."

But my words fell on deaf ears. For at that very moment, I saw the red flashes of four figures moving through the trees towards the parameter of the compound. Agent Fielding and the others had made record time.

"Get radio contact established before everything is blown to bloody hell," the interim director hollered, throwing his hands in the air. "We don't need our people going over that wall and running straight into a trap unaware."

I only hesitated a moment before picking up my phone. No shots had been fired yet. If the signal to Lila's phone had not been jammed, and she had it with her, I might be able to let her know that things were about to go horribly wrong.

"What are you doing?" the man standing near the front of the room demanded as he almost lunged in my direction.

"I'm calling the only person who might be able to help."

"Not on my watch, you aren't," Interim Director Whitman stormed. "Give me that phone. We'll take our chances that Agent Fielding and the others know what they're doing."

"No," I replied as the blood pounded in my temples. "You may not believe in Lila, but I do. Something unforeseen happened after our last communication, or her life wouldn't be in imminent danger now. That's our fault for not intervening sooner. She'll do what she can to stop a slaughter."

I watched as his mouth dropped open, but the phone was ringing, and no one was taking it from me. Perhaps everyone knew we had run out of alternatives. The pulsating sound seemed to drone on forever as we watched whatever was about to happen play out in front of our eyes.

"Lila," I said as soon as it went to voice mail. "Something ugly is about to happen, but you have not been forgotten. Don't let anyone convince you otherwise . . ."

My words drifted off as the phone was removed from my hands. "She's not going to get it, Agent Sinclair. All we can do now is pray."

Every person coming from the hotel had now entered the building and, even from our location thousands of miles away, we could see that they were in a position to open fire the moment one of our agents stepped into the clearing. Someone had let our plans be known.

Agent Barnes was still trying to make contact with Agent Fielding. I wanted to scream out in wretched misery but chose to clap my hands over my mouth instead. No one in the room made a sound as we watched our people climb to the top of the wall and then drop to the ground. But then something unexpected happened. While two of them crept towards the building where Lila, Robert and the others were waiting with their assault rifles pointed at the door; the others went in the direction of the hotel and gaming room.

"What are they doing?" Agent Barnes asked.

That caused the interim direction to rock back on his heels. "I think they've decided to split up. It's a better use of time, but it leaves every one of them more vulnerable. While Agent Fielding tries to find out what's taking place at the meeting, Agent Diaz will make sure the bugs are planted inside the hotel."

"What about the guards on the wall and inside the hotel?" was my immediate response.

"If no one opens fire, they could make it back to the jungle undetected. This was meant to be a stealth mission. That's why we didn't send in a full assault team."

I was just beginning to believe that it might be safe to breathe when the door to the outside building suddenly flew open and someone stepped onto the front porch. Red flashes from the barrels of rifles kept me from seeing who it was, but the person fell to the ground before every image in front of us was moving helter-skelter.

Each blast from an automatic weapon made my heart plummet. It was like some awful movie playing out on the screen in a movie theater, but this wasn't scripted. And then it was over, leaving only an awful, pervading silence that seemed to leech into my soul. I tried to count the number of persons who remained on their feet.

Interim Director Whitman was the first one to collect his thoughts. "Get someone on the phone," he shouted at Agent Barnes. "I'll be damned if I'm going to take this lying down."

"Whom do you suggest?" the competent, but frazzled, agent—who had befriended me and was still trying to reestablish contact with those in the field—asked.

"Get on the horn with the Director Stevens in Bogotá. He'll be able to make contact with any operatives left standing faster than we can."

I sat numbly in the chair, into which I had fallen, while waiting for the interim director to turn his anger on me. He would want vindication for what had happened, and I was his only target. But instead of lashing out at me again, he went into a vacant office and slammed the door. He was on the phone a moment later, but it was impossible to tell whom he was talking to or what he was saying. His countenance radiated nothing but anger and fear.

With my head bowed and my teeth biting into the skin on my hand, an awful realization hit me. The only reason someone would have walked outside the building when an ambush was imminent was to warn the people who were coming. I jumped out of my chair and almost ran the short distance to where Agent Barnes was still working.

"Can you retrieve the video footage we just watched?" I asked.

"Of course," he said. "It's always backed up. What are you looking for?"

"I need to see who was on that porch."

He glanced over at me. "Why? It's not going to bring anyone back."

"Maybe not, but vindication might be the only thing I have left."

"Surely, you don't think it was your friend. There's no reason to believe your message got through."

"Lila wouldn't have left her room without her phone. Even if it was only on vibrate, she would have known I would try to get a message to her."

"That's a long-shot, but who am I to question anyone's instincts or beliefs," he responded. "I just hope you're ready for what you might see. The footage may be too grainy for a positive identification, but we might be able to tell if it was a man or a woman."

He worked his magic, and in a few seconds he had isolated the exact moment when the door to the building opened. He was right about it being unclear, but the person on the front porch was wearing a skirt. It had all happened so rapidly, I hadn't noticed that before.

"Let it play," I said as I tried to reconcile myself to the fact that unless someone could prove otherwise, Lila had given her life trying to warn the very people most everyone believed she had led into a trap.

I could ascertain little from the dark background and colorful images that refused to be still in front of my eyes, but it was enough to know that Lila hadn't been shot in the head. She had simply slumped to the ground. If the bullet had missed her vital organs, and if she received medical attention in time, there was still hope.

And then something truly miraculous occurred. One of the moving images knelt down beside her, and my heart soared with joy as I saw her body being whisked away from the rest of the skirmish. Sam was the only person willing to risk his life to save hers.

I watched the rest of the skirmish play out again. But to my surprise, no one from either side stepped in to offer assistance—not even the guards stationed on the top of the walls. Apparently, meetings similar to this one were a common occurrence, and those not directly involved stayed out of the way. I kept hoping to catch a glimpse of Agent Fielding again but knew he would stay where he was until it was safe to move Lila to another location. It was impossible not to wonder if Robert Evans had been among the casualties, but our people would never be allowed to investigate. Bodies would be buried somewhere on the island, and life would go on as it always had.

Tears filled my eyes as they moved to another pat of the screen where images of persons climbing onto yachts and sailing away was being shown. There was nothing more we could do. My emotional state, ragged beyond belief, forced me to retire to a corner of the room and close my eyes. In that awful moment of hopelessness and despair, the only thing of value I could offer was sending my prayers for deliverance heavenward. There would be no real winners today, just those who were luckier than others.

We waited for nearly an hour for Interim Director Whitman to emerge, and when he did, we quickly assembled. His brow was furrowed and his lips tight. The thing that hit me most forcefully was how methodical and precise all of his movements were. My own boss felt things deeply and sometimes acted on impulse, just as I did.

"The news is both good and bad," he said, and we waited expectantly for him to continue. "Thanks to your meticulous work in locating where everything on the island was located, Sam was able to make it to one of the boats on the dock, hot wire the engine and get back to shore. He has Lila with him. Her condition is critical, and they're life-flighting her to the only place where she can get the help she needs. We're hoping she'll be able to give us something, if she ever regains consciousness. The agent with him wasn't so lucky."

"How did it happen?" someone asked.

"Details are still unclear, but they were trying to get close enough to the building to hear what was going on when Miss Rivers opened the door and stepped outside. Sam recognized her immediately, but before he could get her attention, she went down. The other agent drew the fire in his direction while Sam pulled her out of the way. He's not sure they were even aware of his presence since no one was concerned enough to check for survivors."

"What about the others?" Agent Barnes interjected.

"We're still waiting for Agent Diaz to make contact. We're hoping they were able to put the devices in place while everything else was in chaos. Due to the nature of the transactions conducted, the island has its own set of rules, and the people who come there know it. Our people were instructed to go back the way they had come, but it could be hours until we know if they made it. I'll try to answer any questions, but first, there's someone on the phone who would like to speak to Agent Sinclair personally."

Everyone turned to look at me. I felt the flush of embarrassment rush to my cheeks but didn't let that stop me from hurrying towards the open door. As much as I wanted to hear Agent Fielding's voice, I wasn't sure I was ready for what he might have say.

"It's a good thing we think so much alike, or this whole endeavor could have been a complete disaster," were the first words out of his mouth. "How did you know Lila would try to warn us that the whole thing was a setup."

"I didn't," I responded. "I'm sorry the agent with you didn't make it."

"We all knew what could happened once we set foot on that island. Without any form of communication we had to assume that things would not go as planned. That's why I sent Selena straight to the hotel to plant whatever surveillance equipment she could without being seen. It was nothing but bad luck when it came to the timing. We should have been able to set our own bugs and get away unnoticed. Those guards are basically in place to give the appearance of protection, but they're not going to bother anyone, unless the owner of the island tells them to."

"That seems like a strange way to run a business."

"He can't afford to show favorites. Leaders from any cartel are allowed access, as long as they don't get the authorities involved. Robert seems to think some of the rules don't apply to him, but I'm afraid he's in for a rude awakening."

"So he got away."

"Let's just say he wasn't among the dead at the scene, but what I really wanted to tell you concerns Lila."

I felt my breath catch in my throat. "Is she going to be okay?"

"I got her back to the mainland and will accompany her to the hospital in Bogotá once the helicopter is ready for takeoff. There's no way of knowing how extensive her injuries are. She took two bullets in the back, but she was conscious just long enough to ask for you."

"Say no more! I'll be on the first flight available. Just promise me that you'll stay with her until I get there."

"That's something you don't even need to ask. She's in federal custody, under my protection."

"I understand! Just keep her safe. As soon as they find out she's still alive another attempt on her life will be made."

"Let me worry about Lila for now. You just concentrate on getting to Bogotá. Contact the embassy when you know your arrival time, and I'll make sure someone is there to meet you. That's all the information I can give you right now."

When I explained the ramifications of what Agent Fielding had told me to Interim Director Whitman, he decided to accompany me to Colombia so he could talk to Lila the moment she regained consciousness. He would facilitate her extradition back to the states once she was strong enough to travel. I would have chosen a more personable companion for the trip, but like it or not, we were part of the same team until I was released back to the FBI. On the drive to the airport, I asked him if I could contact my parents so they wouldn't be worried about my extended absence. He gave his permission, as long as I didn't divulge any of the details. Keeping Lila alive until she could be questioned was of utmost importance to him.

My mother was more than relieved to hear my voice. "I've been frantic with worry, Reagan. I heard about the DEA agents being killed on the border. Is that part of the DEA case you've been involved with?"

"You know I can't talk about my work. I just wanted to tell you that I'll be away from my phone for a few days but will call again as soon as I can."

"What about Charlie?"

"He's in good hands for now. If that changes, I'll be sure to let you know."

"Can you at least tell me where you're going?"

"To see a friend who has been seriously injured and is asking for me. I don't know what the outcome will be, but I didn't call to receive another lecture. I just wanted you to know what I was doing."

Her heavy sigh was laced with tears. "When will all this cloak and dagger stuff end? I'm not sure how much more this family can take."

"I can't just walk away, mom."

"So you keep telling us, but we haven't seen you since the first of the year. At least tell me that things are going okay with Trey. I really like that boy."

"We're still seeing each other, but I really can't get into that right now. I'm on my way to the airport, and I'm not alone."

"Then I guess this is goodbye."

"It won't be forever. I love you, mom. Never forget that."

When the call ended, I rested my head against the back of the car seat. It would be several hours before we arrived in Bogotá, and a lot could happen before then.

Chapter 9

I called Assistant Director Bridges before leaving the Dallas International Airport to give him an update. He wasn't pleased that I was going back to Colombia since he had been assure that my assistance in the investigation would be minimal. Nevertheless, he understood my need to see Lila and finish what I had started. He would find out what he could while I was on the plane, and I was to call him as soon as I arrived. I thanked him for his help and support. He assured me that he would be happy when we could put the entire matter to rest. He wanted his agents working for him, not being loaned out to every agency that needed their help.

My first thought after getting on the plane was to try to get some sleep. It had been a gruesome few hours, and I would need every ounce of strength I could garner just to make it through whatever came next. But I couldn't stop the images of what had taken place on the island from swirling through my subconscious. Had I been there, I may have been able to help, but reality told me that I could just as easily become one of the casualties. There were still so many questions I needed to ask, but the interim director was in another section of the plane. We had been lucky to get seats at all.

Fingers of apprehension, dread and foreboding traveled the length of my arms as I retrieved my backpack from the overhead bin a few hours later. I had watched the green of the jungle and the fierce blue-gray of the sky as we made our initial descent into Bogotá. Had it only been less then a year since I first arrived in that country to take Tess Tremaine's place as a governess? So much had happened since then that it seemed like a different lifetime. I wondered what my stay this time would bring.

Interim Director Whitman was by my side as we walked rapidly through the terminal, but he was on his cell phone rather than talking to me. The noise of the other travelers made it difficult to hear his responses, but the deepening of the furrows between his brows let me know that he wasn't pleased with whatever was being said.

"Plans have changed," he announced as we made our way past the last security checkpoint. "You won't be accompanying me to the hospital just yet."

"Why not?" I asked. "My only reason for coming was to see Lila."

"Because it's been brought to my attention that you're needed for another assignment first."

I was going to express my profound agitation and near contempt for the way DEA operations were run when I looked up to see the man who had stolen my heart hurrying towards us. He was dressed in garb similar to what he had been wearing when came to take me to Carlos Mendoza's compound. The two men following closely behind him were dressed in suits. There was nothing clandestine about this part of our mission.

"Interim Director Whitman," he said, after glancing briefly in my direction. "I'm sorry for any inconvenience a change in plans brings. Agents Ahlstrom and Alvarez have been instructed to take you wherever you need to go. But a situation has arisen, and I need Agent Sinclair's help for the next few hours. Director Stevens will explain what we are up against. I can only tell you that our prompt attention is required."

"See here, Sam," he retorted. "I didn't come all this way to be told what to do."

"I understand that, sir, but Miss Rivers has not regained consciousness, and you won't be able to question her until she has.

We have people stationed at every entrance into the hospital and at her door. Trust me when I say that we have everything under control. It's doubtful anyone even knows she's here."

He snorted his annoyance. "I'll give you six hours. Agent Sinclair is a guest of the DEA this time, not one of its borrowed operatives."

"Nothing will happen to her," my former partner replied as he took my arm and led me away from the other men. "I sorry for springing this on you in such a public way, Reagan, but I knew he wouldn't allow your further involvement without some lengthy explanation. He's all about keeping things low-key and manageable."

"Do you really need my help?" I asked once we were on the escalator and heading to a lower level.

"While I would love to tell you that I have nothing but impurities on my mind, that is hardly the case right now. I've learned a few things that might prove helpful, and there are some people I want you to meet. But mostly, I need to know if you really meant what you said before I left Texas, or if you were just telling me what you thought I wanted to hear because you were convinced that I was nothing more than a dead man."

The directness of his question, coupled with the desire in his eyes made my knees weak. I wanted to believe that we could overcome anything after what we had already endured, but love and sharing a child might not be enough.

"I meant it," I admitted as we stood facing each other just inside the terminal doors.

"That's all I needed to hear," he said as the muscles around his lips quivered. "If we weren't standing in such a conspicuous place, I would give you the welcoming kiss you deserve, but that's neither practical nor wise considering the number of potential enemies swarming this city. I'm still waiting to learn if Robert Evans has made it back."

I followed him out into the sun that was partially hidden behind some angry-looking clouds. My ability to recall had never seemed like such a burden. The very air seemed to hold memories of the compound, Charlie's birth, Maria's death, our flight through the jungle and the people who had tried to both kill and help us.

Agent Fielding must have noticed the change in my countenance as we crossed a busy street. "I can still take you to the embassy where someone can oversee your visits to the hospital, but I can't join you. What I'm proposing doesn't exactly have the DEA's stamp of approval."

I had known from the moment I saw him again that he was going rogue. It was how he worked best. The confines of government restrictions and waiting for approval stifled his creativity in solving problems. In many ways, I was just like him, and that didn't sit well with any of my superiors either.

"You talked about wanting me to meet someone," I said as we came to a late-model sedan. He opened the door to the passenger seat so I get in.

"I won't lie to you, Reagan. I haven't thought this through, but if Lila doesn't wake up, we're out of leads. Selena and Travis were able to plant the devices they took with them and make if off the island, but everything else is still up in the air. She's staying on the coast for a day or two to make sure transmissions can be heard, and see if she can recognize anyone who enters the harbor from that direction. But it's my guess that anyone who could possibly help us got away before I did."

"Still, what you did will help the DEA."

He walked around the car and situated himself behind the wheel before answering. "Members from dozens of cartels use that place to launder money and make introductions, but I was hoping for more. It still blows my mind how easily Robert Evans can move from one place to another without being detained. That's another reason I want Selena to stay where she's at. Someone I thought I could trust told him what was being planned. I need to know who it was."

"And what you're planning to do today can help with that?" I asked as the car's engine turned over, and he pulled out of a parking stall.

"Probably not," he replied.

I was intently aware of the tension in his body, and the worry behind his shielded eyes. Just two days earlier, he had insisted that I remain out of harm's way so Charlie would have at least one of his parents coming home to him. Something enormous had happened to make him change his mind.

"You know I have complete confidence in you, but I need to know if Lila is going to make it before we head into the unknown again," I said as I watched another car pull into the traffic behind us. "You were being purposefully evasive with the interim director."

"That was necessary to get you away from his watchful care. He believes he's responsible for you."

"I've already cleared this visit with Bridges. I was supposed to call him when I landed."

"Let's put that on hold for now since I know exactly what he'll say if you even mention leaving the city with me. Lila is in the ICU under heavy sedation. The doctor who operated repaired what he could, but it will be touch and go for the next few days. You can wait in the room with her, hoping she'll wake up, or you can take a few hours to see what we can learn together. I'm on my way to meet Maria's mother. I think I owe it to our son since I'm the reason she's isn't here to watch him grow up."

"But why now?" I asked as my heart began to beat so rapidly I thought I might be having a stroke. This was the last thing I ever expected to hear. "We could come back when Charlie is older and no one is hunting for any of us."

"Because Magdalena Gonzalez left word at the embassy early this morning that she needs our help in finding one of Maria's younger sisters. It appears that she has become affiliated with the newly formed cartel. She refuses to talk to anyone but me. We need to find out if that's true and exactly what she wants us to do about it."

I stared out the window at the passing buildings. How quickly we had gone from a prosperous city into areas of squalor where the poor and impoverished lived. Maria's family resided in a small village. I had no idea how long it would even take for us to get there.

"What if we're walking into a trap?"

"That's most likely exactly what we'll be doing, but I can't afford not to see where this leads. I know what I said about wanting you to stay out of this, but I really don't want to do this alone."

"I thought she specified that you come by yourself."

"She's not going to care once I explain who you are and what you did to help her daughter."

I sat upright immediately, my eyes almost blazing. "You can't tell her about Charlie! His life is in enough danger. What if she wants to see him?"

"That's not even going to be offered as an option, but I am counting on her strong sense of family to get the answers we need. Do you have any idea how quickly our objectives could be met if we could get Leila Gonzalez on our side? She could lead us to everyone else."

I pushed the palms of my hands into my forehead before responding. My decision now could change everything.

"I can see why you don't want anyone else involved. What you're proposing is crazy on so many levels. If Robert Evans knew we were coming to the island, he's going to have his people watching everyone even remotely connected to us."

"You're right, but it will take time for him to regroup after this little snafu. He needed the money new investors would bring to prove what he's capable of doing on his own. While no one on that island wants to become involved in anything that doesn't directly affect them, it won't take long for him to learn that someone, who wasn't supposed to be there, moved Lila's body. I've tried to remain as inconspicuous as possible until now, but there are only so many moves I can still make before someone catches up with me. I'm going to make damned sure they count."

"You could always leave this takedown to someone else?"

"And do what?" he asked. "I'm not going into hiding, and it wouldn't do any good anyway. Unless we do something that tears this entire merger apart, none of us will ever be safe. I don't know about you, but I can't live that way."

It only took a moment for me to reach a very uncomfortable decision. "Then let's see what we can do together. I just wish Lila didn't have to be involved. Isn't there any other place in the entire country where she could have received the help she needed?"

"Can't you just accept that I did what I thought was best and leave it at that? She needed a surgeon I could trust. I know we aren't going to bring an entire organization down in one fell swoop.

They're much too big for that, but if we play our cards right, we can do some major damage."

"Do you have any idea how deep Leila's involvement goes? Affiliation could mean anything."

"The child is barely seventeen. That tells me everything I need to know, and I doubt Magdalena would have risk making that call if her daughter was doing nothing more than attending parties hosted by some of the influential people we know are involved. I can almost guarantee that she hasn't met any of the Seville brothers since they've always been the ones with the brawn who were willing to get their hands dirty but never aspired to roles of leadership. That's why the original merger makes so much sense. Even bringing Alma and Carlos into the mix is a strategical move since they're family and have the right connections. What we need to find out is if she's come in contact with Lupe or Robert Evans. It takes more than just a flair for business to mastermind the kind of operation they're trying to build."

"You make it sound so calculated and cold."

"And you think otherwise? Not every woman, or man, who has children is as compassionate, honest and as good as you, Reagan. That's why I'm glad you're the one raising our son."

I looked at him from the corner of my eye, wishing he could capture the true vision of parenthood. "You should be doing that with me."

He reached over and took my hand. "I would like nothing more than to see if I could make a go of it at being both a husband and father, but I only know how to compute risks and blend in with the bad guys. I've never stuck with a personal relationship for more than a few weeks in my entire life. What if I'm not any good at it?"

His admittance made me sad. It wasn't going to easy for him to chart a new course if we both made it out of Colombia alive—even with Charlie and me around to help.

"People don't fail at anything, unless they give up," I replied.

"I should never have asked you to come with me today. Robert Evans isn't the only member of this joint cartel who is uneasy. More mistakes will be made, and people will become even more vigilant in protecting their people and their assets. I don't want my selfishness taking you away from Charlie."

"Do you think we've been followed?" I asked, glancing over my shoulder at the traffic on the road behind us.

"No! I even switched cars at the hospital before driving to the airport."

"Then let's see what we can learn. I trust your instincts when it comes to Maria's family. I just wish there was something I could do for Isabel and Luis. I know you have them hidden somewhere."

"Not any longer. I was able to find a distant cousin, on their mother's side, who was willing to take them in. She detests Mendoza and doesn't appear to be afraid of him. As far as I know, she has no known ties to any of the cartels. That's not saying their lives will be easy, but at least they will be given a chance at having a more normal life."

I glanced out the window. Both men and women were busy working the fields by hand. They were dressed in shabby attire, and most of them were missing teeth. It made my heart ache. Maize and other crops would soon be planted, but nothing would ever yield the kind of income the production of cocaine did.

"Mendoza will never be okay with that. He was grooming Luis to be his successor."

"That might be the case, but he has more pressing problems to consider."

"Other than the obvious?" I asked.

"You can make light of it, if you want. But can you imagine three highly-motivated, and previously successful, women like Lupe, Alma and Eloise working harmoniously together for long? I'm not a psychic, but I would wager my last dollar that friction in the ranks has already begun."

"They do seem to have rather volatile natures, but how does that help us?"

"What I'm hoping is that they'll destroy each other from within and save us the trouble. But since I know that's asking a little too much, I would settle for enough discord to give us the upper hand for a change. Robert is already in trouble because his planned meeting went sideways. If we could get something else on him, or his mother, the others might decide that another play for power is in order."

It was an interesting thought, but we were past the point where speculation would be of much use. What we needed was something concrete to work with, or everything we hoped to gain would be lost.

We drove for some time in silence. The information in my head was churning around like a riptide, and I was afraid it might pull me under. There were too many questions, and if Lila didn't make it, we might never uncover any of the answers we were looking for. Protecting the people she loved was only part of the reason Robert Evans had been able to get her to go with him. He had something big on her that she didn't want to get out, and it had to be something that had happened since we'd met.

"You're lost in thought," Agent Fielding said as we made our way along a single lane road with small adobe houses spaced at intervals.

I turned to face him, wishing we could talk about a future that might never be ours. "Do you know anything more about Magdalena Gonzalez that just her name?"

"I wish I could answer in the affirmative. Maria and I didn't have much time to talk. But from what she said, her family was comprised of honest, hardworking people who detested what the cocaine industry has done to their country."

"Even if that's still true for most of them, it appears that at least one of her sisters has decided to forgo a life of poverty."

"I've been thinking about that the past few minutes and have no doubt that Mendoza's people have been keeping an eye on all of them since he found out the baby he thought was his son actually survived. He may even be the one who enticed Leila to leave her family behind. I just hope she's still alive when we find her. I would hate for a mother to lose two beautiful daughters."

Using children as pawns was barbaric, but the kind of people we were dealing with didn't just settle scores. They destroyed lives simply because it suited them to do so. "How would he even know where Maria's family came from? It seems unlikely she would have told him."

"There is no end to the number of informants cartels have on their payrolls. But I think we owe it to Maria to if we can help. She gave both of us a very special gift."

I couldn't disagree. I had thought about Maria's family often and wished there was a way I could meet them so Charlie would better understand his heritage. But I wasn't sure the present circumstances would lead to anything good, even if it brought us one step closer to shutting down the biggest cartel I had ever heard of.

Agent Fielding must have noticed my mounting apprehension. "I wouldn't presume to tell you not to worry, Reagan, but we'll know soon enough if it's a legitimate call for help. Their house should be just a few miles ahead. We'll stop before we get there and make the necessary preparations. I've filled the trunk with a small arsenal."

I fingered the revolver at my waist; grateful I had been allowed to carry it through customs and every checkpoint at both ends of the flight. I was no longer afraid of defending myself, or anyone else. We were taking about Charlie's family, and their blood ran in is veins.

Agent Fielding pulled the car to a stop behind the first cluster of buildings in the village of Villavincencio. The sun was trying to come out, and while it was still damp and chilly, it could turn into a rather pleasant day—weather-wise, anyway. There were few people on the street, but one thing I was sure of, everyone would know of our arrival by the time we made it to our destination.

"Are you sure this is necessary?" I asked as he took two semi-automatic weapons from the trunk and handed one of them to me.

"I certainly hope not, but I couldn't get word to her that we were coming. She might not even be at home, but some of her younger children will be. School isn't an option for most of the kids in these villages. They'll work in the fields when they're old enough to help provide for the family—if the cartels don't get to them first. "

"If they're without adult supervision, they might not be willing to talk to us," I replied.

He thrust a lumpy bag in my direction. "I took that into consideration. I haven't met a child yet who could refuse candy. That should keep them occupied while we find out what we need to know."

We were back in the car before I could think of anything to say. The guns would remain in the back seat—underneath a blanket and out-of-sight—but close enough to grab if necessary. We passed a large Catholic church with stained glass windows, a small garden plot and a sizeable graveyard completely overrun with crosses and headstones.

"Maria's family was luckier than most because the local priest took a personal interest in them. That doesn't always happen when there's a big congregation and very little financial support. I'd like to talk to him. Since he's a man of the cloth, he might be more inclined to tell the truth than some of his parishioners."

"Did you want to do that now?" I asked.

He shook his head. "Talking to Magdalena is the reason we're here. If she can't be found, we can do that as a last resort. I really don't want anyone else involved. I feel bad enough about Maria's family. I was hoping that having the baby out of the country would be enough to keep them out of it."

We took several additional turns down narrow, dirt roads to a less desirable part of the village where all the small, adobe dwellings looked much the same to me—old, colorless and rundown. The feeling of desperation and deterioration was hard to miss.

"That should be it on the left," he said as a little girl in a short cotton dress and brown jacket ran into the house he was indicating. "At least the cartel isn't here to greet us with guns blazing."

His cool assessment of the situation did little to alleviate my fears. Gunmen could be hiding anywhere waiting for us to get out of the car. While there were few trees in the yards to offer cover or shade, abandoned vehicles lined both sides of the road. I noticed curtain windows moving when I opened my door. That didn't seem like a very good omen to me.

"People around here don't take kindly to strangers, and interlopers of any kind mean nothing but trouble to their relatively peaceful existence," Agent Fielding said, as if discerning my thoughts.

"And they consider us members of that group."

"Look around you! Does this look like a place where tourists would come? The residents of small villages like this eek out a living the best way they can, and the cartels rule."

I no longer had to ask what he meant and tried to slow my breathing and take in more of my surroundings as he led me up a cobblestone pathway to a wooden front door that was much in need of paint. Natural vegetation that grows so profusely in damp, mountainous regions seemed to encroach on the landscape in a suffocating abundance, making me wonder if the inside of the homes ever felt warm. Overhead power lines assured me that electricity was available but, with the amount of smoke spiraling from chimneys, I doubted it was extensively used. Unlike the other houses on the street, this one had a flowerbed out front.

"I'll make the introductions, and we'll go from there," Agent Fielding said as his knuckles rapped loudly on the door. "I'm sure they know we're here, but . . ."

He didn't have to finish his thought for me. Maria's mother had taken a huge risk by contacting the authorities. If the cartels got word, their retaliation would be swift and brutal.

"Why did she do it?" I whispered as we waited for someone to answer. "She knows what will happen if the wrong people find out."

"I guess she simply ran out of options since she doesn't want the same thing to happen to any more of her children. Death isn't always the worst alternative. I just wish there was some way we could relocate the entire family."

"Is that a possibility?"

"Perhaps! The only problem is that family doesn't stop with Maria's siblings and parents. There are uncles, aunts, cousins and grandparents to consider. No Colombian would sacrifice extended family just to remain safe."

"That's tragic since I doubt Mendoza, or any of the others, would go after the entire clan."

"Are you sure about that? There's no way of knowing just how many of them are involved with the cartels by choice. I only hope our showing up doesn't start some chain reaction we can't control."

I took a step backwards, but his had shot out and detained me. "Leaving now isn't going to do any good. People already know we're here."

The hinges on the door squeaked, and the little girl we had seen run into the house poked her head out. She had beautiful dark eyes that reminded me so much of Maria and appeared to be be no more than five or six.

Agent Fielding spoke to her in Spanish, telling her who we were and asking that we be allowed to speak to her mother. I glanced behind me as I heard a vehicle approach. It didn't stop but slowed down considerably as it passed by the house. I was almost certain I saw the glint of a gun. The automatic weapons Agent Fielding had brought were still in the car, but we both had service revolvers hidden underneath the jackets we were wearing. They wouldn't do much good if we came under attack, but he didn't want to upset Magdalena.

And then I saw her standing just a few steps behind her daughter in a room that looked spotlessly clean. She was small-boned and delicate-looking like Maria, with a smattering of gray at her temples, but it was impossible to tell her age.

"Please come in," she said in almost flawless English. "I have been hoping you would decide it was safe enough to come. While the news available on the radio is not extensive or entirely true, one can hardly miss the amount of turbulence in my country since this new cartel has decided to make its home here."

I followed Agent Fielding inside. There were pictures on the walls, brightly colored woven rugs on the tile floor and a feeling of genuine warmth and friendliness. I could hear the sound of other children coming from an adjoining room, and the little girl who had first come to the door left to join them, but not before she was holding the paper bag we had brought with us. We were asked to make ourselves comfortable on a black leather sofa in front of a raging fire while she poured cups of tea. I took the one she offered knowing I would never drink it, but the warmth coming from the steaming liquid was comforting.

"Maria wrote to us what a fine and honorable man you were, Agent Fielding. That is why I felt I could trust you."

"I am so sorry for your loss," he replied. "Maria never wavered in her devotion to her family. You should be very proud."

"That she was able to get away from this life, yes, but she wrote to us of her life at the hacienda and her troubles with Carlos Mendoza. He is a very bad man—capable of monstrous things. I still cannot believe she became so intimately involved with him, but I suppose things like that happen when one so young is kept away from those who love her. I know you do not hold what she did against her like so many others in the agency. My daughter was not a bad person. She simply got caught up in something she was not prepared to handle, but God has forgiven her and taken her to his bosom."

"Tell us about Leila?" Agent Fielding interjected. "We can't stay long, and we need to know why you believe she has become affiliated with the cartels if we are going to be of any help."

Her downcast eyes let us know that she was hiding something big. "I understand the risk you are taking by even coming, but not even my husband knows what I am about to tell you. It would break his heart and destroy what we have left of our family. He is the most honest and brave man I have ever known and has always refused to give in to the cartel's demands. That is why I married him when my family wanted me given to someone else. I never meant to deceive so many people, but I was very young when I first discovered who I really was."

"And who is that?" Agent Fielding asked.

She didn't answer. She simply set her tea cup down on a side table and rose to her feet.

"I have six beautiful daughters, each very precious to me," she said, advancing to the fireplace and removing a photograph from its mantel before handing it to me. The faces I looked upon reminded me of angels. Each of the girls was dressed in white. Maria was the oldest—the youngest was an infant in her arms.

"They're lovely, but I still don't understand what you're trying to tell us," I replied.

She took the picture from me and put it back in its accustomed place, running her fingers lovingly over the glass before resuming her place in front of us. When she did so, I noticed that there were tears in her eyes.

"Please tell us what is obviously very painful to you," Agent Fielding said encouragingly. "Maria told me what she knew about your past. I am aware that you have been estranged from your family for many years, and that they were heavily involved with the cartels. That is why you ran away from home, and why she joined the DEA. She wanted to make a difference just as you did."

Magdalena sat like a statue on her wing-backed chair, but I could detect a look of hopelessness in her eyes. "I truly believed that my past was buried forever. No one in my family knew where I had gone or whom I had married, and then Leila ran away to Bogotá to seek her fortune as a model or an actress. She had both the looks and the drive to become very successful. I opposed her going, but she would not listen. I knew what she would find if anyone noticed her resemblance to me."

I was more confused than ever but knew I could not rush the telling of her story.

"Leila was soon meeting with an agent who began taking her to parties where she would get the exposure to become famous. He was confident in her ability to make him wealthy, but I believed I could get her to come home. So I went to the apartment where she was living with several other girls. She allowed me to come in, but she would not listen. She only glared at me with the greatest hostility—blaming me for keeping her in a hovel when she could have been enjoying the finer things in life all along. You see, she had met a member of my family—someone long forgotten by me—but someone who had come back to Colombia after spending many years in the United States with her husband and son."

I felt a sort of sickness in the pit of my stomach, and when I looked over at Agent Fielding, I knew he felt it too.

"You're related to Lupe Evans?" he asked.

The tears in her eyes were genuine and free-flowing. She wiped at them with the back of her hand.

"She is my great aunt on my mother's side and one of the most ruthless women imaginable. She learned the business from her father and was more aggressive than either of his sons or his other daughter, my grandmother. She had no intention of ever marrying. She wanted to be her father's heir, but when Walter came to Colombia looking for the backing necessary to start his own operation in New York City, she fell in love with him. The passion she felt was not shared, but she made him an offer he could not refuse. If he would marry her and take her with him, she would use her knowledge and all the family money she could get her hands on to make him the most feared and profitable businessman in America."

The light was beginning to dawn, but the rest of her story needed to be told.

"My family lost most everything, but she was gone, and there was no way of getting back what she had taken. To survive, they joined forces with another cartel."

"Mendoza's," Agent Fielding said.

"The one that has been run by different members of his family for generations. I almost told Maria when I learned that she was being sent undercover to his compound as a governess."

"Why didn't you?" he asked.

"Because I did not much care what happened to my family of origin. They have destroyed so many lives. It was very wrong of me, but I thought I could keep my little ones safe by keeping my secret. Now, I have lost two daughters. I do not want to lose any more. I will tell you all I know of my family. It may not be enough, but perhaps it will help you bring them to justice. My great aunt came back to make amends after her divorce from Walter, but from what I have learned, she now controls the largest cartel in all of Colombia. She always had delusions of grandeur, and now she has the means and the backing to take anything she wants."

"Has she threatened you?"

"She does not have to. She has Leila and will take any of my other daughters if it suits her. Amelia is thirteen and already showing signs of wanting to follow her sister to the city where she knows wealth and prominence exist."

"We will do everything within our power to help. But in case you are unaware, several attempts have already been made against our lives."

"May the Blessed Mother protect both of you," she said. "My home has never been a truly safe place, but I have tried to make it feel that way."

"Perhaps you should tell your husband what you know."

"I will do so when he returns from our shop for his noontime meal. We run a friendly society where fresh produce is sold. It does not bring in much money, but it is good, honest work, and we are respected in the community. He will be heartbroken when he learns of my deception. I have prayed my entire life that he would never have to know where I came from."

"I'm sure he will understand," I interjected.

Her smile was soft and Madonna-like. "I pray you are correct. The only man who knows of my past is Father Xavier. That is why he worked so hard to make sure Maria was able to get away from here and do something important with her life. He would have done the same for Leila, but she was always a willful child and did not want to work for what she got."

"Please go on," Agent Fielding encouraged. "There really isn't much time."

"You are right," she said. "It is just such a relief to talk about what has happened. I never meant to keep my secret forever, but as time went on, it was easier to do so than to tell my husband the truth."

During the next few minutes she related all she could remember about her ancestors and the lucrative business they had once controlled. She had enjoyed many happy times as a child on big estates in both Bogotá and the southern part of the country where they would fly into a small local airport and drive for what seemed like hours over bumpy roads that twisted and turned until they arrived at what could only be described as paradise for a child.

She couldn't remember the exact location, but the lake was crystal clear, the birds colorful and noisy, and the small creatures—like frogs, ducks and monkey—prolific. She was able to run at her leisure and explore where she wanted, as long as she stayed away from the sheds where men were constantly working.

The inside of the house where her grandparents lived was museum-like with statues, painting and artifacts that could not be touched. There were secret passageways, mysterious conversations, and the most delectable fruits imaginable. People came from the small villages nearby to work in the fields. She had never felt intimidated by the iron walls that surrounded the compound, or the men with machine guns until she reached puberty. That's when she began listening to what the servants had to say. They whispered about secret meetings, untimely murders, and the destruction caused by the amount of cocaine being processed and distributed. When she found the body of her personal maid lying face down in the driveway, she realized she did not want to be part of the life her family had chosen and began making plans to escape.

"What about the house in town?" Agent Fielding asked.

"It is still standing at 1511 Coronado Street, but I have not been inside for many years. My parents are dead, and I do not know what happened to my older brother, Salvatore. Perhaps you can find out from some public record."

"We'll see what we can do. Is there anything else you can tell us? I'm afraid you haven't given us a great deal to go on, but we certainly understand your concern for Leila much better. If Lupe Evans indeed has her, she needs to be found."

"That is all I can ask," Magdalena said. "The sins of the fathers always fall on the heads of the children, even when they are trying to do what is right. I already know what my fate will be. I am caught in the middle of something I cannot control. But perhaps you can still protect the rest of my daughters. The estate in the country I visited as a child is not far from where Carlos and Alma were raised. I met both of them when I was small. That is why I fear so much for Leila. They will use her and cast her aside before moving onto someone else. I have photos of many of the places I visited, along with one of my great aunt, but alas, they were taken many years ago.'"

My mind instantly flew back to all the pictures I had seen since beginning my work with DEA. Often some overlooked clue could be found if the right person was looking—like the moles on Alma's chin, the first names on the back of the picture of the Seville brothers, and the painting of the Mendoza ancestral home. The southern estate Magdalena had described sounded promising since there were bound to be other manors in the vicinity that would make suitable homes for the Seville Brothers and even Robert Evans.

"If you wouldn't mind, I would very much like to see them," I said.

"Then I will get them," she responded, leaving us sitting on the sofa in front of the dying embers of a once hotly-burning fire.

"I'm not sure we have time for this," Agent Fielding said. "We need to get the family away from here. I don't have a good feeling about where this might be heading."

"Where can they go?" I asked. "The cartel obviously knows about them. I'm not even sure they would be safe at the embassy."

"You're right," he said, running his hands through his hair. "But we can't just walk away. They're part of Charlie's family, and I would never be able to face my son if I didn't do everything within my power to protect them."

"How long do we have to come up with a plan?"

"None! I've been watching through a crack in the window curtains. That car we saw when we arrived is now parked across the street. I'm fairly certain others have joined it because I haven't heard the sound of children playing since we came inside. That's very unusual for this time of day."

"What do you propose?" I asked, daring myself to glance in his direction.

He reached over and took my hand. "I've always known what to do until now. Every instinct told me not to bring you with me, but I was being selfish."

"You don't have to explain," I replied as tears tickled the end of my nose. If these were indeed my last moments on earth, I needed to use them wisely. "There was no force involved. This was something we both needed to do. If we don't make it home, my family knows exactly what to do. The paperwork is already in place."

"Forgive me for taking so much away from you," he said.

I might have said something in reply, but Magdalena had returned to the room with a small bundle in her hands.

"You must go and take my daughters with you to the church where Father Xavier will get them to safety. I trust him because he has helped me before. I will find my husband and join them as soon as possible."

"I'm afraid that's impossible," Agent Fielding replied. "Gunmen are already on the street."

"So I noticed from my bedroom window. They will not attack the house directly. My great aunt would not allow that. She may be merciless when it comes to others, but I am still family. Her orders will be for them to wait until you return to your car before coming after me. Esmeralda can show you the way to the church through the back streets. If you are careful, no one will know you have gone."

"You must come with us," I replied, just as I had done with Maria so many months before.

She shook her head solemnly. "No! I must stay here and face my past. It is the only way to ensure my younger daughter's safety. Perhaps my great aunt can be reasoned with."

From what I knew about the people involved, I doubted that would be the case, but I wasn't going to argue. Maria might still be alive if she had remained behind at the compound instead of hurrying into the jungle with us.

"Are you sure they will go with strangers?" I asked.

"They will do exactly as I tell them. Please do not be afraid for me. I have lived knowing this day might come for many years. It is a small sacrifice to give your life for those you love."

Her words made the tears flow. She had accepted what I had been unable to. I immediately rose to my feet, crossed the few feet separating us and put my arms around her slim but erect shoulders. This woman would not betray a confidence, and she deserved to know the truth. I didn't even ask Agent Fielding for permission before speaking.

"There is something I must tell you before we go," I said. "Maria's son did not die in the jungle. I was with her when she died, and she asked me to take him home with me and raise him as my own. He is both beautiful and healthy. I wish I had a picture of him I could give you, but all of my belongings were taken to the embassy when I arrived just a few hours ago."

"I think I can help with that," Agent Fielding said, reaching into his pocket and pulling out his wallet. I held my breath because I knew what was coming. I had given him a picture of Charlie before he left Virginia after Neil's death. "There's something else you need to know. I'm the baby's father, not Mendoza; though she had to make him believe the child was his. He was a result of compassion and friendship, not violence and force. I only learned the truth of his parentage recently. I haven't acted the part of a father since learning he was mine, but you can rest assured that your grandson has been loved and cherished by the woman Maria chose for that role."

"Gracious, gracious," she whispered as the package in her arms fell to the floor and she took the picture Agent Fielding offered. "I have always known he was not dead. You have given me hope. I will not give up this fight. My grandson must be proud of me."

"I will tell him all about you," I promised, knowing it was something I might not be able to do. "He will know what a truly remarkable grandmother he has, and some day—God-willing—the two of you will meet."

Her moment of rejoicing soon ended. "You cannot leave dressed the way you are. I am sure something can be found that will help you blend more easily among the villagers, but do not expect any of them to help. They will look the other way if no one is about but are loyal to the cartels and will tell anyone who asks where you have gone."

She led me into a bedroom that was obviously shared with her husband. Like the main living area, there was a large cross on the wall and many photos of people I would never know. I wished I could take some of them with me. I had given serious thought as to what I might find when I met Maria's family, but nothing had prepared me for the extraordinary woman who might well be sacrificing her life to save those of her younger daughters. I felt both humbled and awed by her gracious acceptance of the hand fate had dealt to her. If I made it home to my family, I would come clean about everything—even the love I felt for a man they already believed was totally wrong for me.

I removed my pantsuit and lay it across the end of the bed. The white peasant blouse she provided was beautiful with red, gold and blue trim. It was little too snug in the wrong place, but that wasn't a great concern. The skirt came just below my knees and had generous pockets. I could put my revolver in one and my badge and money clip in the other. The shoes were hopelessly small and could never be worn, but no one would notice the ones I put back on my feet once they were covered with dust from the road. There was a red shall to cover my head and upper body.

By the time I emerged from the bedroom, Magdalena had a much-larger fabric parcel ready for me to carry, but I wasn't going to complain. It knew that a gift from a grandmother to a grandson had been added to whatever she already wanted us to have.

Three young girls were waiting beside their mother—the oldest about ten, the youngest not much more than three. They all looked scared, but I knew they would be brave.

"Amelia has gone into the village without permission," Magdalena explained when she noticed my expression of concern. "I will find her and bring her to the church. I have instructed my children to do exactly as they are told. They will not give you any trouble.

She kissed each little girl who stood there with a single object in her hands. They were dressed as if they were going out to play. I hoped they would be warm enough. It looked like it was going to rain.

We were taken into the kitchen and a door leading to a root cellar where vegetables and fruit were stored was opened. It smelled of dank earth.

"Few people know this entrance to the house exists. My husband had it built because I complained so loudly when he brought produce for me to store if there was a delay getting it to the shop. I like my home orderly."

She took the hand of the youngest child and helped her down the stairs into the cold semi-dark. A single light bulb hung suspended from the ceiling. I shivered as the first blast of cold air brought back memories of our flight through the wine cellar when we escaped from Mendoza's compound into the jungle.

"The door at the other end opens behind the vegetable garden. I pray no one will see you. Once you have cleared the back wall and are in the alley, you can look up and see the church steeple in the distance. Esmeralda knows the way. She will not get lost."

"Thank you, Magdalena," Agent Fielding said. "We will guard your children with our lives."

"They are all I hold dear," she replied. "I hope we will meet again."

I wanted to say something encouraging, but the situation was much too grim. Despite what had been said, I had no doubt that the gunmen on the street would shoot to kill if they got the chance, and any villager who saw us would not remain silent if asked if we had been seen.

It didn't take long for us to make it to the back door of the cellar through an assortment of potatoes, turnips, beets, corn and carrots. Much to my amazement, it moved silently on its hinges.

"Be safe my darlings," Magdalena told her daughters as she ushered them out into the daylight. "Do as you are told, and all will be well."

I waited for a tearful farewell, but it didn't come. Without turning around for another look at her mother, Esmeralda took her youngest sister by the hand and led us through an orchard where trees stood dormant awaiting the arrival of spring. I wanted to reach out to the middle child. These were my son's aunts, and my need to protect them was strong, but I knew that despite our best efforts something awful and unforeseen could happen. I wanted to know all of their names, but that inquiry would have to come later. Perhaps once we had made it to the safety of the church.

Nothing was said as we moved forward as fast little feet could take us, but I knew Agent Fielding was totally aware of our surroundings. He looked like he belonged to this land, just as he had when we first met. Magdalena had given him a sombrero that partially covered his face and a poncho to hide the cleanness of his white shirt so he would fit in better.

Just watching the way he moved made me realize, yet again, that the allure of having his own family might never be enough to pull him away from the life he had chosen to live. He liked helping people in distress, and right now, I felt exactly as he did. Leaving these little girls in the hands of a priest I had never met seemed more than impossible. I wanted to take them home with me, but they had to stay where they were. And I had to believe that they would soon be reunited with their mother.

I thought about the revolver in my pocket as we moved from the first street to the next one wishing I had extra ammunition in case it was needed. But angry voices coming from somewhere behind us took my thinking in different direction. I couldn't risk letting anyone know I had it while the children were with us. They had to be protected. That meant I couldn't stop walking or turn around. By the time we were two blocks away, I noticed that people were milling about as they usually did, and children were playing in the streets. Still, I kept my head down—just as I had done when we entered the village where a rickety plane was waiting so Agent Fielding could fly us away from the jungle where Maria's baby had been born.

"It's going to be oaky," he whispered in my ear as he came to walk beside me. The three little girls were only a few steps ahead. "Maria's mother knew what could happen when she walked away from her family. We have to believe that she planned carefully for this eventuality, even if she did leave her husband in the dark."

"Do you think he will forgive her?"

"Forgiveness is not an easy thing, but perhaps in their case, love will conquer all."

I hoped he was right. Magdalena Gonzalez deserved to see her children again and have her family intact.

A cool breeze lifted the hem of the blue skirt with colorful embroidery I was wearing. I would have reached down to make sure that my revolver was still inside the right-hand pocket, but the bundle Magdalena had given me was heavy and the muscles in my arms were beginning to burn from the tension brought on by our unexpected flight. I knew there was at least one large book inside, but even though my fingers moved across the surface, I was unable to tell what else the package contained. All I knew was that my son's grandmother had prepared it for him, and I would safeguard the contents with my life so he could grow up with a real sense of his rightful heritage.

But I couldn't keep my mind on fanciful thoughts for long. I needed to remain as alert as Agent Fielding who had moved away from me again. I knew he was allowing me to carrying the package because taking it from me would give our presence away faster than any other gesture. Men in villages like this one did not do the work normally assigned to women.

So I let him walk in front of me a little closer to the children. Surely Magdalena knew that Robert was next in command to his mother. He had killed his own father to secure that place of dominance and would not give a second thought to killing his cousin if she did not comply with any demands he made. Perhaps that indisputable knowledge was behind her insistence that we take the children with us.

Each ruffle of a leaf, bark of a dog, or unexplained movement made me shiver and want to increase my pace, but our best defense was not calling attention to the fact that we were in a hurry. I was amazed that no one seemed to have noticed our escape through the root cellar. Any mercenary sent to take care of business would make sure every entrance to the house was clearing visible so escape was futile.

I had to muffle an unwanted vocalization when the church bell began to ring. I knew from the position of the cloud-covered sun that it was time for afternoon siestas. God certainly moved in mysterious ways because no hostess in a place like this would allow her guests to leave without refreshment and rest during the early hours of the afternoon. Perhaps the gunmen outside were even taking advantage of the daily ritual. If so, our disappearance might not be discovered before we had time to get away—although I wasn't sure how far we would get on foot.

Leaving the car behind, with an arsenal of weapons in the truck, would be frowned on by our superiors. But the choice had been taken out of our hands the moment the second car stopped in front of Magdalena's home. We might never know if it had followed us from the airport, but we were in a great deal of danger now.

The little girls' skirts and bare feet were covered with dust, and they looked so tired and scared I wanted to take all of them into my arms at once, hold them tight and explain who we were, but I kept my distance. These beautiful children deserved so much better than being separated from their home and their mother because the cartels were mad at us, but any display of affection on my part would only confuse them and perhaps cause a scene we couldn't afford to make.

I worried continually as we made our way past numerous shops where clothing, housewares and various sundries were sold. But even the people entering and leaving the cantinas, where brightly-colored fluorescent lights displayed the kinds of alcohol that was served, didn't seem to notice us. The order we were walking in, along with the way we were dressed, made us look like any other family in the village. I wished I knew more about the Catholic faith and how to address Father Xavier when we met him, but I would have to rely on Agent Fielding to make clear why we had come.

There was no one in sight as we approached the sun-baked walls of the largest building in the village. The belfry tower loomed above our heads, and the bell had quit tolling the hour. I knew this was a house of God where people worshiped the only way they knew how. It was also considered a neutral zone—even for the ruthless vigilantes who were sent to enforce the unwritten laws of the cartels—but that didn't mean the hallowed walls would not be desecrated if the reason for doing so was great enough. I had no doubt that the capture or death of two federal agents would qualify. We had been a thorn in both the Mendoza and Seville cartels for long enough.

"Here goes nothing," Agent Fielding whispered as he pulled a mammoth wooden door open to expose the insides of the cathedral. It took a moment for my eyes to adjust to the darkness, even though the day outside was gloomy. The first thing I saw was a large crucifix with a replication of Christ's bruised, broken and bleeding body nailed to it on the wall behind an ornately carved pulpit. There was a crown of thorns on his head and nail prints clearly visible in his hands and feet. It made me shudder because the men who would soon be coming after us would not hesitate to inflict whatever torture they thought appropriate to get the answers they wanted.

The three little girls hurried inside as if they knew exactly what must be done. How I wished Charlie would someday meet them. I couldn't help but admire their courage and complete devotion to their mother. But harsh reality told me that this day was all we would ever have, and the only tangible remembrance would come from inside the package I still carried in my arms. I pulled it closer to my body as the heavy door slammed shut behind us. The darkness was only broken by a few stained glass windows and the lighted wall sconces that hung between them.

Esmeralda made her way cautiously down the isle between two long rows of wooden benches to the front of the chapel. Her younger sisters followed without making a sound. I noticed there were no doorways on either side until we got right in front of the pulpit. While Agent Fielding and I watched, she pushed back a heavy, velvet curtain and rapped lightly on a door. I stood as if transfixed, hardly daring to breath, until it opened and a man dressed in a long, brown, woolen robe with a cream-colored rope around his waist poked his head out and motioned for us to come inside.

Once we were standing in a chamber that looked like a combined library and living space with a desk, books, single bed and washstand, he spoke.

"I feared this day would soon come. So many members of my flock are being lulled away by the riches the cartels offer that there seems to be no time left for God. Did Magdalena give you any further instructions? She has been my most faithful parishioner since the day she arrived in the village many years ago."

"We were told to bring the children to you. She trusts that you know what to do and will see that they remain safe," Agent Fielding told him as I continued to survey the room that looked like it belonged in the 19th century.

Surely the Catholic church could afford better accommodations for its priests, but then maybe Father Xavier knew the importance of fitting in with his flock. They would not come to him for confessions, services or advice if they felt he was not one of them.

"I have people ready to take them away from here and make sure they are protected, but we must move swiftly. Members of the newly formed cartel are already in the village looking for two federal agents."

For a split second, I detected a look of sorrow, mingled with distrust, cross his otherwise expressionless face. I couldn't blame him for how he felt. We had brought more danger and possibly death to some of his parishioners, but we had done so unintentionally.

"We came because Magdalena asked for our help," Agent Fielding continued. "She wants to keep all of her daughters safe, even the one in Bogotá who has chosen to become involved with the cartel. I knew Maria after she went to work for the DEA."

"Ah, Maria," the old priest said. "Such a lovely, young girl—so bright, compassionate and strong. I had so hoped she would bring great honor to her family, but alas, even after such careful training she could not resist what the enemy had to offer. To bear the child of a drug lord is a very reprehensible thing."

Agent Fielding shook his head. "Please do not think unkindly of her, Father Xavier, she never lost her faith and her son did not belong to Carlos Mendoza. That was something she was forced to make him believe."

I looked over at the three little girls who stood so straight and tall, even though I knew each one of them wanted to cry. Their entire world was collapsing, and they would likely end up being raised by strangers. It was only then that I relinquished my package to a nearby table and advanced towards them. I needed to hold them just once before saying goodbye, but I had no idea what their reaction might be.

It seemed like my arms remained open for the longest time before the youngest, whose doll had dropped to the floor, walked over to me. When she put her arms around my neck, I felt my spirit soar. God would protect this little band of strangers who had come so fleetingly into my life.

"Please do not be afraid," I said in my best Spanish as the other girls looked at me suspiciously for a moment and then joined her. "I know you do not understand all that is happening today, but I am raising Maria's son. He did not die as you thought but is a beautiful, strong baby who resembles all of you in such a striking way. I wish he could be here to meet you, but I promise that he will know all about his brave little aunts who did what their mother asked, even though their hearts were breaking."

I held them until I felt Agent Fielding's hand on my shoulder. "We need to find a way out of the village, Reagan. It won't be much longer until our location is discovered, and we can't bring peril into a House of God."

When I looked up, I saw that the priest's countenance had softened.

"I am not sure what I can do to assist you," he said. "All we have is an old truck that is used to haul produce to people who are bedridden or otherwise unable to travel."

"We'll make it do," Agent Fielding said. "The car we arrived in is parked in front of the Gonzalez house with cartel members watching it. They might discover the weapons hidden inside, but if they don't, they could be sold or used however you see fit. At any rate, the papers for ownership are inside. I purchased it with my own money, so no one will come looking for it."

While the priest contemplated the proposed transaction, I rose to my feet. Most of my cash and traveler's checks were in the backpack Interim Director Whitman had taken with him to the embassy, but I had at least fifty dollars in American legal tender in a money clip in my pocket. If I gave that to Esmeralda, it would go a long way in providing for their needs until they could return to their family. But the barefoot girl in a white blouse and multi-colored skirt looked almost frightened when I extended it in her direction.

"Please take this, Esmeralda," I told her, knowing she would need help getting it turned into Colombian currency. "Maria would want you to have it so you can help provide for your younger sisters."

"I will see that she knows what to do," Father Xavier said, giving me just a hint of a smile. "The truck is behind the church loaded with produce that must be delivered to another village today. The key is in the ignition. My driver has not come in, and it would be tragic if so much food was lost to those who so desperately need it."

"Just tell us where it needs to go, and we'll make sure it gets there," Agent Fielding responded. "I have been in this country for many years and have a profound respect for the people who are fighting the cartels."

A few more words were spoken, and then we were led out another door to the back of the church where an ancient, flatbed truck had been loaded with fresh, loose produce. Father Xavier gave us directions to a small village that lay in the same direction as Bogotá and only a few miles out of our way.

"No one will suspect who are you as long as you drive slowly. Our deliveries are set and people expect to see the truck on the road today."

I hoped he was right. The number of prying eyes behind window curtains could not be calculated, and most of the people lived under the rule of the cartels and knew what would happen if their loyalty was ever questioned.

"We'll make sure the truck is returned to the church somehow," Agent Fielding told him. "And thank you for your help. I know it is a lot to ask."

"I pray God go with you," Father Xavier replied. "We do all we can to stop our people from joining the cartels, but there is so little we can offer as an alternative. Most of the people in my congregation see nothing wrong with raising coca as a crop. It has been done for centuries. What many of them do not understand is what happens once those crops are gathered. They are like children in so many ways, and I fear for them. Satan delights in preying on the innocent."

"That he does," I replied as Agent Fielding climbed into the driver's seat of the truck. I looked around to say good-bye to Maria's little sisters, but they had disappeared in another direction.

"Do not worry about the little ones," Father Xavier told me as he opened the door so I could climb into the passenger seat. "We have known this day was coming and adequate preparations have been made."

I didn't know what else to say except "gracious". The children's welfare was out of my hands. I clutched the parcel Charlie's grandmother had given me tightly as the truck's noisy engine broke the stillness of the afternoon. The day had been bittersweet, but I was glad I had come. I was taking something to cherish home to my son, and with God's continued intervention, I would soon be holding him in my arms again.

Chapter 10

I glanced out the back window of the flatbed truck hoping to catch one last glimpse of the little girls as Agent Fielding set the gear. The grinding noise almost made my teeth ache. I had seen the poverty of the Colombian village people before, but this time, it had become much more real. I blinked back tears of remorse for not being able to do more to help Charlie's family. Past experience and common sense told me that Magdalena had been living on borrowed time since the day she decided to leave her family of origin behind, but I still hoped our coming had not brought them added harm.

"I think you'd better stay out of sight until we're away from here," Agent Fielding said as the truck jolted forward. "Women would not accompany their husbands on a delivery run here. I wish I could trust the good Father since men of the cloth are supposed to have given their lives to God, but I caught a glimpse of the people hoeing in the garden as we said our brief goodbyes. They were watching us, and any one of them could have taken this load of vegetables. I hope we aren't driving into another trap. Our car will be of little use to him, even if he gets to it before it's burned."

Without making some disparaging comment, I lay down on the seat and clutched the cumbersome package to me as my stomach began a serious round of churning. He wasn't the only one to notice that all of our movements had been observed. Even the nuns who had spirited the children away moved stealthily and missed nothing.

"Maybe be he was just switching with us to be kind," I said as the gears creaked again and we picked up speed.

"I hope that's the case, but it wouldn't be the first time people affiliated with religious organizations have been on the cartel's payroll. You saw how everyone lives. Some of the people are okay with it, but those who have been to the city know there is more to living than mere existence. Offering information on where we have gone could make some peasant a relatively wealthy man."

I closed my eyes against his cynicism. I didn't want to believe that good people could give way to evil just because an opportunity for easy money came their way.

"But they know right from wrong," I insisted as I looked at the worn knees of his pants and the scruffiness of his shoes.

He knew exactly how to assimilate into this culture, and I had best listen to him if I wanted to return to Charlie. True help was nonexistent right now, and I had given away all the money I had that could have been used for bribes.

"I'm not downplaying anyone's religious or moral convictions, Reagan. I'm simply stating a fact of life around here. Despite good intentions, people get sick or hurt and need extra money. The cartels help the downtrodden when the chips are down—if they're willing to give something in return, that is."

"Do you really think someone will tell them where we've gone?" I asked as he shifted into another gear. We didn't appear to be moving any faster. From the number of times the tires rotated over the ground we couldn't be moving more than 15 or 20 miles per hour.

"Unfortunately, that's pretty much a given. We'll drive out to the main road, ditch the truck, and hopefully find a different way of getting back to Bogotá before the people who are after us make it this far."

My head shot upward, but his hand came down on top of it preventing me from being seen. "What about the produce?"

"There are plenty of people who can benefit from the extra vegetables, and the truck will be returned to the church as soon as everything is gone."

I let out a sigh of frustration and worry. "What about the little girls? Will they be okay?"

"No one will come looking for them, as long as Magdalena cooperates with her great aunt's wishes."

"And what will those be?"

"Acceptance of what has already happened and a return to the family fold where each of the little girls will be groomed to play very important parts in soliciting new business and preserving old connections."

"Magdalena would never agree to that!" I exclaimed. "She asked us to come so we could find a way of getting Leila back to her."

"She knew that was never a possibility, just as I did."

"Then why did we risk coming?"

"Because we owed it to her, and I wanted both of us to meet Charlie's family before it was too late."

"That's not a good enough answer."

"It's all I have. Magdalena knew what the outcome of her life would be if her aunt ever returned to Colombia and found out where she was. Anything, but complete family loyalty, will not be tolerated."

"But she doesn't remember anything that could hurt them."

"It doesn't matter what she's consciously aware of. She told us everything she knows because she wants a better life for all children. It's just too bad this happened before each of her daughters was old enough to make informed choices or protect themselves."

I knew what he was telling me, and my heart suddenly felt as if it would break for the beautiful woman who was my son's biological grandmother.

"She's not going to walk away from this, is she?" I asked.

Without even looking up, I knew he was shaking his head. "She will stand by her beliefs. She wanted the information she had to get into the right hands while there was still a chance of doing so. She did it in a public way so there would be no misunderstanding as to where her allegiance lays. I'm sure her house has been under surveillance for months. You can sit up now. We've left the village limits."

"What will happen to her husband and Amelia?" I asked as I straightened my back into an upright position.

His jaw hardened. "They will be given a choice. I know what the daughter will do, but I am not so certain about her husband. He may not value his wive's idealism as much as she thinks he will when he finds out his entire marriage was based on a lie."

I slumped into the door of the truck and rested my head against the window. "She was trying to protect him. Surely he'll understand that. Isn't there something more we can do to help?"

"We did the only thing she desired by getting her three youngest children away from home where they may have a chance at a better life. I'm sure she made her selection of where they will go carefully. They may not even remain in the country."

My brow furrowed. "Children deserve to be raised in a loving family. They will never be happy, even if they are safe."

"That wasn't our call to make, Reagan. I know you would like to take them with you, but getting Charlie out of the country was nothing short of a miracle. Something like that will not happen again."

I knew he was right, but Magdalena's sacrifice in sending her little ones away when she knew she would never see them again was breaking my heart. That heaviness only intensified as we drove along a two-lane road where there was very little traffic. The sky was nearly black. It had started to rain, and I was wearing a thin cotton blouse with only a light shawl to cover my head. Once we left the truck, we would be at the mercy of both the elements and people who wanted us dead.

"Were going to make it, Reagan," he said, turning to me with a half-hearted smile. "Once we get back to the city, I'll see what can be done. We're no match for a guerrilla army on our own, but we have information that may be useful to the authorities. Aren't you the least bit curious about what's in the package Magdalena sent? I'm sure it's not some great family treasure, but it has to be something she wanted protected. It might even have clues that will lead to the cartel's demise."

I was just about to untie the knot when he slammed on the brakes, nearly propelling me through the windshield since seat belts were unavailable.

"We'll leave the truck by the side of the road and catch a ride with that load of chickens and pigs. They have to be going fairly close to the city, and even if they're not, we can't afford to remain in a vehicle that only goes thirty miles an hour."

He jumped from the front seat, raced into the middle of the road and began waving his arms frantically. By the time I reached the edge of the asphalt, the angry-looking driver—with his hand laid unmercifully on the horn and swearing profusely—was pulling to a stop.

"Give me a moment to make the arrangements," Agent Fielding said, touching my arm reassuringly. "I wish you hadn't given everything you had away, but we'll make do with what I have."

He was approaching the driver before I could reply. At least he hadn't openly chastised me. I had been thinking with my heart instead of my head, but I had just said goodbye to Charlie's family knowing I would never see any of them again. I waited until a few bills had exchanged hands, and then he motioned for me to join him at the rear of the truck. Other people were already in the back with the animals. It wasn't an usual way for any villager to travel.

"Climb in quickly," he said, hoisting me upward as I grabbed for a side railing with my free hand.

The stench of wet manure was almost overpowering, but now was not the time to be squeamish. Before I had time to sit down on a bail of rotting hay, we were underway. The peasants already assembled gave us curious looks before going back to their own conversations—that were both loud and puzzling—since the local dialect scarcely resembled the Spanish I knew.

Agent Fielding pushed a goat that was trying to get at the hay aside and sat down beside me. "I'm sorry it has to be this way, but we have to keep moving."

"I understand," I replied as the first drops of heavy rain hit the top of my head. I pulled the shawl I was wearing over the package I was carrying and bent over it hoping my body would protect whatever was inside from getting wet.

I was scared, and not just for the people we had left behind. Everything Magdalena had said reminded me that all actions had consequences. While some of them could be predicted and planned for, the majority had to be dealt with as they arose. The only comfort I could draw from was knowing that members of my own family were still safe.

"Try not to worry," Agent Fielding said as his arm came to rest around my shoulders. "I tried to get you a place up front, but the seats were already taken. I told the driver that our truck had developed engine trouble, and we didn't want to be caught in a storm. I'm not sure he believed me, but money still speaks more loudly than words."

"He doesn't know who we are, does he?"

"He might! News travels fast in these parts, and even the poorest day-laborers seem to have access to cell phones. But we won't be with him long enough to make any real connections. We'll get off with the first group of people. It might take us longer to reach the city, but we can't afford to remain in one place for too long."

"You wouldn't be doing this if I weren't with you," I said as the muscles in his arm tightened. "You'd be back in the village trying to help Magdalena."

"Maybe, but I won't leave our son an orphan. I'll contact headquarters as soon as I can and let them know what happened."

"You don't really believe that will do any good."

"They'll send agents to investigate, but it's doubtful anything will be found. The cartel lost credibility when their meeting was interrupted. They have to prove that they can still be trusted."

"By doing what?" I asked.

"My guess is that they will try to placate the people who were considering becoming part of the team by making exorbitant promises they'll never be able to keep. And to keep members within their own ranks happy, they will demonstrate their ability to manage business affairs while still covering their tracks."

"That means Lila isn't safe."

"She's well-guarded, but no, she isn't safe. Once Robert finds out she didn't die at the scene, he'll move both heaven and earth to make sure she's eliminated."

"Even if she doesn't know anything."

"What she knows is irrelevant. She got the upper hand by leading us to that meeting. Her betrayal will be avenged."

"Is there any chance the Mendoza's, or even the Seville brothers, will react negatively to what happened and try to seize control on their own?"

"Interesting theory!" he responded as the rain beat down even more forcefully. "They could plan another takeover, but it would be hard getting the necessary backing since the new cartel isn't fully developed yet."

"But it could happen with the right incentive?"

My mind had begun working again. If we could get members of the inner circle to start doubting each other, like Agent Fielding had alluded to earlier that day, they might destroy themselves. But for that to happen, we needed information—whether true or contrived—that was powerful enough to cause dissension.

It wasn't long until we stopped at a small roadhouse and several male passengers got off. We disembarked with them, making sure to stay behind the truck so the driver would not see us. I was cold and completely soaked when we stepped inside. The lights were low, the music blaring and most everyone was seated at the bar with bottles of beer, or other alcoholic beverages, in their hands.

"Too bad you don't drink," Agent Fielding said, taking in the entire room with one sweeping glance. "It's just what you need to get warm."

"I'll survive," I told him, trying to minimize a full-body shiver. "Do you think they have a phone we can use? I left mine in my backpack."

"Smart girl," he replied. "I threw mine into the brush before leaving the church. Even when they've been turned off, their location can still be traced. I'm sure there's one somewhere, but I need to get you settled first. In case you haven't noticed, you're the only woman here who isn't getting paid for the services rendered. I would hate for someone to make a proposition that meant retaliation on my part. Things could get ugly in a hurry."

His concern made me smile, but I had no intention of talking to anyone. My accent alone would give me away. I just wanted to get back to the city, check on Lila and return home to my son. If I didn't do that soon, I might end up making the same sacrifice for Charlie that Magdalena had made for her daughters. Passing him off to others wasn't how I intended for him to grow up, and it wasn't what Maria had wanted when she asked me to raise him and keep him safe.

Agent Fielding led me to a corner table while I sniffed back tears I hoped he wouldn't notice. "Don't make eye contact with anyone. We can't be sure who any of these people work for."

I nodded my head in agreement, and then watched him walk away. There were fifteen or twenty men present in the small room. They all looked scruffy and gave me the chills, but perhaps that was only because they spent a great deal of time on the road. The tavern was too far away from a village to be a local hangout, and the men didn't exactly look like fieldworkers.

I fingered the package I was holding underneath the shawl. I wanted to see what it contained but couldn't exactly spread its contents out on the table. Too many prying eyes were watching.

The door opened again, and two men walked in. Their clothing alone told me they were not itinerant laborers, or even truck drivers. I lowered my head even further, wishing we were still in the back of the truck with the animals and remaining peasants. We were not that many miles away from the church, or the truck we had abandoned by the side of the road.

Agent Fielding immediately disappeared. I contemplated joining him, but if these men were looking for us, we stood a better chance of not being recognized if we were apart. They took a studied look around the room, and I felt their eyes linger on me for longer than was necessary.

Without moving anything more than my fingers, I reached for the gun in my pocket. I might be able to take both of them out if I was able to fire the first shots, but I couldn't be sure how many other men in the room were armed. My breath seemed to catch in my throat when one of them leaned over to ask the barkeeper a question. He would give us up in an instant for a very handsome reward.

The seconds ticked by slowly as I sat tensed and ready to make my move, but there were no raised voices, suspicious looks or movement in my direction. If the man wiping glasses before stacking them suspected who we were, he was keeping it to himself. I listened as the conversation ended and their feet moved back across the floor more slowly than they had done when entering. Then I waited until the door slammed shut.

The noise, that had ended rather abruptly when the two men entered the establishment, resumed. I glanced up in time to see Agent Fielding return to the room, but he didn't come directly to my table. He stopped to have his own conversation with the barkeeper, and I saw a small wad of bills exchange hands.

"I can't be sure those men were looking for us, but I've paid for the use of one of the upstairs rooms and arranged for a small meal. It's the safest place we can be right now," he said a few moments later as he sat down in the chair next to mine. "I also contacted headquarters. Giving away our location isn't something I would normally do, but public transportation is no longer an option. It's going to take an hour or more for help to arrive."

I followed him down a narrow hallway to the back of the building where a staircase led upwards. The paint was peeling from the walls leaving an ugly exposure of crumbling stucco and wood. The carpet was soiled and matted, and the smell of alcohol and stale cigarette smoke made my stomach wrench. I could hear laughter and bed springs squeaking as we made our way to the end of the hall. Apparently, the barkeeper had a very lucrative side business.

"I'm sorry I can't offer you anything better," Agent Fielding said as the door closed behind us blocking the unwelcome noise but not the smell.

"Please don't apologize," I replied while trying to decide if it was safer to stay standing or risk sitting on one of the chairs. The bed was definitely off-limits, and it wasn't only bedbugs I feared. "It's just good to be out of the rain."

"I would suggest a shower to warm up, but even I would be hard-pressed to use it. This really is a terrible place."

His honesty made me smile, and I decided that I could either complain or be pleasant. Either way, we had been given more time and there was a great deal to discuss. "Do you think it's safe to talk? The walls don't appear to be very thick."

He moved towards the window, parted the curtains and looked out. "I doubt anyone pays attention to what goes on up here. I can see the main road. We'll be able to keep an eye on any new arrivals."

I put the package I had been carrying on the table and removed the shawl, laying it over the back of a metal chair to dry. "Do you want to open what Magdalena sent, or should I?"

"You do the honors," he replied, turning from the window and joining me. "I really am hoping there is something useful inside so we can both go home to our son."

His words made my heart race. I would like nothing better than to see if we could become a real family, but we had to get out of Colombia first. My fingers fumbled with the knot that had become small and tight. But after a few attempts, it released, and I was able to spread the fabric away from the contents inside.

"What's this?" Agent Fielding asked as he reached for a large family Bible whose black leather cover was worn almost thin at the edges. "I may not be religious, but even I know that people keep track of births, marriages and deaths in these."

I shared his enthusiasm for such a gift but for a very different reason. Magdalena had given Charlie her most sacred, family treasure. It was only further confirmation that she recognized her fate and trusted that her grandson would cherish it as she had.

"Just be careful," I cautioned as he lifted it into his hands. "The pages might be very fragile."

"I understand its value," he replied as I glanced at the other items on the table. The family photo that had been on the mantel had been included, along with a crocheted blanket, a crudely carved wooden horse and a necklace and earrings of beautiful turquoise. Each item told me of a grandmother's love for a grandson she would never meet.

Tears ticked my nose and I began to cry, great sobs of mourning that wouldn't stop. The woman and girls we had met that day were part of our son's family. How could we have left them behind?

"Let it go," Agent Fielding said, putting the Bible back on the table and pulling me into his arms. "You have every right to be sad.

What we witnessed today were complete acts of selflessness and bravery. I promise to do everything in my power to find out where the little girls have been taken and make sure they're okay."

It felt good to be held close as his fingers traced a line across the back of my neck, but I knew he couldn't promise the same thing for Magdalena. She would stay true to her convictions, but I had a feeling that Amelia would chose to follow Leila, rather than go with her little sisters. There was no way of knowing what her husband would do. Betrayal, in any form, was hard to take.

"I didn't mean to fall apart," I said, once the tears had stopped enough that I was able to control my speech again. "I suppose tension and lack of sleep are contributing factors."

He kissed my forehead. "Don't ever lose your compassion, Reagan. Sometimes I feel like I've been playing these games of survival and deceit for so long that I've forgotten how to feel human. There is never a shortage of bad guys. "

I looked up into his dark, brooding eyes, only this time they seemed to be caressing me. "I don't think you've forgotten. You just need to be reminded that it's okay to have needs and desires and someone around who really cares."

"And you still care after all I've put you through?"

"More than you'll ever know," I admitted.

"I wish I could carry you over to that bed and show you just how much you've changed my life, but I want our first time to be special, and that certainly isn't here."

Despite my desire to reaffirm that we would have a first time, it could never happen unless certain conditions were met, and now was not the time to be talking about us.

"Maybe we should take a look at that Bible," I replied, pulling away from him. "Magdalena sent it with us for a reason. Were you able to tell Director Stevens what we learned? I'm assuming he's still the one in charge here."

If he was upset by my response, he gave no indication. "There wasn't time to give him much more than the basics. He'll have agents at the scene as soon as possible, but these people work fast, and they never leave survivors. As for the old family property, there are literally hundreds of estates scatted through the mountains and valleys of southern Colombia. That place could be anywhere."

"So we're back to where we started."

"Not quite," he said. "The director mentioned a huge gala being held at the Hotel Grande Ballroom tonight to celebrate the opening of a new musical comedy. Everyone of influence will be there. If we get back to Bogotá in time, he'd like us to attend."

"For what purpose?" I asked. "Aren't we already on everyone's hit list?"

"I most certainly am, but it's doubtful anyone in the city—who is not hiding from the law—even knows what you look like. You haven't met any of the Seville brothers or Robert Evans."

"Have you?" I asked.

"Not officially, but thanks to your diligence, and the photo Neva had in her possession, we know what they look like. If we could make contact with Leila Gonzalez, and describe what happened to her family today, perhaps she would give us something useful on her double-great aunt."

"Magdalena said she was very angry when they last saw each other and practically threw her out. Why would she be willing to help us now?"

"For two reasons. First, while she may not feel kindly towards her mother, she will not want to see her little sisters given to strangers."

"And the second reason?"

"Despite her enjoyment of the good life, she's still a village girl who was raised to abhor the cartels. She knows how they operate, and when she finds out that her own mother has become one of their victims, it will motivate her to seek some sort of revenge."

"You're basing a lot on the character of girl who has already proven that family values mean little to her."

"I'm trying to see her as Maria did. Leila was considered the great beauty of the family, as you can see if you look closely at the picture Magdalena sent, but she had no desire to do anything useful. She knew she could use her looks and her body to get anything she wanted. Maria was always worried about her but said she had a kind heart and would choose the higher ground when presented with the right options."

"Even if Maria was right, how do we convince Leila that we are more than just federal agents who want to bring down the people who have given her the life she always wanted?"

"I was worried about that myself until a few moments ago, but Magdalena gave us the perfect weapon to use in convincing her daughter that our interest in her family's welfare is genuine. It has to be one of those miracles you're always talking about."

My confusion was sincere. "If you're talking about the picture, we can't exactly brandish that around at a party."

"Not the picture, Reagan—the earrings and necklace. If she sees you wearing them, she'll know we've have personal contact with her family."

I glanced down at the gift Magdalena had sent for her grandson. "She could just as easily assume that we stole them and tell someone about it."

"That wouldn't be so bad! At least we would finally meet some of the people we've been looking for. I know this isn't the perfect plan, but it would certainly ease my conscience to be instrumental in reuniting Maria's sisters. Besides, we have the element of surprise this time, and no one would cause a scene at a big event like that, not even Lupe Evans. She knows the government turns a blind eye to much of what is going on, but any public disturbance must be dealt with."

I wasn't sure I agreed, but having something that belonged to Magdalena would certainly go a long way towards making an introduction. "We wouldn't have to mention Charlie, would we?" I asked.

"I don't see how that's relevant. No one in the family seemed to know of his existence until you told his grandmother."

"Was I wrong in doing that?"

He ran the back of his hand down my cheek in a most sensual way. "It was one of the most compassionate and courageous things I've ever watched you do. I know how dedicated you are to keeping our son safe, but she deserved to know that her daughter left a personal legacy."

"Still, she'll never get to know him—no one in the family will. I wish there had been time to explain how everything happened."

"She learned what was most important. We can talk more about today another time. But right now, we need to figure out what we're going to do next."

"You don't have to convince me that attending this party is the right thing to do. But I am surprised your boss would even want my help. He knows how unreasonable I can be."

"Maybe he considers it a form of payback, and maybe he just recognizes that you're the only one in a position to help."

I sank down into the nearest chair. "I guess his reasons don't really matter. My life became indelibly intertwined with the DEA the moment I agreed to assume Tess Tremaine's identity. I doubt that's going to change any time soon."

"That's my girl, and you won't be working alone. We'll be in this together, just like we've always been. The details haven't been finalized yet, but they want this cartel dismantled before it takes over the entire country. Those stealth planes Robert has commissioned are a worry to everyone because they can't be tracked in the usual way. I'm hoping that by this time tomorrow we've put such a huge dent in their operation that they'll have no choice except to call it quits."

He was acting overly-confident for my sake, but I loved him even more for giving me hope. There were so many things that could go wrong, even in a large crowd of people. And there was no guarantee that Leila would even attend the gala. All the worry and preparation could come to nothing.

"Why don't we take a look at the Bible," I suggested for a second time. "If you're right, we might find names, dates and places that could benefit everyone."

"Not until we've eaten something," he replied as we heard footsteps in the hall. "But I need you to slip into the bathroom while I see who's at the door. We don't want to give anyone a reason to talk."

I did as he asked, and once the chain on the door was removed, Agent Fielding accepted a covered platter and two bottles of water. I heard the man delivering it apologize for taking so long.

While we ate hot tamales, we tried not to talk about anything work-related. But I couldn't keep my mind from wandering. I didn't even know the first names of the two youngest girls we had left at the church, and I doubted that Magdalena's husband would be given any leniency. She may not have explained her background to him, but they had been together for over thirty years. That meant he would be considered a threat.

The food was good, and I consumed enough to keep my stomach from making very unladylike sounds, but my heart was heavy as the pages of the Bible fell open. It was easy to see that it had been read many times over the years, and I wished my own scripture study had been half so intense.

But if I thought any more about God, his many blessings or the reunion of family members—whether on earth or in heaven—I might not make it through the rest of the day. I needed a clear head if I was going to do as Agent Fielding had asked.

"Well, that was a bust," Agent Fielding said as he pushed himself away from the table after running his finger down a lengthy lists of names, dates and events. "I guess it was too much to expect an inventory of land holdings, even though the Bible appears to have come from Maria's side of the family."

"That's not exactly what Bibles are used for," I lightly chided, realizing that this might be the first time he had actually looked at one. "Not only do we know who Magdalena's ancestors are for multiple generations, including her great Aunt Guadalupe, but we also have accurate information about her husband and each of their children. I can't begin to tell you what this might mean to Charlie one day. But on a more practical side, if those names and dates were taken to a hall of records, deeds to many properties might be found."

"We'll hand the book over to someone who can work that angle while we attend the party tonight. I wish it were more of a cause for celebration, but I'll take whatever opportunity presents itself to be with the woman I love." He put his hands on my cheeks and kissed my lips. "I don't know how I ever survived in the field without you."

Despite of our dismal surroundings, and the thought of what activities usually took place within its walls, I felt a moment of complete happiness. I was with the man who had come to mean more to me than I had ever imagined possible, and I knew he felt the same way about me.

"You survived because you're the smartest man I've ever met and the most handsome too."

"Sweet-talker," he replied as the edges of his lips turned into a smile. "I'm the last person in the world your God-fearing, Christian parents would want you to bring home. Can you even imagine the chagrin of your overly-protective brothers?"

I was about to give my response when we heard a car stop in front of the roadhouse. Agent Fielding left my side and moved swiftly to the window while I reached for my gun. Regardless of what he'd said about the relative safety of the room we were in, there was no escape from the second level of the building—other than through a window or back the way we had come.

The look of relief on his face when he turned around was irrefutable. "Director Stevens came himself. He must have driven like a bat out of Hades to get here this quickly."

"You're sure it's him?" I asked.

"Couldn't miss that authoritative face, even if I wanted to. Sorry we can't continue our conversation, but maybe we can pick up where we left off after the festivities tonight. We haven't even touched the list of things I'll have to change if I want to be with Charlie and you on a more permanent basis. But know this, I am committed to giving it everything I've got."

"That's all I need to know for now," I said with a playfulness I wished could remain, but I was learning to take my moments of joy when they came.

He helped me repackage my bundle, but instead of hurrying me to the door like I supposed he would, he pulled me back into his arms. "I meant what I said, Reagan. I know I've never been a virtuous man, but I do want to change."

"Then it will happen," I said, pushing myself upwards until my lips were on his. I had loved Trey in my own way, as I had Neil, but Sam Fielding was the man I had been waiting for.

He returned my kiss, but as if on cue, the rapping came.

"You in there, Fielding?" Director Stevens asked. "Hope I'm not interrupting something important, but daylight's burning, and we have things to do."

Agent Fielding squeezed my arm. "My work will never be done here, but I promise it won't always be like this. I'm thirty-seven. I think I've remained a bachelor long enough."

My face flushed scarlet. If that was his idea of a proposal, it was a lame one indeed, but it really didn't matter. He was thinking long-term, and for now, that was all that really mattered.

Chapter 11

"Good afternoon, Agent Sinclair," Director Stevens said when I stepped into the hallway with the package I meant to protect hidden securely beneath my shawl. I would let the people at the agency have the information the family Bible contained, but I would not turn it over to them. This gift was meant for my son, and without it, I would never be able to put together a very important part of his family tree. "I wasn't expecting to see you back in Colombia after what transpired a few months ago."

"No, sir," I replied, daring myself to look at him. He appeared even more formidable than when I had demanded to take Mara's son home, but the decisions he made and the steps he took could determine the fate of a nation. "Circumstances change, and these are certainly unusual ones."

"That they are," he responded. "So why don't we try to make the most of them and get you back home before Assistant Director Bridges has my head on some proverbial platter."

Nothing else was said until we were standing outside the roadhouse in a light mist left over from the rain. Few people even glanced our way as we walked through the cantina. If they were sympathetic to the cartels they would relay what they had observed.

Otherwise, they would go about their business as if nothing unusual had occurred.

"Why don't you ride up front with the driver, Agent Sinclair," he suggested as we approached the black car that was waiting for us. "Sam and I have some strategizing to do."

"Please don't exclude me from that, sir," I said.

He frowned in my direction. "I see that your impertinence has not improved, Agent Sinclair. You're still as outspoken as ever, but since you are part of this, I suppose your input should not be discounted. I have people on the way to the Gonzalez home, but it's unclear as to what may be found. Our belief is that we're in the middle of some standoff. The men won't move until they're told to, and Magdalena will not give them any reason to storm the house until she knows her daughters are safe. It still boggles my mind that one of our own had direct family ties to Lupe Evans. What the hell was Maria's mother thinking by not informing her of that?"

"She thought she was protecting her family," Agent Fielding told him as I got into the passenger seat and smiled half-heartedly at the driver.

"Well, it was a damned foolish move!" Director Stevens replied. "If we'd known sooner, we might have been able to save more lives— including that of her daughter—and dismantle this latest threat before it had time to unleash some of its venom."

"Have you decided anything more about this evening?" Agent Fielding asked as soon as we were underway.

"Invitations to the gala have been secured for both you and Agent Sinclair, but one misstep on either side could result in a lot of innocent lives being lost."

"We'll do our best to make sure that doesn't happen. Has a place been located where Leila can be kept, provided she's there and can be persuaded to talk?"

"She wouldn't miss an opportunity like this, and a room at the hotel is being secured until we can get her to a safer location. I trust your instincts and capabilities, Sam, but if we fail to get our hands on her, the entire operation will go so far underground we may never get another lead worth pursuing. I also worry that you're too well-known to be seen in public. If Lupe knows what happened today, and who was involved, she will have people waiting."

"Then we'll just have to be ready for them. Agent Sinclair and I have in our possession a Bible belonging to Lupe Evans' family. It lists past ancestors for generations. If we could match those names to old family holdings, perhaps we could find out where the Seville brothers, the Mendoza's and even Robert Evans have relocated. I'm not saying they'll all be at the same location, but it is a place to start."

"I'll have my people look into it as soon as we get back to the city, but central records may have been doctored or pulled. Our best bet is still getting Leila away from her aunt and finding out what she knows. She's the only member of the Evan's family, other than Robert, who goes where she wants without worry of being arrested. We think she is being used to pass information."

While they talked about the layout of the building, possible escape routes, and what they hoped to accomplish by sending us to the gala, I copied the information from the Bible onto a sheet of paper. If I relinquished this family treasure into the director's hands, it would become government property and end up in some guarded facility as evidence—never to be recovered.

I refrained from making additional comments on the drive back to Bogotá, but I listened intently and fretted about the advisability of having both Agent Fielding and me at the gala. I was prepared to die in defense of my country, or even for some innocent individual, but I didn't want to be tortured and leave Charlie an orphan. He deserved better than never knowing what had happened to any of his parents.

When we got to the Colombian embassy, I was escorted to the room I had used before and left alone to prepare for an evening that might not net the results we hoped for. Even if Leila Gonzalez was at the gala, it was doubtful she would be alone. And I feared it would take more than a necklace to convince her to talk to me. She was an angry teenager who believed her parents had kept her from the life of glamour she had always wanted, and there was no way of knowing what she may have become involved with that would hamper her judgment.

The backpack I had brought through customs was sitting on the floor just inside the door, and a small tray of refreshments was waiting, but neither of those things interested me right now. I set the package Magdalena had given me on the nearest chair and untied the bow. Director Stevens had not been happy when I refused to turn the Bible over to him, but he had accepted the piece of paper with names and dates on it.

A black, form-fitting dress, along with a shoulder bag large enough to hold my service revolver, had been laid across the bed. Without even picking it up, I knew it would fit. Agent Fielding was completely intuitive when it came to securing things for me to wear. Accompanying stiletto heels stood on the floor.

After the emotional day I'd had, I wanted to call home and tell my parents how sorry I was for all the tumult I had unwittingly caused, but nothing I said right now would bring them any comfort. When I got home, I would face them directly and try to undo some of the damage my choices had caused.

Everything I needed to prepare for the evening had been set out in the bathroom, including fragrant body wash and lotion. I hurried as quickly as I could, but it was hard not thinking about everything that could go wrong. We were making far too many assumptions about people who had given us no reason to believe they were capable of normal, human feelings.

I brushed through my hair, applied what little makeup I had brought with me, and then pulled the dress over my head. The silky fabric seemed to glide down the entire length of my body like a snugly-fitting glove. I stared at my reflection in the oval, free-standing mirror for a few seconds before putting on the necklace and earrings Magdalena had sent. She had meant them as a gift for her grandson, not trinkets to be used in apprehending her daughter.

When Agent Fielding knocked on my door, I was ready. He was freshly shaven and looked wonderful, but he was not wearing a tux.

"What's up?" I asked as he brushed past me into the room.

"There's been another change. I know we were planning on doing this together, but Director Stevens has managed to convince me that the two of us walking into a room filled with possible cartels members together will only get someone killed."

"Unfortunately, I agree with him," I replied. "So what are we going to do?"

"I'm going to watch from the sidelines while you confront Leila. There isn't time to involve anyone else, and what is said must be completely believable, or she'll bolt without giving us a chance to explain."

"And you think I'm capable of doings that?"

"Just remember the look on Magdalene's face when she said goodbye to her daughters if you start to feel yourself waver. We're doing this for Charlie's family. We have to remember that, even if everything else goes sideways tonight."

"What about Lila?" I asked. "I came here to see her, not get messed up with the cartels again."

"Let's just say she's still alive, and Interim Director Whitman is there to make sure she stays that way until she can be questioned about what really happened in Texas. He wants her back in the states. Her testimony will be vital in prosecuting the men responsible for killing his people. He's not going to let anything happen to her."

"That's a little naïve, don't you think? We've both seen what the cartels are capable of doing. They tried to kill Charlie, you and me, but they succeeded with Maria, Angel, Edward and Neil."

He took my hands in his. "I would take every ounce of your pain away if I could, but even the most careful laid out missions come with no guarantees."

"So why bring Lila to Bogotá at all when you knew this was where she was most vulnerable? There had to be hundreds of other hospitals where the surgery could have been done."

"You're right! There are hundreds, probably thousands of hospitals in Colombia, but this was the only one where Dr. Perez is licensed to practice. You do remember him?"

My mind whipped back to the little clinic in a very undesirable part of the city where Agent Fielding had taken Charlie and me when we first came out of the jungle.

"Of course, I do. He was kind and helpful, although I don't remember many of the details surrounding those few days."

"I won't even state the words that come to mind when I think about my attitude back then," he said as the muscles in his jaw tightened. "I was so furious with you for sabotaging years of undercover work that it was all I could do to keep from shooting you myself, but if you hadn't been a woman of insurmountable strength and conviction, I would never know I have a son."

"I shouldn't have brought that up now," I said. "I'm sorry."

He shook his head solemnly. "I'm not, though I suppose it's not the most ideal time to talk about how we've both changed. There are so many noble and trustworthy people involved in this fight, and that includes the doctor who operated on Lila. He and his wife were instrumental in saving dozens of lives before she was gunned down, along with their only child, for being in the wrong place at the wrong time. I thought he might go into hiding, or take the law into his own hands after that, but he continues to risk his life helping others. He was absolutely the best chance she had. Anyone else may have let her die because it was what the cartel wanted."

"There's still so much I don't understand," I admitted. "The merry-go-round that has become my life is exhausting."

He kissed my hair. "I feel like that most of the time myself. I never should have asked you to come, but I will get you home to our son."

"I know you will, but I am the best chance you've got of getting Lila to talk when she does wake up. She won't say anything to the interim director. He's much to brusque."

"That thought did cross my mind, though it wasn't the deciding factor. By the way, you look ravishing. The necklace and earrings are the perfect touch."

"Do you really think Leila will recognize them?"

"I guess we'll soon find out."

He led me down the hallway. Our hands remained intertwined until we made it to the top of the staircase where we saw Director Stevens and a woman waiting near the front door.

"His wife, Veronique, will accompany you to the ballroom door, but you'll be on your own after that. A command center is being made ready in one the guest rooms. Your job will be to get Leila to leave the festivities and join you on the balcony or an outside patio.

From there, we'll get her away to a safe place where, hopefully, she'll be willing to cooperate."

The blood in my veins seemed to throb unmercifully as we made our way down the stairs. He was oversimplifying the entire mission for my benefit. I knew how hard it would be to separate Leila from her companions, if she even showed up. She would have been well-trained on keeping what she knew to herself and avoiding anyone who might pose a threat.

"I'm glad you're still willing to work with us, Agent Sinclair," Director Stevens said when we were standing in the entry hall with them. "I know what we're proposing is a deviation from what was discussed on the drive back to the city, but if anyone believes Leila is being escorted from the room against her will, there will be an exchange of gunfire. Your job is to make sure that doesn't happen. Once we have her in custody, we'll make arrangements for you to go home to your son."

"Not without seeing Lila," I reminded him.

"We'll make sure that happens. My wife will explain more about the young woman you'll soon be meeting on the drive to the hotel. She's become quite a celebrity the past few months, despite the occupation of her benefactor. The cartels need public support and will get it any way they can."

I looked from him to the woman at his side. Her skin was tinted a beautiful shade of gold, and her gown was of rose-colored silk. There was a strand of pearls around her neck, and she appeared to be about my age. It was impossible not to wonder how they had met and how long they had been married.

Without saying anything more, Agent Fielding removed a cape from the coat rack by the door and slipped it around my shoulders. The night was cold but, as promised, a limousine was waiting. The chauffeur held the door open for us.

"You can rest assured that this decision was not made lightly, Agent Sinclair," Director Stevens said as we drove through the guarded gates and into the streets of the city. "We weighed our options carefully, and you stand a better chance of approaching our target without calling attention to yourself than any of the rest of us. A fresh, young face is always a novelty at affairs like this, and Leila will be drawn to you—if for no other reason than determining just how much of a threat to her social life you may become."

"I do not wish to disagree because I support whatever decision you make, my dear, but I have been watching Leila's rise to fame," Veronique Stevens interjected. "I do not believe she would feel intimidated by any other woman. She has been groomed carefully and knows how desirable she is. Agent Sinclair's best way of reaching her is by appealing to her sense of family honor. Despite what she has become, she loved Maria. Knowing that you were with her sister when she died and have given her son a home is the best way to reach her heart and move her to the desired action."

I felt the bile rise to my throat. That was something I had no intention of doing.

As if intuiting how I felt, Agent Fielding reached for my hand. "Since the child we are talking about belongs to both Reagan and me, and several attempts on his life have already been made, I'm not sure that is our best course of action. We'll use the necklace and earrings to draw Leila away from the crowd. They belonged to her mother, and given what has taken place today, I think they will be just as effective."

"I did not know of your personal involvement, Agent Fielding, but then my husband does not share everything with me," Veronique said, taking a sip of champagne from a tall, crystal glass the director handed to her. A mini-bar had been built into the back of the limo, but I was no longer surprised by luxuries like that.

"I should have been more forthright," Director Stevens replied. "I figured you would have heard that by now."

"You forget that I seldom listen to what the servants, or agents, are saying when it does not concern their duties. Life would become much too complicated if I did, but I would never knowingly endanger the life of a child. I was just trying to be helpful. Leila is not going to be easily swayed. Her picture has been in all the tabloids lately. She has become quite the celebrity, and you can be certain that despite her aunt's seeming leniency, she is being kept on a very short leash. Getting her away from the photographers, and the people who will be watching her, will be no easy task."

"Perhaps I should be carrying a camera," I responded.

"I doubt you would get close enough for a personal conversation if you were. If there is time, give Leila the opportunity to make the first move. If her people believe she is in control, they will be less likely to interfere."

"What would you suggest as an opening remark to get her attention?" I asked.

"My advice would be to say nothing until she approaches you. Let the necklace you are wearing speak for itself. I could not help but notice how truly stunning it is, and I believe I have seen it before."

"And where would that be?" Agent Fielding broke in.

"Around the neck of Guadalupe's mother in a photograph that was taken nearly one-hundred years ago. I have always had an interest in the rich and famous, especially those in my own country. It offers a harmless diversion from the more weighty matters we are forced to deal with almost daily."

"Please go on," her husband encouraged.

"Along with all the bad they have done, the Costa family has always been a great supporter of the arts. That is why I know Leila will be there tonight. Maintaining the proper public image is what keeps Lupe Evans insulated from the rest of the world, but you must be extremely cautious. That necklace is very valuable and disappeared many years ago. Everyone believed it had been stolen, but the police were never able to determine who had taken it."

"Surely you don't believe Magdalena was responsible!" I exclaimed. "She would not have given it to us if it was stolen."

"How it came into her possession will not be the issue, as long as it is returned to the rightful heir."

"You're talking about Lupe Evans. Why would she even want it? She must know Magdalena has it, and she can buy anything she wants."

"Seeing it around a stranger's neck is all it will take for her to want it back. Public image means everything to her, as does avenging family honor. I wish I could be there to help guide the conversation since I am familiar with Leila's interests and personality, but I do not think my presence would be an advantage. People in this city know who I am and what my husband does to stop corruption and take the cartels down. I pretend I am not afraid, but that is not how I feel inside. That is why we have decided not to have any children. The thought of bringing them into a life of danger, where they could end up alone, is totally abhorrent to me."

She began sipping on the slightly-tinted liquid in her glass while I leaned back on the seat and tried not to frown. Her comment about children cut deeply, although I doubted it came from a place of insensitivity or malice. Being a mother was hard work, but the dividends that came from feeling totally connected to someone who needed more than just physical care made up for every moment of fear, frustration or panic. Magdalena understood that fierce and unshakable bond between mother and child. That's why she had given me something so easily recognizable to take home to Charlie. She knew I would recognize its dual purpose and use it to help free her daughter first.

Agent Fielding reached squeezed my hand as the driver pulled to a stop in front of the Hotel Grande. Lights inside were blazing, and people were hurrying up the marble steps to be met by a doorman in full uniform. His show of concern and familiarity in front of his boss touched my heart, but it also let me know that he had made another decision I wasn't going to like it.

"I think Reagan should handle this alone," he said. "Seeing her with your wife will only make people question who she is."

"But she's never gone undercover on her own before, and you told me yourself that she can be a liability in social situations. What makes you think she can pull this off alone?"

"Because she has more to lose than the rest of us if something goes wrong. She won't make any mistakes."

I bit my bottom lip to keep the tears from forming. I didn't want to walk into a room filled with murderers, imposters and thieves where our enemies would know exactly who I was the minute they saw what I had around my neck. There was little doubt that news of what had happened in Villavincencio had reached the ears of everyone who wanted to get rid of us.

"I see where you're coming from, Sam, but this is the only shot we have at getting to Leila Gonzalez before her aunt closes ranks," Director Stevens responded. "If she loses control of the situation . . ."

"That won't happen, sir," I interjected before he could say anything more. "I understand my limitations, but these people have unleashed havoc when it comes to my family and friends. I can assure you that no one is more committed to seeing them stopped."

He gave me a look of admiration. "In that case, we'll give you an earbud with radio transmission capabilities and see what you can do. Some of our agents are already inside the building, but they have been told not to offer assistance unless directed to do so. Sam and I will be in the command center. Get Leila to come to us, and we'll take it from there."

The lobby of the Hotel Grande was warm and inviting with it's rich colors, dark wood and multi-hued carpet that was so thick and luxurious my feet made no sound as I crossed over it to the most opulent ballroom I had ever seen. White marble pillars extended from the floor to help support an ornately painted ceiling with images of angels, gardens and blue sky. There was a dais where the producers, director and stars of the musical were stationed to receive congratulations and probably a little extra monetary support. Heavy velvet curtains covered each ceiling-high window and French doors opened onto a warp-around patio from several locations. There was music, laughter and the clinking of champagne glasses.

My first inclination was to search out the nearest place to take cover should the need arise, but if government officials, law enforcement and cartel members all felt safe attending the same function, no one would risk violence unnecessarily. They would wait until the affair was over to take care of business. I couldn't help but notice that few people with cameras had been allowed inside the hotel. This was a very formal and dignified event.

After leaving my wrap at the coatroom and giving my ticket to one of the persons stationed at the entrance to the ballroom, I stepped inside. I had been told to let Leila come to me, but without Agent Fielding by my side, I felt naked as a newborn.

And then I heard his voice through the bud in my ear. "This is a social event, Reagan. Dignitaries from all walks of life are here, but they are no better than the commoners they so openly distain. They just have more money and power."

"I would say that gives them an edge," I whispered back.

"No doubt," he replied. "Most of the federal agents will be easy to pick out since they'll only be pretending to consume alcohol and fit in. Cartel members, and the people who protect them, will be a little more difficult to spot. They're bank presidents, socialites, doctors, patrons of the arts, judges and members of the police force. The lines become blurry when trying to decide who is actually on our side."

"I don't know how you've survived the deception and games all these years. I've barely held it together the few times I've been asked to help."

"Most of the time, I find the work both stimulating and gratifying. It only gets complicated when rules are discarded or broken."

"That's quite an admission coming from you," I said as a waiter advanced towards me with a silver tray that was filled with glasses of sparkling champagne. I shook my head when he extended it in my direction.

"I can't deny that Maria might still be alive, and we wouldn't be facing the most ruthless and extensive cartel in DEA history, if I had done things differently. She was beautiful, smart, intuitive and would never have allowed her sister to become involved with their grandmother's sister if she'd had even an inkling of what was going on."

"You can't know that for sure," I said as I watched the people in the room circulate. "As much as we might like to believe we're in charge, we can't control what anyone else is going to do."

"I suppose, but you have to know that I would be with you now if I felt it was the right move."

"We're playing it cautious, and there's really nothing to fear. I just have to trust that the necklace I'm wearing will be enough to draw Leila to me because I'll never recognize her. She could look very different from the girl in the photo."

"Trust your instincts," he replied. "We came later than the other guests because we didn't want to be waiting around for a no-show. Hold on for a moment. We're getting something from one of the other agents."

I walked further into the room, my eyes alert to everyone around me. This evening couldn't come to an end fast enough for me.

"Look for someone in a red dress with a diamond choker around her neck. Leila has changed the color of her hair from black to blonde, but the roots should give it away."

And then I received what could only be described as divine intervention. When I turned around, I saw the woman Agent Fielding had just described standing in the center of a group of admirers.

"I've got her," I said a little too loudly. "She doesn't look much like her sister. At least the softness isn't there. I'll see if I can get her attention."

"Just move slowly and don't attract any undo attention."

I did as he asked, but I had nothing to offer Leila—except for the fact that three of her younger sisters had been sent into hiding simply because her mother had taken a dangerous stand. I wasn't even sure if Magdalena was still at the family home. Instinct, along with the basic nature of the people we were working against, told me that she had either been taken prisoner by her aunt or killed.

When I got to the edge of her circle, I released that assuming she would even glance in my direction would be a stretch. This young woman was flawlessly beautiful and commanded the attention of everyone around her. If I didn't want to stick out like some awe-induced groupie, I would have to make my presence known.

"You're Leila Gonzalez," I said in my best Spanish. "I have heard so much about you. You are even more lovely in person."

The group of men around her parted, and she looked over at me. Her eyes caught the necklace I was wearing almost immediately.

"Where did you get that?" she demanded. "I know it belongs to my mother."

"If you will come where I can explain, I would be more than happy to tell you."

"Why would I do that?" She raised her arm as if to call someone over, but before doing so, she seemed to change her mind. "You do not belong here. I would recognize you if you did. You are not even Colombian."

"I came here to meet you," I said, knowing the direct approach was the only thing that would work with her. "I knew your sister, Maria."

She didn't say anything for the longest time, and I knew she was weighing her curiosity over what I had to say with her allegiance to Lupe Evans. Even the entire DEA working together would not be able to save me if I was taken before the dreaded matriarch. She would have me killed the moment she knew who I was.

But even as the terror of what might happen continued to ascend, I didn't break our gaze. She would not tolerate weakness. I could tell that from the way she held her head and the straight line of her back. All the men who had surrounded her had moved away, except for one. He was young, but there was something very familiar about him. He whispered something to her that I could not hear.

"Do not worry, Henri," she said as her fingers trailed along his arm. "I am not a fool. I will see what she has to say and turn her over to you if the need arises."

His dark eyes held such contempt and loathing that complete recognition was almost instantaneous. This was Eloise Seville's youngest son. I had always thought of him as being a pampered child and not personally involved with the family business, but the man standing in front of me would not hesitate slitting my throat. Something about his time in prison must have hardened him, or perhaps he had finally come of age and was seeking his rightful place alongside his older brothers.

"What's it going to be, Leila?" I asked. "I am sure your boyfriend is only concerned for your safety, but I mean you no harm. I just want to talk about your family. We don't even have to leave this room. The balcony above will give us the privacy we need."

"Henri is not my boyfriend, though we have become close recently," she retorted. "He works for my aunt and accompanies me to many social engagements. It is not always safe for a girl in my position to be alone in a room filled with many strangers."

"I'm sure your concerns are justified. There are many people who prey on innocence."

She studied me for a few moments, but her face was too controlled to read. "I will come with you to the balcony and give you five minutes to tell me why you are wearing the only pieces of valuable jewelry my mother has. If I do not like your answer, you will hand them over to me and suffer the consequences."

My bravado was rapidly vanishing. Leila Gonzales was not as indifferent to her family as she might pretend, but she was not afraid either. She knew what her place in the cartel would be if she followed orders. It would take a great deal to convince her to walk away, and five minutes was barely enough time to explain how I had known her sister.

"That's all I'm asking," I said.

"You will wait for me here, Henri," she told the man who had not left her side. "If I have not returned in the specified amount of time you know exactly what to do."

"It is not wise," he cautioned. "We know nothing about her."

"I can take care of myself, and this is not a request. I mean to find out why she is wearing a family heirloom. This is between the two of us."

Lights flashed as she walked in front of me across the room and up the staircase to the balcony like some regal princess who knew all eyes were still upon her. I noticed that both a man and a woman took a few steps closer to where Henri Seville stood. They might be able to stop him from following us, but there would be plenty of others ready to step in and keep us from taking her away.

"Explain why you have something that does not belong to you," she said once we were alone. "My mother would not give what she holds dear to anyone she does not know and trust. Her wish was for her oldest grandchild to have it."

Her astuteness astounded me. She was no longer a naïve village girl. She knew how to store and sort useful information as easily as I did.

"I saw your mother this morning. She fears for her life because she will not back down in defending what she believes is right. Your three younger sisters have been sent away. I turned them over to Father Xavier myself."

A look of shock passed quickly over her face. "My mother may not agree with my desire for a good life, but she cannot dissuade me from it."

"You don't care that she may have already been killed?"

This time, her eyes were blazing with anger when she turned them on me. "I would have been told if that was being planned."

"Men were parked outside of the house. When your mother said goodbye, she did not believe she would ever see your sisters again. Surely you do not want them to live with strangers for the rest of their lives."

"I will find them and bring them here with me."

"That is not what your mother wanted."

"Do not tell me about my mother's desires. You said you knew Maria. How can that be since you are an American? I can tell by your terrible accent."

"I was with Maria in the jungle. She did not want this life for you either. She died for her convictions."

She grabbed my arm, and her acrylic fingernails bit into my flesh. "Henri was right. You are no friend. You are a DEA agent who wants to take away what I have found. I will not betray my aunt. I would rather die than go back to a life of poverty."

"I don't work for the DEA, Leila, and I am Maria's friend. I saw Carlos Mendoza shoot her. He didn't even care that she was carrying his child."

"That is not true," she almost hissed. "I have spoken to him in person on many occasions. He is a great man who loved my sister, even after finding out who she was working for. She was killed by the DEA because she would not betray him."

I shook my head slowly. I wanted her to surrender peacefully. "Maria was trying to get away from him. He was going to kill her the moment the child was born. The same thing will happen to you. It is only a matter of time."

"I do not believe you," she spat out, ripping the necklace from my neck with her free hand. "You stole this from my mother in an attempt to get me to believe something that is not true. Lupe Evans would not harm a hair on anyone's head."

"She arranged for Robert to kill his own father because he betrayed her. That doesn't sound like a compassionate woman to me. She may demand the same from you. Could you kill your own mother or one of your sisters? Your new life will not come without a cost. You will be asked to prove your own loyalty."

"No!" she screeched as her fingers left my arm. I hardly noticed that it was bleeding. "We have discussed this. I am her protégé. I will run everything with Robert. His wife will give him a divorce. We will be married, and together we will rule an empire that was meant to be ours."

Her outburst left me speechless, but while my mind was searching for another comeback, two strong arms reached out from behind a curtain. One hand covered her mouth, and the other one drug her away.

"Run down the back stairs as rapidly as possible," Agent Fielding said. "A car is waiting in the alley."

I didn't even wait for further directives as I darted towards the exit sign. Footsteps were already pounding up the staircase. I threw my shoes aside before the heavy door had even closed behind me and ran as fast as my feet would carry me down cold, tile steps. When I got to the the main floor, I picked up a stool and wedged it underneath the door handle. It would not stop my pursuers for long.

The smell of delectable food led me to the kitchen. I brushed past chefs, busboys and waiters as I moved beyond shelves of dinnerware, stoves and basins filled with hot, soapy water. I head the sound of breaking glass and oaths being shouted in my direction, but I didn't stop to apologize. When I stepped outside, pebbles, and other sharp objects, grazed the soles of my feet as I hurried down wooden steps and into the dark alley.

"This way," I heard someone shout from the back of a motorcycle. I hesitated, but the tires spun in the debris that covered the alley floor. "I am Agent Ramirez from the embassy. We could not risk having one of our cars seen."

Putting my life in the hands of someone I didn't know wasn't easy, but I climbed on behind him and put my arms around his waist anyway. No sooner had my body made contact with his than the door I had just walked through opened and gunfire erupted into the still, night air. I heard bullets whizzing around my head as we moved towards the end of the alley, took a corner much too sharply and drove through oncoming traffic to another side road.

"God help me," I prayed as we picked up speed. I was freezing, and I had no idea where we were going. I watched buildings go by at such a rapid rate of speed that it made my heart race and my head spin. If I had made an error in judgement, no one would ever know what had happened to me.

I rode behind him for several miles as the wind whipped my hair away from my face and goose bumps covered my arms and legs. There were no stars overhead, and the traffic was horrid. But he didn't seem to mind cutting in and out between vehicles or riding into another alley when a traffic light kept us from making the needed progress. I would have called out to see if Agent Fielding could still hear my voice, but somewhere during our flight, the ear piece had literally flown out of my ear. The only thought that gave me any comfort was knowing my service revolver was still inside the evening bag that seemed to sail through the air behind my left arm.

And then without warning, he abruptly stopped near a park where the leafless trees cast grotesque shadows in the light of widely-spaced street lamps.

"I'm sorry there wasn't time for any advanced warning, Agent Sinclair. Sam anticipated a hiccup and told me to be ready."

"What happened?" I asked. "I thought everything was going according to plans."

"Before I answer your question, we need to get you warm," he responded, removing his jacket and handing it to me. "It is thirty degrees outside, and I am not sure how long we will have to wait until your ride gets here. I would take you back to the embassy myself, but the alarm announcing our presence was sounded the minute you left the ballroom floor. You can be sure someone saw us leave. The entire hotel was swarming with Lupe Evans' people."

"Will Agent Fielding be able to get Leila away?"

"My assignment was to wait in the parking lot for his call. Smart move mentioning Henri Seville's name. He wouldn't have been the one accompanying Leila if a setup wasn't expected."

"So nothing we did came as a surprise. I thought only a few people were even aware of tonight's mission."

"I can't tell you what I don't know," he responded. "But if someone doesn't arrive within ten minutes, we're to head out of the city to a safe house."

"Is that where they'll take Leila?"

"Director Stevens will make that call, but it is doubtful they made it to the tenth floor where we had a temporary command post set up. What you did tonight was gutsy, but there will be a price to pay."

I was about to ask him what he thought that price would be when two headlights turned down the street towards us. We were still sitting on the motorcycle, but there wasn't time to make another getaway. I reached for my gun, knowing I would be able to fire at least one shot before being hit.

"Do not worry," Agent Ramirez said as the sound of a loose muffler dragging along the street made my ears vibrate. "I would recognize that old clunker anywhere."

I returned his jacket and climbed inside. The ride back to the embassy was noisy, but no one made a move against us. The driver, who preferred to remain anonymous because he was working undercover in a gang unit, told me that the streets were already crawling with gunmen hired specifically by the new cartel to protect their investments. Leila Gonzalez's abduction would be handled swiftly and without remorse for anyone who got in the way.

He also told me that I couldn't be taken directly to the embassy. It was being closely watched. I would be dropped off several blocks away and have to make the rest of the way on foot. Since it was a rough neighborhood, I would need to dress in the workman's jacket and pair of pants on the backseat and use the cap to cover my hair. I was given a password that would get me through the servant's entrance on the north side of the compound.

To say that he stopped to let me out would be an exaggeration. He merely slowed down and told me to jump. It was by God's grace alone that I didn't break something as I tumbled onto the sidewalk, but I understood the risk he was taking in even delivering me this far. I needed to look like nothing more than a drunk who had been tossed aside.

So I staggered down the sidewalk, clinging to walls as I went. That wasn't exactly a hard thing to do. My body ached and my bare feet throbbed. Vehicles passed by on the street a few yards away, vile words were shouted and even a few objects thrown in my direction. But I didn't slow my pace or lose my concentration—even when an inebriated man grabbed my arm and asked for something to drink. I simply brushed him aside and continued on my way.

I had not been on the street that ran behind the embassy, but the delivery entrance was clearly lighted. I knew a security detail was in charge of opening the gate and hoped I had been given the right password. Nothing about this night had gone as expected, but Agent Fielding's attention to details, along with his genuine concern for me, could not be discounted. I was only alive because his mind never ceased working.

I delivered the password and waited for admittance. The man behind the metal bars and thick adobe walls seemed to take his time before pushing the button that made a side gate creak open.

"Give me what you are wearing so it can be disposed of and then enter the main building through the servant's entrance," he instructed. "Once inside, you can take the back elevator to the floor where the guest rooms are located. Do not let anyone see you. Your presence cannot be made known until certain preparations have been made. The entire city seems to be on fire tonight."

His message was both cryptic and disturbing, but I took it to heart. After crossing a pebble driveway where delivery trucks brought needed supplies, I came to a heavy back door that opened into a hallway. The sound of voices let me know that people were still working, but since I was alone, I pushed the button to call the elevator and then hurried inside. When I turned around, I noticed bloody footprints on the once-clean floor.

The ride up was too short to access the damage done to my feet, but when I arrived at my destination, I looked for the nearest linen cabinet and then wrapped two clean towels around my feet. I don't know why keeping the hallway floor clean seemed so important to me. It wasn't my fault the DEA mission had turned out so badly. But when I got to my door, I heard a movement inside. I made sure my gun was ready to use before turning the knob.

"It is only me," Veronique Stevens said from a corner of the room where she was sitting in a chair in the lamplight. She was still wearing the evening gown I had seen her in just a few hours earlier. "I have been waiting forever for you to arrive."

I stepped into the room and closed the door before the shivering began again. "Can you tell me what's been going on?"

"I am still in the dark as to what happened once you left the floor of the ballroom. We will find out what we can as soon as we get you warmed up and see to your injuries."

I wanted to argue, but as I wrapped my hands around my arms I knew I would crash if the proper precautions were not taken. "A quick shower is all I need."

"As you wish," she responded. "I will come back with a warm robe and the needed medical supplies."

She left me alone, and I headed into the bathroom where I turned on the water and removed my torn and soiled dress. I didn't bother looking into the mirror. My reflection would only confirm the fact that I was lucky to be alive.

The scratch on my arm—inflicted by Leila's fingernails—had quit bleeding. But the water did not run clear. It would take time for the cuts and abrasions on the bottom of my feet to heal.

Veronique dressed them as best she could and gave me something for the pain as I sat on the edge of the tub. Once she had finished, she led me to the bed and made sure I was comfortably settled.

"Please do not blame anyone for what happened tonight," she said. "So much of what we do cannot be controlled. There will be serious repercussions, and you must be out of the country before that happens. Guadalupe Evans has always believed that no one would dare make a move against her. That is why Leila has been allowed to wander."

"It sounds like you don't always agree with the decisions your husband makes."

"William works very hard to stop the drugs in my country, but what he does is dangerous. I live in constant fear that I will lose him. I do not wish for you to share the same kind of life, but Sam Fielding is a man not many women can resist."

I wanted to ask her what she meant but felt it wise to keep my personal feelings to myself. "Do you know where Leila will be taken now that the hotel cannot be secured? I might be able to help."

I had seen a glimmer of the girl Maria had once known when she talked about her little sisters, but Leila had completely embraced her new life. I believed she would sacrifice anyone to keep what she had found. What she didn't seem to understand was that the DEA played for keeps too. They would not let her go, and they would use any tactic necessary to get her to tell them what she knew.

"No one must learn of her location until she has decided to cooperate. I do not like to believe there are traitors within the DEA, but that would be foolish. Members of my own family are involved with the cartels. Life here is very complicated, and even those of us who are trying to make the streets safe face serious barriers."

"I'm not sure I could do it," I replied.

"You are still very young. I just wish you did not have to fear for the life of your child. I cannot imagine the depth of commitment you have made to him with your heart."

I leaned back against the soft pillows and tried not to think about Charlie. If what Veronique had said was true, I would be sent away without even knowing what had happened to his father.

"Try to rest, Agent Sinclair. There is no way to know when anyone will return. I will let you know as soon as someone has contacted me."

There was nothing I could do except follow her instructions, but rest seemed very far away. So I pulled out the family Bible Magdalena had given me and began thumbing through its pages. My fingers became almost rigid when several sheets of very thin paper materialized between two of the pages. The handwriting was neat and small, but it was in Spanish, and I wasn't sure I could decipher it correctly on my own.

"*My Dearest Family,*" it began. "*I do not know how to express the deepest feelings of my heart. I have known for many years that my secret would come out, and when it did, lives would be destroyed or lost. Still, I kept what I had learned to myself, not wanting my own shame to hang as a cloud of darkness over my husband and daughters. I renounced my heritage as a way to* cover the disgrace I am forced to bear, but I fear discovery is near, and my sweet Leila has been drawn into the same trap as my mother. I pray it is not too late to save her from some terrible fate. I tried to tell her of the evilness of the people she had become involved with when I went to the city, but she has been blinded by the promise of power and wealth and does not want to understand . . . "

It hit me with perfect clarity that Magdalena had written the letter, but why hadn't she mentioned its presence when giving the Bible to me? I quickly returned to my reading as a sense of foreboding swept over me.

"But I digress from what must be said because it causes so much pain. I am not who I pretend to be. My mother's death was not an accident, and I am the product of an illicit affair perpetrated by a wicked and dangerous man who has now gone to meet his maker and suffer for his many offenses towards God and many others. Walter Evans lured my mother into his bed while he was courting my great Aunt Lupe. She was no more than a child and already promised to the man who raised me. When she told him she was carrying his child, he threatened the lives of everyone she loved and made sure the marriage took place before she turned fourteen.

"She told no one what had happened, not even the man I believed to be my father. I found her suicide note, quite by accident, when I was ten and began plotting my own escape. I kept the horrible truth to myself until after Maria was born. I feared for her life if someone should discover the truth behind my parentage. Father Xavier promised to keep my secret and see that my children were protected if anyone found out. My husband does not even know of the great burden I have been forced to bear. When I learned that the man who had violated my mother and helped give me life was dead and found out that Robert was my half-brother, I knew that my time had run out.

"I have kept the suicide note. It will verify what I have written. I pray God will have mercy on my soul when I meet him in heaven. My daughters do not deserve the disgrace I have heaped on their heads. *I have loved them with my entire heart. Magdalena Gonzales.*"

The vileness of what I had read made it hard for me to think, and the pages slipped to the bedcover before I even glanced at the last one—my son's great-grandmother's suicide note. The implications were more than horrifying. My son was a direct heir to one of the most powerful drug cartels in the world. No wonder I hadn't been able to read Magdalena's face when I told her she had a grandson. She was thrilled to know of his existence, but it only meant that his life would always be in danger. She had sent the Bible with us because she trusted that Agent Fielding and I would know what to do with its contents.

It was hard to suppress the tears, but I couldn't allow emotions to override reason. If I turned the pages over to the DEA they would be used as weight to get Leila to turn on the cartel, but they could also push her over the edge. I hoped she and Robert had not already become intimate, but that was not the thought that made my heart race. If Lupe Evans learned of Charlie's connection to her late husband, she would have him killed.

I hurried to the bathroom as the bile rose to my throat. I had always prided myself on knowing the right thing to, but I was confronted with an impossible situation. I leaned over the white porcelain bowl as my head began to spin and everything left in my stomach came spewing out. The entire journey of the past nine months could come to an evil and inhumane end if I revealed what I knew. But if I didn't . . .

Without even attempting to stand up, I rocked back on my heels and closed my eyes. I couldn't express what was in my heart because my mind was already telling what I needed to do. But it would be on my own terms. I was through having people I did not work for give me orders and expect me to follow them.

The note Magdalena's mother had written paralleled what I had already read. The only new information was how completely her violation had cankered her soul, but she had never been strong enough to take a stand. She only hoped that the Blessed Mother would forgive her cowardliness, and she would not have to spend eternity in hell for taking her own life.

I hid the notes underneath the mattress before dressing in the one change of clothing I had left. I would demand to speak with either Agent Fielding or Director Stevens before revealing their contents.

Since my feet were wrapped in bandages, I didn't bother with shoes. I simply ran down two flights of stairs, past several agents who were on duty, and straight to Director Steven's office. A faint strip of light was coming from underneath the door. I rapped loudly before one of the agents caught up to me.

"The director isn't here. You need to go back to your room."

"I can't do that," I shot back as my nostrils flared. "I need to speak to someone with authority immediately."

"I'm afraid that's impossible," he replied, and then the doorknob turned.

"What seems to be the trouble?" Veronique Stevens said as she poked her head out

of her husband's office. It was nearly two in the morning.

"Just tell me where Agent Fielding or your husband is. What I have to say will not wait."

"But that cannot be done," she replied. "They will be detained for as long as it takes."

I pushed my way past her into the room. "I do not mean to be impolite after the help you have already extended tonight, but I know you can reach someone in case of an emergency."

"Please tell me what you think he needs to know, and then we can make a decision together."

"No!" I retorted, and I saw her lips twitch. "I might not be a member of the DEA, but I am a federal agent, and I will be treated with respect."

By this time, two other agents had joined the one who had spoken to me.

"Contact him, or I will," an agent by the name of Lopez said.

"You do not know what you are asking," she challenged him. "Interrogations are being conducted as we speak."

"I am well aware of what is going on."

"Then you know he cannot be disturbed. I am only trying to protect and help him."

"That's all any of us are doing."

"Very well," she sighed, picking up her cell phone and touching the screen. "However, you must know that I will not be held accountable for his displeasure at being interrupted."

"Do what you feel you must," he replied, taking the phone from her.

I hoped the director would answer because my gut told me that Agent Lopez had been bluffing when he told Veronique that he knew what the director was doing.

"What is it?" I heard an irritated voice say before the phone was handed to me.

I cleared my throat before answering. "It's Agent Sinclair, sir," I said in my most commanding tone. "I've discovered something you need to be aware of."

It had suddenly occurred to me that I didn't need to mention my son at all. The only information he needed was that Walter Evans had impregnated Magdalena's mother, and she was the result of that coupling. That fact alone was enough to turn the young woman I had met earlier into a raging militant, even if the unthinkable hadn't happened between her and Robert yet.

"I'm listening, but make it fast. Leila claims she would rather die than betray those who have taken her from a life of indigence and who love her more than anyone else ever has."

"She's not going to feel that way when she learns what I have to say."

"You have something useful."

"Oh, more than useful, sir. I believe it could blow the entire operation apart, but I need to be the one who tells her."

"That's impossible. We're all living on borrowed time as it is."

"Then let me help the way I have been trained to do."

"So now you're claiming to be an expert at interrogation. If I can't get her to cooperate, what makes you think you can?"

"Because we shared a momentary connection, and I believe I can build on that. I don't want to discuss this over the phone. It's much too personal."

"Very well," he responded. "I wouldn't even consider your audacious demand if it meant leaving the embassy, but there wasn't time to make other arrangements after the fiasco at the hotel. We have her in the basement. Agent Lopez can bring you here, but don't expect another miracle. This girl believes her elderly aunt will move both heaven and earth to make sure she's returned to the life she was meant to have."

"If that's what she thinks, her world is about to be shattered. I'll be there as soon as I can. Is Agent Fielding with you?"

"He's with Henri Seville. Our people grabbed him before all hell broke lose in that ballroom. I'm still waiting for a report of hospitalizations and deaths. I had hoped this could be done without violence, but it didn't turn out that way."

I told Agent Lopez that I needed to get something from my room. He followed me up the stairs but didn't say anything. Veronique Stevens was clearly upset at not being included in what was about to happen, but this was none of her business. I would do what I had to, but I would not let my son become involved again.

Agent Fielding was waiting for us in the dimly lit basement. It felt like a prison, but I knew that keeping persons of interest from escaping was part of the reason it had been constructed. He took me forcefully by the arm and led me a discreet distance away from the others, making no mention of the fact that I wasn't wearing shoes.

"I hope you know what you're doing," he said. "Getting Leila to tell us what she knows may be the last chance we have at bringing these people down. They're going to close ranks and relocate, but not before they've taken care of us."

"Read this, and then tell me that I'm making a mistake," I responded, thrusting the sheets of paper I held securely in his direction. "I found them quite by accident a few minutes ago but know with complete assurance that Magdalena meant for us to find and use them."

My heart seemed to pulsate like the roaring of a lion as I watched the expression on his face change with each line read. It was obvious his feelings of repugnance and concern equaled my own.

"Do you really want to go through with this?" he asked. "The backlash could be astronomical."

"What other choice do we have? I may not have translated each word correctly, but the idea behind what happened couldn't be missed. Incest and rape within the confines of Lupe Evans own family will not be tolerated, nor will the residual outcomes. Can you even imagine the amount of cruelty she's capable of unleashing when she finds out that the woman she thought was her niece is really her husband's illegitimate daughter? And Leila told me herself that she and Robert plan to be married and rule together once he's obtained a divorce. I don't even want to think about what that might mean. But if Lupe and Robert can be defeated, the Sevilles and Mendoza's will not be able to stand on their own. Carlos and Alma have already shown too much weakness by joining forces with them, and the Seville brothers haven't gotten their feet wet in the Colombian underworld yet."

"What about Charlie?" he asked.

"The only way we'll ever be able to watch him grow up is to get rid of everyone who has a reason to bring him harm. I would rather deal with it while we have the upper hand than take a chance with someone who does not share our personal interest in the outcome."

"You really have changed," he said. "I'm proud of both the woman and the agent you have become."

"Then help me do this for Charlie and the members of his family who deserve to be free."

"Okay," he relented. "I'll do what I can, but Director Stevens has to be included."

During the next few minutes we discussed what we could, and then I moved into the room where Leila Gonzalez sat handcuffed to a heavy, metal desk that had been bolted to the concrete floor. The look of defiance in her eyes let me know that she still felt as if she was in control, but that would not last for long. Agent Fielding and Director Stevens would watch what transpired from the other side of two-way mirror.

"Why are you here?" she asked. "I will not tell you anything."

"I don't expect you to, Leila. I only want you to listen. I have brought a letter from your mother. Would you like to hear it?"

"She is dead to me! Why do I care what she says?"

"Because a mother's love for her daughter does not end just because there has been a disagreement over how one decides to live her life."

"How could you possibly know of such things? You have not disappointed anyone."

"That's not true. No one is above making mistakes. Do you think my mother was happy when I chose a career in law enforcement? She wanted me to get married and raise a big family just as she had done. Your own mother has made mistakes she is not proud of."

"That is not true! My mother is a paragon of virtue. She would never hurt anyone."

"But still she has. You are hurting, and part of that is her fault for keeping a secret her daughters had every right to know. Surely you would recognize something that was written by her own hand."

I held the first sheet of paper in front of her eyes, but it was too far away for her to reach it. "I found this a few minutes ago in the family Bible she gave me for safekeeping. She meant for you to see it, but she does not want you to judge her too harshly for a decision she made when she was not much older than you are now."

"Give it to me," she demanded. "You do not have a right to touch anything she has written."

"Maybe I don't, but I already know what it says. The contents have me both concerned and puzzled. How can a mother not know that her true parentage will affect her children?"

"Stop playing games. I will not believe anything you are saying."

"Not even if I tell you that your grandfather is not who you think he is? Even Father Xavier knows you have been living a lie. You have every right to claim your heritage, although the reason behind that might surprise you."

She was thrashing around almost violently now. I was afraid she might hurt herself, but I had to keep going if we were going to get the desired reaction.

"I will kill you when I am free," she shouted.

"That may be true, but it won't happen before I tell you that Walter Evans is your real grandfather, not some poor peasant who had less than a peso to his name. He lured your grandmother into his bed while he was engaged to Guadalupe Costa. She was thirteen

—no more than a baby herself. And when she tried to fight back, he told her he would kill anyone who stood in his way. So you see, your connection to the family empire is very real. However, there is one problem. How do you think your benevolent Aunt Lupe is going to react when she finds out that her husband's biological granddaughter plans to marry her son?"

She didn't even ask to see the letter for confirmation. She simply put her head down on the table and didn't move for the longest time. I was afraid my sordid revelation may have shattered her fragile link with reality. I waited for someone to join us, but when that didn't happen, I knew I had to continue.

"Is there something you would like to say now?" I asked. "You can read the letter yourself. I also have a suicide note from your grandmother as confirmation."

When her head came upright, and I saw the look on her face, I realized that this girl was more like Walter Evans than I ever would have imaged. "If I give you what you want, can I walk away a free woman and keep what is rightfully mine?"

"I'm not here to negotiate a deal, Leila, but I'm sure something can be arranged. A life behind bars, in a woman's prison, is no place for a beautiful girl."

My work was done. I had opened a door, but I would never feel good about doing it. The papers were still in my hands when I left Leila behind. Like her grandfather, she knew how to survive, but the cost to her soul was enormous.

"Good job," Director Stevens said when I was standing in the hall again. "I don't know if you're lucky or blessed, but we can take it from here. Go back to your room and try to get some rest. We'll make arrangements to get you back to the states first thing in the morning."

Chapter 12

It was after four in the morning when I lay down on my bed and closed my eyes. The events of the past twenty-four hours were swirling around in my head so rapidly that I was unsure of what was truth and what was merely a figment of an overly tired mind. It seemed impossible that my beautiful, innocent son had a direct link to the formidable cartel we were trying to bring down. What would happen when Robert Evans learned that Magdalena was really his half-sister, and he was planning to spend the rest of his life with her daughter?

But of more immediate concern to me was Charlie's safety. I had done the only thing I could, but if word got out about his true lineage, there was no way to calculate the amount of danger he could be in. Lupe Evans would hate him, and if we couldn't bring her empire down, untold mayhem would be released. I had put the letters back within the pages of the family Bible and secured it in my backpack. There was no physical evidence to tie him to Walter Evans, but I wasn't the only one who knew Magdalena's secret now.

I must have fallen asleep because the sun was up when a knock on my door brought my head from my pillow. I was still wearing the slacks and shirt I had worn to interrogate Leila, and my feet were still swathed in bandages.

"Who's there?" I called out as I struggled to stand.

"Director Stevens is in his office. He asked that I bring you to him directly."

I didn't recognize the voice, but my response was immediate. "Just let me wash my face, and I'll be right there."

"There is not time for that. He is leaving in a few minutes and said he needed to speak with you first."

I hobbled to the door. My feet hurt much worse than they had the night before, but I managed to make it down the staircase without tears. He was sitting at his desk and didn't seem to notice my disheveled appearance or the way I was walking.

"It was good of you to come on such short notice. I wish I had better news to report."

I sank down into the nearest chair deathly afraid of what might be coming. "Has Leila changed her mind about cooperating?"

"She's still in a state of shock. What she just learned has tremendous moral implications because of her family's religious beliefs, but she's told us where everyone is living. I'm mobilizing forces, and we'll raid each compound simultaneously, but that doesn't mean she was telling the truth, or that she didn't keep some pertinent piece of information to herself."

"What happened in the past wasn't her fault—at least not all of it."

"Tell that to a grieving, betrayed woman! We're moving her to a place where we hope she'll be safe, but that's not what I need to tell you. Your picture is all over the news today. The family is requesting help in finding the woman who was last seen with Leila Gonzalez. A very hefty reward has been offered. I'm afraid you won't make it through airport security without being detained and questioned, perhaps even arrested."

His words hit me like a sledgehammer and shattered what little hope I had left. "They think I abducted her?"

"They think you aided in her disappearance. There is a slight difference."

"What about Henri Seville?"

"He isn't a national celebrity. This was an unfortunate oversight on our part, but we were told no photographers would be allowed inside the hotel."

"So what am I supposed to do?"

"Our plans our basically the same. We will get you out of the city by car, and then arrange for a private plane to take you to Panama. From there you will be on your own. I have talked to Assistant Director Bridges. You are to call his private line from a pay phone when you arrive, and he will tell you what has been decided."

"What about Lila?" I asked. "My entire reason for coming was to see her."

"Interim Director Whitman agrees that would be a very foolish move. However, Miss Rivers is awake and said she will speak to no one but you. We need her cooperation in case Leila's information is less than accurate."

"Then what are we waiting for?" I asked.

His smile was unexpected. "What you lack in experience, you certainly make up for in tenacity. I can see why Sam admires you so much. Why don't you get what you brought, and let's see if we can salvage a reunion. No one is aware of Miss Rivers presence in the city yet, but we need to be prepared for that eventuality."

I was trying to get my feet into a pair of shoes when Veronique appeared at my door. Her presence was mystifying after the way I had treated her the night before. She had a large woven bag and a few items of clothing in her arms.

"Please come in," I said. "I'm sorry for my past behavior, but I had information that couldn't be shared."

She walked into the room and unceremoniously dumped what she was carrying onto the bed. "My husband says I take too many liberties because I am his wife. In that way, we are very much alike. We care what happens to the men we love."

Arguing semantics with her was futile. Married or single, loving someone made taking risks and overstepping boundaries much easier to do.

"You're right," I said. "We all cross lines at times, but that doesn't mean I don't respect you or your husband. The DEA is lucky to have both of you."

"Sam is just the same," she replied. "He works very hard to do what is right. Maria was a truly beautiful woman and a very dedicated agent. I thank you for your compassion, and your willingness to give her child a home. I am sorry her family has become involved in all of this. It is the last thing she ever wanted."

"Maybe they will be okay," I said.

"I pray you are right, but you must hurry. My husband has arranged for a car to take you to the hospital. I do not know the details of what will happen from there, but he will make sure you are safely out of the country before nightfall. Please do not come here again."

She left the room before I could ask why my presence so disturbed her.

I was going to wear the dress and shoes she provided but something stopped me. Instead, I put on the white blouse and skirt Magdalena had given me the day before and put my service revolver back in the right-hand pocket. After securing the red shawl around my shoulders, I pushed the things I was preserving for my son into the shoulder bag, along with the identification I would need to get back into my own country legally. Then I piled everything else neatly on the bed so it could be removed from the room when cleaning was done.

No one came out to wish me goodbye or good luck, but Agent Perez was there to drive me to the hospital in an unmarked car. This was not how I had envisioned my return trip to Colombia. My intention had been to see Lila and make it home without getting into any trouble. Now my picture was being shown on the news, and I had unearthed another life-altering secret.

"I am sorry I cannot go inside with you, but I was told to return to the embassy directly after bringing you here," Agent Perez said when he pulled into the main parking lot at the hospital. "You should be safe as long as you remain inconspicuous. The interim director from Texas will tell you what you need to do next. He and your friend are in room 517."

My heart was heavy as I looked at him. He was about my age—inexperienced, enthusiastic and filled with unrealistic hopes and dreams.

"I never thanked you for helping me last night. I hope it didn't get you in any trouble."

"I have dealt with problems like that before. The director's wife is a good person, but she tends to think her authority is synonymous with that of her husband."

"So you trust her?"

His shoulders rose as he spoke. "How can anyone really trust someone else in the line of work we do? But I like giving others the benefit of the doubt until they prove me wrong. I wish you were working for us. There is something very different about you."

"Maybe it's because I still believe there is a God who loves his children and has a plan for their growth and happiness."

"I quit praying ages ago. We were trained to rely on our own abilities when our superiors were not around."

Without conscious thought, I reached out and touched his arm. "What we learned is important but not all inclusive. I pray continually for strength and help. It's the only thing that keeps me moving forward."

"Perhaps I should reconsider my relationship with God," he replied, looking both flushed and embarrassed. "I often feel the need for added direction when receiving some of my orders."

I made sure the heavy, wool shawl was covering my head before I stepped out of the car and watched him drive away. There were no easy answers to anything we did. Manipulating situations and lives might seem like a game, but everyone I knew was playing for keeps.

Tears tickled my nose as I made my way towards the elevator doors, but I felt a pang of fear reach my heart when I saw a rather mottled image of myself on a television screen that hung suspended from the ceiling. The caption read: "Woman wanted for questioning in the disappearance of socialite, Leila Gonzalez, who disappeared from the Hotel Grande Ballroom last night."

The picture was grainy and dark—most likely captured on someone's cell phone—but anyone who looked closely would not miss the resemblance. I realized quite suddenly that not wearing the clothing Veronique had provided was helping me blend in with the most prolific part of the crowd.

The elevator stopped on each floor. I stood at the back where I could watch as people left and entered. All it would take was one person to sound the alarm, and I would never see Charlie or my family again. But I couldn't dwell on my own struggles right now. I would only have a few minutes with Lila so the questions I asked needed to count.

No one else got off when I did. I thought that unusual because it was a big hospital with six elevators in almost constant use. I looked around to see if anyone I recognized was waiting for me, but the only people in view were the nurses working at their station. Not wanting to be recognized, I advanced quickly along the hallway towards room 517. And then I was standing at the foot of Lila's bed. The number of machines keeping her alive were hard to miss.

"It's me, Reagan," I said, brushing the shawl away from my face. "I've come to see you because I believe in your innocence and want the man who did this to you punished. But that won't happen unless you're willing to answer some very difficult questions."

I heard the interim director clear his throat, but I didn't turn to face him. His only reason for being here was to make sure she stayed alive long enough to be extradited back to the United States to face a jury and be put in a cell for the rest of her life. I wasn't going to let that happen.

"You're really here," Lila whispered as her eyes opened and she tried to focus on her surroundings. "I've been praying you would come because I want you to know what really happened. You're the only one who will understand."

"Just rest," I said, dropping the shoulder bag to the floor and brushing the damp hair away from her forehead. "I'll stay for as long as I can."

"Please do not endanger your own life by staying here with me. You need to be with Charlie."

"Why would you say that?" I asked.

Her words were slurred by grogginess, but she was fighting to remain lucid. "Because Robert will get even with me for betraying him. He heard my phone buzz when you called. I wasn't supposed to have it with me. Have you found him? I want this to be over."

I solemnly shook my head. There was no reason to lie. She understood what he was capable of doing even better than I did.

"We don't have time for unnecessary chitchat," Interim Director Whitman said in an irritated tone from the corner of the room. "I need to know who was responsible for the deaths of my people and how I can keep it from happening again."

Lila tried lifting her head from the pillow, but it fell back limply. "I told him you were the only one I would talk to."

I glanced over my shoulder at the man who had accompanied me to Colombia. He looked exhausted, but badgering Lila wasn't the way to get what he wanted. Her condition was critical, and there was no way of knowing just how long she would remain conscious.

"Please give us a few minutes alone, sir," I said.

His eyes narrowed, but surprisingly, he took a step towards the door. "I'll give you what I can, but time is running out, and we both know it."

I took Lila's hand the moment he was gone. "Don't let him get to you. We're all past the point of complete exhaustion."

"I never meant for any of this to happen, Reagan. You have to believe that. I only went with Robert because he threatened to kill Charlie and you if I didn't."

My breath caught in my throat, but I couldn't afford to lose focus. "Then give me something I can use. The authorities are only interested in finding answers. How long have you known Robert Evans and how does he even know about Charlie and me?"

"We didn't actually meet until he came to my hospital room in Mexico City, but I knew something about him because he was all Angel every talked about when we were alone at the Rios ranch. He was supposed to be this magical god who was going to deliver her from the awful monster she had married and give her the life of love and fulfillment she always wanted."

"Go on," I encouraged.

"It's a rather long and complicated story, but it began the afternoon of the ball when I overheard a phone call she was having with Robert, and it's why I accompanied you to the hospital when I thought you were losing your baby. I didn't do it to be kind. I needed to get away before someone found out what I had done."

"I'm afraid you're losing me. What was said that had you so frightened?"

"That they were going to meet before the party to finalize their plans in making sure Walter got what he deserved. They were both tired of living in his shadow and taking his orders. I knew I had to figure out what they were up to so I followed her to a corner of the estate where he was waiting. There was an ugly exchange because things didn't go as she anticipated."

"Are you saying that Angel had something to do with her own husband's death?"

"She was part of the entire takeover and expected a lover's tryst. But what she got was news that his wife was expecting another child, and Robert couldn't possibly leave her until after it was born. She flew into a rage and informed him that she was tired of waiting. If he was going to desert her after all they'd been to each other, she was prepared to destroy the entire legacy he planned on building for his family. That's when she told him she had records outlining every business deal both he and Walter had made over the past ten years, and she had given that information to someone who would know what to do with it. Robert was visibly shaken and tried to placate her by saying that she would still be the one ruling by his side. He just had to make his mother understand first because she was the one in charge until he had gained everyone's trust."

My head was filled with anger and confusion, but I couldn't let Lila to see how much her deceit was affecting me. If she had just come clean sooner, some of the horrors of the past few months could have been avoided. "Why didn't you tell someone what you overheard?"

"Because I was scared. I recorded the entire conversation on my phone and knew what would happen if anyone found out. I waited until they had gone back to the house, but Angel saw me return and asked where I'd been. I gave her some lame excuse about going to visit the horses."

"Did she believe you?"

"I didn't exactly wait around to find out. I hurried to my room, hid my phone in a secret compartment in my suitcase, and got ready for the party. When Edward asked me what was wrong, I told him I was just worried about the shipment. I kept hoping Angel would forget even speaking to me. That was a common occurrence when she was using. But when I saw Walter and her come down those stairs and head straight to the patio, I knew she hadn't forgotten anything. As soon as she and Robert finished with him, they would come after me."

"But Robert turned on her too."

"I should have known that would happen. I had been doing a little checking into his family when I got bored. I was aware that his mother had returned to Colombia where her family had once been at the top of the cocaine industry."

"But that doesn't explain why he approached you in the hospital."

"I think he was on a fishing expedition to see if I knew anything about the book Angel had mentioned. He knew we'd been friends in the past. And he came rather cleverly disguised in a priest's garb claiming to be there to give me last rites."

"But you didn't know anything more about the book than I did back then."

"Robert had just killed two people! The only way I wouldn't become his next victim was to play stupid but helpful. I told him this big sob story about being alone in the world with Edward and Angel gone and not knowing what I was going to do. He suggested we form a sort of alliance. He was looking for something Angel claimed to have. I told him we had been friends for years and perhaps I could help him find it."

Her hand had become limp and almost cold. "It's okay, Lila. I'm not going to judge. Just tell me what happened after that."

She took a labored breath before continuing. "I poked around a little after I got out of the hospital just so he would believe me. But when I didn't find anything useful, I thought he would go away and leave me alone. I promise I never gave him either Neva or Tristan's names."

"You were playing a mighty dangerous game."

"That's how I've lived my entire life. I came to Washington D.C. to tell you what I knew, but soon discovered that his goons were still watching me. When he found out I was going to Mexico City as a possible witness, he said he needed me to keep him informed about what was happening with the trial. I thought he was just interested because of his father."

"When did you figure out what was really going on?"

"Not until right before we left the city on the helicopter. I asked him about the bombing to get Carlos out of prison and was informed that I needed to mind my own business and continue working with him or see Charlie, my daughter and you die."

I leaned over and kissed her forehead. "What you did was both stupid and heroic, but we can get you into witness protection where you'll be safe."

"No one can protect people like me, or even you," she replied. "He knows the FBI has the book Angel mentioned, and that I've been helping you. They've managed to nab a number of the people he was counting on for support in building his new regime. That's why the meeting on the island was planned. He needed to recoup his losses, and he wanted me to pay for the part I had played in messing up his plans."

"Why not just kill you?"

"I asked him about that. He said he wanted me to suffer something more excruciating than death. And knew, from what he had observed over the months, that the best way of doing that was by destroying all the good I had been trying to do since committing to get clean. But it would be done in a public way where the very people I claimed to be helping would question everything I had ever done."

My knees came close to buckling. That's why he'd made sure she was at the place where the first shipment of cocaine was exchanged. He was destroying her credibility.

"What about your cell phone?" I asked. "Does the confrontation you taped still exist?"

"The phone, the money I've been able to save, specific instructions and my written testimony are all in a safety deposit box at the US Bank six blocks from my loft. I hid the key in what I hoped would be a safe place and know Robert's people didn't find it while ransacking my home, or I wouldn't be laying in this bed. I can tell you where it is, and you can take it to the bank. The number on the box is 11025."

"Oh, Lila, " I said. "My partner found the key, but we weren't able to figure out what it belonged to. Do you know where Robert is now?"

Her head moved ever so slightly. "No one stays in one place for long."

"But there has to be a central location. Have you been to his mother's estate or met his wife?"

"Robert only talked to me when he needed my help. I was guarded both day and night. I can only tell you that his wife has not been part of this, but she is too afraid to oppose him. He has her stashed away in some country estate but seldom visits either her or their children. He has a mistress somewhere in this city who is very young and beautiful."

"Did you know her name?" I asked, thinking back to Leila Gonzalez and the conversations we'd had the night before.

"No, but he is beginning to tire of his mother's constant demands and has begun doing things without her knowledge."

"Like what?" I asked.

"He purchased a second stealth plane using money she had earmarked for something else. That's why he needed the backing of the men he was meeting on the island. Carlos Mendoza is keeping it hidden on one of his properties, and one of the Seville brothers has been taking lessons so he will know how to fly it."

I was pushing too hard, and she was beginning to lose her power of concentration, but I could't stop yet. "Are they planning another shipment?"

"Most likely. He needs money badly and was returning to Colombia after our trip to the island. When he finds out I am still alive, he will send someone to finish what he was not able to do."

"So Robert was the one who pulled the trigger."

"He said he was tired of my games. I didn't step out on that porch to warn Agent Fielding and the others. I was pushed from behind to draw the fire and then shot in the back."

Without warning, her face contorted with fear. "Something isn't right, Reagan. I don't feel so good."

I looked down to where her hand had gone. Blood was beginning to saturate the sheet where it covered her abdomen. But before I could call for help, the door opened and the interim director walked back into the room.

"Times up," he said. "I hope you've learned something useful."

I gave him an angry look. "Your sarcasm and distain can wait until later. Lila's bleeding."

He moved rapidly to my side and pushed me away from the bed. "I'll take care of this. Your escort has arrived, and you are going to leave."

"Not like this," I replied.

"Do not question my authority, Agent Sinclair. I will see that Miss Rivers is cared for, but you are to go directly to the front of the building where a delivery truck from Pedro's Floral will take you to the edge of the city."

"Don't you want to know what I learned?" I asked as Lila's eyes closed and one of the monitors began beeping.

"There's no need for disclosure. A microphone was planted under the edge of her bed. Assistant Director Bridges will be informed about the location of the safety deposit box, and I will take care of everything else. Now get out of here before this room is swarming with hospital personnel trying to save your friend's life."

I wanted to say something denigrating and derogatory, but the sight of Lila's ashen face made me reconsider. I couldn't help anyone if I was locked up in a Colombian prison where I would likely be executed before a defense lawyer could even be hired. That thought was the only reason I was able to reach down and pick up the bag I had tossed to the floor.

"What you did was despicable, sir," I retorted.

"I do whatever is necessary to get the job done. You should know that by now."

I stepped back as the door opened so I wouldn't be in the way and could make an unobserved exit, but instead of many hospital personnel rushing in to take care of Lila, only Agent Selena Diaz entered the room.

"Where's the doctor?" I demanded. The last I'd heard, she was supposed to be on the coast.

"No time for smalltalk," she responded, tossing a pair of pink scrubs onto a chair. "There's been a breach. Robert Evans' people know Lila is here. We've got to move her immediately, and I'm going to need your help to do it."

I felt every muscle in my body tense but knew she wasn't kidding. When I looked up at the television in one corner of the room, the words flashing across the bottom of the screen were explaining how a woman had been rescued from an island off the coast of Colombia and taken to a hospital in Bogotá.

"What do you need me to do?" I asked, instead of demanding to know what part she had played in the breech. Too many secrets were becoming common knowledge, and only a handful of people were aware that Lila had even survived.

Agent Diaz was unplugging equipment as she gave her response. "Put those scrubs on so you won't look like some bullfighter, and then get Miss Rivers to the ground floor where hopefully Sam will have an ambulance ready. The interim director can clear the way to the freight elevator while I find the doctor. I told the personnel at the desk that everything was under control. Damned inconvenient that one of the monitors had to go off like that. I hope you're both ready for a fight because members of this new and improved cartel have already entered the hospital. They're asking questions, moving swiftly and don't seem to care who knows they are here."

I looked to the interim director for help.

"Just do what she says," he almost snarled, pulling his gun from his holster and moving into the hall. "Miss Rivers is no good to anyone dead."

Nothing about this seemed right to me, but I had seen enough the past few months to know that even a moment's hesitation could be deadly. So I hurriedly put the scrubs over the skirt and blouse, slid my revolver into the drawstring waistband of the pants, and then pushed the bag onto the shelf underneath the bed. The blood on the sheet was spreading rapidly now, and Lila hadn't moved since telling me that she knew something was wrong.

"I'll meet you downstairs," Agent Diaz said. "I know you have no reason to trust me, but Sam will explain everything if we make it that far."

She was gone before I could make my reply, but I still kicked the lever that kept Lila's bed in place. Her life had been tragic in so many ways—too many foster families who were only in it for the paycheck and bad influences she had not been taught how to resist. I marveled again at how blessed I had been being born into a loving Christian family.

"How good are you at avoiding bullets, Agent Sinclair?" Interim Director Whitman called out as he hurried back into the room before I even made it to the door. "We have no idea who our real friends are, except for the doctor. I'll try to keep the way to the freight elevator clear, but you'll be on your own getting her to the first floor. Hopefully, things will be in place by the time you get there."

"I'm ready," I said, taking a deep breath of stale, hospital air. Lila had not moved, nor had she reopened her eyes, but the movement of her chest told me she was still alive.

"It's a clear shot right now, but it won't stay that way for long," he continued. "Give me a fifteen second lead. I may have to draw the gunfire away."

The door opened again before I finished my countdown. "What is going on?" a nurse demanded in crisp Spanish. "You are not assigned to this floor."

She was small and young. I could take her down easily if I had to, but there wasn't time, and I couldn't afford the commotion if any of Robert Evans' people were already on their way to our floor.

"Don't just stand there," I said, deciding in a split second what I needed to do. "Can't you see this woman is bleeding? I'm taking her directly to surgery. If your incompetence results in her death, you will be prosecuted. Where were you anyway when this emergency arose, chatting it up with some young doctor or orderly away from the nurse's station?"

The stunned look on her face told me that my bluff had worked, and I wasn't even wearing an identifying badge. Without saying anything else, she held the door for me while I pushed the bed into the hallway.

I couldn't see the interim director, but I heard the beeping of buttons as I passed in front of the main bank of elevators. I would feel much safer when I was off the floor where Lila was being treated. If anyone who had been involved with her care was on the cartel's payroll, he or she would capitalize on it.

The fact that blood was clearly visible on the sheet covering Lila's body made my ruse more believable, and the young nurse who had interrupted our getaway seemed intent on making sure we made it to our destination without intervention or delay. I followed her lead, and when we got to the freight elevator, she used her own card to swipe the security pad. I knew then that nothing about this plan had been thought through because the uniform that had been stolen for me hadn't come with one.

"I will go with you," she said as I pushed the rolling bed inside. "I never meant to do any harm. I was only away from my post for a moment."

"That won't be necessary," I replied as I watched her frightened eyes. "Just stay here and make your excuses to your supervisor."

"Please see that she is okay. I cannot lose my job. It is all my family has."

"I'll do what I can," I told her as the door closed over runs that were in need of oiling. I hated hurting anyone, especially when they had likely done nothing wrong, but my instructions were to proceed to the ground floor without delay and hope someone I knew was waiting.

I tried to clear my mind of useless thoughts as our descent continued. Robert Evan's people would have no trouble overtaking an entire hospital. If he found out what Lila had said about the video tape, I doubted there was anything the DEA could do to stop him from killing anyone who knew about it. I needed to get out of the country without delay, but I needed to take both Lila and Agent fielding with me.

Daylight was coming from somewhere when the door opened on the ground floor. I pushed the bed into the hallway. Lila hadn't made a noise, but there wasn't time to make sure she was still breathing. I could hear the sound of voices coming from almost every direction, but no one was physically present to tell me what I was supposed to do.

We were near the emergency room. That much was clear from the types of noises I heard once I was able to clear away the sound of voices in my head, but there were too many doors to determine which one I should take. That dilemma was solved when the one to my right opened and Agent Diaz stepped through it. On the floor behind her were the bodies of two men with blood pooling underneath their bodies.

"This way, Reagan," she said. "I had hoped for a clear getaway, but I guess that wasn't in the cards."

The sun was nearly blinding when we stepped outside. It took a moment for my eyes to adjust, but while I was checking to see if we had been followed, Agent Diaz had more to say.

"Don't look so worried. This isn't the first time we've tried something like this. Sam and I make an incredible team, and I don't see that changing, despite what he may have told you. I've called the embassy. Director Stevens is on his way south with a couple of teams to check out the leads Leila Gonzalez gave us. He's left Sam in charge of making sure you get out of the country, and I will assist him any way I can."

Fingers of agitation made me involuntarily quiver as the truth behind her words settled. She hadn't given up on Agent Fielding. I was simply a distraction that needed attention, but I would stay with Lila until I knew she would recover and go home when I felt it was right.

I followed her a few feet to the back door of an ambulance that swung open at her command. Dr. Perez and Interim Director Whitman were inside. I could see Agent Fielding sitting behind the wheel, but he neither turned in our direction or acknowledged my presence. I knew he was keeping track of what was going on in front of us so we wouldn't get blocked in.

The two men lowered the gurney to the ground and then proceeded to move Lila onto it. While they worked, I retrieved the bag from underneath the bed and made sure my gun was ready to use.

Dr. Perez was at her head when they lifted her inside. "This is very bad. I will do what I can, but I cannot give you any guarantees. If she is bleeding internally again . . ."

"Fair enough," the interim director told him as he placed his foot on the running board. "I saw half a dozen suspicious-looking people on my way out. It won't be long until they figure out what we've done."

"They will move quickly, and they leave no survivors," Dr. Perez said. "I hope you know a place where we can operate. We must do it soon, or she will not make it."

"Sam will take care of everything," Agent Diaz replied as she pushed me towards the others. "I need to be upfront with him."

I didn't even bother expressing my displease. I simply took the hand the interim director offered, but the door was still open when four men with assault rifles came running into view and the first shot rang out. I fired twice before the door swung shut.

"Please, Heavenly Father," I prayed as more bullets hit the metal covering. "Help us make it out of this."

The doctor was bracing himself against the wall, and the interim director was hanging onto a bar that ran the length of the enclosure, when we rounded the first corner at such a high rate of speed that the gurney slid sideways pinning me to the opposite side of the ambulance. I could hear gunfire coming from the passenger side of the cab and knew that Agent Diaz was returning fire.

When I looked down at Lila, her eyes were closed, her face the color of parchment paper, and her breathing almost non-existent. I knew she was unaware of what was happening, and for that I was grateful.

By this time, the doctor was able to move to her side. He readjusted the IV and opened the black bag he'd brought with him. He checked her pulse and blood pressure and then looked over at me.

"I hope you believe in God," he said as he made the sign of the cross. "He is the only one who can save her now."

"How much time do we have?" I asked, knowing that it wasn't always enough to believe in God. If it was Lila's time to go, there was nothing anyone could do to save her.

"Not long!" he replied. "We must get the bleeding stopped and see what damage has already been done. Even then, it might be too late."

"And there isn't any place in the city where we'd be safe? Bogotá is a huge place," Interim Director Whitman interjected as he tried to remain upright.

"Perhaps there is a place we could go," Dr. Perez replied as he pushed himself towards the cab of the ambulance and slid the connecting window open. "Take a left on St. Sebastian's. It is about a mile ahead. There is an animal clinic three blocks down on the right. It is closed for the Sabbath and has a sterile operating room. We might not be detected if you pull into the back alley."

Agent Fielding picked up speed, making it nearly impossible for the doctor to resume caring for his patient. We might have a head start, but it would be virtually impossible to outrun anyone in an ambulance that weaved spasmodically back and forth through the heavy traffic. I had nearly fallen to my knees several times, and the interim director looked like he was going to be sick.

"Someone will have to assist me," the doctor continued as he tried to keep the tubes going into Lila's body from being torn loose.

"You do the honors, Agent Sinclair," the interim director shouted, taking a firmer grip on the rod as we rounded another corner. "I'm sure I'm the better shot, and someone will have to keep guard."

I didn't say anything as vivid memories of the last time I had been asked to assist in a medical procedure came rushing back. I was no longer that newbie agent in the middle of the Colombian jungle where my son had been born and Maria had lost her life, but I knew nothing about the kind of medical procedure necessary to save Lila's life.

There was a moment of inactivity before the ambulance made an abrupt left turn and then came to a dizzying stop. I saw Agent Diaz move into the driver's seat when Agent Fielding jumped out. A moment later, he was pulling the back door open and helping lower the gurney to the ground.

I waited to say anything until he took my hand. "Is this the way our story is going to end?" I asked as the two men pushed Lila closer to a back door that had been stained by the removal of what I knew had to be gang-related graffiti. "I don't think I can say goodbye to you again."

"Then don't," he responded. "Just say my given name. I don't think I've ever heard it cross your lips."

"Why should that matter? All you need to know is that I love you."

His laugh was gentle as his fingers traced a searing path along the edge of my jaw. "You are fiercely loyal to the people you care about, but I don't want to be Agent Fielding to you any longer. I just want to be Sam."

"Are you sure, Sam?" I said as I had made a commitment that would haunt me for the rest of my life if he didn't come back to me. "It might change everything between us."

"That's exactly what I'm hoping. I will be back to get you, Reagan. I don't know how or when, but we will both get to see Charlie again. Now give me a kiss because I've got to stash that ambulance somewhere."

His lips touched mine with an intensity that let me know a love like ours only came around once in a very lucky lifetime.

"Come on, Sam," Agent Diaz called out. "We've got to get out of here."

"Not yet," I said. "You need to know what Lila said."

"That can wait until we see each other again. My job is to make sure no one finds out where you are."

He sprinted away, and I heard a door slam shut. Then I watched as the tires of the ambulance stirred up little tornadoes of dust while leaving the alley. I took a deep breath before looking at the sign above my head. The letters were nearly faded, but we would be using Jose's Animal Clinic to try to save Lila's life. I didn't bother to ask how they had gained admittance when Interim Director Whitman held the door open for me.

"Good of you to join us, Agent Sinclair," he said, slamming it shut and securing a deadbolt. "Why the long goodbye? Is there something you should be telling me?"

"We cannot waste any more time," the doctor said, keeping me from having to fabricate an answer.

The light in the room was dim but it showed that the enclosure was used for storage and the cages of animals that were recovering from surgery. Most of them were too weak to do anything more than whimper.

"Are you sure no one else is in the building?" I asked as he opened another door that led into an operating room.

"Everyone will be attending Mass for the next hour or so, but someone will be back to check on the animals before returning to their homes."

"Then it will be my job to detain them, by force, if necessary," Interim Director Whitman responded. "How long is this going to take?"

"I do not know what the problem is yet," Dr. Perez said, opening drawers and cupboards as rapidly as he could and pulling out a few trays and other objects. "Have you had any medical experience, Agent Sinclair?"

"None," I replied as I removed the shoulder bag Veronique Stevens had given me from underneath the sheet that covered Lila's body and set it aside where the contents would not be damaged. Then I took the gun from my pocket and put it on a nearby shelf.

"That is too bad. I can do the surgery, even in these less than ideal surroundings, but you will have to give me the instruments I need. I will tell you when to suction and when to pack."

I had no idea what he was talking about, but he didn't ask if I was even willing to try. He simply gave me a gown and a mask and told me to put them on. While I was doing that, he pulled a surgical kit from the large, black bag he had brought with him and began arranging instruments on a rotating tray in the order he would need them. He added some kind of sedative to the IV bag and hung it back in its hook, along with a bag of "O" type blood. Then he handed me a suctioning tube and some packing gauze, pulled back the blood-soaked sheet and lifted Lila's hospital gown. I saw his jaw lock as he made the first incision through sutures he had put in place just a few hours before.

All of the color rushed from my face as I looked at my friend's torn flesh, but I willed my hands not to shake as more of the deep red mixture came gushing out. The light bulb that hung above our heads did little to illuminate what he was doing, and I had no idea how I would ever be able to help him.

But as his fingers flew, he instructed me when to stand back, when to check the monitors and when to suction away any extra blood. My mind seemed to slip outside of my body, and I soon became aware of nothing except the sound of his voice and the commands or reprimands he was giving. I had no idea what my superior was doing. He made no comments and didn't come near the table where we were working.

We went through enough packing gauze to fill a trashcan before he found the site of the bleed and was able to stitch it up. Lila's heart stopped once, and I had to stand back while he shocked it back into rhythm. She didn't move, but the clicking of the monitors let me know that she was still alive.

And then he was stitching up the incision he'd made. I had no idea how long the process had taken. I only knew that my entire body ached, I was covered from head to toe with blood, and I had just been part of something I had never imagined myself doing.

"There is nothing we can do now except wait," Dr. Perez said as he checked Lila's vitals and moved away from the gurney. "She is in God's hands now."

While he was removing his soiled gloves, he instructed the man who had been standing guard to help me clean up the operating room so there would be no evidence of our being there.

"This isn't in my job description," Interim Director Whitman muttered before going into the hall to look for cleaning supplies.

I didn't much care what he thought. I only cared that the people I loved survived.

"I'm sorry you got pulled into this again, Dr. Perez," I said while he was gone. "I know you might never be able to return to the hospital."

"That is the least of my worries right now. I can still practice my profession, even if I lose my license and have to travel to remote villages to do it. There is no end to the suffering in my country. I have been honored to help the DEA, but if I am to die for helping others, it is of no real concern to me. At least I will be reunited with my wife and child. I miss them every day."

I saw tears come into his eyes. They tugged at my heart. "You need to know, Dr. Perez, that the baby whose life you saved when we brought him out of the jungle is well, happy and very much loved. I have adopted him legally, and Carlos Mendoza is not his biological father."

"Sam told me of his connection to the baby. He is more than distressed by his actions, but you must not judge him too harshly. He is a man of conviction and action. No one else would keep coming back to help us when his life is in constant danger. Listen to what he tells you to do. He has proven his loyalty many times. I am not always so sure about the others."

I was about to ask him what he meant when the interim director returned to the operating room with a broom and a bucket filled with rags and cleaning supplies. While he mopped the floor, I picked up everything that had dropped to the floor and wiped down walls, cabinets and any object that was splattered with blood. It seemed to be everywhere, even on the light fixtures above where the doctor had been operating. I tried not to look in Lila's direction. Now that Robert Evan's knew she was still alive, there wasn't a safe place anywhere for her recovery.

I wished others could see her the way I did. Her metamorphose had been consistent, if not always recognizable. It had begun when she cautioned Angel about being so vocal in talking about the ledger and urged me to get away from the Rios ranch and take my husband with me. But I knew I was in the company of a woman who really wanted to change the first time I stopped by her loft in Washington D.C. She was wearing jeans and trying to decide how she was going to make the open space livable.

"This isn't at all what I'm accustomed to, but I'm so excited to be doing something different with my life," she had said after making a 360-degree turn in the large, bare room that was easily twice the size of my apartment. "I lived in a penthouse, very costly and beautifully furnished, when I was with Edward, and before that . . . Well, let's just say that I rested my head wherever I could until Angel came along. She knew how to make things happen, but she wasn't always wise when it came to personal involvements. She would still be alive today if she hadn't become so infatuated with Walter. I don't want to end up like that."

"Let's not talk about sad things today," I told her as I walked over to a tall window that looked down on a very busy street.

"I'm not trying to be morbid," she replied. "I'm simply acknowledging the fact that everyone's luck eventually runs out. I've had few friends over the years, and losing even a pretend one is a terrible loss. Angel could have kept her mouth shut about so many things. That's what you do when you're involved with organized crime. I know I would give anything if I could go back to the day my daughter was born. I would quit using and hanging out with the wrong people. I would wait tables or cashier in a store to keep a roof over our heads. But it's too late for any of that now. I may not even get to meet her because the past will never leave me alone."

"We all have regrets, Lila," I told her, wondering if a time would ever come when I was no longer afraid.

"Oh, honey," she replied. "You have no idea what regrets are until you've spent as many years as I have looking for the next fix and then not remembering what happened when you got it. If I hadn't been involved in that kind of life, I might have found someone who could have given me a real home and family, and Edward might still be alive to watch his children grow up."

I reached for her hand when she came to stand beside me at the window. Lila was a good person, and I didn't have a lot of friends either. All the deceptions I had been involved with since bringing Charlie home had seen to that.

Whenever I expressed doubts about anything after that day—even when Charlie was in the hospital—she would give me a hug and remind me how we couldn't afford to get all negative and morose over any of life's challenges. We simply had to acknowledge our mistakes and try to do better.

"You're attacking that cupboard like it did something to you personally," Interim Director Whitman said. "We'll get you out of this. You won't become a statistic on my watch."

"I'm not worried about that," I assured him, tossing my rag into the large, black, plastic bag that was now ready to be sealed and thrown away. Other than our presence and some missing supplies the room looked as if it had never been used. "I just wish help would arrive. Dr. Perez has done all that he can for Lila, and someone will be back to check on the animals."

"Most likely before we've gone," he replied. "I only hope all of this has been worth it. I know I seem unreasonable in many of my demands, Agent Sinclair, but there is a great deal riding on this. Miss Rivers is a material witness in two homicides, and we can't be sure she was telling the truth about the recording. It wouldn't be the first time she's lied."

Before I told him how I really felt about his attitude and constant derogatory statements about my friend, I moved to Dr. Perez's side. "How's she doing?" I asked.

"She is still alive. That is the best we can hope for right now. I have given her another shot of morphine and her vitals are stable, but we cannot stay here much longer. I keep praying that reinforcements will arrive, but there is no way of even knowing if Agent Fielding and his partner have been successful in alluding the people who were after us."

"They made it," Interim Director Whitman said from the other side of the room. "Otherwise, we wouldn't still be standing here. My question is whether or not they'll be able to come back and get us. I need Miss Rivers back in the United States as soon as she is ready to travel."

"What about Agent Sinclair?" the doctor asked. "Her help has been invaluable today."

"She will be extracted by whatever team has been put in place to complete the task. I have Director Stevens assurance of that."

"I'm afraid whatever arrangements he made came to an end when we left the hospital by ambulance," I interjected. "Agent Diaz told me he was on his way to the southern part of the country to follow up on some leads he was given last night."

"Then I guess it's up to us to find a way out of this mess. Why don't you try to do something about your appearance, Agent Sinclair? I'm sure everyone has a full description of the way you left the hospital by now."

Chapter 13

I left the two men alone while I sought out the closest restroom. It was useless to argue with either of them because I didn't know what was going to happen myself. As I scrubbed the blood from my arms, hands and face with paper towels and bacterial soap from a hand dispenser, I tried not to rehash every moment I had spent in Colombia during the past forty-eight hours. From the room on the other side of the wall, I could hear the plaintive cries of animals. It was a miracle our activities had not already been discovered.

After I was as clean as I could get without taking a shower, I took off the scrubs and was happy to find that the clothing Magdalena had given me was only rumpled, not soiled. It would be heavenly to sit down and rest. The bottoms of my feet were throbbing, but there wasn't time for that. We still needed a plan that would get all of us to safety.

With the soiled scrubs in my arms, I made my way back to the room where the doctor and interim director were watching over Lila. But when I pushed open the door, I knew their disagreement hadn't stopped. Both men looked agitated and angry.

"Is everything all right?" I asked as I shoved what I was carrying into the top of the open garbage bag and slipped my revolver into the pocket of Magdalena's skirt.

"Why don't you ask the good doctor," Interim Director Whitman said. "It seems he alerted some of his people as to what was happening before we left the hospital. Now, he wants to tell them where we are. I refuse to leave my life in the hands of a man I barely know."

"I'm afraid we're left with few options since Director Stevens is unavailable, and Agent Fielding would have come back to get us if he could," I responded. "I trust Dr. Perez completely. He has sacrificed home, family and profession to help the DEA when no one else would and has never asked for anything in return."

The interim director gave me a hostile look. "That's a nice speech, Agent Sinclair, but it doesn't alleviate my fears since there is no place in this country where we'll be truly safe now that Robert Evans knows Lila is here."

"All the more reason for us to listen to what he has to say. This is his home. He knows the city and people better than we ever will. Please tell us what you have in mind, Dr. Perez."

He looked down at Lila before turning his attention to us. "I meant no disrespect to anyone, but this is not the first time the DEA's hands have been tied during one of their missions. That is why I alerted my people. They do not know where we are, but there are places in this city where people can be kept safe for a few hours while other arrangements are made. We have no transportation, and you can be certain that the cartels have their forces on high alert. If the owner of this clinic comes back and we are still here, the authorities will become involved. None of us are innocent in the eyes of the law, and the judicial system will not stand behind us after all we have done. My people are waiting for my call."

"Then make it," I said, without looking at Interim Director Whitman for approval. His displeasure could be dealt with once this crisis was over.

While we waited, I made another sweep of the room to make sure nothing had been overlooked. It seemed like only moments until there was a rapping on the door opening into the alley.

"Let me check it out," Dr. Perez said. "I did not ask where my people were when I called."

We were partially hidden behind the door leading into the operating room, but instead of remaining where I was, I pulled my own service revolver from my pocket and went to stand next to the interim director. He had already dimmed the lights. We would not be able to defend ourselves for long with two hand guns, but we would make every bullet count.

It seemed as if all the air in my lungs lodged in my throat as I heard the lock on the back door turn and rusty hinges creak open. But when nothing was said, I knew we still in the clear.

"This is my nurse and trusted friend, Juana Hernandez," Dr. Perez said when he returned to the darkened room. "She works with me and has brought her brother, Rafael, to help us."

"Thank you for coming," I told the woman I had met at the clinic several months before. "I am sorry for all the trouble my presence has brought into your already tumultuous lives. What you do for others cannot be equaled."

"We each do what we can. I have spoken to Agent Fielding. He has advised me that it is best to separate before leaving the clinic. I am to take Lila to a safe house on the other side of the city, while my brother escorts Agent Sinclair to a location where she can be extracted from our country without detection. I have brought what clothing I could for the journey." She tossed a paper bag in my direction. "I have included a tortilla and a few pieces of fruit. There may not be time to stop for something to eat."

The meaning behind what she had said hit me with such force that I was unable to do anything more than mumble a polite word of thanks. I was being sent away while the interim direction would remain with Lila. I might never see her again. I might not even be informed as to what happened to her or to the man who now controlled such a huge piece of my heart.

"When do we leave?" I asked, looking at the man who would be taking me into an unknown future.

"Immediately. We have taken every precaution, but that does not mean our movements have not been noticed."

I touched Lila's hand before retrieving the shoulder bag I had been trying to keep track of all day. "Be safe, my friend, and know you are loved. I will prove your innocence and make sure your daughter is safe."

"There is an old van waiting outside," Nurse Juana told the doctor as he prepared Lila for transport. "It is the best I could do on such short notice. Try to get her settled while Agent Sinclair and I check for anything that could lead the owner, or anyone else, back to us. I will leave some money where it can easily be found."

She took out a cloth and began wiping down surfaces I had already cleaned while the men wheeled the gurney Lila was on into the alley. I noticed through the open door that the rain had let up, but the sky was nearly black.

"Please try not to worry," Nurse Juana told me as I tied off the top of the large garbage bag and pulled it towards the hall. "Dr. Perez will do everything he can for your friend, and my brother will make sure you get out of the city."

"Do you know who will be meeting me?" I asked.

"I am only told what is necessary, but I can assure you that Rafael will not leave you alone. He will stay until he knows you are with the right people. Once you are away, you must never come back. The cartel will not forget what you have done to disrupt their lives."

I wanted to ask her so much more, but that would only delay, and perhaps destroy, plans that had already been made. When we stepped into the alley, she pulled the door to the building shut while her brother dumped the garbage bag into the trunk of the car we would be taking. She bid him a brief farewell before climbing behind the wheel of the van. I noticed that the interim director was in the passenger seat. I watched as she backed down the alley wishing I'd had time to thank the doctor for all he had done.

Occasionally, during that sober drive through the city in a car that was dented and needed a fresh coat of paint, I let my eyes drift to the dark-skinned man—wearing a heavy coat and tan pants— sitting beside me. If asked to describe him, it would be almost impossible. He seemed unremarkable in almost every way, but his ability to blend into the crowd was his best defense in staying safe.

"I am sure you have questions," he said after we had been driving for some time. "I cannot tell you much, but I am happy to share what I can."

"Perhaps you can start by telling me where we are going."

"I have been asked to deliver you to a garage in a small village a few miles to the west of Bogotá. I should have preferred to wait until the storm that is coming had passed, but my sister told me that you must be gotten to safety immediately."

"Do you always do as your sister asks?"

"She has dedicated her life to a worthy cause. I am not so selfless, but I help when I am able to do so. Our government has been trying for many years to bring additional tourists to our country to help stimulate an impoverished economy. Colombia is filled with many beauties from its majestic mountains to its pristine beaches, but alas, much of the world still views my home as a place of violence and fear where cartels flourish, and the people who are trying to stop them are making very little headway."

"Perhaps we will be able to stop this latest one by working more closely together," I replied as a gust of wind seemed to move the car to the right. I gripped the door handle hoping he wouldn't notice. "What is it you do for a living?"

"I fix small planes mostly. It brings in enough money to take care of my wife and five children, but the private airport where I worked was sold recently. When I asked the new owner if I would still be able to work on his planes, he told me that most of them would be grounded because he was moving in a new direction."

"Really?" I asked, trying to keep my mind from exploding. A private airport meant hangars and the ability to take off and land at will. "What was his reply?"

"That he would keep me on the payroll to service the planes he would still be using, as long as I did not mind running errands and keeping what I saw or overheard to myself. I am a simple man, but not a naïve one. The airport is not monitored as it should be, and it is highly-guarded both day and night. There are places where I am not allowed to go, but I do not mind. I am able to adapt to most anything."

"Does your sister know about your new job?" I asked.

If Robert Evans had purchased an airport, surely someone at the DEA had to know about it. It certainly didn't bode well for me if the man who was supposed to get me to safety was working for the very cartel we were trying to bring down.

"My employment has always been kept separate from the work she does. It is like that for many people in my country. While we abhor what the cartels are capable of doing, they are the only ones who pay enough to support a family. And they offer a kind of protection no one else is able to give. Every time I do something for Juana, I am risking the lives of the people I love."

"Then why do you help her?" I asked.

When he looked over at me, I could see the torment in his eyes.

"You have not lived in my country, Agent Sinclair. Most of us do not get to choose the kind of life we will live, especially people who grow up in villages like the one where Juana and I were born. They see nothing wrong with raising and harvesting coca leaves. They are used in many religious rituals and are mixed with lime and chewed as a stimulant to keep warm since it is cold in the higher elevations much of the year."

"I appreciate the fact that it has many practical uses when it is not mixed with chemicals that turn it into cocaine," I replied, knowing I needed to be careful since I wasn't entirely sure where Rafael Hernandez's loyalty stood.

"Then you understand my dilemma when it comes to separating customs that have been in place for thousands of years from what has only been going on for a few hundred. I would discourage anyone from becoming involved with the cartels. It is a vile and ruthless business, but I do what I must to take care of my family. My sister is often forced to look the other way, but she knows she can trust me with certain tasks when no one else is available."

"Thank you for your honesty, Rafael. I wish your family only the best."

"As I do yours. Juana told me about the baby you rescued from the jungle and smuggled out of our country so he would be safe. I know that has not been easy. Carlos Mendoza is a vindictive and cruel man, but that does not stop people from following or helping him."

"Is he the one who purchased the airport?" I asked.

Rafael glanced quickly in my direction. "I do not know who owns the business. It is run by a manager, but there are often secret meetings and private phone conversations. I do not listen in or become involved. I simply do my job, keep my opinions to myself and run a few errands. My family would not survive without the money I am making, and I am no longer in a position where I can walk away. I am only helping Juana today because she could not do everything herself. I hope you will not use what I have said against me or my family. People in my country do what is necessary to survive."

"I wasn't asking you to divulge information," I replied. "I know what it's like to live under a magnifying glass."

"Then you also know that people do whatever is necessary when backed into a corner. Go home to your family and do not look back. I have seen the news reports today. The cartel will not forgive your part in Leila Gonzalez's abduction."

I turned my attention back to what was happening outside my window. The rain and wind had increased, making it difficult to see the road. And the man behind the wheel was hemmed in by circumstances beyond his control. My inquisitiveness may have inadvertently sealed my fate.

To keep from saying anything more, I allowed the drive to continue in silence until he left the freeway and turned into a narrow, rural road with trees along the edges that towered above our heads. It was getting darker, and the shadows seemed to dance grotesquely as the car lights hit the leafless branches. I was armed and no longer hesitant about using my weapon for protection, but the idea of inflicting pain on another human being who was only trying to take care of the people he loved was still abhorrent.

I glanced at Rafael's profile as the tires of the car hit a major rut. He was not some day-laborer without an education who was living hand-to-mouth as so many of the people I had met in Colombia were. If he knew how to fix airplanes, that meant he had been to school and had other options for providing for his family. Something had convinced him that working for the cartels was an acceptable vocation. Juana might trust him, but I was rapidly beginning to feel like some animal caught in a dangerous snare.

"How soon will be there?" I asked, allowing my fingers to touch the smooth surface of the gun in my pocket.

"The garage is less than a mile ahead. I will drop you off at the door, but I must return to my home. With all the unrest brought about by this new cartel's rise to power, it is not a good idea to be unreachable by my employers."

"Then I can only thank you for seeing that I made it out the city. I had hoped that no one would recognize my photo, let alone link my presence at the gala back to the DEA. As far as I was aware, there were only two people in the country who knew of my existence before my return—Carlos and Alma Mendoza—and they have not been part of anything major for many months now."

The ripple along his jaw was almost imperceptible, but I had been trained to notice such things. "You have been given the chance to get away from my country and return to your family, Agent Sinclair. I would advise you to make haste in doing so and stop interfering in matters that do not directly concern you. The cartel will send a powerful message now that two of their own have been captured. If I were you, I would not want to be anywhere near when that happens."

"But why should the cartel care so much about two young people who roam the streets freely and do exactly what they want? It's not like they were privy to any major plans."

"Often the ones who have the least amount of practical knowledge can do the most damage. They tend to speak without thinking. Perhaps the cartel merely wishes to silence them after all the trouble they have caused."

I felt my body lurch forward as he pulled to an abrupt stop in front of a dilapidated building that stood at the end of a dark street. Several vehicles stood in the gravel parking lot, but it was impossible to tell if anyone was inside. No lights were visible anywhere.

"Are you sure this is the right place?" I asked.

"My sister's instructions were clear. However, I will not be going inside with you." He reached his arm in front of me and pushed the door open. "You may not agree with how I have chosen to live my life and provide for my family, but any attack against me, or my employers, will lead directly back to Juana and the good doctor who cares for so many of your people when they are in trouble. Please keep that in mind when you are helping your associates plan their next move."

I felt my feet hit the ground and my body stand erect, but before I could say anything more, he pulled the door shut and drove away. I hung the bag Veronique Stevens had given me at the embassy over my shoulder and advanced towards the front door of the vacant-looking shop. The raindrops were falling fast and furiously. It would only take a few moments until the wool shawl that covered my head had absorbed all the moisture it could. I would have to take my chances as to whom might be waiting inside.

My stomach was growling when I tried the doorknob of the less-than-inviting building. It had been a long, emotion-driven day, and the paper bag filled with tortillas and fruit that Juana had brought to the animal clinic was on the floorboards of the car. Rafael had not given me time to pick it up. It was impossible not to wonder how he would explain his actions when he saw his sister again. Maybe he would simply tell her that our trip had been interrupted, and he was unable to help.

"Is anyone there," I called out as a door with a very dirty, glass window swung inward. The fact that it had not been locked only added to my anxiety. "I am not here to cause anyone harm. I am merely seeking shelter from the storm."

When no one answered, I moved into a room that appeared to be a combination reception area and office. Fumes from paint, oil, gas, heavy-duty cleaners and welding torches assailed my nostrils and made my eyes burn. There could be no better place for a person to disappear than this remotely-located, automobile repair shop at the edge of a very small town.

I removed my service revolver from the pocket of my skirt and held it out in front of me as I moved cautiously towards a desk where I hoped to find something that would tell me where I was. I doubted there would be a phone available so I could call the embassy, but if this turned out to be an ambush, I would not give up without a fight.

My footsteps fell softly on what I knew was a grim-covered floor as raindrops continued to pelt down on the tin roof. My hand was reaching for the first stack of papers when I heard a movement from the far side of the room. I looked up to see a pinprick of light turn into the glow of an overhead, fluorescent fixture.

"This way," Agent Selena Diaz said. "Sam and I have been waiting for you but didn't want anyone to know we were here."

"Why not?" I asked, taking a tentative step in her direction. "I was led to believe everything had been arranged."

"Sam asked one of his colleagues to make arrangements for you to be brought to this location, but there was no way of knowing if it would happen. We were talking about how long we should wait when we heard you call out. It isn't safe to stay in one place for long right now."

I sidestepped tools, automobile parts and pools of sticky substances as we made our way through the repair part of the garage towards a back room. "Has something happened I should know about, Agent Diaz?"

"I'll let Sam explain what we've been dealing with since we dropped you off at the clinic. I hope everything is okay with your friend. I know how fond of her you are."

A reply wasn't necessary. She wasn't really interested in Lila's condition. She just wanted me to know that I would never be part of what she and Agent Fielding shared. And then I saw him standing in what appeared to be a private residence. At least there was a refrigerator, a sink, a table and two chairs and a cot.

"Glad you made it," he said, barely glancing in my direction since he was busy loading a semi-automatic rifle "I don't like leaving anything to chance, but in this case it was unavoidable. Where's Juana's brother? She assured me you wouldn't be left alone."

"On his way back to his family, I hope. Were you aware that he's working for the cartels?"

"That's not unusual. People around here often have divided loyalties, but that doesn't mean they can't be trusted. I would never have agreed to Juana's proposal if I thought there was anything to fear."

I wanted to believe him, but the entirety of my conversations with Rafael Hernandez had left me with feelings of doubt. While I didn't want the wrong people to know he was helping the DEA, there were certain things that needed to be discussed.

"I'll leave my opinion about that until later. Right now, I want to tell you what he said. I tried to downplay its significance, but I can't deny that it it certainly gave me something to think about."

"There isn't time for lengthy explanations," Agent Diaz said. "Just give us the abbreviated version, and we'll be the judge as to whether or not it may impact what we are planning to do."

I fought back the need to retaliate since it would serve no useful purpose. "The small airport where he works as a mechanic was sold a few months ago. Most of the planes have been grounded. Security has been increased and flights are not being monitored by the government as they should be. Lila also told me that Robert bought a second stealth plane with money his other had earmarked for something else. Is that succinct enough for you?"

"It would be, if I knew who the new owner was," she replied.

Agent Fielding just frowned. "I believe I know where Reagan is going with this. If Robert has purchased another stealth plane, he needs a place to store it and people who will look the other way when he decides to use it. Did he say anything else?"

"Nothing we haven't heard before, except for a warning that any move made against him, or his employers, would directly impact Juana and Dr. Perez. He seems to think that the cartel's only interest in Leila and Henri is making sure they are silenced for good."

"And you believe him?" Agent Diaz asked.

"He isn't some uneducated peasant who works in the field. He is articulate and knowledgeable. While he gave a plausible explanation as to why he was working on planes for the cartels, I don't know his exact relationship with them. But there is a reason he practically pushed me from the car, with the warning that I should take the gift of life I had been given and use it wisely."

"Then we need to respond accordingly," Agent Fielding said as he tossed one of the weapons on the table to the woman who had been his partner while I took care of his son. "Selena, I want you to find out where Rafael Hernandez has gone and keep an eye on him while I get Reagan away from here."

"Don't you think we should be doing that together?" she asked. "There's no way of knowing what either of us might run into."

"Then stop by the embassy and get some backup before proceeding. While you're doing that, make sure someone checks out the safe house where Lila has been taken. They might need to make another move before morning. This storm will offer some protection, but if Rafael has any intention of betraying us, he's going to do it when the payoff will be the greatest. I don't want anyone caught unaware when that happens."

"But we came together," she replied.

"You take the car. I'm sure I can get something here running. There really is no other way if we want all of our basis covered."

"Why don't we just contact the embassy by phone before going rogue? Someone there will know if there's any reason to worry. The cartels are notorious for planting information that keeps us chasing our tails."

"I would do that if Director Stevens wasn't leading a task force somewhere in the southern part of the country. He's the only one who knows the scope of what we're dealing with right now. And quite frankly, he's the only one I trust."

"I could go with you," I volunteered.

Agent Fielding shot me an annoyed glance. "That's out of the question. My first priority is getting you out of the country. After what you just said, you'll be the first one Rafael gives up. That may even be the reason he left without making sure you made it safely inside."

I'd had the same impression as to what the man who had brought me here might have in mind. Warnings were merely indications as to what was being planned.

"Then I suppose we have no choice since Reagan managed to get her picture taken when she was told not to draw any attention to herself," Agent Diaz said as I heard the sounds of water dripping in the sink. "It's amazing how one person can be at the epicenter of so much turmoil when she just came to check on her friend."

"Reagan isn't responsible for any of this, Selena. Besides, I'm the one who asked her to come. She just lost one friend without being able to say goodbye. I didn't want to see that happen again."

"We all have to worry about losing our partners and other people we care about. No one is invincible. Just keep your cell phone active so we can stay in touch. I really don't like the idea of working on this alone, Sam."

After letting the air slowly out of her lungs, she walked towards the back door. Agent Fielding followed her. "I wish it didn't have to be this way, Selena. You're an incredible partner."

The look she gave him betrayed what she was feeling inside, but it was the way she ran her hand down his cheek that caused my heart to race. "I would never betray you, Sam. Working with you the past few months has been the dream of a lifetime. Please don't take any unnecessary risks. I want you back in Bogotá, unharmed, so we can continue this fight together."

The ease with which they were interacting made it hard for me to believe that many of the lines they had crossed would ever be forgotten.

He went with her when she stepped outside. Instead of listening at the door, I used that time to look for something to eat and drink. My stomach was empty, and the throbbing in my head was getting worse. I would worry about the harsh realities of unrequited and impractical love later. Right now, I needed to keep from getting ill. I found several bottles of water in the refrigerator and a package of saltine crackers in the stand-alone cabinet next to it. I was trying to choke one of them down when the back door opened again.

"I can't tell you how sorry I am that things did not go as planned, Reagan," Agent Fielding said. "I didn't even ask about Lila. Is she going to be okay?"

I took a sip of water before answering. "I helped Dr. Perez with the surgery, but she was still unconscious when they left for the safe house. Do you really think my life is in imminent danger? Like Selena said earlier, I'm only a bit player in all of this."

"Not to me," he responded. "You're the glue that's holding everything together. That's why I want you out of this country. The trick will be finding a place where you won't be detained."

"Is there such a place in Colombia right now?" I asked.

"I have a few ideas. I just wish we knew where Rafael's inherent loyalty lies. If his comments are indicative of what is really going on at that airport, we could do some major damage to the cartel by getting inside the hanger where the second stealth plane is being hidden. Can you imagine Robert's reaction if he lost something his mother didn't even know he had? That internal dissension we talked about could blow everything sky high."

"You should be with Selena instead of babysitting me," I replied. "I know how you feel about being where the action is, and this is beginning to feel like a reenactment of what happened the last time I was here."

"Nothing about this is the same, Reagan, and please don't worry about Selena. She's trying to hang onto something that never was."

"Have you told her that? I saw her reaction just now," I replied.

He put his arm around my shoulder. "I know I have no right to expect your understanding or forgiveness for many of the things I've done, but they have nothing to do with my feelings for you or our son. I want a life with both of you, but we have to get out of this predicament first. Now, why don't we see if we can't find something that will run. Our best bet for getting you home is finding an airport as far away from Bogotá as possible."

I followed him into the main part of the shop where he began checking out the vehicles that were awaiting repairs. Some of them had parts strung across the floor and others wouldn't start when he turned the right key in the ignition. I wanted to help, but my knowledge about how a vehicle ran was limited to watching the lights on the dashboard for any sign of trouble and changing a tire.

"What about the ones parked outside?" I asked. "Surely the owner would have something customers could use in an emergency."

"I'm not sure anything in that category would get us where we need to go, but what the heck, there's nothing inside that will do us any good. Why don't you grab those crackers, and anything else edible you can find, while I take a look. The noise coming from your stomach could wake the entire village, and I'm not sure it would be a good idea to stop anywhere, even if we managed to find some fast food establishment that was open this time of night."

I knew he was lashing out because he was afraid. He had sent Selena back to the city because it was the right thing for the DEA, but by doing so, he had left us vulnerable to an open attack with no means of getting away. So I hurried back to the kitchen and began going through every cupboard on the premise. In addition to the crackers and bottles of water, I found a tin of sardines, a half-eaten package of jerky and a bag of pork rinds. Everything else needed a can opener which I was unable to find.

The lack of supplies made me wonder just how long it had been since the shop was open. Perhaps it had been deserted when one of the cartels made its sweep. That would certainly explain why Agent Fielding had known it was available for his use, and reminded me of what had happened at both Dr. Perez's clinic and the village in the mountains. When things were no longer needed, they simply disappeared.

By the time I had everything stowed in the top of my shoulder bag, he was back to tell me that he had hot-wired an old pickup truck. It might not take us very far, but anything was better than staying where we were. He picked up the remaining semi-automatic rifle before leading me outside into the damp and chilly air.

Nothing was said for the longest time as we rolled across uneven surfaces, guided by two headlights that were so faint it felt like we were moving through some oppressive and otherworldly tunnel. I clung to the door handle, trying not to jump whenever we hit a pothole or something appeared to be darting across the road in front of us. I knew he was trying to make sense of everything we had learned during the past few hours. But there wasn't a pattern to anything that had happened. It was like trying to fit square pieces of a puzzle into round holes.

Quite suddenly, he slammed on the brakes and pulled to the side of the road.

"What's wrong?" I asked as my heart seemed to lodge in my throat.

"We've got this all wrong," he responded as his eyes seemed to bore into mine, even though I could barely see them. "We've spent all our time talking about killing the dragon, but what if we've been focused on the wrong monster?"

"You're losing me," I said. "I thought you believed Lupe Evans was at the head until Robert was ready to assume control."

"Maybe that's what the real kingpin wanted us to believe so we would spend our time running in circles instead of looking at on what's really going on. Don't you think it's strange that no one has succeeded in killing us? They claim it's what they want, and they've certainly had plenty of chances."

"Neil's dead," I reminded him.

"I don't mean to be insensitive since I know how close you were, but what if that was just collateral damage? Who is the common link in all of this? The one person who already has a foothold in this country, and the connections necessary to facilitate a great deal of change. But the one we keep overlooking because he lacks the right financial backing—or the personality—to move to the possession of prominence he's always felt he deserved."

"You're talking about Carlos Mendoza. I know he had grandiose ideas and felt he was unstoppable, but he was also a spineless coward who killed innocent women and let other people take the fall for him."

"All that's true, but he was able to manipulate the prison system twice and get away with it. That means he has support from people in some very high places who are able to overlook some of his flaws. You didn't know him the way I did. There was a period of time when I was more than just one of his hired assassins. We would spend hours playing chess in his library. He said I was the only man he had ever met who could outthink his strategical moves, and if we were not on the same side, he would love to see what I could do in a real game of life and death."

"That's a mighty big leap."

"Think about it, Reagan. Why was nearly everything in the house at the compound removed, and an entire village dismantled, by the time our people went back to do any serious digging?"

"He didn't want to give us a reason to go back."

"Bingo!" he replied. "Carlos was a creature of habit, and that compound was his baby. He owned thousands of acres in the jungle and had plans for every foot of it. I know where I'm going with this might not make a lot of sense, but let's lay out all the things we've learned since your return. I think if we put them alongside what we already know, we'll see a very interesting pattern emerge. I don't want to make another bad judgment call anymore than you do, and I think this is worth looking at."

"I work better when I'm able to write things down," I responded.

"So do I, but we can work through this in our heads if we try, and we start by eliminating everyone who isn't a serious contender for leadership, and that begins with Leila Gonzalez and Henri Seville."

"Why them?" I asked.

"Because they were left out in the open where we could get to them. That means they have no knowledge that could seriously hamper anything."

"What about Leila's involvement with Robert?"

"A very revolting occurrence, and one that could have been avoided if the right people had been paying attention, but hardly relevant. Robert has always been a playboy. I would imagine he's had quite a number of mistresses over the years who were cast aside when he was through with them. Just look at what he did to Angel, and his wife, if you need proof as to the kind of man he really is. But we'll get back to him in a minute. As for Henri Seville, did he look like a gangster to you? He likes to talk big, but he was given the task of keeping track of a girl whose greatest delight was dressing up for a photoshoot. They were nothing more than obvious distractions."

"What about Magdalena?"

"I believe she wanted to be a good mother and a law-abiding citizen to help make up for the sins of her family. But she chose to hide, rather than take the kind of stand that fosters true change."

"You do understand that you're talking about our son's grandmother."

"I'm not denying that her heart is in the right place. I just hope she hasn't been captured by her family because I'm not sure she will be able to withstand the type of torture they'll inflict to get her to see things the way they do."

"Do you think she'll tell them about our visit?"

"She'll try to get them to see reason by appealing to their sense of family. But what she doesn't understand is how truly heartless and immoral these people have become. If they even suspect we are closing in on them, they'll pull out every stop and no on will be safe."

I found myself leaning into the door and trying not to tremble. "That means no one in Charlie's family can be protected."

"We'll do what we can, but it may be too late for some of them. This ugly business had been going on for generations, and we should all be a little scared as to where it might lead."

"Even you?" I asked.

He reached over and took my hand. "I'm able to compartmentalize and hide most of my feelings, but that doesn't mean I don't have them. The only way to save our son, and anyone else who is even remotely involved, is to decimate this beast until it can no longer rise again."

"Then let's do it together," I said.

"That's not practical, Reagan."

"Why not? You have an idea of what needs to be done, or you wouldn't have brought it up."

"My thoughts are still germinating, and what I need from you is an honest opinion as to whether or not they have any merit. My people here can be mobilized to do whatever is necessary to get the cartel shut down once we have a solid plan in place."

"Okay," I said, not wishing to belabor any issue since I knew I would make my own decision about staying or going when the time came. "What else have you been thinking?"

"That the Sevilles brothers are nothing more than ghosts who have never aspired to roles of leadership, despite what their parents may have had in mind for them. Why else would they be willing to take up residency in a country where few people know who they are? They followed their friend, Robert, because he shared his father's ability to get other people to do the risky and dirty work while he evaded the authorities and lived the good life."

"Where's the payoff in doing that?"

"Some men are natural-born mercenaries who flourish in the shadows. Monetary compensation is secondary to the rush they get from waging war against the establishment, eliminating people who step out of line and taking what they want. I've known hundreds of men just like them over the years. The Sevilles are out of their element here. Who is going to listen to what any of them have to day?"

I felt my brow furrow. "They have been the one anomaly that never seemed to fit. But if their goal was to remain invisible, why take the risk of getting Eloise and Henri out of jail? Like you said, he's practically useless, and Eloise left the remains of her cartel up from grabs by moving to a foreign country."

"They still need contacts in Mexico to help move product across the border, and no one has ever been able to determine just how far the Seville's holdings go. We can't even be sure all the older brothers are still Colombia. A mass exit may have been staged simply as another way to throw us off. I'm not saying I have the right answers. I'm just trying to figure out who is really at the top, and Lupe Evans doesn't fit the profile of the person we're looking for."

"What about her hatred for Walter?"

"I'm sure there was no love lost between them, but she hasn't played an active part in the distribution of drugs for decades. For her to rise to the top at this stage of her life, she would need the support of people who have been involved in the game recently."

"That's where Mendoza comes in."

"Despite his lack of finesse in certain areas, he always manages to land on his feet. Can you really see Robert Evans running an organization successfully for long? He's impulsive, self-absorbed and makes decisions without consulting others. Even if Lupe is in charge, she's not going to turn her empire over to someone who does things behind her back. And it certainly isn't going to sit well when she finds out that the girl she took under her wing—whom she thought was her great niece—is really her ex-husband's granddaughter. The backlash when that information goes public will be astronomical, and we need a plan in place before it happens."

My body fell backwards as the totally of what we might be facing hit me. This wasn't just about taking down a ruthless cartel any longer. It was about protecting our son, and the lives of everyone even remotely connected to him. "Just tell me what you think we should do."

"We need to find out if the compound is the home base for the cartel and if Carlos Mendoza is running it before I let anyone else know what I'm thinking. Whoever is behind this enjoys playing games and keeping the authorities running around like chickens with their heads cut off. That's the criminal I went undercover to stop. I should have known what he was doing long before now."

"You can't blame yourself for any of this."

"Like hell, I can't," he responded, pulling his hand away from mine. "He was laying out clues all along, only I was too involved with my own fixations to see them. Well, that ends now! If he wants a worthy opponent, he's going to get one."

I swallowed back a new rush of fear. This was the man I had known in the jungle—the man who cared about nothing except completing his mission.

"You can't do it alone."

"That's the way I work best. I'll find someone to get you to an airport, and then I'm going to give Carlos Mendoza the fight of his life. His reign of terror is over."

"Stop it, Sam," I shouted, as the sound of the pickup truck's motor pounded in my ears. "I'm no longer that newbie agent who had no idea what she'd gotten herself into. I can take care of myself, and you're going to need help covering all the basis without getting caught. Running off alone, and half-cocked, is exactly what Mendoza anticipates. And you can bet your last dollar that he'll have a trap in place to keep you from leaving the compound alive. You can throw me out of this truck if you like, but that's the only way I'll let you leave me behind again."

"What about Charlie?" he asked. "He deserves having at least one of his parents alive to raise him."

"Charlie deserves more than that, but he's too young to understand the fight we're in to protect him. Carlos Mendoza was the first one to threaten his life, but there have been others, and they'll just keep coming until we make them stop. Now, quit trying to be chivalrous. Let me give you the backup you need, and then we can go home to the child who needs both of us."

"Are you sure, Reagan? I have no idea how I'm even going to get to the compound. If he is there, he'll have the entire area under constant surveillance."

"What about going back the way we got out?"

"It would take too long. Besides, he'll be expecting a covert attack because it's what I do best. What we need is a plan he won't anticipate. I've been thinking that we could fly into Manuel's village with a load of supplies. There are a couple of vehicles available to take canned goods and medical supplies from one village to another. Transports were always coming into the compound. Alma usually oversaw the deliveries, but if she isn't there, we might be able to get past whatever servants are on duty. I'm sure he's using many of the ones he had in the past. Not many people want to live in the jungle, and he likely had them tucked away in anticipation of a new rise to power."

"You make everything sound so cold and calculated."

"Mendoza is known for his ability to get results. If you really are with me on this, we have a lot to do before morning. It isn't safe to fly into the mountains at night, especially during a storm. Is there anyone at the compound you think might be willing to help? I wasn't exactly on a first name basis with most of the household staff."

"Rosa would do what she could, but she relies on the money she makes to support her family. What about Father Francis? I know he works for Mendoza, but as a man of the cloth, he couldn't possibly condone his actions."

"I'm not sure we could get him to turn on his benefactor. He runs an entire monastery and is responsible for the souls of all the peasants who live and work in the area. He would never jeopardize being there for communion and final rites. However, he is a frequent visitor, and many of his people come and go at will. If we could get our hands on a couple of monk's robes, we might be able to blend in enough to get inside and find out what we need to know."

"Then let's do it," I said.

He set the gear, and we were back on the road. I tried not to worry as we made our way through the rain and the dark. Our plan had more holes in it than a spaghetti strainer, but I had no doubt that by working together we would be ready by morning.

Chapter 14

We drove for what seemed like forever in a dark and oppressive silence. I knew Agent Fielding was making plans for our return to the jungle. But my mind was thousands of miles away with Charlie. What would really happen to him if I didn't make it home again?

My coming to see Lila had plunged me even further into a web of deceit, mystery and violence that no one could have anticipated. If the DEA could find the plane and Robert Evans, the recording Lila had made might go a long way towards having him incarcerated. But if his family wasn't running the show, that meant another showdown with the Mendoza's, and I was personally familiar with what they were capable of doing. I was about to mention my concerns when Agent Fielding drove up to the side of a building and turned the key in the pickup truck's ignition.

"Is that what we're going to use in the morning?" I asked as I looked at the outline of the single-engine plane that stood next to the tree line. It looked uncomfortably familiar.

"Supplies are delivered to the village where Manuel lives every Monday morning. Lucky for us, that's in a few hours. If we can get it off the ground at first light, it should give us time to set our plan in motion before anyone even discovers it's gone. Many of the people here are not early risers."

"Are you telling me that no one is watching it now?"

"Why should they? Everyone in the area knows this landing strip belongs to the cartels. It would be suicide to disturb anything. Why don't we go inside, eat something and try to get a little rest. Tomorrow will be anything but pleasant."

I slung the bag I had been keeping track of all day over my shoulder and slid to the ground. The rain was still pelting down on my head and shoulders, but at least my feet didn't hurt quite so badly. Either the wounds had not been severe and were starting to heal, or my emotional trauma was keeping me from feeling physical pain. Agent Fielding was holding the door open by the time I made it around to the front of the building. A musty odor that seemed to consist of damp moss, rotting wood and stale tobacco assailed my nostrils when I stepped inside.

"I'm sorry I can't offer you a better place to sleep, but at least it's not as bad as the huts and cave we stayed in during our time in the jungle with Charlie," he said, putting a match to the wick of a kerosene lamp that sat in the center of scarred, round table. "There's a bathroom in the back, and a cot we can use. I hope you don't mind sharing it with me."

"Not at all," I replied, surveying my surroundings with more than trepidation. The flickering light let me know that it was in much the same condition as the living quarters at the garage and the room at the tavern where I had felt much safer standing. "Just give me a minute to wash up, and then we'll eat what I was able to find."

"Take your time," he responded. "I'm going to make sure everything is on the plane. If it isn't, we'll need another plan for getting to the compound. You should be able to find something a little warmer to wear in one of the cupboards next to the cot. A skirt and light top won't cut it where we're going. You'll freeze to death."

"Thanks," I said as he moved towards the door. "I'm starting to get used to wearing other people's clothing. Do you think Lila made it to the safe house okay?"

His sigh was heavy when he turned to face me. "Listen, Reagan, we can't waste time worrying about anything other than what we've committed to do. Despite how it might seem at times, the DEA knows how to take care of its assets and act on new information in a timely and appropriate manner. Lila will receive the best care possible until she's well enough to leave Colombia, and Interim Director Whitman will make sure no one gets close enough to harm her. That said, I wish I had never asked you to come. You should be home with Charlie, not traipsing through the jungle with me again. If you're having any reservations, just tell me. There's still time to get you away from here."

"I'm not going to change my mind."

"Then let's concentrate on making sure this mission is successful. If the plane is ready to go, we'll discuss how to proceed, once we land, when I get back."

The door slammed shut, and I was left in a place I really didn't want to be. But instead of giving in to irrational fears or self-doubt, I dug through the cupboards until I found something warmer to wear. No one would ever recognize me in the coveralls and plaid shirt I pulled from one of the shelves, but I wasn't entering some pageant. I was preparing for what could be the worst fight of my short career.

I didn't even try the light-switch to see if the power was on when I went into the bathroom to change my clothes. Agent Fielding had used the lamp for a reason, and that was good enough for me. By the time he returned, I had our limited amount of food sitting on a paper towel next to the lamp. We ate what we could, and then he turned off the lamp and led me towards the cot in one corner of the room. My heart was racing when he pulled me down beside him and secured a wool blanket around us.

"It's going to get cold before morning, and I need you close to me for the next few hours," he said, drawing me into his arms as he had during the time we had been at the Rios ranch.

Turning to face him was impossible the cot was so narrow, but I made sure my fingers were intertwined with his. "There is no place in the world I would rather be, except for having Charlie with us in a place where we would all feel safe. You haven't told me what your thoughts are for after we arrive."

"That's because I don't know what we're going to find. Manual is loyal, but I can't be sure about anyone else. You saw how quickly news reached the village after the raid. What I failed to tell you is that Mendoza's men travel to and from that village regularly. It's a hub for getting processed cocaine down the mountain."

"So this landing strip really is under the cartel's protection."

"It is, and the fact that the plane is filled with fresh produce and boxes of assault rifles and ammunition is all the proof I need that the compound is no longer abandoned. Mendoza is back, and he's resurrecting his business and his army. We can use that to our advantage by delivering the weapons ourselves, but there's a ninety-five percent chance that someone will recognize me before we get through the front gate."

I let the air out of my lungs slowly. "Perhaps this would be a good time to tell you what I learned from Lila before her incision ruptured. It might give you hope that not everything in the universe is working against us."

His lips brushed the back of my head. "I love your optimism, but I'm afraid we need another one of your miracles—something not unlike the parting of the Red Sea."

"So you do know a little about the Bible."

"Grandma Winnie used to tell me stories. I always thought they were in the same category as Grimm's Fairy Tales, but you're beginning to convince me otherwise."

"Good to know! Lila didn't become involved with Robert by choice. She was trying to save Charlie, her daughter and me."

"That's old news. You've always believed in her innocence, despite the fact that she's made some very unfortunate decisions."

"She had good reason to make some of them. She recorded a conversation between Robert and Angel right before the ball. They outlined Walter's murder and talked about her contributions and rewards for helping set the takeover in motion. She left it in a safety deposit box in a bank near her loft, along with her written testimony outlining everything she had done to keep people safe. The FBI already had the key. They just needed the location."

"Our Lila is certainly filled with surprises. If a recording does exist, why didn't she give it to you when she first returned to the states? We might not be sitting where we are now if she had."

"You know the answer to that. She needed emergency leverage. Robert contacted her while she was in the hospital in Mexico City. He wanted to know about the journal and figured she might know where it was."

"This story just keeps getting better," he said, pulling me even tighter. "How was she able to convince him she didn't have it? She was the logical choice."

"Because she really didn't know where it was. She wasn't even sure Angel was being truthful when she said she had it. She came to D.C. to tell me what she knew, but Robert was having her followed. He knows about Charlie, my family and me."

"Have you been able to get this information to Assistant Director Bridges?"

"Not yet," I admitted. "Interim Director Whitman had a microphone installed under Lila's bed and said he would take care of everything. But that means the FBI will be left in the cold because he believes the DEA is in charge of everything."

"Not in this case," Agent Fielding replied. "This is one heck of a time to be without a cell phone, but we have to trust that he will play by the book on this one. Our only other alternative is to forgo this mission and see if we can't get word to your boss ourselves."

"No," I said. "We make this trip, find Mendoza and see that he ends up where he belongs. Then you can take care of the others while I go home to our son."

Despite knowing what must be done when morning came, I allowed the comfort of his arms to lull me into a far-from-restful sleep. What we were doing had little chance for success, but I had never believed in him more.

The next thing I knew, he was shaking my arm and telling me the sun would soon be up. He had found two heavy jackets for us to wear and two hats—the kind the guards at the compound wore—to put on our heads. It wasn't much of a disguise, but at least we would be warmer.

"Has the rain let up?" I asked as I got to my feet and stretched.

"Enough that it's safe to travel. I've already put your bag in the plane. I figured we couldn't leave it here."

"Thank you," I said, pulling on the heavy boots that had miraculously appeared beside the cot. "I wish I had a good reason to believe that Charlie will see the things Magdalena meant for him to have."

"Don't give up on me now, Reagan. We'll leave it tucked inside the plane while we go to the compound. Manuel will make sure no bothers it."

"Will he also make sure it gets back to the embassy if something happens to us?"

He closed the short distance between us, put his hands on my shoulders and looked into my eyes with an intensity that made me want to back away. "Our only goal is to make sure Mendoza is there. We'll leave his capture to someone else."

"What if that isn't possible?"

"Then we deal with it. I know life is precious, but I'm tired of playing these miserable games. If a confrontation occurs, someone will die."

I felt his pain and uncertainly as he turned and walked away. He was trying to be optimistic for my sake, but Carlos Mendoza was a cruel and driven man. If we were caught, he would make sure our deaths were slow and painful.

Despite my misgivings, I wound my hair into a bun and tucked it inside the hat I would be wearing. Then I followed him from the building. The air was so heavy with moisture I found it difficult to get air into my lungs without coughing. The green foliage that kept the makeshift runway hidden hung close to the ground, and there were pools of water everywhere. I shivered as my boots made sucking sounds in the mud leading to the more solidly-packed earth. There would be no sun today. The best we could hope for was making it to the village before the clouds burst again.

Agent Fielding didn't bother with pleasantries. He merely tossed me an apple as he climbed into the pilot's seat and then maneuvered the airplane into position. There was no one on the ground to tell us we had been cleared for takeoff. Where we were going, we would have the sky to ourselves.

I glanced behind me at the boxes containing weapons as fuel was sent to the engine. Then my eyes closed as my body hurled backwards in the worn seat. I didn't want to be scared, but I was.

The sensation of having weight press against me continued as we climbed upwards. I didn't even bother to look out the window as the trees below us became nothing more than a smear of green before disappearing. We needed a better plan than driving up to the gate in a truck and hoping we would be admitted without being shot. If Mendoza was at the compound, he wouldn't be alone. And he would have the home-court advantage.

Manuel came out of a hut when the plane landed. If he was surprised to see Agent Fielding instead of the usual pilot, he made no mention of it. A few men helped with the boxes of weapons while the women scurried away with the commodities that were necessary to sustain their lives.

"I am glad to see that you are still alive," Manuel said after the last box of rifles had been loaded on an old, flatbed truck and secured for the drive with heavy chains. "I was afraid my people would go hungry after Mendoza was driven from his home. They are not so industrious, but their hearts are good. Father Francis sees to that."

"How is the padre?"

"Very well. He was here yesterday to give us the sacred communion. He will be at the compound for the next few days. That is why I know people have returned."

"Is this the first load of weapons that has been delivered?"

"To this location, yes, but we are not the only village who aids in what the cartel does. Why have you come back? There is still a price on your head."

"I am only here on a mission of discovery. I need to know exactly who is at the compound."

"So you intend to deliver this load of weapons? I would not advise going back, but I know you are not a man who will listen to reason when there is work to be done."

"My reasons for going are my own. Is there anything you can tell us that might aid in our safe return?"

He glanced in my direction, but I was unable to tell if he recognized me as being the woman who had entered his village eight months earlier with an infant in my arms.

"Unfortunately, I have not been to the compound recently, but you can be certain that if Mendoza has come back it will be highly guarded. There is only one person who might be able to help—my niece, Rosa. She was called back into service a few weeks ago, along with her youngest sister. They work inside the house. My worry for them only increases the longer they are there. Rosa can take care of herself, but Anna is much too young to be away from home."

I bit my bottom lip to keep from crying out when I heard her name. That meant she had not been killed in the original raid, and Mendoza did not suspect that her loyalties were not with him. But Anna was young and naïve, and Mendoza was always looking for another conquest. He had even tried to make a move on me.

"I have met Rosa before. She was a good friend to Maria," Agent Fielding said.

"Then you know she can be trusted."

"I would prefer not involving civilians in this, Manuel, but I will try to make sure they are safe."

"Then go with God," he replied. "I will make sure that no harm comes to the plane while you are gone."

Little more was said as we climbed into the cab of the flatbed truck. Agent Fielding lay two machine guns on the seat between us. I couldn't bring myself to look at him as we set out on a narrow road that was filled with enormous potholes and tire tracks so deep that keeping a wheel from becoming lodged in one of them was a constant battle. It was impossible to hear the sound of anything above the noise of the motor's grinding, but I knew the kinds of animals and insects that lurked inside the perimeter of foliage. I had stared into the eyes of many of them knowing that death was only milliseconds away. And I only had to open a window and reach out my hand now to touch something indiscernible that would end my life as surely as any bullet could.

What we were doing was ludicrous on so many levels. Nonetheless, I understood Agent Fielding's need to to finish what he had begun when he first entered Mendoza's compound. I wondered what he was thinking now as each moment took us closer to a deadly showdown if the man he had once worked for was there.

He didn't speak to me until we reached the village where the happy children had been the day of my arrival as a pretend governess to Isabel and Luis. I didn't know how long we had been driving, but the position of the sun, behind lingering clouds, let me know that it had been more than a couple of hours.

"We'll stretch our legs before going on to the compound," he said, shoving his door open and climbing to the ground.

I waited for a few moment before joining him. There was no sign of movement anywhere. "And just what are we going to do when we get there? You haven't said a word to me since we left Manuel, and I think I have a right to know how we're going to proceed."

The look he gave felt like a blast of frigid air. This wasn't the man who had held me in his arms the night before. This was the angry, insensitive and determined man who had led Maria and me into the jungle after I had unintentionally ruined his mission.

"I must have been possessed to allow you to come," he almost snarled. "This is no place for an FBI agent, regardless of how intuitive she believes herself to be. Now, I have to worry about keeping you safe instead of completing this mission like I've always done—alone and unhampered by someone who has no idea what she's up against."

I caught his arm before he stomped away from me. "Don't give me that crap about always working alone. I may not be like Selena Diaz when it comes to giving my all to the cause and knowing how cartels operate, but I'm not stupid, and this isn't my first time in the jungle. I know how to survive. I've been doing it the past eight months with no help from you. Now, quit acting like I'm going to mess up and tell me what you need me to do. I intend to make it home to our son—with or without you."

"Was that your idea of a reality check?" he asked when his eyes stopped blazing and his breathing returned to normal. "I didn't mean to upset you."

"That's a lie! You wanted me to know who was in charge and get me to cower to your wishes like I've always done, but that's not how this relationship is going to work any longer. We're partners in more than just an insane desire to break up this cartel. I've been thinking that I should be the one driving when we get to the compound. No one, other than Mendoza and a few of the household servants, have ever seen my face. Once we're inside, we can slip away while they're unloading the guns and enter the house through the back door. There's a hallway that leads directly to the main entry. If we're careful, we might even make it to the library. Father Francis conducts Mass and takes confessions whenever he comes. That should keep most of the staff occupied. At least they should be thinking about absolution from their own sins and not our unexpected arrival."

"Driving that beast of a truck is no picnic, Reagan. Don't you think they're going to question a woman delivering weapons?"

"Not if you play along. Women can be just as inhumane and unprincipled as men. Haven't we already seen that with Alma, Lupe and Eloise? It's the best chance we've got. We're both dead if anyone recognizes you."

He didn't say anything more. He simply returned to the truck, but this time I was the one behind the wheel. Gears screeched as we moved forward, but Agent Fielding didn't offer any censure. I knew he was busy planning our route into the house and what obstacles we would face once we were inside. We couldn't exactly go in unarmed, but carrying an automatic rifle would alert everyone to our presence. And there had been no time to discuss how we might be able to make our escape.

"Don't worry about saying anything to the guards," Agent Fielding said when we could see the walls surrounding the compound. "They'll be expecting this delivery. Just park where they tell you to, and then wait for my signal. If they're stockpiling in the usual place, we simply take a quick turn to the left and follow the driveway to the back door."

"Won't that leave us exposed?"

"Dressed the way we are, we'll fit right in. We'll have no more than ten minutes to make it back to the truck. People making deliveries are not allowed to stay, and anyone wandering around without authorization will be executed. Are you still glad you came?"

My heart was hammering when the gate clanged and banged its way open, and then a guard with an assault rifle pointed in my direction came to side of the truck. I rolled the window down but didn't look up when he spoke to me.

"Take the truck to the holding warehouse," he said in Spanish. "Our people will help you unload."

I didn't reply, I just put the truck into gear and let the tires roll forward. I could see guards placed at several vantage points along the top of the rock wall, but they didn't seem particularly interested in us.

"Hang a right," Agent Fielding said before we had gone more than a few hundred yards. "The place you're looking for is at the far end of the compound. Mendoza never leaves weapons where they can easily be found. Fortunately for us, it's right next to the house. Once you're out of the truck, move to the left side of the building. I'll join you there."

The men in charge of deliveries were standing in front of the warehouse when we arrived. I slipped one of the automatic rifles sitting between us over my shoulder and then let my feet drop to the ground. The sound of the door slamming shut seemed to reverberate through the heavy, cold air. I noticed that Agent Fielding kept his head down as he lowered the tailgate on the truck and then moved aside so the others could unload close to fifty wooden boxes. I had no idea how many weapons each carton contained.

I moved when he did, and we were soon hurrying towards the back of the house. The scarred, metal door we came to wasn't locked. He pulled it open and stepped inside. Once he had ascertained that we were alone, he motioned for me to join him.

Now that I had regained my bearings and knew exactly where we were, I moved forward as rapidly as I could past the elevator that went to the second floor, the wing where the servants lived, the stairway leading to the wine cellar, the pantry and the walk-in freezer. I paused momentarily as we came to the kitchen door.

"Just keep moving," Agent Fielding whispered. "We don't want any unnecessary confrontations."

The soles of our boots made no sound as we moved across the entry hall with the enormous chandelier. Not everything had been returned to its original place, but it was apparent that someone who valued the residence had returned. A fire was sending out rays of warmth when we entered the library. Agent Fielding told me to stand watch at the door. He would be the one searching for documents that told us what Mendoza's part in the new regime really was and where everyone else was hiding.

Now that I was back where my life-changing journey began, all past memories resurfaced with such intensity that I almost wished Carlos and Alma Mendoza would appear so we could take care of them permanently.

As if someone heard my inner thoughts and immediately responded, the door I was standing next to with my automatic rifle in my hands swung inward knocking me off balance. By the time I regained my footing, losing the hat I had been wearing in the process, a very familiar voice was speaking.

"Please do not stop your snooping on my account, Jorge," Carlos Mendoza said as he advanced into the room wearing a black, velvet smoking jacket with an ascot tied deftly around his neck. "Quite the clever move coming back to my home on a delivery truck. You have been a very competent opponent, but alas, we have updated our surveillance since you were last here. Facial recognition programs are available for people on both sides of the law."

"But I'm still the one holding the gun," Agent Fielding replied.

"Not the only one, Jorge. You can tell your parter to come out from behind the door. You are both too honorable and inquisitive to shoot me before you get the answers you are looking for. I understand that congratulations are in order. The son I thought was mine actually belongs to you. Our Maria was a very naughty girl, along with that agent who thought she could deceive me. I suppose you have had your way with her too. She was a spunky thing— although none too bright. You should both be very concerned if you think you can keep that baby safe from me. I will destroy all of you."

"Your threats mean nothing to me because you won't be walking away this time, Carlos. We're taking you in and will see that you're put in a facility where setting off another bomb will be impossible."

By this time, I had moved further into the room with my gun pointed at Carlos Mendoza's head. He didn't even bother to glance in my direction. He merely laughed in that sickening tone I remembered so well.

"We both have tactical moves that could be made, but only one of us will be victorious. I have used our time apart to gather an army that will not fail me, and you have come here without adequate backup. That was always your biggest flaw, Jorge. You never liked being told what to do, even when you were working for me."

"That may be true, but you can hardly expect me to believe you singlehandedly control the most powerful cartel in all of Colombia after only a few months time. We all know Lupe Evans and her son, Robert, are in charge. Any power you may possess has been granted to you by them."

I knew exactly what Agent Fielding was trying to do, so I took a few steps closer to the two men. We might be holding the guns, but if we opened fire, or tried to get him out of the house without his consent, we would meet with opposition of the most brutal kind.

"You are just trying my patience now, Jorge. Why not sit down and have a drink while we discuss other options. Even with all your past interference, you could yet assume a place of prominence by my side. I need someone ruthless and cunning who knows how to play both sides. You might find it not such a bad place to be."

"That's not going to happen," Agent Fielding said as Mendoza filled two goblets with amber liquid.

"Perhaps I have not stated my case clearly enough, Jorge," Mendoza replied, extending one of them in his direction. Much to my surprise, Agent Fielding took it. "I will have Anna bring us something to eat while we discuss what we both have to lose if we do not come to a reasonable compromise. She has become quite important to me since my return. Man was not meant to sleep alone."

I watched numbly as he pushed a button on his desk. He was bringing her in to use as a hostage. I had to make sure that didn't happen.

"You are nothing but a repulsive animal who preys on the innocent," I said as my finger tightened around the trigger. "How can you live without yourself after molesting a child? No one would blame me if I ended your life right now."

He took a long sip from his glass before turning very slowly and deliberately to face me. "So the other fool decides to speak. I figured you would on your way home to that bastard child you are raising the moment your face appeared on every newscast in our country. You see, I have been appraised of your comings and goings lately, Agent Sinclair. It seems you are no longer that timid mouse who appeared at my door pretending to be a governess. But you have chosen the wrong game to play this time. I only have to decide which one of you will live longest—the parents or the child."

"No one is going to die today," Agent Fielding said.

"That is not true," Rosa calmly responded as she stepped into the room. She was holding a large, crucifix in her hand and Father Francis was not far behind her. "I have just been to confession where I have admitted to all of my sins and was coming here to rectify an impulsive decision, but I fear it is too late."

"What are you talking about?" Mendoza demanded.

"You will be on your way to hell very soon now for defiling my sister, Señor Mendoza. That liquor you are so fond of drinking and giving to your guests has been laced with a generous portion of cyanid that one of your most loyal men told me where to find. I am surprised you not feeling the effects already."

He clutched his throat as his eyes grew large with fright. "You will die for doing this."

"That may be so, Señor Mendoza, but I am ready to pay for my sins. Are you?"

It was almost as if everything moved in slow motion after that. Agent Fielding dropped his untouched glass to the floor and then there was a loud crash as Carlos Mendoza's body hit the side of his desk.

"Get the women out of here," Agent Fielding told Father Francis as he knelt beside the man whose heart was no longer beating. "I will take care of things here. There is a plane waiting at Manuel's village. Tell him what has happened, and he will make sure they are both taken to a place of safety until other arrangements can be made. Is there anyone I can trust here?"

"Anna will be willing to help, as will Tomas Rivera. They are childhood friends. Everyone else is loyal to the new cartel. But you must know that Alma is expected to arrive later this afternoon. I am not sure who will be accompanying her."

I opened my mouth to tell Agent Fielding that I would not leave him alone, but the movement of his hand stopped me.

"This isn't the time for a heartfelt goodbye, or for demanding equal rights. Go with Father Francis and raise our son. I promise to make it back to you, if that God you so fervently believe in feels I am worth saving."

Father Francis took my arm, but not before Rosa had removed the machine gun from my arms, and escorted me from the room. She closed the door to the library and followed us.

"Please do not be afraid," she said as we passed by the door leading into the kitchen. "Father Francis carries a gun when he travels. These mountain roads are not safe for anyone, but he has been granted a certain amount of leniency and protection because of his position. I know my actions will not go unpunished, but I heard most of what was being said. I will do what I can to make sure you are reunited with Maria's child. He does not deserve to suffer any longer for what his parents have done."

Father Francis threw a wool blanket over us after we crawled into the back of the van. "Do not move until we are far away from here. I will tell the guards at the gate that I have been instructed to bring more honey from the monastery. I am not in the habit of lying, but I am sure the Holy Father will forgive me this time."

Somehow, we made it through the gate and were soon bumping down the rutty road I had driven over just a few minutes earlier. It was raining heavily. Perhaps that was why no one had tried to search or detain him. But even with Anna and Tomas's help, a body could not remain hidden for long, and Alma would demand to speak to her brother the moment she arrived. Agent Fielding had sacrificed himself so I could go free, just as he had always done.

Rosa held onto my hand until Father Francis told us it was safe to leave our hiding place.

"I did not mean for anyone else to get caught in my plan to rid the world of Señor Mendoza," she said, straightening her back and leaning against the outside wall of the van. "Perhaps if he had never returned, but the knowledge of his crimes have haunted me for many years. I saw him push his wife over the balcony, and then did as I was commanded in covering it up. I did not even warn Maria when she became involved with him. I could not allow the same thing to happen to Anna."

"You don't have to explain. Carlos Mendoza was an evil and cruel man," I told her as I pushed myself into a sitting position beside her.

"I am not so worried about what will happen to me, but my family must be kept safe."

Telling her that everything would be okay was both unnecessary and unwise. She had abandoned her post and a man was dead. It wouldn't take long until everyone inside the compound was asking the same questions.

It was almost dusk when we arrived back at Manuel's village. The strained look on his face when he saw Rosa only confirmed my belief that the next wave of violence would soon begin. Father Francis told him what had happened in the library.

"I feared this move was much too bold to make," was his reply. "Take Rosa to the monastery and keep her safe until we get word from the compound. Agent Fielding will do all he can to set things right. I will return the plane myself. We must move with precision and haste."

Before anyone else came to the airstrip to inquire as to what was going on, Rosa had returned to the van with Father Francis and the plane was in the air. I sat huddled in the passenger seat as the huts in the village soon disappeared.

Manuel did not address me during the entire bumpy and stressful flight, and there was nothing I could say to him. People took risks because they believed in what they were doing. It was as simple as that.

When we finally landed, he told me to pick up the bag that had been left in the cargo hold and climb into the pickup truck Agent Fielding had left beside the building the night before. He would take me as far as the nearest airport, but there was nothing else he could do. He must return to his village and try to protect his family.

My mind, which had been in a dazed kind of stupor, suddenly came alive when he left me in front of the doors leading into a small terminal in what seemed like the middle of nowhere. It was doubtful any planes would be leaving before morning, and I would have to take my chances when it came to a destination. But I needed to get to Charlie. What Mendoza had said about killing him could not be ignored.

The first flight I could book was to Honduras. I paid for my ticket with the only credit card I carried. It could be easily traced, but I doubted anyone would come looking for me for a few days. My biggest concern was getting word to the Colombian embassy in Bogotá about what had happened at Mendoza's compound. It took several tries, using a pay phone on the concourse, before a connection was made. Much to my surprise Veronique Stevens answered.

"I have been worried about you ever since Agent Diaz arrived alone last night. I do not know if she has been able to do what was asked. She has been away all day, and my husband has not yet returned."

The time for worrying about her loyalty had passed. "Is there any way you can get a message to him? I cannot give you any details, but Agent Fielding is at the compound in the jungle. Mendoza is there, and Alma was expected to join him before nightfall."

"Say no more, my husband will hear of what has happened immediately. I will not ask how you know this. I can only hope you are on your way out of our country. The media is still covering Leila's abduction and Miss River's survival. The cartel will not stop looking for either of you."

"I won't come back," I told her. "Just promise me that your husband will do everything he can to help the people who have given all they have to this cause."

While waiting for my flight, I went into the women's bathroom to tidy up. I looked like someone from a refuge camp in my oversized coat, heavy, muddy boots and torn coveralls. It was a miracle I had been allowed to purchase a plane ticket at all, and anyone who saw me would remember. For that reason, I removed what I wearing and replaced it with the clothing Magdalena had given me. Then I ran my fingers through my hair before putting the shawl over my head and joining the other passengers.

From Honduras, I purchased a ticket to Washington D.C. I didn't have the funds to keep hopping from one airport to another, and I needed to be home. I tried to rest on both flights, but it was impossible not to think about what might be happening to the people I had left behind or what I might be facing when I landed. While Mendoza could no longer make good on his threats when it came to Charlie, Alma would seek revenge. And there was no way of knowing what Lupe or Robert Evans would do when they learned of his relationship to them.

My innocent baby was in the middle of this barbaric nightmare, and it was up to me to make sure no one ever found him.

Chapter 15

The terminal was filled with noise and people when I landed on American soil, but there was no one to greet me. Neil was gone, my boss didn't know I was back, and my family had to be protected.

As I saw it, I had only a few hours to make some crucial decisions. Assistant Director Bridges would offer protection for as long as he could, but there was a limit to what he could do now that the Colombian government was involved. If they discovered who I was, they would demand extradition so I could answer some very difficult questions. I no longer believed that anyone could protect me if that happened.

I hailed the first available taxi and told the driver to take me directly to FBI headquarters. There was no logical reason to believe that Assistant Director Bridges would be in his office, but from past experience, I knew he rarely went home before midnight.

My thoughts turned to Sam and Lila as we passed darkened buildings and tall streetlights on our way through the city. I didn't know if they were safe or even alive, and my son's grandmother . . . Well, her life may have already ended. So many people had given their all trying to stop the production and shipment of cocaine, but it would never be enough.

Whatever impulsive or humanitarian decisions I had made in the past had to be accepted, learned from and resolved—even my childish fantasies about Agent Fielding. He was not some romantic figure out of a novel or movie. He was a flawed, but extraordinary, individual who was more committed to his career than to the people who were supposed to be part of his life. If I did what I knew must be done, I could say a permanent goodbye to all my unrealistic dreams. But maybe that was how it was supposed to be.

The cabbie pulled up in front of the building at 935 Pennsylvania Avenue. I gave him the required amount of money, slung the heavy bag containing the things Magdalena wanted her grandson to have over my shoulder and climbed out. Once I saw the assistant director, every part of my life would change.

The doors were never locked, but a minimum of two guards were always stationed at the main desk to make sure no one without clearance was admitted beyond the metal detectors. While I hardly resembled an FBI agent in my flared skirt and red, wool shawl, lengthy explanations were neither required nor expected. I simply produced my badge and then waited for admittance.

Somewhere between landing at the village and my return to civilization, my service revolver had disappeared. That had come to my attention rather jarringly when I passed through the first security check in Colombia on my way to Honduras. I was fairly certain Manuel had it, unless he had allowed someone else to riffle through my bag. I would explain its disappearance when the time came.

It was after eleven when I made my way past a silent and empty bullpen and up the stairs to Bridge's office. My head was pounding and my knees weak, but that was to be expected since it had been nearly thirty hours since I'd last slept. No one was in his outer office, but I could see a light coming from underneath his door. I rapped loudly on it while telling him who I was.

"I don't even know where to begin," he said as the door opened, and he motioned for me to come in. His eyes were red-rimmed, his light-blue shirt crumpled and the muscles around his lips twitching. I was surprised that he was not alone. My partner, Agent Howard, was seated in one of the chairs facing his desk. I slid into the other one without saying anything.

"Director Stevens called earlier today," he continued. "Otherwise, I might be home in bed right now. I sent you to Texas at the DEA's request because I believed it was the right thing to do, but I am incapable of understanding how, or even why, you would allow yourself to be drawn back into this horrible situation after all you've been through. If something cannot be done to squelch these claims regarding your involvement in a supposed kidnapping, it could erupt into an international incident. What in the world were you thinking?"

"I guess I wasn't thinking, sir," I replied. "Lila had been shot, and there was reason to believe she wouldn't survive, so I went."

"I am not questioning your loyalty, Agent Sinclair. What I want to know is why you didn't go directly to the hospital to see Miss Rivers with Interim Director Whitman, instead of spending over ninety-six hours with Agent Fielding stirring up trouble none of us needs."

"Lila hadn't awakened from surgery, and he wanted me to meet Charlie's grandmother. It was supposed to be a fast and simple trip. I know you can't condone what I've done, but Carlos Mendoza is dead, and some solid leads have been established that could bring the entire organization down."

"It's going to take more than my forgiveness to get you out of this. The state department is asking for our full cooperation since an American was involved. Who is Leila Gonzales, and why did the DEA want her so badly they involved a member of my task force in a kidnapping?"

"It's a long story, sir," I replied.

"Then enlighten us. We can't help if we don't have all the facts."

"Director Stevens didn't tell you about the contents of a letter I found in the Bible Charlie's biological grandmother gave us?"

"There wasn't time. He was following another unsuccessful lead. He only said he was making arrangements to get you out of the country before your identity was uncovered and you ended up in a Colombian jail."

"What about Interim Director Whitman?"

"Not a word. Why?"

"Because I'm the one who doesn't know where to begin now. I could tell you everything that happened in Colombia, but it's not entirely relevant to the situation here. The interim director promised to contact you after planting a bug in Lila's hospital room so he could overhear a conversation we had three days ago. That key Agent Howard found belongs to a safety deposit box at a US Bank. In addition to a signed affidavit as to the part she played in all of this, it contains a videotaped conversation between Angel and Robert Evans outlining their plans to kill Walter and much more."

"Damn it," Assistant Director Bridges swore. "After all we've done to help the DEA, I can't believe they would keep something like this from us. I suppose it's unrealistic to believe it might still be there."

"In all fairness to the interim director, he may have been a little preoccupied. The last time I saw him, he was on his way to a safe house with Lila after she was operated on for a second time in a veterinarian's clinic. I know because I assisted the doctor before being sent to a mechanic's garage."

"Where you disobeyed even more directives . . ." he interrupted. "I'm not even going to ask if you accompanied Agent Fielding to Mendoza's compound. You wouldn't be dressed the way you are if you'd done what you were told."

"Please don't blame him for my actions, sir. I was fighting for my family."

"We can discuss that later. Right now, I want Agent Howard to gain access to that safety despot box and make sure it has not been disturbed."

"What about me?" I asked.

"You're going to wait in conference room three until I come to get you."

He didn't elaborate, and I didn't ask any questions. I simply left his office and made my way down the hallway. When I got to the specified room, I left the light off and dropped into the nearest chair. With my elbows on the table, I rested my forehead in the palms of my hands. There was no reason for outbursts of any kind. What had happened wasn't any one person's fault.

Even so, I couldn't help but wonder why God had not pulled me back when he knew where I was going to end up. I didn't want to face what was coming. I had suffered enough trauma and loss to last a lifetime, but denying his many miracles was futile. He had carried me through hundreds of situations I would never have survived on my own. Asking for more divine intervention now seemed both selfish and a little cowardly. But if I did what I knew I must, I would be leaving everything familiar behind.

My contemplation came to an end when Assistant Director Bridges returned. He flipped on the light. His look was anything but encouraging.

"I spoke with Director Stevens again. He assures me that Lila is in stable condition. Interim Director Whitman will remain with her until it is safe to bring her home. He also gave me a brief rundown on how you assisted in getting three of Magdalena Gonzalez's daughters to safety and the role he asked you to play in getting Leila into DEA custody. What I don't understand is why this new cartel is so interested in the family of an agent who died in the line of duty months ago, regardless of the fact that Carlos Mendoza once believed her child belonged to him. The men who followed you to Villavincencio picked up Magdalena's husband and remaining daughter at their vegetable stand, after she had gone with them willingly. Perhaps you could fill in some of the blanks so I can handle things on this end more effectively."

"You really want to know all the sordid details that have ruined what was left of my life?"

"Only the ones that will aid in making certain difficult decisions."

"Then you need to know that Walter Evans had an affair with Magdalena's mother while he was courting Lupe."

The look of shock on his face let me know that he didn't need any further explanations. "So Charlie's grandmother is Robert Evan's half-sister."

"That's only part of it. Maria's sister, Leila, was planning to rule by Robert's side once he got a divorce. I fear any help she may have offered the DEA came from a place of revenge and not a sense of duty to correct any personal wrongs. She truly believed she had found the life, and the people, who would make all of her dreams come true."

Assistant Director Bridges sat down and put his arms over his head. "I feel sorry for the girl. Becoming involved with a man she didn't know was her uncle must have been devastating. But we can't ignore the elephant in the room by focusing on anyone else right now."

"What about Agent Fielding?" I asked.

"Director Stevens got your message about him needing help, but it isn't easy getting to the compound—let alone getting inside without massive casualties. Why didn't you just tell his wife that Mendoza was dead? He seemed quite surprised by the news."

I forced myself to look at him and not the tabletop. "We didn't kill him, sir, if that's what you're thinking. We went to the compound simply to see if he was there. Agent Fielding and I both believed he had more to do with the operation than previously thought, but we needed proof."

"Did you get that?" he asked.

"I can only tell you that we found him, and he seemed very pleased with himself. He was building an arsenal and had increased security surveillance. He walked into the library while we were looking for something we could use."

"If neither of you shot him, how did he die?"

"He was poisoned. One of the servants had witnessed him murder his wife and torture Maria. When he moved on to her youngest sister, she took matters into her own hands. Mendoza's law are the only ones that exist in the jungle. Agent Fielding said he would try to contain the situation while the priest got Rosa and me to safety. I probably should have been more forthright with the director's wife, but . . . "

"You needed to give Agent Fielding the space necessary to perform some of his magic. I understand your allegiance to him. I probably would have done the same thing, but the fact remains that he may be beyond anyone's help by now."

"Don't you think I know that, sir," I replied. "Leaving him alone in that library with a body to dispose of and one of his greatest enemies on the way was the hardest thing I've ever done. But we both knew what would happen if we went looking for answers."

"Then you need to know that no one has heard from him, but we can no longer disregard the price you have on your head—or the one that will be on Charlie's when Robert or Lupe Evans find out who he is."

"I'm prepared to do as you say, sir," I responded.

"That's good because we need to make both of you disappear, and I've already started the process."

"Exactly what have you done?" I asked as the blood rushed to my head making it difficult to think.

"I'm having your apartment cleared out as we speak. By morning, there will be no trace of you ever having lived there."

It was too late to stifle my gasp of honest horror. "What about my family?"

"You knew the chance of going into the witness protection program was real when you brought Charlie to the United States. I'm surprised it hasn't happened sooner, but it's unavoidable now. I'll have an extra team keep an eye on your family, and have them moved to a different location if necessary. But you cannot contact them. If anyone recognizes who you are from that image being blasted across all the television sets in Colombia, you will have more than just the cartels to worry about."

"Where will I be sent?" I asked.

"We have several properties across the country ready to be occupied, but it will take a few hours to create new identities and make arrangements for transport with the federal marshals. Due to the sensitive nature of this operation, only Agent Howard and I will know the specifics of your relocation. I hope you trust him the way you did Agent Southwick because your life is literally in our hands now."

"I do," I responded. "Has he been able to get inside the safety deposit box? I would like to know if the information has been secured before I leave."

"I'm still waiting to hear from him. Meanwhile, I want you to go the VIP suite to shower and rest. I've made sure it's available and has what you need. I'll make arrangements for Charlie to be brought to my office when preparations are complete. This is hardly the way I wanted this to end, Agent Sinclair. You had a very bright future with the FBI."

There was nothing I could say in reply. I had broken too many rules to ask if I might be reinstated when the current situation was resolved. So I picked up the key he left on the table and took the elevator to the right floor. A terrycloth robe hung on a hook in the bathroom. I would worry about what I was going to wear when someone came to get me, but that happened sooner than anticipated.

"Who's there?" I called out, forcing myself from the bed where I was trying to rest.

"It's me, Agent Howard. I've brought a few things from your apartment."

I pulled open the door, realizing that this was first time we had spoken directly to each other since my return. The largest suitcase from my closet was sitting on the floor beside him.

"This may be a little presumptuous, Reagan, but after seeing you in Bridges's office, I thought you might appreciate having some of your own clothes to wear. I promise I didn't go through any of your drawers. I had one of the women assigned to clearing things out pack a few things and leave them at the front desk. Everything you own should arrive at your new place eventually. At least that's what the assistant director is working towards."

"Do you agree with him about this being the only option I have left?"

He slid the suitcase inside the room before answering. "I've never worked with anyone who had to go into hiding before, but it seems like a logical plan."

"So I really am going to be in the custody of the United States government—possibly for the rest of my life."

He touched my arm reassuringly. "You can't look at it that way. There are thousands of men and women in two agencies who will be working tirelessly to bring the people who have threatened every part of your life to justice, and I will be among them. The DEA should be honoring you for meritorious service. Hell, you weren't even a member of their team, and you still gave them everything you had."

"It's not like I didn't have a few debts to pay. Were you able to get into Lila's safety deposit box?"

"Everything inside is being catalogued and secured as we speak. That video, along with her confession, will go a long way in getting Robert Evans put away."

"He still has to be found. I wish I could see what she wrote."

"No, you don't," he responded. "She laid out everything in explicit detail. Just remember her as the person she had become who made a sacrifice for the people she loved. Now, you need to get dressed. The assistant director wants you in his office in thirty minutes. He needs you out of the city before it gets light."

The first person I saw when I walked back into Bridge's office was my son standing on the floor holding Amanda's hand.

"He doesn't like to be held quite so much now that he knows he can go places on his own," she said.

I felt a familiar lump of regret lodge in my throat when he looked up at me and smiled. Between my time in Texas and Mexico, I had been gone for over ten days. "How long has he been walking?"

"He's still learning, but I've never seen such a determined child. I videotaped everything and put it on a disk. I'm so sorry about what's happened."

"Me too," I replied, dropping to my knees and pulling him into my arms. He squirmed around but didn't protest.

"I hate to cut this reunion short, but there isn't much time," Assistant Director Bridges said. "If you will excuse us, Agent Cole. It's not that I don't trust you, but the fewer people who know about this the safer everyone will be."

She looked over at me as the tears formed. It wasn't easy being a woman in the FBI, and she had helped me understand both my limitations and my strengths after Neil's death. I was going to miss her.

"I understand, sir," she replied as she gave me a quick hug and kissed Charlie's upturned cheek. "Be safe, and know there are a lot of people working and praying for your quick return. I'll get

Charlie's things. I've made sure you have everything you need for the next forty-eight hours. I hope that will be enough."

"You've been amazing, Amanda. I couldn't have asked for a better friend."

"This is the worst part," my boss said after she left the room with Agent Howard. "I've secured transportation, new birth certificates for Charlie and you, a driver's license, and a bank card with enough to keep you going until your new job as a longterm history sub starts to kick in. It might not be the ideal situation, but it was the best that could be done on such short notice. All the information you need is in that manila envelope. Guard it carefully. Agent Howard will make sure you make it to the state line where the U.S. Marshals will meet you at a place called Granny's and escort you to your new home in Kansas City. Everything should be ready by the time you get there."

"But a teacher!" I exclaimed, since it was the only thing that seemed to register. "I'm not sure I can do that. I remember how horrible kids were in high school."

"I'm sure they're even worse now, but with your training I have no doubt that you can keep them under control. I've already contacted Director Stevens with the information you gave me. No one is going to let this slide. We'll keep working until you're able to come home again."

"I know that, sir, but I have to admit that I'm scared. Are you sure it wouldn't be better if I just stayed here? Charlie could remain with Agent Cole, and I could work every angle possible until Robert Evans, and everyone else involved, is in custody. I wouldn't even have to go home. I could stay right here at the agency."

His smile was sympathetic. "Your help would be invaluable, but we can't be sure there aren't additional moles in either organization. Like it or not, you are in the middle of all of this, and I will not lose another agent. I'll give you a burner phone, but I hope the only call that is made is the one telling you that it's time to come home."

"What do I do now?" I asked.

"You wait while I make sure everything here is in place. Just leave your badge and your service revolver on my desk. They'll be waiting when you come back."

"About that," I said, unclipping my badge. "My gun seems to have disappeared somewhere in the jungle."

"Then let's hope it remains lost," he replied. "You'll be under constant surveillance by the U.S. Marshals, and I'll issue you an unmarked gun that cannot be traced. You can carry it with you. Agent Howard will make sure you have ammunition."

"Thank you, sir. I'll keep it hidden."

"That's what I'm counting on. I know this is hard, but it isn't the first time I've helped someone start over. You're going to make it through this latest challenge, and when it's resolved, you'll be back working with the unit. Just have faith in the process, and even if you don't, use your religious beliefs to keep you focused. I may not share them, but I do recognize their benefits."

"I'll do that," I told him as an amber-colored envelope was pushed in my direction.

"Everything I've told you about is in there, along with a phone that has been set up in your new name. Please don't get it mixed up with the burner. I'll update you if I can, but for this to work, you have to accept that you're not going to know anything besides what comes out on your local news channel or in the papers. You absolutely cannot go off chasing some lead on your own."

I glanced over at my son who was rapidly making his way across the floor towards a large, potted plant with trailing vines and made a swift move to grab him before he got there. "I won't let you down, sir. You helped give me the greatest miracle of my life."

"Just remember that when you get discouraged. You have the potential of becoming one of the best agents I've ever worked with, but we've got to keep you alive for that to happen. Hang tight for a minute, and we'll have you on your way."

I left the safety of the FBI building a few minutes later in an unmarked blue Ford with Agent Howard at the wheel. I sat in the passenger seat with Charlie in the back. Amanda had fed him breakfast. He was dressed for the day, but it wasn't quite time for his morning nap. I handed him a bottle of juice after strapping him in and hoped for the best. Our suitcases had been put in the trunk, and the envelope containing everything I needed to know about my new life was in the shoulder bag sitting beside my feet.

"Aren't you going to check out your new identity? I know I would be more than a little curious about the life the government had concocted for me," he said as we merged into a steady stream of traffic.

The sun was just beginning to rise over the tops of the tall buildings that surrounded us. It was going to be another pleasant day in the city—weather-wise anyway.

"That can wait," I replied, turning my head to see what kind of vehicle was in the lane behind us. "I'm more concerned with making sure we're not being followed."

"I know what I'm doing, Reagan."

"This isn't just some routine assignment. My son is with us. His safety is my most pressing concern."

"I get that," he said, glancing in my direction. "I wouldn't trust anyone with my kids either, but you have to know that Bridges is a master at what he does. He will leave no stone unturned when it comes to the wellbeing of his agents."

"I just wish he could give me a timeline of when this will all be over. I feel utterly disconnected and useless."

"You are an integral part of everything that is happening. That's bound to make anyone jumpy, but you can't afford to be reckless after all the work that has gone into making this happen. You take unnecessary chances, and while they often yield great results, they don't always go as planned. There are thousands of competent agents in the FBI and DEA who know exactly what they're doing, but only one person can be Charlie's mother. If I'd gone though what you have in getting him, I wouldn't risk being able to raise him, not when you know who is coming after you."

I felt my heart leap. He had said coming—not who might be coming. "What do you know that I don't? My hands may be tied when it comes to actively participating in bringing these criminals down, but I don't deserve being left completely in the dark."

He realized his mistake immediately and tried to correct it. "I'm just taking a proactive approach. The authorities are closing in on some very ruthless people, and they will retaliate. You need to be ready for that. There is no doubt in my mind that you will be called to testify when this is over, and it won't be in Mexico. Just keep that in mind whenever you feel this isn't necessary."

It took little more than ninety minutes for us to arrive at Granny's where we were to meet the two U.S. marshals, Farmer and Hastings, who would take Charlie and me to our new home. I wasn't the least bit interested in what it might look like. My very soul was in turmoil as I tried not to dwell on all I had lost—from Neil, family and friends to my job and ever feeling safe again. But mostly, I just tried to keep my thoughts from drifting to Sam and the strong likelihood that I would never see him again.

No one appeared to have followed us. For that I was grateful, but I still kept the gun Bridges had given me where it could be reached quickly. I knew he was making the only decision he could when it came to our safety, but I wasn't ready to accept a new kind of normal yet.

The two men waiting for us were dressed in street clothing like Agent Howard. They produced their badges and gave the proper password before I was allowed to step out of the car. They greeted me cordially, but there was an unmistakable air about them that let me know this wasn't the first time they had accepted displaced agency persons into their program.

I tried not to think about the future as suitcases and Charlie's infant seat were switched to their car for the rest of the drive. Since there were two of them to do the driving, we would not stop for the night. It would be up to me to make sure my son was cooperative. Thankfully, Amanda had packed sufficient formula, snacks and toys to help him survive the ordeal. He was't fond of traveling by car.

"I guess this is it for the time being," Agent Howard said as he stood next to my door before closing it. "I promise we won't give up until you're home again."

There were tears in my eyes when I looked up at him. He was my last link with anything familiar. "I'm going to hold you to that."

"Wouldn't have it any other way," he responded, giving me an unexpected hug before turning to my companions. "Take good care of them. They're some of the best."

The door slammed shut, and I heard the bang of his fist on the top of the car. My heart was racing when we pulled out of the parking lot. It would be several hours until we stopped for something to eat. The federal marshals wanted to put as much distance between us and Washington D.C. as possible.

While I understood that the witness protection program saved a great many lives, it wasn't infallible. Watching Neil die in what was supposed to be a safe house had shown me that. The best I could do was to follow the rules and remain vigilant. Everything else was in God's hands.

"What can you tell me about the place we'll be staying?" I asked when I could stand the silence in the car no longer. They were not talking, and the radio had not been turned on. "I know I'm supposed to be teaching history at a local high school."

"We'll see the house at the same time you do," Marshall Farmer, who was riding shotgun, said. "It's supposed to be in a quiet, suburban neighborhood with an apartment above the garage. The marshal who will be living on site is moving in now, and a connecting door to the main house is being installed to make surveillance easier. We can't exactly hang around a single woman and a child without drawing undo attention. Tracy Sullivan is about your age and very competent, but we'll never be too far away. The rest of what you need to know should be in the papers that were sent with you. I suggest you become comfortable with everything before we arrive. It will make the transition easier."

That reminded me that I had yet to open the manila envelope Bridges had sent. I was almost afraid to see what it contained. Regardless of the direction my life had gone, I liked who I was and couldn't imagine being anyone else. According to my new driver's license and birth certificate, my name was Randi Morley. The brief background story I was to commit to memory said that my husband's name was Vaughn. We had been married for three years, and he was a Marine stationed in Afghanistan. Our son Charles Christopher—thank goodness I would still be able to call him Charlie

—had been born on August 12. No mention was made of it having been a natural birth or an adoption. It would be up to me to come up with something believable, that I could live with, as to why our blood types didn't match and why I was still a virgin when I had been married for several years.

I had a new social security number, a bank account, and a military insurance card that would allow either Charlie or me to be seen at any hospital or clinic and minimize questions. Other than a few minor details that would help in solidifying my cover story, I could invent anything I desired. But keeping the lies to a minimum was a priority for me because it was too hard to keep them straight.

I asked for a pitstop when necessary, ate when my companions were ready, and tried to sleep when Charlie did. My comments and questions were limited because the responses I got were always short and rather curt. I knew the men I was with were only doing their job, and protecting another federal agent who had as much baggage as I did wasn't going to be easy, but a little reassurance would have made the trip less difficult and lonely.

We arrived in Kansas City late the next morning. The house I was taken to had been built during the beginning of the twenty-first century. I could tell that much from the construction materials and design. There was a long front porch, river rock on the bottom half and vinyl siding on the second level. There was nothing pretentious about it, but then a young, married woman whose husband was in the military wouldn't have the resources for a home in a more expensive neighborhood.

A late-model minivan was parked in the driveway, and the windows facing the street in the apartment above the garage were open. I could hear music playing when I pushed my car door open and tried to climb out.

A girl wearing shorts and a tank top came hurrying down the outside stairs with a bright, welcoming smile. She didn't look any more like a federal agent than I did, but then that was part of the rouse to keep us safe. She had her arms around my neck before I even realized what was happening.

"Don't look now, but there are people on this street who are going to want to know everything about us," she said. "I had a couple stop by last night with a plate of cookies to welcome me to the neighborhood. I told them I was renting the upstairs apartment from my cousin who would be arriving today. They know your pretend husband is in the Marines and this is your first home off a military base. A moving van should be arriving later today with your personal belongings. The house has the essential furniture. My job is make your transition as painless as possible while keeping both of you safe."

I didn't know what to say. She had already started to spread the lie that was now my life.

U.S. Marshal Farmer had unbuckled Charlie's car seat by the time my embrace with Tracy Sullivan ended. "I'll put your suitcases on the front porch, but we won't hang around to chat. I don't want anyone remembering that we've even been here. Additional surveillance will be in place within the hour. Until then, just sit tight and don't leave the house. We'll be in touch after we've checked in at the field office."

"All right," I said, turning my attention to Charlie. He was awake and starting to cry. The next few days would be incredibly hard for both of us.

I stood beside my new protector as they drove away. There was no one on the street, but that didn't mean someone wasn't watching. From this point on, I was Randi Morley—wife of a Marine, soon-to-be history teacher, and the only one who could keep my son safe.

"Charlie is adorable, Randi," Tracy said, stepping right into character as she walked beside me carrying the car seat and diaper bag. I had my son in my arms with the heavy and soiled bag I had carried all the way from Colombia over my shoulder. "I'll try not to intrude on your private time, but my job is to make sure you remain safe. I know I don't have to worry about you doing something stupid that will blow your new cover."

"Most certainly not," I replied. "Safeguarding my son is my only concern."

"Then we should get along just fine. I know I'm young, but this isn't my first assignment."

She led me inside through a door that already had a security camera in place. To the right of the tile entry—and the staircase that led to the floor above—was a spacious great room with a large bay window and gas fireplace. Beyond that was a dining room and a sunny kitchen overlooking a spacious backyard with a wooded area behind it. There were beautiful trees all around the property.

"This is nice," I told her as I watched a small deer nibble at grass that needed to be cut.

"My thoughts exactly," she replied. "The master bedroom is on the main level behind the office. There are three additional bedrooms upstairs. A connecting door to the apartment above the garage has been cut into one of them. I'll be using that room at night so I'll be closer. We don't have to share meals unless you want to. I have a fully functioning kitchen. My job is to make sure no one gets close enough to cause any harm and watch Charlie while you're at work. I come from a big family so I know what to do."

"You don't have to explain your qualifications," I responded, setting my son on the floor where he immediately began exploring. I put the bag containing Magdalena's Bible on the dining room table. "This may be very new to me, but I do understand why it's necessary. I will maintain my cover and keep from causing you any trouble. Do you know when I report to school? The instructions I got were rather vague."

"First thing in the morning. Plans are underway to make that position permanent, but it will take some time. I'll bring the suitcase inside and put the car seat in the van while you get settled. I've been instructed to be your chauffeur for a few days. We can make adjustments as warranted or necessary."

I took my time looking around the house. It really was a lovely place with plenty of sunlight, clean carpets, adequate furnishings, fresh paint and inlaid flooring in the living area. The master bathroom had a jetted tub and huge walk-in closet. There was a brick patio with an outdoor fireplace and flowers like the ones my mother grew at home in the back yard. With a little care, it would be the perfect place to raise a family, but I didn't want to look at it that way. I needed to believe that people who had any interest in us would soon be caught.

We had soup and crackers after I had unpacked the few belongings Agent Howard had made available for me. I explained

Charlie's schedule and what he most liked to eat. She warned me about Brown Recluse and Black Widow spiders and where they would most likely be found. She also showed me pictures of local poisonous snakes like the timber rattler, cottonmouth, pygmy rattler, massasauga and copperhead and told me to be careful when I was walking around outside. I told her I had been raised in the south and knew how to be careful.

My trepidation at pulling off a stint in the classroom proved to be less challenging than I thought it would be. I had a natural affinity for my students, loved the subject material, and the faculty and staff were friendly and willing to help—especially with the new computer programs for reporting grades, keeping in touch with parents and integrating everything that was taught into a digital format so lesson content could be accessed by students at home.

I worried that too many questions about my family and home life would be asked. The lies I was already telling were cumbersome enough, so I told my new acquaintances that I was an only child whose parents had been killed in a car accident several years earlier. My cousin was staying with me to help out around the house and watch my son, and my husband was in special forces so I really had no idea where he was or when he might be coming home. I hoped the rumor mill would do the rest and people would think it insensitive to pry any further into my life.

I couldn't exactly produce a wedding picture, or even one of my pretend husband, but I wore a simple gold band and put a photo of Charlie on my desk. My students and colleagues seemed to enjoy listening to stories about the things he was learning to do. It was all I could safely talk about without backing myself into some corner. Tracy continued to assure me that fitting in was an illusion best perpetuated by making it appear that I had nothing to hide.

While we were both dedicated to the work we had committed to do, our personal relationship took a beating from the beginning. She was open and friendly and wanted our ruse as cousins to remain believable. But to her, that meant meant sharing a bottle of wine or drinking a can of beer in the evening, speaking exactly what was on our minds and watching movies or television shows with enough violence, sex and profanity that I always ended up excusing myself and leaving the room. It didn't help when she asked for an explanation. I tried to put into words my stance on everything from alcohol, tobacco and caffeinated drinks to attending church services and blessing the food we ate.

She agreed that we both had the right to believe as we liked, but she was a self-proclaimed agnostic who saw nothing wrong with enjoying all the pleasures life had to offer. That's why my stance about not having sex until my wedding night caused her to throw her hands in the air and decide to spend most of her evenings alone. I wasn't trying to be difficult, but I couldn't change how I felt. I needed my relationship with God to remain intact. He was the only reason Charlie and I were still alive.

It took five days for the moving van to arrive. Charlie was too big to be put in a dresser drawer again, so I had him sleep in the king-sized bed with me. It wasn't the safest solution, but he enjoyed the freedom of rolling around while he slept. I had a blanket in place to keep from falling off, but my own rest was minimal at best. The moment his crib was unloaded, I created his own space in what was supposed to be an office.

Setting up a new home, starting a new job and trying to fit into an established neighborhood kept my mind and body occupied the first few weeks I was in Kansas City. I managed to make it through Easter, plant a small vegetable garden in the back yard when the weather became warm enough, and survive both Mother's and Father's Day without falling apart. But by the fourth of July, my nerves were so raw I began spending part of each night clutching my blanket and screaming into my pillow over the injustice of being separated from the people I loved simply because I was trying to do my job.

Adding to my discomfort were the nightmares that refused to stop. I longed to know if Lila had recovered and was back in the Unites States, but mostly I worried about my son's father. He had sent me away so I could keep Charlie safe, but I had fully believed that it wouldn't take long to dismantle the rest of the cartel now that Mendoza was dead. I tried several times to sketch his likeness, but I wasn't an artist, and I couldn't begin to replicate his image as it appeared in my mind.

I even contemplated driving to Maine and breaking into his grandmother's house to lay claim to the scrapbooks she had made before anyone else found, and perhaps even destroyed, them. But as it was, I couldn't go anywhere until my own ban was lifted, so I did my personal suffering in silence.

Regardless of my desire to follow every rule, I felt like I was living in some meandering maze never knowing when someone evil might come looking for us. I questioned the sincerity of everyone I met from the teller in the bank, to the clerk at the store and the receptionist at the pediatrician's office. I rarely let Charlie out of my sight, except for the time I was required to be at work. It was an injustice to his developmental growth, but I was afraid of failing Sam.

Charlie's first birthday come and went with little fanfare. I baked him a cake, decorated the house, purchased a few presents and took numerous pictures, but only Tracy and I were there to help him celebrate. Had we been able to go home, his special day would have been shared with grandparents, aunts, uncles and cousins. There would have been a huge dinner, followed by silly games, unwrapping a veritable mountain of presents, and eating copiousness amounts of cake and ice cream. Charlie would have loved it.

And then it was fall. I had heard nothing from Assistant Director Bridges for nearly six months. I avidly followed both print and broadcast news at home and at school but without clearance to access any government databases, what I gleaned was minuscule. The very people the FBI and DEA were trying to bring down were fueling, at least in part, much of what was being seen and heard.

Chapter 16

It was late on Thanksgiving evening, and I was sitting on the sofa in my living room staring blankly at the television screen without even knowing what program was on. It had been a long day. I had cooked a twenty-pound turkey with all the trimmings. I would never say that my pie crust now rivaled that of my mother, but at least I was mastering a few culinary skills. Tracy had eaten with us and had helped clean up the kitchen.

Our past differences had mostly been resolved. She had even consented to attending worship services a couple of times since she knew how important they were to me, and she didn't like sending me away from the house on my own. We were spending some of our evenings together again watching much milder forms of entertainment. She was in her apartment above the garage now. I was supposed to be reading a book, but my mind was rarely still long enough to remember what had been read. That's why the television was on. If I could find something to capture my interest, it was a much-needed release from fighting the demons that had yet to leave me alone.

I would go back and change so many things about my past if I could, but that wasn't part of the plan God obviously had in mind for me. I couldn't even say that Charlie had been given a raw deal by being born in the jungle and being related to members of one of the most nefarious drug cartels ever created—one who took innocent lives as easily as they paid bribes and didn't let family ties get in the way. He was my joy, my hope for a brighter future and my only contentment with what wasn't such a horrible life. I just needed to get passed the huge hole in my heart—the one left because I could not be with all the people I loved.

Eight months in exile seemed like a lifetime. Charlie was running all over the house now, and it was a constant struggle to keep him from getting into things he shouldn't. His vocabulary was expanding at a tremendous rate, and I knew he understood nearly everything I said. I loved hearing his voice first thing each morning as he chattered and sang in his crib, and his hugs and kisses still made my heart soar. He was a well-adjusted, happy toddler who knew he was loved, and he rarely got sick—despite the weakness his body had displayed after such a traumatic birth.

I talked to him constantly about his extended family. That included his biological mother, grandmother and aunts. I prayed for them each day, just as I prayed for his father. I kept the emergency phone Assistant Director Bridges had given me charged and in a place where I wouldn't miss his call. But with each passing day of silence, my expectations of hearing something positive diminished. This war with the cartel could go on indefinitely, and I might never know what had happened to anyone from my past.

Without conscious thought, I dimmed the light, lay down on the sofa and pulled the blanket that had been covering my knees up to my shoulders. I had spent many nights in the great room of my home recently. It was easier than climbing into bed where I always fought for sleep to come. I would enjoy the next three days with Charlie, doing everything I could to make him happy, and then return to the classroom on Monday. I had been given a full-time job that fall, despite not having the right credentials. I might have to satisfy state regulations eventually, but for now, I was just grateful no one had come looking for us.

I listened to the ticking of the grandfather clock in the entry hall as my eyes closed. I had become an expert at using both breathing and counting techniques to stop my heart and mind from racing, but when sleep did come, it never lasted for long. Since I couldn't afford to see a local therapist where I might reveal something I shouldn't, I was keeping a daily journal. In it, I explored   every feeling I was having. Nothing was too insignificant. I might be the only parent Charlie ever had, and I needed to be a positive and productive one. I thought about Neil and Maria often. I knew they were helping me from the other side. I could feel one, or both, of them in the room with me when I felt I could no longer go on alone.

I was just slipping into that hazy fog of forgetfulness when I heard a loud pounding on the stairs.

"Get up, Randi," Tracy shouted as her bare feet hit the tile. "We've got company. Take Charlie into the bathroom and lock the door."

"I didn't hear anything," I responded, shoving the blanket to the floor.

"Well, I did. There's a car parked on the other side of the street, and someone is approaching the front door."

"Is he alone?" I asked as I moved into the hall with her. Charlie's bedroom was at the front of the house.

"He was when I saw him through my window, but that doesn't mean there aren't others with him. Just do as I said. There wasn't time to alert the field office. You weren't expecting anyone, were you?"

"Most certainly not," I responded. "I've kept a very low profile, and my social life is nonexistent."

"As it should be," she said.

Her gun was pointed at the front door, but I didn't feel an urgency to leave her alone. If someone truly dangerous approached the house, it would be through the wooded area behind the back yard.

She gave me an angry look when the doorbell rang. "It's after midnight, and why the hell isn't that camera on the side of the garage working? I checked it out myself before heading to my apartment for a single nightcap."

"Just use the peephole," was my reply. "I'll make a quick sweep through the lower level just to make sure everything is secure."

But before I even made it to my son's door, she was calling me back. "He's in a military uniform. I think you should take a look."

During the brief moment it took to return to her side, every horrid thought imaginable seemed to rush through my mind. "Are you sure?"

"I know camouflage fatigues when I see them."

She stepped away from the door, and I put my eye to the hole. Instant recognition made my knees buckle.

"We've got to let him in," I nearly shouted. "It's Charlie's father."

I had the door open before she could stop me. The tears were rolling down my cheeks when I threw myself into his open arms, nearly propelling both of us to the ground. He swung me around in the air before placing a not-so-soft kiss on my lips.

"I was hoping for a pleasant reunion but never expected this," he said as I took a step backwards so I could see his face. "Are you going to invite me in, or do I have to stand on the front porch to explain why I've come?"

"I'm sorry," I said, fearing that if I let go of his hand he would turn into a mirage. "You're the last person I ever thought I would see again."

"So my feisty, little agent missed me," he replied, running the back of his hand down my cheek. "That's good because I plan on staying for awhile."

His eyes were sparkling, but he looked so thin and incredibly tired. "Does my boss know you're here?"

"Of course! How else would I know where you were? He wanted to let you know I was coming, but I told him I needed it to be a surprise."

"Why? You knew what my reaction would be."

"I only knew what I hoped it would be, but it's been over eight months. That's plenty of time for you to fall in love with someone else. I had to see for myself that nothing had changed between us."

"There's never been anyone but you, Sam."

He tilted my chin upwards so he could kiss my lips again. "I know that now because you used my first name. Is it okay if I pull my car into your driveway? I didn't want to make any assumptions."

While he ran across the street, Tracy stepped outside with me. Her gun was still in her hand. "So that's the illusive Agent Fielding. I figured he was dead."

"So did I. His coming back is nothing short of a miracle."

"I don't believe in miracles of a religious nature, but he certainly appears to have more lives than any cat. If you're sure it's okay, I'll leave you alone to get reacquainted. From what I've seen, I doubt you'll be able to call yourself a virgin come morning. That man has been waiting a long time to have you back in his arms."

"We know what we're doing," I responded as the sound of a car engine rippled through the night air. "There's too much at stake to go into anything blindly just because it might feel good."

"But he's Charlie's father, and you love him."

"That's why I'm willing to wait. I want a real family, not just a lover's tryst that has very little chance of surviving once emotions have calmed down a bit."

"If you say so," she replied. "But I certainly wouldn't let a man like that get away. From what you've told me, he's someone anyone can count on."

"That he is," I said, watching him take a duffle bag from the back seat before locking the car. "He's the most remarkable man I've ever met, but something made him feel it was necessary to come here. I need to find out what that is before doing anything else."

Introductions were made once the three of us were inside, and then I asked to be excused while I found a robe. Tracy told me she would keep Sam company while I was gone. I decided to take my time. They needed a few moments to get to know each other since we would be sleeping under the same roof—at least for now. And I definitely needed time to decompress.

Once she had gone upstairs, we stood by Charlie's crib, hands entwined, and watched him sleep.

"Does he always look this peaceful and beautiful?" Sam asked. "I'm not sure I'll be able to tear my eyes away from him. I've never seen anything quite so perfect. I thought my life had come to an end when you walked out of that library at the compound. I almost came after you but knew I had to trust that someone would make sure you made it down that mountain and back to our son. I think I may have said my first prayer ever that day."

"Does that mean you now believe in God?"

"I've seen too much these past few months not to believe that someone is helping to orchestrate our lives. I had no idea what I was going to do. Mendoza was dead, Alma was on her way, and there was an army of men waiting in the courtyard outside with enough ammunition to take down an entire village without breaking a sweat. I just knew you couldn't be a part of it."

"I understood what you needed to do and why. That's the only reason I didn't fight you about leaving. I don't want to spoil this moment unnecessarily, but I know you're not here for just relaxation or pleasure. What's going on?"

Before answering, he brought Charlie's hand to his lips and kissed it. "I don't know how I could have ever believed he wasn't worth trying to save. He's all I've thought about during the months we've been apart. He's not even going to know who I am when he wakes up, is he?"

"Charlie is open, intuitive and loving. I tell him about you every night. I just didn't have a picture so he would know your face. It won't take long for him to accept who you are."

"I hope the same thing applies to his mother. You're the strongest, most forgiving and truly extraordinary woman I've ever known, Reagan Sinclair. I can't believe I'm lucky enough to be standing beside you again. I certainly don't deserve it after all the horrible things I've done."

"Let's not talk about that part of our past. And in case you didn't get the memo, I've been going by the name of Randi Morley. My husband, Vaughn, has been in Afghanistan."

"Why do you think I'm dressed like this? I didn't want the neighbors talking when I came to your front door. But do I really look like a Vaughn to you? I think your boss has watched too many reruns of Alias on the tube."

"Don't knock it. That was one of my favorite shows during high school and college."

He led me to the great room where we both sat down on the sofa. I curled my feet underneath me and leaned away from him. Otherwise, I would have found myself in his arms.

"The beginning is always the most difficult part of the story for me," he said, taking his cue from me. "I don't want to overwhelm you with all the grizzly details."

"Then just tell me that everyone who wanted to hurt us has been dealt with, and we can finally go home. I don't know if my family will ever forgive me for all the trouble I've caused, but I won't quit trying until they do."

"You don't have to worry about that. I have it from a reliable source that they're all safe and love you dearly. You even have a new sister-in-law."

"Who told you that?" I asked.

"Your partner, Agent Howard, has been keeping an eye on them. I met him briefly when I stopped by the assistant director's office to update him on what's been going on in Colombia. I'm afraid he couldn't have told you much if he had called. The DEA has been very secretive about all of its missions lately. I wish I could tell you that everything has been resolved, but I'm afraid we still have one person missing. Robert Evans has never been found."

I allowed my breath to leave my lungs slowly. "He's the one I've been most worried about."

"That's precisely why I'm here. I told Director Stevens that I was tired of chasing my enemies all over the southern hemisphere when my family, who had been forced to live in exile, needed me at home."

"Your family," I said.

"Don't look at me like that," he replied with a mischievous twinkle in his eyes. "You know that's how I've felt for a long time now. I just needed to arrive at a point where I was ready to leave all the other stuff behind."

"Is it pretty dull around here."

"That's not what I meant. I want to watch my son grow up and spend time really getting to know the woman I love. I couldn't do that in a body bag or some shallow grave that no one would ever find, and I could see the handwriting on the wall. It wasn't easy convincing Alma that she could come with me willingly or end up like her brother. I even had to throw in a few words about Luis and Isabel—not that she'll ever get out of prison to see them—but despite what she's done, I really believe she loves them and wants to be part of their lives."

"I can't believe she didn't fight back."

"Anna and her friend helped me set up a little presentation for her arrival. It seems that not everyone in the household was as committed to their employer as we were led to believe."

"I don't even want to know what that may have looked like. What about the men outside?"

"With a little encouragement, she told them that her brother was having a heart attack and needed to be flown directly to the hospital in Bogotá. By that time, Father Francis and Rosa had returned. She said she couldn't leave me alone to cover up what she had done. She came down the mountain with us in one of Mendoza's private helicopters. Her presence had a lot to do with what could have been a much different outcome. In her very calm, but commanding way, she let Alma know that Carlos had already gone to meet his maker and would end up in hell where he belonged. But she still had time to confess her own sins and receive a much-needed pardon."

"That certainly doesn't sound like the woman I knew."

"She was a broken woman by the time we landed. I almost felt sorry for her. After an initial interrogation where we learned nothing of value, Director Stevens had her sent to a private institution in Ecuador. I spent several weeks trying to get her to talk, but to my knowledge, she hasn't uttered more than a few words since leaving the compound."

"Perhaps she believed more strongly in God than we gave her credit for. What will happen to Rosa, Anna, Manuel and all the others?"

"Rosa will be allowed to return to her family, but I'm not sure how any of them will survive. The government has seized control of the compound, and this time, they will make sure that no one returns. There was some talk of letting the servants turn it into a refuge for all the displaced persons in that part of the jungle. It could be a viable plan, if they're willing to work together to keep it afloat."

"Wow," I said, sinking back into the folds of the sofa. "It's hard to believe we no longer have to worry about either of the Mendoza's. What else can you tell me?"

"I won't keep the important stuff from you, but please don't get upset if some of my answers are less than complete. My past is part of who I am, but I would much rather concentrate on the present. For the first time in nearly two decades, I really believe I have a future that is not defined by the DEA."

"Does that mean you're resigning?"

"Let's just say that I'm taking a leave of absence from active duty. Director Stevens understands my reasons for needing to get away. He even said he'd put in a good word if I wanted to work as a trainer at the academy. Apparently, he thinks I would be ideal because there is little I have not seen."

"He's right, and you have my full support in anything you decide to do, but I still need you to tell me about . . . "

"You don't have to finish that thought," he said, as the bulb in the lamp flickered. "I really thought I would find you with stacks of papers all over the house trying to figure out what you had missed."

"I tried doing that the first few months, but it was a futile effort after losing all clearance when I brought Charlie here. But that doesn't mean I ever quite praying for any of you, especially Maria's family. I feel connected to them, and not just because of our son. I know Magdalena was only trying to keep the people she loved from becoming involved."

He reached over and took my hand. "I wish I could tell you that she survived. Lupe tried to bring her into the fold, but she refused to cooperate—as did her husband who was completely devastated when he found out what she had been keeping from him."

"What about their daughters?"

"Leila is still in protective custody. I spent a great deal of time with her after I left Alma. She eventually told us everything she knew, but it wasn't soon enough to find the Seville brothers or their mother. I searched for them over half of Colombia, and even went back to Mexico, but I suspect they'll remain in hiding while they decide if it's even worth the effort to start over. Robert's mismanagement caused them to lose face with their suppliers, and

Eloise lost a lot of their backing when she attacked you. Henri is still in DEA custody. If he knows anything, he's not telling us. As for the rest of Maria's sisters, they've been reunited somewhere."

"They might be able to grow up together, but they shouldn't have to do it without parents."

"Come here," he said, pulling me towards him. He brushed the tears from my eyes when I was close enough. "Nothing about this war on drugs is fair for the innocent, but it's a reality that must be faced. Thanks to Leila, I stood in Lupe Evans' presence at her villa and confronted her about all the evil she's unleashed on the world by wanting revenge for a cheating husband who not only married Angel but impregnated her own little sister. I shouldn't have brought it up so abruptly but figured she already knew."

"So Magdalena didn't tell her anything."

"I'm afraid I'm the one who let that cat out of the bag. We needed help finding Robert. Selena was able to find the plane he purchased without his mother's consent, but no one would admit to knowing where he was. Do you want to know what I got for being willing to take another calculated risk for the greater good—a letter opener in my gut. A noise coming from the other room distracted me from the unofficial interrogation, and Lupe used it to her advantage. I grabbed for her arm when I saw what was coming but wasn't fast enough. I've spent the last two months in the hospital. I would have bleed out on the floor of her sitting room if Leila hadn't acted quickly enough."

"I had no idea you'd been through so much. Shouldn't you still be recovering?"

"That's part of the reason I'm here. I could use a little TLC, but I also want to keep an eye on you and Charlie until Robert is in custody. I'm not sure we have anything to fear from him. He's on the run because his entire empire has crumbled, but that doesn't mean he isn't dangerous."

I made a bed for him on the sofa. He wanted to be close to both Charlie and me but knew my stance when it came to the kind of intimacy he really desired. He told me we would talk more in the morning. I kissed him goodnight and returned to my room, but while I lay in bed until I heard someone moving about in the kitchen, I didn't sleep. My mind was busy rehashing everything he had told me and how it might impact the rest of my life. I wasn't ready to make the kind of decisions I knew were coming.

Tracy left the next afternoon. After calling the field office and letting them know that my former partner had arrived, she was told to report for a new assignment. I gave her a hug and expressed my appreciation for her dedication and selfless service when I hadn't always made it easy. She only wished us good luck and gave Charlie a final kiss after her bag was packed.

A taxi picked her up at the curb. Sam stood by my side in the driveway while we waved goodbye. He was still wearing the fatigues he had arrived in and made sure he had his arm around my waist when one of our neighbors went to the mailbox. We needed to be seen together as a newly-reunited married couple if our rouse was going to continue undisturbed.

He and Charlie hit it off immediately. I can't say that my son intuitively knew that Sam was his father, but he definitely enjoyed the male attention after months of being with no one besides Tracy and me. He loved being tossed into the air and having someone who would spend hours on the floor or in the back yard playing with him. I fixed meals, and did the usual amount of cleaning and laundry, but we took time each day to do something special as a family.

At first, I resisted leaving the safety of the house Charlie and I had been confined to for so many months. It had been drilled into my head about the necessity of keeping a low profile, but something about having Sam with us made me feel less afraid. We started small by taking a walk around the block and speaking to everyone we passed. He carried Charlie and held my hand. I was the one with the gun in my pocket because we didn't want our son that close to a loaded weapon, but we knew it wasn't wise to go anywhere unarmed. From there, we went to a park, a restaurant and then to the mall. Charlie needed more normalcy and freedom to grow up unafraid.

On Monday morning, I went back to the classroom and left them at home. We had discussed how we were going to handle the situation all weekend. He would sleep on the sofa or in Charlie's room on a cot and watch him while I was at work. I would let the people at school know my pretend husband had returned and would continue being the supposed breadwinner since he couldn't exactly look for a job when the only identification he had was real.

It seemed like a good plan theoretically, but each day it became more difficult to keep a safe distance. We felt like a couple and a family, and I found myself watching both of them sleep. Sam was quickly becoming an integral part of my daily life. He didn't just watch Charlie during the day, he cleaned house, fixed meals and looked for ways to make me feel appreciated and loved. I tried to respond in an appropriate manner but knew what he both needed and wanted because it was how I felt too.

I was aware of everything about him—the way his hands moved, the tilt of his head when he was thinking, the set of his jaw when he didn't quite know what to do, and the way it felt to be in his arms. Sometimes, we would lie on the kingsized bed, fully clothed, but wrapped in each other's arms. I would listen to the beat of his heart and the intake and release of his breath and knew I wanted to share every part of my life with him.

He suggested a trip to the house in Maine for Christmas. I questioned the advisability of going since the weather was unpredictable, and we would have to drive. He told me the car had good tires and we could stop as many times as we liked. I had two weeks off from school, and it would be the only break we had until spring. Besides, no one had come looking for us, and Vestie Jennings wouldn't tell anyone we were there.

I finally consented, hoping he knew what he was getting into. Charlie wasn't the best traveler, and I was physically and emotionally drained after endless months of anxiety and sleepless nights. I wasn't particularly worried that anyone in Boothbay Harbor would recognize us. I had only left the house a few times, including the trip to the library where we'd found Angel's sister, Neva. My thoughts often centered on her, and the way I had been forced to betray her confidence. If the right time ever came, I would try to find her. She might never forgive my actions, but she deserved to know the entire story, not just the things the authorities would have told her.

It was snowing when we arrived on the twenty-third of December, but the house was warm and inviting. Sam had called Vestie from a payphone at the motel the night before to tell her we were coming. It was safer than showing up unannounced. He had even given her a partial explanation as to why we were together and a warning about keeping our arrival from becoming part of the town's gossip mill. We would only be there for a few days, and while she was welcome to stop by for a long overdo visit, he couldn't explain anything more than he already had.

"How do you want to celebrate?" he asked me after we had turned Charlie loose to explore. Knickknacks were plentiful, but most of them were too high for him to reach without climbing. I caught his dark eyes gleaming as his chubby legs carried him towards a tall ceramic giraffe that stood in one corner of the living room, but Sam placed a restraining hand on my arm. "Let him go. There isn't anything of real value here except memories."

"You haven't been here for a long time, have you?"

"Not since right after my Grandma Winnie died. She would be thrilled that we're here together. She always told me I would have a family, but I was determined that nothing was ever going to slow me down."

"Are you sorry you're not still actively working at a job where you get paid?" I asked.

He pulled me into his arms and rested his chin on the top of my head as we watched Charlie move from place to place almost too overcome to touch anything. "I've never missed anything less. I just wish my work didn't have to follow us wherever we go. I keep thinking there should be something more we can do to move things along. I want us to have a real life—white picket fence and all."

"I don't need that illusion of happiness. I have almost all I need just being with you and Charlie."

"You still miss your family."

"More than you'll know. My home was always filled with wonderful smells and laughter, but never more so than at Christmas. That's when all the extended family got together. We would sit around the tree and read the story of Christ's birth. Then we would drink eggnog without any alcohol, sing carols and open one special gift. It was the one time of year when petty grievances were forgotten, and we could concentrate on what was most important—the life and mission of our Savior—and what we needed to do to become more like him. Maybe someday you can join us."

"I wish that could happen this year, but maybe we could make Christmas special in our own way. We certainly have the weather for it, and I noticed a parking lot full of trees when we pulled into town. I'm sure there are still a few things at some of the stores to add to what we brought with us."

"Don't you think it would be better if we just stayed inside? We've been very lucky so far."

"I doubt anyone would notice another father going out to buy a tree. Why don't you make a list of the things you need to make the kind of Christmas you're envisioning happen, and I'll see what I can do. It might not be the most spectacular, but it's our first one together as a family. I intend to take lots of pictures so we won't forget."

"Just don't get one that's too big. We have nothing in the way of decorations," I replied, not wanting to think about the future because this moment was all we had.

He turned me in his arms and kissed my eager lips. "I think Grandma Winnie has that covered. I doubt she threw a useful thing out in her life. Why don't you check the attic while I see what I can find on the main street of town. You and Charlie can sleep in the master bedroom like you did before. I'll set the crib up and sleep in my old room. I don't want you feeling uneasy about anything while we're here. I just want you to relax and try to have some fun."

"Thank you," I said. "I've never known a man quite so wonderful as you."

"I doubt that's true, but it's still nice to hear," he said before following Charlie into the kitchen. "I guess we should see what Vestie has left in the fridge. I know she wouldn't leave it empty."

While he went to look for a tree, I unpacked what we had brought and made a list of the things I needed to cook Christmas dinner. I decided we should invite Vestie, if she didn't have other plans. She had stocked the refrigerator and pantry with the things she thought we might need and left a note telling us to call when we were ready for a visitor. We would keep things simple, but she needed to visit with Sam and see how much Charlie had grown. I couldn't worry about her feelings for me after the way I had left so unexpectedly.

Sam was humming when he carried a beautiful, Douglas fir into the house. It was a sound I never tired of hearing. He had it in a stand that would hold water and asked me where I wanted to put it. I snatched Charlie away from its protruding branches and told him it needed to go in front of the living room window. I had already cleared a place for it.

The boxes he brought from the attic—since I had done nothing more than locate the ones labeled Christmas—were dust-covered, but the items inside were truly priceless. Some of the strands of lights didn't work, but he was still able to illuminate the tall, full-branched tree that was really much too big for the allocated space, but I wasn't about to complain. Charlie was more of a hindrance during the tree-trimming process, but he loved every moment spent wrapped in strands of garland, carrying toy soldiers around the room, and being swooped out of the way before he stepped on something that might get broken. It was truly a magical evening, but we were all exhausted, so I excused myself at the same time I put our son to bed. I was on the verge of giving in to mounting temptation.

By the time I had Charlie bathed and dressed the next morning —he had slept much longer than usual—Sam had already been to the general store and purchased everything on my list.

"You don't have to go to all this trouble," he said after placing the last load of plastic bags on the kitchen counter. "I'm sure a restaurant will be open somewhere."

"But I want to cook," I replied as I started to organize the perishables.

My intention was to put a thinly-sliced ham in the oven on Christmas day, but I was going to bake pies and rolls today. Part of it was a desire to show him how much I cared, and part of it was having something to do that didn't involve physical closeness like watching a movie, playing with Charlie or putting a puzzle together. I'd had incredibly sensual dreams about him the night before.

His crooked smile made me realize I had made the right decision. "I'm always ready for a home-cooked meal, although that's not at the top of my list as to what makes a successful relationship. What can I do to help?"

By early afternoon, I had two pies cooling on the counter and rolls ready to go in the oven. Vestie stopped by with a fruit basket. I wanted tell her the truth about my relationship with Sam so she wouldn't think we were living together in the usual sense, but that was a luxury I didn't have. So, I smiled and thanked her for such a thoughtful gesture. I was about to invite her for Christmas dinner when she said she was on her way to spend the holiday with an old friend and needed to get an early start. It was still snowing and some of the roads might be closed soon. I promised we would get together when she got back.

"That gives me an idea," Sam said when she had gone. "There's an old sleigh in the garage. Why don't we take Charlie sledding? No one is going to come looking for us today."

"Isn't he a little young?"

"Maybe, but he's strong and healthy, and it's not that cold. Besides, we won't be gone long. I just want to do as many things as we possibly can while we're here. There are no guarantees about tomorrow."

I knew he was right so I bundled Charlie up as best I could and found an old blanket to use for added protection. One of us would be holding him anyway. We drove a short distance to a hill where children of all ages were playing and took turns sliding down with him. He was definitely his father's son because while I was terrified for his safety, he was shrieking with delight.

"Why don't we take him to see Santa before we go home. I'm sure there's one somewhere in town. After all, it's almost Christmas Eve."

"He's too little to even know who Santa is," I reminded him when we were back in the car.

His sigh was heavy. "I know, but I've already missed out on so much of his life. I can't believe I ever thought chasing bad guys was more important than being a father. I don't know how you put up with me."

"That's easy! I do it because I love you and because you're the best man I've ever known."

"I'm not a good man, Reagan, but I am trying to be better."

"Then let's find that Santa and take another picture. I keep forgetting that all of this is new to you. It feels like we've always been together after the past month."

I asked Sam if he would read the story of Christ's birth as I held Charlie in front of the twinkling lights of the tree that night. He was tired and ready for bed, but I needed this time to think about the only gifts that had ever mattered to me this special time of year—life, health, something to believe in and being with the people I loved. Maybe next Christmas we would be with the rest of our family.

Sam carried Charlie to his crib after he'd opened one gift—a stuffed puppy he could sleep with.

"I hope you're not quite ready to turn in," he said as we watched him sleep. "I wouldn't mind a little company and maybe even some hot cocoa and marshmallows. It's all I have to offer since I'm know you're not interested in the bottles of wine in the cellar underneath the house."

"Cocoa will be fine, but I don't want to keep you from all your pleasures. You've given up so much lately."

He took my hand and led me out of the master bedroom. "I don't consider any of this a sacrifice. I'm exactly where I want to be, but I saw how uncomfortable you were when Vestie stopped by earlier. You don't want anyone believing that we're living together in sin, even though we share a son."

I smiled up at him. "It couldn't be helped."

"Maybe not this time, but it doesn't have to happen again. I want to protect you from everything, not that I've done a very good job of it in the past."

We were standing in front of the fire next to the tree, and I felt the heat radiate through my extremities. "No one else could have kept us alive, and I'm more than grateful we've had time to get to know each other better."

"I suppose that's a byproduct of not being able to include anyone else in our lives right now. I just hope you're not too disappointed by what you've learned."

"How could I be? You've just shown me what I've known all along."

"And what's that?"

"The person you are when you don't always have to be strong and in control. You genuinely care about others, and you're not afraid to accept new challenges, even when they come in the form of changing diapers and getting your son to eat his vegetables."

"What about the deeper issues like inherent values and learned behaviors? I know I'm not the kind of man you really want."

"But you're the kind of man I need. I'm not saying that as a way to cop-out. I know we still have issues and difference to work through, but I can't imagine not having you in my life. And past experience tells me that we're not so different inside. We both want a family that stays together, and we're willing to do whatever it takes for that to happen."

"Then let's take the next step," he said, reaching into his pocket and producing a ring whose diamonds were so bright they nearly took my breath away. "A reprieve wasn't the only reason I needed to come here. This ring belonged to my grandmother. She wanted me to give it to the girl I married. Will you be my wife, Reagan Sinclair? There's every reason in the world for you to say no, but I'm hoping, and yes praying, that you won't. I can't imagine us being separated again."

This was it—the moment of truth when I could embrace the future the man of my dreams had to offer or back away. He wouldn't ask me again.

"Yes, Sam, I will," I said before I had time to change my mind.

"You really mean it?" he asked before slipping the ring on my finger. "I don't want to push you into anything."

"You're not pushing," I said. "This is where I want to be too. I've known you were the only man for me since the day Charlie was born. You've complicated my life in more ways than you will ever know, but you've also complimented it. I can't imagine loving anyone else the way I love you."

"What about your family? I'm not sure your brothers will ever accept me."

"They'll grow to love you almost as much I do, though I'm sure they might not be too pleased in the beginning. After all, I am their baby sister, and they've spent their lives trying to protect me."

"That's my job now," he said.

"That's both of our jobs. I can't tell you how many times I've wanted to hold you in my arms but was afraid to follow my heart because of where it might lead."

"Then let's not wait to make it legal."

"How do we do that when at least one of us is living under an assumed identity?"

"I have a friend who's a former judge. He and Grandma Winnie used to be quite tight. He'll marry us and file the paperwork personally if I ask him to. It doesn't even have to be put in the paper or be done at the courthouse. He has a housekeeper and a butler who can act as witnesses. They're old but not senile. No one will even know it happened, unless we tell them."

"You're sure he'd be willing to do it? Aren't there supposed to be blood tests and a license?"

"He'll take care of everything. You know rules were just made to be broken by people who know how to do it. All it takes is a call. He's been following my career and would be thrilled to know that I'm finally settling down."

Sam made that call, and we were married Christmas afternoon at Judge Donnelly's home with members of his home staff as witnesses. There was no time for preparations, but the judge had decorated lavishly for the holidays so he performed the ceremony in front of a tree trimmed in white bows and silver tinsel. I wore the only dress I had with me—the red one I had packed hoping Sam would be amenable to a attending a religious service commemorating the holiday. He wore a white shirt and the best pair of pants he had. I cried when we were pronounced husband and wife, not because I had any regrets, but because no one I knew was with us.

Several pictures were taken on our phones before his housekeep produced a large tray filled with glasses of champagne so toasts could be made. I held mine as the judge wished us a long and happy future. Sam took a sip to be polite, but he hadn't had so much as a bottle of beer since he'd come to be with us. Charlie didn't know what to think and clung to my leg when I wasn't holding him.

"You've given enough service to your country," the judge said when we were ready to leave. "Now it's time to build your own life, and I can tell that you've chosen not only a beautiful young woman to share it with but a sensible one too. Winnie would be very proud of the man you've become, and would she ever enjoy playing with that little boy of yours. Odd thing is that he doesn't look much like either one of you."

"That's a story for another time, but I can assure you that he's ours," Sam told him. "You'll make sure the paperwork is filed discretely?"

"I'll take care of it first thing in the morning. No one will be in the courthouse, and I know where everything is. I'll have a notarized copy of everything you need here at the house by tomorrow night, and the originals will be tucked away from prying eyes. I know you might not be staying for long, but I do hope you'll come for a long visit when all this unpleasantness is behind you. Damned shamed good people's lives have to be messed up for doing the right thing, but I suppose that's the price of being a hero."

"No hero's here," Sam replied. "Just people who want to forget the past so they can enjoy the future."

Charlie tore open his presents when we got home. There hadn't been time to do it earlier. He was more interested in the wrapping paper than the small gifts inside and played until it was time to eat dinner. We took dozens more pictures, and then Sam set the table while I finished preparing the meal that would be our first one as husband and wife. He said all the right things—even though the ham wasn't as moist as I hoped it would be—and then we did the dishes and put our son in the crib we had pushed into the hallway so we could have some privacy.

I didn't have anything sexy to wear, but when I stood in front of my husband in a worn t-shirt and pajama bottoms it suddenly didn't matter that our courtship and marriage were far from conventional or even normal. Someday, we would laugh when we told Charlie about it, but just for tonight I was going to put all the danger and difficulties aside and go to the man I loved in complete surrender. He had certainly waited patiently long enough.

"You're beautiful," he said as he opened the sheet for me. I could see his bare chest and the way his muscles rippled in the soft lamplight.

"I hope you don't mind that I'm just a little scared but in a very pleasant way."

He turned on his side and ran his finger seductively down the side of my face. "I promise to be gentle, but you have to understand that this is a new experience for me as well. I've never made love to my wife before."

"I hope I won't disappoint you."

"Never," he said, and I could see tears in his eyes. "You're more precious to me than anything in this world, and I've never loved you more. This is our journey of discovery. I pledge my life and my heart to you and not just for better or worse. I pledge it to you forever. I don't care what I have to do to make that a reality. I only know that from this moment on I will live my life for you and Charlie and a child of our own that I hope we have one day. I don't want our son to grow up alone."

When his lips found mine, I knew I had truly found my rightful home in the arms of the man who had been my competitor, my protector, my confident, my support and my friend before we even realized that our relationship might become something more. I let our passion take us where it would, and I was soon enveloped in a beauty I had never known existed outside fairy tales and romantic movies.

I wanted to express my complete love and devotion over and over again. And that's exactly what we both did until the soft fingers of a bright dawn peaked through the window curtains. We fell back into each other's arms as Charlie's voice began calling for us.

Epilogue

Our day of release from hiding came exactly three months after Sam and I were married. It had been a magical time, despite obvious worries and daily routines. He was an amazing husband and father—patient, attentive and loving towards both of us. But it was when I fell into his arms at the end of each day that I knew I had truly found heaven on earth. Giving myself to him completely and without hesitancy came easy. He made me feel like a woman in every way, and I often found myself smiling unexpectedly in the middle of some lesson I was giving at school.

We made it a point never to take what we had found for granted and tried not to dwell on matters beyond our control. I didn't talk about religion, unless he asked a specific question. I simply continued doing what I had always done—reading my scriptures, blessing the food and saying my personal prayer every morning and evening. I knew he would accept the truth about Christ's mission and the Plan of Redemption when he was ready. Until then, I would continue extending my unconditional love and letting him know how much I appreciated all he had given up so we could be a family.

I was fixing dinner and Charlie was playing with a stack of blocks when the call came. Sam put the deposable phone that had been silent for eleven months on speaker so we could both hear what Assistant Director Bridges had to say.

"This has been a long time coming, but I just got word from Director Stevens that Robert Evans is in custody."

My knees went weak, but Sam's strong arms instantly offered the support only he could give.

"It's about time! What happened?" he asked my boss.

"I didn't ask for details. I figured you could do that. I just wanted you to know it's finally safe to come home."

Now that my head wasn't spinning so fast, I knew exactly what I wanted to ask. "Tell me about my family and Lila. Is everyone still okay?"

"Your family is safe, and Lila is actually working for us as a confidential informant. She's proven her worth, just like you always said she would. We'll do everything we can to make sure she has a long and prosperous life, but she has a colorful past, and there's always the chance someone will figure out what she's up to. She says she's willing to accept her fate, as long as Charlie and you can come home. I think she has some news of her own to share."

"When can we expect to make that move?" Sam questioned as tears slid from the corners of my eyes.

"Give us a few days to make sure he doesn't get lose—that seems to happen occasionally—and then give the school your notice. They may want you to stay until the end of the year."

"I can do that, as long as I can talk to family my again," I said, looking up at the man who had come to mean everything to me. He knew I meant no disrespect to the family we had created for ourselves, but our news couldn't be shared over any phone. "Will you call again when everything has been settled?"

"You can count on it, Agent Sinclair. I'm not the only one in this office anxiously awaiting your return."

Sam and I had already discussed our work-related future, and mine did not include returning to active duty any time in the foreseeable future. He would take the job in Washington D.C. as an instructor at the academy—if it was still available—and I would stay home to raise Charlie and the new little brother or sister we hoped he would have before much longer.

"Are you ready for this?" he asked when the call ended. "I wish it was Charlie's bedtime so we could have a real celebration."

"I'm sure we can coax him into his crib a few minutes early." I said as he nibbled my ear sending rivulets of desire everywhere. "I'm rather glad I bought a few special things for dessert tonight."

"My goodness, Mrs. Fielding," he said, his eyes sparkling with the physical longing I so loved to see. "You never cease to amaze me. I think I'll bathe Charlie while you finish with dinner. I can't wait to be alone with you."

I kissed his lips and ran my hands slowly over his shoulders and down his arms, feeling every muscle tense at my touch. I would never grow tired of loving him.

Watching them leave the room, I knew it wouldn't be easy facing my family after everything I had done, but I hoped they would understand and forgive. As to how one of the potentially most treacherous cartels in Colombia had finally been completely overthrown, I could live with a few unanswered questions. My life had been anything but ordinary, but trusting in God's plan had paid huge dividends.

I slid an enchilada casserole into the oven and went to join my husband and son. I could hear shrieks of enjoyment coming from the bathroom. If I knew the two men in my life, there would be water everywhere to clean up.

That's all of the story for now . . .

Other Titles From Jan Hill Books:

Coming Soon!

A new series about women who meet life's challenges with courage, strength and conviction. Each individual story will give you hope, encouragement and a desire to rise above your own trials. I hope you will enjoy them.

Indecision's Flame - Book 1: by JS Ririe

Brylee Hawkins was prepared to enjoy a bright, hopeful future until her fiancé convinced her to return to the Australian Outback to confront the father that had driven her away. On her own again in a harsh and unforgiving land, she is forced to face a mottled and unsavory past and an even more disturbing and dangerous present. As unrelenting lies, secrets and cover-ups – including a family she never knew about - continue to unfold, Brylee soon learns that both decisions and indecision are bringing her closer to a point of no return. Will she find the strength to fight the darkness, or will it seep into her soul and take away everything she had come to treasure?

Lost - Indecision's Flame - Book 2: by JS Ririe

Torn between her family and the obligations of a promise made to her father, Brylee longs to return to the United States and to her fiancé who is patiently waiting for her, but fate seems to have other plans. Jake, the brother of her father's wife, decides to take her under his wing and teach her the ropes of running the ranch - mostly in an attempt to get rid of her. His mockery and ridicule are only enhanced when she learns of her father's legacy and the part she is to play if she wants to help keep it alive. Unable to make a decision about leaving, she is left to wonder if the outback will consume her before the next harsh blow comes.

Exposed - Indecision's Flame - Book 3: by JS Ririe

With LeAnn gone from the ranch because she is unable to accept her husband's death, and the aftermath of the flood to deal with,

Brylee is forced to assume more responsibility than she is prepared for in raising her little brother, Trevor, and trying to keep the family heritage intact. Her troubles deepen when a secret she was keeping from her fiancé is revealed through an unexpected source, and she must learn to accept the fact that her feelings for Jake, the incorrigible, yet handsome ranch hand and family member who has the uncanny knack for seeing into her heart as no one else has been able to do, not even Ben, are beginning to change. A chance encounter on the beach proves just how much she has to fear. Uncle Ned delivers unsetting news about the fate of the ranch, and LeAnn learns about a priceless gift that turns the family upside down and causes Brylee to accept the reality that her life may never turn out the way she planned. Could a bleak present become an even more desolate future?

Betrayal - Indecision's Flame - Book 4: by JS Ririe

Despite a fractured heart over Jake leaving the ranch, Brylee must forge onward in support of her cousin, Molly, who has suddenly decided to get married, inviting Beth to be her maid of honor. Helping to plan an unexpected wedding is prickly, but the reception is even worse when Jake's appearance confirms what she has known all along. Tension and violence quickly ignite in the outback when a nugget of gold is found on a neighboring homestead and a man is killed for not revealing its source, forcing Brylee and Jake to put aside their differences and pretend to get along as they are pulled deeper into a web of misunderstandings, cover-ups and danger. A desperate ride down a mountain on a saddle less horse helps Brylee arrive at an important deduction that could alter her future, but will providence intervene before she can make good on a promise? Every hope for her future is put to the test.

Reawakening - Indecision's Flame - Book 5: by JS Ririe

Jake's cryptic note, when leaving the sinking ranch for a second time, forces Brylee to reconsider the advisability of remaining in the outback where personal heartbreak and unrelenting responsibility are reducing her to a shell of the woman she had once been. But fate intercedes in a most curious way, bringing with it an old aborigine from her past who sincerely believes in the mythical Rainbow Serpent and whose revelations about her childhood and omens about the future of her family shake her fledgling beliefs unmercifully.

A short holiday in Sydney to see her ex-fiancé, Ben, surf in a national competition comes to an end with an unexpected moment of closure and news that both Beth and Jake are in a hospital in Brisbane after a critical car accident. Part of Hawkins' family livelihood is destroyed by a pack of marauding dingoes, and Brylee contracts a mysterious illness that even the experts at the disease control center are unable to accurately diagnose. Her near death causes a recovering Jake to re-evaluate his priorities and decide what he really wants to do with his life.

Unraveling - Indecision's Flame - Book 6: by JS Ririe

After months of disastrous confrontations and ill-fated choices, Brylee and Jake are finally at a place where the future doesn't seem quite so grim, but navigating through the maze of obstacles that have already set in place to keep them apart isn't going to be easy. It's a test of survival, heart and commitment as they race against time, elements and devious plotting to rescue Trevor from the hands of a deranged madman, search for answers and try to keep LeAnn from becoming a sacrificial lamb. Unforeseen circumstances force Brylee to the edge of a precipice where the decision she makes will determine if everything she believes in and holds dear is worth the sacrifice she is about to make.

Destiny - Indecision's Flame - Book 7: by JS Ririe

Beth's arrival at the ancestral home effectively ruins what Brylee and Jake hope will be the beginning of many happy Christmas days, but the much-anticipated holiday turns to complete ruin when Raymond Tucker interferes in a most galling way. It's a battle against family feelings of betrayal, sinister alliances and catastrophic news as NJ returns to the outback armed with a plan that has the potential of upsetting the very balance of nature. Ongoing confrontations and unmitigated pressure force LeAnn to rethink what is right for her and her children, and Brylee wrestles with feelings of self-doubt and a very uncertain future while trying to keep the family together. Will Jake's final decision bring her the closure and peace she so much desires, or will it turn to ashes everything they have been trying to build?

About the Author

JS Ririe is the pen name for Jan Hill who spent her youth in the country where she learned to appreciate solitude, making her own fun, and reading romance novels from some of the masters like the Bronte sisters, Louisa May Alcott, Victoria Holt and Phyllis Whitney. She penned her first novel as a teenager but never pursued what is now her greatest passion until becoming the lead witness in a federal case brought against the school district where she taught broadcasting and journalism. Reagan's story is her second series after writing Indecision's Flame and its sequels as she waited two years to testify. She lives in Utah and has two children and two living grandchildren who bring meaning and joy to her life.

A Note From Jan

Thank you so much for reading this novel. I'd love to stay in touch with you. Please consider joining my MAILING LIST so I can send you periodic newsletters about upcoming book releases, special offers and more. The link to sign up is: http://eepurl.com/dCPYVf . I promise not to spam you or sell your email information to anyone. It will be treated with care.

One last favor: Your rating/review of this book helps promote my work and encourages me to keep writing. A short, but honest review would mean a lot. It shouldn't take more than a minute or two. You can reach the page directly at http://bit.ly/IFReview

Thank you again.
JS Ririe

www.JanHillBooks.com
For contacting the author: JSRirie@JanHillBooks.com